D. Z. Church Reviews

Saving Calypso — "In the tantalizing prologue of this twisty thriller from Church (*Head First*), the enigmatic Calypso Swale decides to leave her home for the second time in six months...Readers will keep turning the pages to see what brings Calypso and Grieg together in the present day. Lisa Unger fans will be pleased." – *Publishers Weekly*

Perfidia —"Church manages, quite impressively, to maintain a sense of hidden but perpetual threat... Overpowering dread and a leery protagonist make this a suspenseful read." --*Kirkus Review, Indie Book Worth Discovering*

Cooper Vietnam Era Quartet:

Dead Legend—"Church writes in a muscular prose that never loses its noirish register...there's something compelling about the milieu and the language that keeps the reader engaged, particularly as the mysteries of Mac Cooper begin to unravel." --*Kirkus Reviews*

Head First — "This sequel continues the saga of the Coopers, a Navy family grappling with its past against the backdrop of the Vietnam War... Church's prose is precise an often subtly lyrical, asking readers to pause and sit with every scene...an intriguing family saga." --*Kirkus Reviews*

Pay Back — "This wartime thrill ride turns the waning days of the U.S.'s involvement in Vietnam into a pulse-pounding, smart tale of suspense." – *BookLife Reviews*

Books by D. Z. Church:

Perfidia
Saving Calypso
Booth Island

Cooper Quartet:
Dead Legend: 1967
Head First: 1972
Pay Back: 1975

Coming Soon:
Don't Tell: 1975

Booth Island

D. Z. Church

A Bodie Blue Books original

Cover design © 2020 D. Z. Church (using BookCreative)
Photograph: Jon Church

ISBN: 978-1-7355208-0-3

Dedication

For my husband, Alan, and his family,
and their island.
And for all our Canadian friends.

Table of Contents

Map of Lower Bay

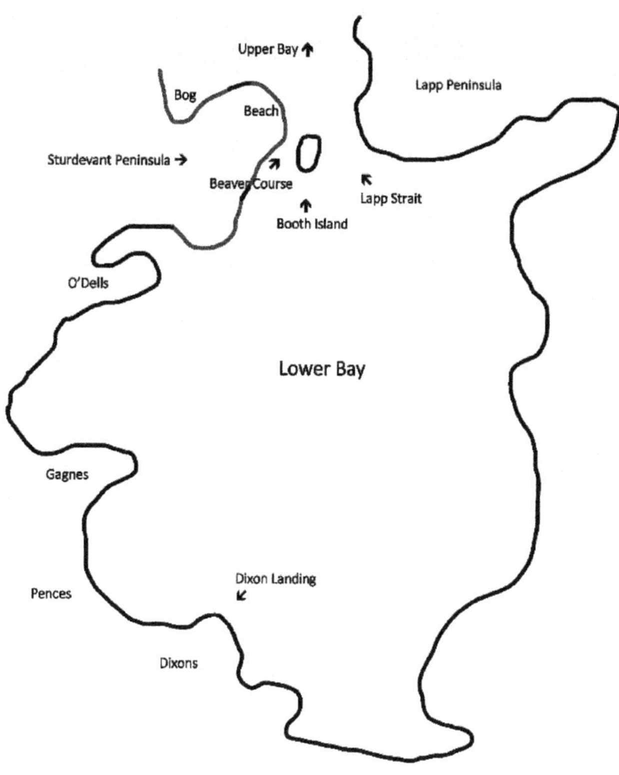

Boo Treader

i

MY CLOTHED BODY BUMPS off granite rocks as it descends into the frigid depths of a Canadian lake. A swirl of red drifts on the bubbles escaping my lips. I watch each pocket of air grow smaller as it ascends toward the surface. A concussion rams my hip against a cement post. I glance to my left. Another body bobs next to mine. Recognizing it, I reach out...

I woke with a jolt knowing I was out of my depth again. I chose to believe that was the message of the dream. The nightmare, really, had haunted me at random intervals since my brother, Roy, drowned at the age of seventeen. I was fifteen at the time. We had been a team.

Roy died on Booth Island. Our family-owned island sits in a long bay that hooks off one of the largest inland lakes in the Canadian province of Ontario. Booth Island divides the long, cove cluttered body of water into Upper Bay and Lower Bay. The quarter-mile passage to the east of the island is charted as Lapp Strait. The much narrower channel to the west is Beaver Course, inhabited by its own industrious beaver. The beaver lives on the banks of Booth Island in a tidy lodge built of sticks, chinked with mud, and anchored to the steep rocky shore.

1

On occasion, the wind drives the waters down the three-mile reaches of Upper Bay with such ferocity that as the bumptious water passes through the two channels, Booth Island appears to steam into Lower Bay like an ocean liner. When we were still a family, we would run en masse to a wooden jetty at New Landing on the north of the island and hold hands as though we were on the deck of a passenger ship. Say the RMS Lusitania. Torpedoed like our family.

My smartphone chirped its distinctive ring from the nightstand next to my bed. The photo card I had received yesterday rested against my clock. My eyes locked on the image of my brother, forever young, leaning on the railing of the deck my mother had built after his death and christened *Roy's Deck*. I robo-answered my phone, knowing Roy's photo had sparked my dream.

"Boothe Treader speaking." My mom added the e to her surname, Booth, to make my given name feminine. Dad called me Baby Girl until I was twelve. My brother, Roy, called me BG to annoy me, now my dad does it for the same reason. Everyone else calls me Boo, like the note inside the photo card, scrawled in my brother's distinctive hand: *Boo!*

The card had been sent from a photo service in California. The return address printed in the left corner read: Roy Treader, Booth Island, Ontario, Canada. It was true he resided there under a handmade marker of cement with words etched in it by my father.

"Hey, Boo, Penny Withers, here." As though I knew more than one shiny Penny. "I know it's early," she rattled on, "I know you're due to arrive the day after tomorrow, but..." How could Penny sound so upbeat at 7:30 in the morning? How could anyone?

A tussle ensued as the phone changed hands. I was fully awake by the time the tug of war ended, my antenna twanging. Something was up. I fingered my brother's face, knowing the photo had been shopped like the others received over the past five years. The boy who killed my brother had been a photographer or played at it. Punished for his bit of malicious mischief by forced enlistment in the U.S. Marines. For all I knew, he was dead. And even if he wasn't, why torture me with these cards? I had nothing to do with his guilty plea or sentence. Besides, photo postcards seemed more like something Roy would do for laughs, thinking it was all a great joke via the astral plane. If so, it was nice that Roy was still enjoying himself.

"Ms. Treader? This is Joe, Joe Withers. Penny and I thought you should know that the OPP, sorry, Ontario Provincial Police are on Booth Island. A body got hung up on the palette at Old Landing last night. Tim O'Dell found it at dawn when he brought the generator around for you." Tim O'Dell managed Booth Island year-round. I had spoken to him a few days ago, letting him know I would be summering over.

"Who?" I croaked, sitting on the edge of the bed, my feet dangling like I was fifteen again, my stomach hollow with fear. This edgy pain in my gut was why it had taken me so long to face my brother, though the psychiatrist my mother paid had been urging me for years, babbling on about closure. I dropped the shrink, instead.

A day later, the first photo card arrived. From that day on, a postcard appeared on June 1st of the last five years. Always of Roy, always alive. I held them dear, telling no one I had received them, including my parents. Why would I? They were addressed to me, and my mother already thought I was nuts.

I am not. At least, I think not.

"We had a bad storm on the lake last night." Joe said, "So far, no one has raised a hue and cry about a missing person, suggesting the body might be someone from Upper Bay. Whoever he is, he will be missed sooner than later, then someone will report it to the OPP."

"What do you need from me?" I stood, walked to my bedroom window, Roy's photo in hand, and gazed out over the Gettysburg battlefield, sloping lawns, ancient trees, deep green, and still. My mother's family had been here during the battle, and we remained.

"Nothing, Penny thought you should know since you're all but on your way. No need to make any sort of heroic effort to arrive early. Unless..."

Off phone, Penny hissed, "For heaven's sake, Joe! Just stop." A brief scuffle, then Penny's voice. "Men! It is a male in his twenties, late twenties. That's all we know."

Penny and I had been friends since she waddled up to me at two years old and put her index finger on the end of my nose. We were summer besties from the moment she fingered me through the troubled summer that led to Roy's death and on to this day. She was lying.

I joked, "What? I suppose someone's spread ketchup on the sleeping bag on the bed and plunged a knife into the mattress?" I had the photo, sent a few years ago, Roy, one hand on the knife. Never mind that he was years dead by then.

"No, thank heavens, none of that in years. A beaver. On your new dock. Eviscerated. That is the word, right, Joe?" Joe must have answered in the affirmative. "Tim's cleaning it up."

"That's all?" I breathed a sigh of relief, realizing I had tensed in anticipation of worse. It had been nine years since I made the summer trek to the island, mainly because of Roy, who bothered me everywhere but haunted me there. The upcoming trip was an attempt to come to some agreement with him; peace seemed like a longshot. The beckoning, beseeching nature of the newest photo underscored Roy's need to be freed.

"I will be there tomorrow. I'm already packed. I just need to shove everything in the car and take off, unless you don't think I should come at all. Pen?" I waited for Penny's answer, worried she would warn me away, knowing I would ignore her if she did. Roy needed my help to transition to the next plane if only to stop him from posing for photos. Trust me, it sounded stupid, even to me. Still, Roy needed to go; he really did. I was less sure I could convince him. In life, Roy ran stubborn to obstinate.

"Don't be silly, Boo, I can hardly wait to see you. Call Meg with your time of arrival. Tim will meet you at the dock whenever you arrive, but mid-day would be perfect, so you'll have plenty of time to get all your goods up to the cabin and set up housekeeping before dark."

Tim O'Dell lived with Meg Dixon in the Dixon farmhouse at the bottom of Lower Bay. I met Meg when I met Penny. We endured the same tragedies, including losing a brother, though Meg's brother still lived.

After Roy's death, her brother, Brad, left home to travel the seven seas before settling in Australia, buying a sheep station, marrying, and having children. So, it was a joy when Meg found happiness with Tim, who was a couple of years older. A Lake boy, he grew up on a thumb of land that jutted into Lower Bay a little southwest of Booth Island.

"Okay, Pen, what else haven't you told me?" It was a guess, a good one by the long sigh that followed.

"A branch broke off in the wind last night and split Roy's grave marker. Tim says it can be fixed."

"Seems propitious." The marker was Roy Treader's only memorial. It seemed cruel that a branch disfigured Roy's last foothold on earth right before I arrived for our long-postponed, much-needed talk. Unless Roy sensed I was coming and was signaling his unwillingness to debate the issues that shackled him to the island.

Well, he could try. This summer was for us, the opportunity to free me of my charming, athletic, semi-adorable though pesky dead brother. He needed to cough up why he continued to throw me into deep water, forever struggling to grab what was beyond my reach. Had it been the other way around, him up, me down, he would have expected the same of me.

Joe responded, "Accidents, Boothe. Nothing to get steamed up about. Tim will have the marker fixed. Nothing much has changed since you quit summering here. Bodies still float up, trees still get blown over, and the occasional animal gets in the way of a boat propeller. You take care on your drive. Penny can hardly wait to see you. And I look forward to meeting the heroine of so many of Penny's escapades."

"Anything else?" I asked.

"As you know, squatters arrive with the spring thaw. Tim saw lights across Beaver Course on the Sturdevant property. Tim and Mike plan a safari to scare off any homeless. It's an annual event involving hot dogs and beer on Sturdevant Beach."

Mike Gagne, Penny's brother, lived in one of the houses on the Gagne property. Mike and I had been a thing when we were both too young to know what being a thing meant. All the promise ended when Roy's body bounced off the boulders clustered on the north side of the island.

"It's not Finn Sturdevant, is it? You know he killed my brother, right? I mean, really, tell me he's not the squatter, and he hasn't killed again."

Joe laughed. I was working out what was so funny when Joe added, "No, Boothe, drowned fisherman, dead beaver, tree branch, squatter, that's all," Joe answered. "Remember to let Tim know your estimated time of arrival."

I was still deciding whether to trust a man who called me Boothe when Joe hung up.

ii

OVER THE SUMMERS ON Booth Island, my mother and I learned to pack a season's worth of clothes and household items into the maw of our trusty SUV while leaving just enough room for a cooler and groceries. Now, I had the whole passenger seat for overage, including the metal Star Wars lunchbox containing the full set of Roy's postcards.

Two hours after the telephone call, I drove down our tree-lined lane. At the main road, I turned left to catch US-15 north. I had a carefully prepared grocery list for my food stop in Watertown, New York, before crossing the Thousand Island Bridge into Ontario and a gift list for a stop at the Duty Free Shop on the Canadian side of the St. Lawrence River.

I tuned the radio to a news talk program and zoned out until my stomach let out a growl. I heeded its demand, stopping for lunch at the flagstone faced, early-1960s diner in Roscoe, New York.

In the car, I shuffled through the photos in the lunchbox for the one of Roy holding the diner's door open. He wore a happy smile on his young face under the roadside sign, redesigned since my mother and I last lunched there. I asked inside when the new sign had been installed. The answer was four years ago. And, for the life of me, I couldn't think of anyone other than my immediate family who knew that lunching at Roscoe's was a tradition.

While I waited for a table, I asked if anyone recognized the boy in my photo. No one did, though one person pointed out how retro Roy's clothes were. Yes! The picture had been photoshopped. I knew that! I also knew I was being gaslighted. I got it. But Roy needed me. I got that, too.

In the middle of a Reuben sandwich and French fries, I noted how late it had gotten. It would be dark before I made Dixon Landing. I called Meg Dixon. No one answered. So, I left a message that I planned to stay the night in Gananoque, Ontario, on the St. Lawrence River, then be at Dixon Landing by ten the next morning. I asked for a return call if the time was inconvenient.

As I drove north for the first time since graduating high school, I considered how Roy's death had changed my world. The suddenness and manner of Roy's death had wobbled me off-kilter as though my axis had shifted. I think it tilted Dad's, too. He and his new wife moved to Montreal as soon as they married, only six months after Roy's death. The signatures on my parents' divorce were barely dry.

Mom and I kept the ancient schedule for three more years. We arrived at Booth Island two days after school recessed for the summer and returned to Gettysburg two days before school began.

Mother kept to the Booth tradition of throwing a dance party at the end of each week. Party nights, people boated to the island from around Lower and Upper Bay to enjoy food, drink, and dancing under the stars. Roy enjoyed them, too, from his usual perch in a hickory tree that hung out over his deck. Mom brushed her shoulders whenever she stepped onto the deck. I gave a wink into the branches. And though he was there, visible to me, island summers were never the same.

Nine years is a long time to go without dancing. According to Tim O'Dell, the unused dance floor rotted until it teeters rakishly on its foundation. In the intervening years, Meg Dixon's father died, leaving Meg the family businesses of farming and maintaining Dixon Landing. Penny Gagne went to college for a semester returning with Joe Withers. Mom went for her MBA and fell in love with hospitality management. A natural fit if there ever was one.

Mom and I graduated from college the same year. Mom got her dream job days before I started work as an editor for a prestigious publishing company. After a few years, I snuck editing gigs in on the side, sending my book recommendations to various publishers. I developed a reputation for readable, publishable books that occasionally made the bestseller lists.

As of last New Year's Day, my gigs became my job, finally freeing me to return to Booth Island for the summer. The island was far enough from New York

City, where I had worked, and Gettysburg, where I now lived, that a casual weekend or even a two-week visit was out of the question. I kept up my friendships via phone, social pages, and letters. Until one day, I realized I was in hiding, as though I had hied myself to a nunnery and that I missed the summer migration and lake friends.

The lack of reliable cellphone and internet reception on the island was the only stumbling block to spending the whole summer up there. I did my research. A café in the closest reasonable-sized town to the island offered internet. I planned to make all calls, upload and download new gigs, do all my emailing, and grocery buying during weekly trips into the village.

In between, I would rely on the gas generator to provide electricity. At my mother's request, Tim installed one just outside the kitchen door. Mom paid Tim to wire an outlet in the cabin's kitchen, another in the front room, and an electric light in each of the cabin's three rooms. So, with a flip of a switch, I could charge my computer then edit anywhere on the island, like the front porch, Roy's Deck, or the promontory. Roy was free to join me, though he never could spell worth spit.

I would miss my mother's company. Liza Booth Treader dropped my father's surname as soon as I hit eighteen. When I announced my business, Mom took wing. Now, Liza Booth was the majordomo for a movie star owned eco-resort in the Caribbean. The fact that the movie star and my vivacious, rambunctious mother were of an age tells the rest of the story. I expected to be invited to some weird ceremony on a pink sand beach before the end of the year.

Three days ago, as Mom and I sat in our beat-up

SUV awaiting the movie star's private jet, she handed me an envelope. In it was the deed of transfer for Booth Island. Mom paid the necessary transfer taxes and this year's property taxes, or the movie star had. Either way, the family island was mine. As Mom exited the car for the waiting jet, she said, "Booth Island is precious. Give a long think before you decide its future."

By the island's future, Mom meant keeping it or selling it. That decision depended on Roy, not me. No sale was in the stars until we resolved his status and mine, too, for that matter.

My father, Dr. Jack Treader, is an anthropology professor at a university in Montreal and a sought-after field site manager. His wife of eleven years, Misty Lapp, is busy raising the second set of Treaders. A pair of twin boys, the Treader version of an heir and a spare. One to replace my brother Roy and another, in case one died--like Roy. The twins, Jake and John, or as my mother called them, Jake and Flake, were ten and barely human.

I didn't like Misty, never had. She took my dad from me. I still found it hard to believe that Dad left Mom, or maybe not. Dealing with my over-the-top mom might make a man long for someone more grounded. Misty qualified; she could stop a lightning bolt cold.

Dad knew I was summering on the island. He seemed glad of it, muttering something about finding the one fossil that resolved history. Though I had no idea what he meant, I sometimes felt like a fossil, dried up, empty, and waiting to be discovered.

Roy's death stopped my progression. I was unfinished. Everyone but me had moved on, Meg, Penny, Mom, and Dad. Mom's oft-repeated wisdom was that one should continue to write new chapters until the book came to a climactic but satisfactory end. I make my living editing other people's endings. Sometimes I rewrite or rework the closing scene until it is memorable. Happily working out other's woes, I ignore my own story and drift.

Okay, I am a mess.

I still struggle with how readily my parents accepted my brother's death. It was unseemly to me that they split, found new lives, new loves, pushed me away, and, in my father's case, made new sons.

Oh, whine, whine, whine. Some would say I was lucky. I was free to spend my summer at a place and with a brother that I loved and who loved me. I had editing gigs lined up. The first was for my favorite romance author, who, like other romance writers, contracted with me to shape their novels. Perhaps they appreciated that I liked my heroes relatable, a little silly and everyman, not six-packed hunks with flowing blond locks.

iii

AFTER MY GROCERY STOP in Watertown, NY, and at the Duty Free Shop, I parked under the porte cochére of a chain hotel in Gananoque. It was dusk as predicted. After a quick seafood dinner at the onsite restaurant, I returned to my hotel room and phoned Penny.

Her husband, Joe Withers, answered, "Tim got your message. He'll keep an eye out for you starting at 10:00 tomorrow morning." Dixon Landing was in clear sight of the Dixons' white clapboard farmhouse situated on a hill overlooking Lower Bay. "The OPP identified the body. Fisherman. His boat was bobbing around in the marsh in Upper Bay north of Sturdevant Peninsula. He was fishing alone. Lots of beer cans floating in the bottom of the boat. The beaver apparently tangled either with a fisher, our version of a big weasel, or a boat motor."

"You're not buying fisher?" I asked, amused that Joe felt he had to define fisher for me.

"The capabilities of fishers to kill everything from vampires to cattle are somewhat overrated," Joe chuckled. "Though, the crazed carnivores *are* hell on porcupines. I vote for boat motor."

"Do you think..."

"Everyone on Lower Bay knows you're coming to the island for the summer. But do I think any of what happened has anything to do with you? Doubtful, Boothe. It has been twelve years. Finn Sturdevant was a teen when your brother died. Besides, this *is* the last place on earth he would show up, eh?"

"I suppose you're right? And there is that restraining order stopping him from being anywhere near anyone in my family."

I knew Joe was right. I knew it when I asked the question, but in my drowning dreams, the face floating just out of reach was that of the dark-haired, dark-eyed outsider that killed my brother. Okay, accidentally killed my brother. Pranked him to death. Splitting hairs, Roy was as dead as if Sturdevant had held him underwater while enjoying the view above the waterline until the last bubbles escaped Roy's lungs.

"If it makes you feel better, the OPP thinks some fisherman found the beaver floating, and, not wanting it to stink up his boat, hefted it onto New Landing, assuming it would be found. And it was. Honk for Tim when you arrive. And Boothe, everything is fine here."

"Call me Boo, Joe, please? And, say, hey, to Penny for me."

"Penny is currently working on her list of things to do, beginning with the moment you arrive. If I were you, I would worry about getting any work done. She is primed to fill every available minute of every available day."

Penny was as effervescent as my mother, except rounder. Her curves made her adorable with her reddish hair, blue eyes, and gamin grin. From the moment we met at two, one chubby, one lanky, we were inseparable. Penny was a full-time mother now, which had only softened her more as displayed in photos and during live chats. I grinned, thinking of a whole summer of Penny time.

I turned the hotel room television onto a channel carrying my favorite Canadian series. Unless I went to Penny's house and watched hers, this was the last television I would see for months. I woke, the TV still on, three episodes later in the series, and crawled between the hotel's crisply clean Egyptian cotton sheets, those, too, would be the last for the summer, and slept.

I dreamed of my brother's grave on the eastern promontory of the island with its view across Lapp Strait to the cliffs of the Lapp Peninsula. Beneath the cement marker, a predominantly red cookie tin decorated with Christmas elves held each family member's precious reminder of Roy. In my dream, a dark-haired head with dead, black eyes rose up from the grave, cleaving the cement marker into two pieces with the sharp point of the single horn that grew out of his forehead.

Roy would have been twenty-nine this year; he never saw eighteen.

Day 1

iv

I GOT UNDERWAY AFTER a late breakfast. The day sparkled, cool with a breeze, the sky was filled with scudding cumulus, their underbellies dark with damp. Hills rippled by highlighted by outcroppings of the crystalline rocks of the ancient Canadian Shield. The road flowed in and out of basins scoured by glaciers, highlighted by streams flowing with water, and filled with every sort of wildlife. Tall trees arched over the roadway. Lush green fields pockmarked with golden rolls of hay and brick houses with lawns mowed to perfection flashed by outside the car with a sigh. Small towns of clapboard houses and small shops invited me to stop. Instead, I kept driving, opting for the most direct route to Lower Bay.

At Dixon Landing, I pulled my SUV onto a triangular lawn. Directly opposite across Lower Bay, Booth Island hunkered between the two channels like a stopper in a bottle of champagne. I pulled the car under the canopy of a towering hickory tree, parking in the traditional spot. I glanced up at the farmhouse. Meg Dixon waved from the front lawn then strolled to the side yard, joining a man in a baseball hat currently twirling two laughing children on a tire swing hung from a walnut tree.

Tim O'Dell, who I recognize from a live chat, knelt at the end of the dock tinkering with the Booth Island motorboat, part of the island goods transferred to me. I gave him a shout. He stood and waved, his blond hair pulled back in a ponytail, broken ends floating over his ears. He sauntered up the dock displaying a loose-limbed gait. The smile on his even-featured face emitted waves of competence. I popped open the rear gate on my SUV, a package of chips fell to the deep grass.

Tim handed me the tortilla chip bag, then turned for a red storage shed, returning with a heavy-duty plastic wheelbarrow. He unloaded the trunk of my car while I hauled my suitcases down to the boat. Soon, Tim rumbled the wheelbarrow up the pier to join me. Between us, we managed everything into the boat. Tim readjusted my suitcases and one heavy grocery bag to balance the load, leaving room for me at the tiller.

"Follow me out to the island," Tim suggested, slinging a leg over a dayglo green personal watercraft. "That way, I can be on the new pier when you nose the boat in for the first time."

He roared off, leaving a rooster tail in his wake. After nine years, I was a wee out of practice but soon was in hot pursuit. It is nearly a mile from Dixon Landing to New Landing on the Upper Bay side of Booth Island. Lower Bay, a goodly sized body of water, can be choppy. It was a deep blue and so like glass today that it mirrored the clouds overhead.

I was eager to both see and tie up at the new aluminum dock. Though I had already seen it via a photo sent of my dead brother sitting on it, dangling his feet in the water. The pier could be retracted like the bridge over a moat to keep the winter ice from ratcheting and grinding it away. When up, it provided a modicum of security. The pier was another improvement my mother made to our underused island. I often wondered if she had it constructed for Roy, but the truth was, Roy rarely occupied her thoughts.

I planned to leave the pier in the water all summer as an invitation to visitors, then have it raised and locked in place when I left at the end of the season. Though I should check with Roy first. If Roy stayed in residence, he might enjoy some off-season visitors. Just another negotiable item between us.

Tim waited for me on the new pier. The pier was hinged to a fixed aluminum landing cemented into the prominent granite boulders on the island's north side. Pylons driven deep into the lakebed supported the leading edge of the deck. Two additional pylons at the floating end of the dock provided stability. Yellow buoys warned boaters of the stanchions' existence and indicated a slow zone. A gantry arm held the winch, cable, and hook used to raise the arm out of the water. When lowered, the I-shaped dock accommodated up to three boats—one at the top and one on each side. Tim's watercraft was tied to the end. I guided my boat into the near side. Tim grabbed the prow line, then the stern, and tied off the boat.

In addition to the dock, a slanted metal rack held the old wooden canoe. Aluminum stairs climbed up the steep gneiss rock face to the top of Booth Island. The stairway had two landings, one midway up the incline, the second at the top, and nearly level with the cabin further up the path. A four-by-four-foot cage attached to the handrail clung to the left side of the stairs. Tim and I off-loaded suitcases, bags, boxes, one from the Duty Free Store, a case of Labatt Blue Label beer, and my new single-cup coffeemaker.

Seeing my head cocked at the cage contraption, Tim fingered me over. With a flick of a switch, the cage rode down the outside of the handrail. "Joe Withers contrived an electrical lift system. Mike Gagne built it."

As I studied the lift, Tim loaded my goods onto the floor of the cage, then took the stairs two at a time and flipped another switch. The lift chugged up the railing. Tim unloaded the contents onto the top landing. I huffed up the stairs to join him. Over the years, my family had humped groceries, clothes, toys, and a Sailfish sailboat up the steep slope from Old Landing to the cabin. Now, with Joe's amazing contraption, the first twenty-five feet of the hill took the switch on the gas generator filled from four, five-gallon containers of gas locked in an aluminum cage under the stairs.

Joe's lift was a big deal. Booth Island rises straight up out of the lake. We paid taxes on three and a half acres; the useable portion was no more than two. The rest of the island was cliffs and mountain goat territory had there been mountain goats. More than once, one of us had grazed, twisted, or bruised an ankle making the climb from the anchored wooden pallet that served as Old Landing. No more. Now, one just rolled the goods from the lift to the cabin over a gently sloping, manicured path lined with decorative white stones and solar lights. Even so, Tim and I were sweating like Egyptian slaves by the time we transferred all the food, summering over paraphernalia, and beer to the cabin.

The cabin occupies the peak of the island's rocky acres. My great-great, or so, George Booth built it at the end of World War I from half-logs hewn from the indigenous bitter hickory tree with help from the O'Dell and Gagne families. All the timber, furniture, appliances, well, everything had to be floated across the water or hauled across the winter ice in sleds, later by truck, and carried up the cliff.

The twenty-by-twenty-foot house has a kitchen and a bedroom to the back, and a front room the length of the back two. Outside, facing Dixon Landing, an eight-foot-wide porch fronts the building under a shed roof held up at intervals by log posts. The cabin sits on a raised foundation, leaving plenty of room to store the summer screens, the sailboat, and any other odd long flat thing beneath it.

When I was young, everything rolled off the front of the porch into the dirt. The slope was much worse now. My coffee mug knocked over in the bustle of stashing items on the porch, rolled sideways before wobbling off with a thump.

In the back, the new generator purred away on a concrete slab outside the kitchen door. The refrigerator and stove ran on propane, as did the remaining gaslights in each room. Three thirty-pound propane tanks supplied the stove and refrigerator from a second cement pad. Currently, the valve was open, and propane hissed through an aluminum hose into the kitchen.

I lit one burner on the range to check the gas flow. The refrigerator in the front room gave a muffled huff then hummed. I lit a propane sconce on the kitchen wall. It flickered then caught. Satisfied, I turned the burner and sconce off.

A schedule tacked by the kitchen door indicated the days Tim would check and refill or replace the gas and propane tanks. If I needed refills sooner, I was to signal and Tim would replenish my gas supply within a day.

Signaling meant clicking out Morse Code on the Aldis Lamp, a signal lantern installed when the cabin was built. Aldis Lamps were commonly used for ship-to-ship communication; ours was aimed at the front window of the Dixon farmhouse.

The year after Roy died, Mom had a cantilevered deck built on the prow of the island in my brother's honor. She christened it with champagne and a brass plaque that read *Roy's Deck*. Tim waited for me on the deck in the same location where Roy had posed in his most recent postcard. I stopped by the refrigerator, located in the front room by the kitchen door, to grab two beers. As I stepped through the screen door onto the porch, I noticed the traditional spiral-bound guest notebook open on the front room table.

Each Labor Day weekend, when we packed out, we left a new spiral-bound notebook on the front room table with a pencil attached by string and the cabin open for visitors. Those adventurous enough to scramble ashore at Old Landing and climb to the top of the island could, if they wanted, leave us a note. For over a hundred years, people used the island, kids, fishermen, couples out for romance. And they respected it except for a few notable incidents, the ketchup blood and knifed mattress being a prime example.

We wrote the year on the cover of each notebook, read then filed them, oldest to newest, the minute we arrived the next summer. The notebooks contained whole histories of the kids who came up the hill on a lark, came back to drink, then to romance, then to show their own kids where they fell in love. We rarely met our off-season visitors, but we felt as though we knew them through their hastily penciled notes. It was nice to know that someone had maintained the tradition in our absence.

I set the Labatt Blue Label beers on the picnic table, then flipped a switch. Bulb lights strung between the poles at each corner of the deck lit, announcing to all and sundry that the Booths of Booth Island were back in residence.

Tim occupied a seat at the picnic table in the prow of the deck. We sipped our beers communally. Fishing boats trolled up to an old landslide that formed a point off the southeast corner of the island and anchored for a night of fishing. The metal boats swayed in the lake's current, the oarlocks clanked, the anchor ropes squealed, lazy, calming sounds.

"Best view on the lake," Tim commented, with a dip of his beer bottle.

I nodded, took a slurp of beer then asked, "Does Meg have a visitor?"

"Her brother Brad showed up with his brood three days ago. I offered to stay at my folks until Brad leaves. Meg begged me to stay."

"I saw two kids playing on the rope swing. Brad's then?"

"A boy and a girl. Eight and seven. Pesky with adorable Aussie accents. His wife has some bigtime job in Cairns, so she stayed down under." Tim's world would be out of whack until Brad returned to his cattle station. I got it, not from experience, but from editing romance novels.

"When I called Meg to let her know I was coming for the summer, there was no mention of Dave visiting."

"Meg didn't know until Brad parked outside the

farmhouse door," Tim explained. "The greeting was darned reserved, considering it has been twelve years since they've seen each other. The chill prompted my offer to bunk with my folks. Like I said, Meg begged me to stay."

"Begged?" A hickory husk bounced off the tabletop. I checked the interlocked branches overhead for Roy, noticing that the breeze had become a wind. Tim's eyes followed mine before he returned to his beer with a shrug. Which I took to mean he felt the other presence, too. But maybe not.

"Begged. Meg was about to get on her knees. So, I stayed. Brad is in the room we share, the kids in Brad's old room, and Meg and I are bunking downstairs in the backroom. She hasn't slept in two days. And there's no romancing with two kids wandering loose."

"Having Brad home must drum up a whole host of unhappy memories."

"Oh, I don't know, Boothe. Accidents happen on the lake all the time. Roy was one. I remember Mike and Brad being interrogated off and on for a good while after Roy's accident. But the Alberta oil fields were calling to me. Eventually, I just packed up and went. I got a job in a day. Plus, I never ran with the gang of three, so I hardly knew your brother, more a passing acquaintance."

The gang of three, Mike Gagne, Brad Dixon, and my brother, Roy. Meg's dad dubbed them that when the three boys were barely out of diapers.

"Roy wasn't the only death that summer. Finn Sturdevant's father, Don, drowned, too. I always wondered what Don Sturdevant did to tick off his son."

"Nothing, poor kid," Tim said. "His father went fishing and ended up floating face first in a stump bog.

Finn was inconsolable, as he was with Roy.”

“Oh, right! He never showed an ounce of remorse.”

“His dad’s death tore him up. My folks offered Finn the room next to mine. He chose to stay in the cabin on the Peninsula and fend for himself. Your dad and mine paddled over to check on him from time to time; otherwise, he was on his own.”

“To watch, take photos, and lay in wait for Roy?”

Tim narrowed his eyes, choosing his words carefully. “I was in Kingston the night Roy died. I had a run-in with the gang of three about two days before. Nothing important. Macho stuff. They ruled Lower Bay. Being a few years older generally kept me out of their sphere of influence. I was nothing but glad I wasn’t on the lake the night of Roy’s accident.”

“It wasn’t an accident,” I said, punctuated by a confused bobble of my head.

“Malicious mischief, then.”

“How’d you and Meg get together?”

Tim sipped his beer and relaxed. “I worked that job out in Alberta, up by Fort McMurray. Fort Mac. Gorgeous country. Huge skies. I came home on R&R six years ago, and there was Meg. I stayed. That’s the long and short of it.”

“Now you’re working the farm while Meg takes over the Township?” I kidded, though I was curious. Meg had run for Councillor from the Township a few years ago and won. According to Penny, Meg was a force on the Township Council. Her platform included slowing new building to conserve the quality of life on the lake. Thanks to her, the Township had purchased several available plots of land as easements.

When I called to let Meg know I was coming for the summer, she reminded me that I needed deeded lakefront access to sell Booth Island, should I choose. This bit of Canadian pique drove U.S. island owners nuts since many used public facilities for their boating needs.

My family had relied on the Dixons for lake access since my great-great, George Booth, bought the island in the early 1900s. If something happened to Meg or Brad Dixon, my family would have an island, no boat storage, or lake access on Lower Bay. Making now an excellent time to acquire some shoreline and increase the value of Booth Island, whether I sold or not. If I did sell, Roy's plaque and cookie tin would leave with me. A ripple of wind deposited the huffy end of a twig on the table. Roy's vote. No, at a guess.

Tim grinned, playing with the fallen leaves. "Meg's got plans to save the lakefront from further development, sort of get things back in balance, that's for sure. It keeps her busy. I farm and caretake. It's not a bad life, Boothe."

"Boo," I corrected.

I offered Tim dinner as thanks. He got another beer instead. When the first loon called, I accompanied him to New Landing. He squeezed my right bicep, a friendly, asexual, comforting gesture, mounted his watercraft, and roared off with a wave of his hand.

I checked the bowline knots that held my rocking boat to the pier, then fished my overlooked cosmetic bag from under a seat on the floorboards. The zipper was half open. I sat on the platform and inventoried the contents: a brush and comb, shampoo, toothbrush and paste, a pack of disposable razors, multi-vitamins, and aspirin. Everything was there. I dangled my feet in the water. A fish nibbled my toes from time to time while I listened to the hushed words of nearby fishermen float on the night air. Meanwhile, the memory of Roy swung a feather-light arm over my shoulders.

When the familiar lopsided Big Dipper appeared among the myriad of stars overhead, I climbed the stairs, cosmetic bag in hand. The LED lamps, ordered online and delivered to Meg, lit the path from the dock to the cabin. The dense canopy of the trees affected the brightness of the lights in spots, but even dim light was appreciated.

I hung my cosmetic bag on a nail above a shelf lodged between twin tree trunks that had served as our vanity since Prohibition days. I tugged the bag once to make sure it would stay the night, then swung through the screen door into the kitchen. The ten-by-ten room contained a plank counter, deep aluminum sink, a white four-burner propane stove and oven combo, and shelves on any open walls. The walls were painted yellow and always had been. This looked like a fresh coat. The only other furniture was a 1950s aluminum and Formica table for food preparation jammed in the corner under the kitchen window opposite the stove.

After Dad ran off with Misty, Mom installed a water system. Carrying buckets of water up the steep slopes from Old Landing was onerous with Dad and Roy to haul them and impossible without them. Now, a flip of a switch pumped water from Lapp Strait into three 125-gallon drums laid horizontally on pedestals, each tank connected to the next. An enclosed wooden trestle supported the barrels above and fed a sun-warmed gravity shower under the last tank in the line. I flipped on the pump switch by the kitchen door. The pump revved up, then idled, indicating the drums were full thanks to Tim.

I unboxed a single-cup coffeemaker and plugged it

into the kitchen's one electrical outlet. Feeling efficient, I filled the water reservoir from a filter pitcher I brought, worried that the drinking quality of the lake water had degraded in the intervening years. Even nine years ago, despite the ban on two-cycle engines, oil sometimes slicked the lake surface. And, of course, there was the odd dead beaver found floating on the waves.

Happy at the prospects of a great cup of coffee come morning, I readied for bed, brushing my teeth at the forked tree. As I stepped back into the kitchen, a shadow wavered across the ancient glass of the front room window. I rushed into the room, the screen door batted close, I tore through it, fluttering the pages of the open notebook on the table.

I leaped off the porch just as a foot disappeared down a grassy path to the left of Roy's Deck. My left foot caught one of the solar lights. I tumbled head over heels landing awkwardly. I stood—pain shot from my left foot into my head. I grabbed a sapling for support, balanced, took one step, and decided neither foot nor ankle was broken.

Hobbling to the porch, I used a post to leverage myself up the one step, reached for the doorframe, and swung through the door into the nearest chair at the front room table. The ankle was swollen and more than a little mottled. I figured it for a sprain, not one of those leave you limping for a month pulls, but a couple of days off your feet and off you go twists.

I stood and leaned, rather than stepped, to the refrigerator, hoping for ice. Tim, bless him, had filled both ice trays. I emptied one tray into an empty bread bag from a basket of bags kept on the bookshelves that lined the wall, then wrapped the bag around my ankle.

Installed at the table in the front room, my foot up, I pulled the notebook over.

BOO! covered the page in the clownish letters that kids draw, fat, and shaded in graphite. Greeting or threat? I whispered Roy's name in case the backhand message was from my left-handed brother. No answer, not even the swish of a branch on the roof.

I traced the word with a finger. This was Roy's corner. Night after summer night, he sat here in the glow of the propane lights, sketching out some cockamamie idea or other. The island was littered with his crazy improvements. A huge slingshot meant to keep invaders at bay. A plank between two tall beech trees used as a diving platform. A hammock of slatted wood strung together with twine lashed thirty feet above the ground between two hickory trees, reachable by boards nailed onto a third tree. According to the court filings, Roy had been climbing the island's rocky north face under the diving plank when Sturdevant scared him to his death.

It was a Friday night. On Fridays, husbands who worked drove down from Ottawa, over from Toronto, or up from Kingston to be with their summering families. Boats raced up and down the reaches of Upper Bay. Dances were held for the kids, purportedly to keep us out of trouble. I loved being on Lower Bay, hanging out with my summer friends, being in demand because of my fun-loving brother.

There was no dance party on the island that Friday. Mom was mopey about something and canceled it. So, Penny, Meg, and I attended a social at a church on Westport Road. Ice cream, grilled meat, corn on the cob, all the end of summer fare, and boys from as far as the village of Westport and town of Perth.

We dressed for the occasion in tight shorts and sleeveless shirts, some with ruffles at the shoulder. We were fifteen and ignoring our escort, Meg's grandmother, Mildred. A spry, wise woman in her sixties. We all called her Dred, including Meg. Dred had a tone to her voice that made you obey her every command in dread of whatever the punishment might be. And we were too afraid to find out.

That night, in the dusky light, fireflies began their mating dance, little bursts of light flitting randomly above, in, and around stalks of corn. The town boys circled us. The summer boys approached. We all knew summer love never came true, mostly from movies and songs and, of course, our mothers.

As young as we were, the Lower Bay girls, Meg and Penny included, were looking for a mate, which meant a boy from the area with prospects. Each dance was an opportunity to meet someone from outside the Lower Bay community and a chance to escape to a more prosperous life.

The Lower Bay men who farmed did okay. The men who lived off the summer lake people did well, too. But the rest, the ones who were disinterested in or unable to build docks, fix and repair cabins, or sell wood scraped by. Their sons left for the cities--Kingston, Perth, Ottawa, even Toronto--and never returned. If you were lucky, you were the Lower Bay girl they took with them.

We flirted, danced, and laughed until Dred pointed to the car. We giggled away the drive home, rating the boys we had met on our three scales, looks, personality, and bod. Warm air rushed over us through the open windows of the car. It was a night to remember.

When we took the corner onto Lower Bay Road,

lights blazed from the Dixon farmhouse. A yard light lit people milling about the Dixon Landing dock. Two boys, one dark-haired, one light, sat on the pier oblivious to the bodies and hubbub. Shadows of neighbors rushing to join the group mingled with the quaking of tree leaves.

Dred parked. We hopped out in our getta-boy wear. The boys on the dock shifted their eyes to us. One was Penny's brother, Mike, the other, Meg's brother, Brad.

Mom picked her way through the crowd across the shadowy, rough ground to me. Her face was the same shade as the waning moon. Dad was nowhere. Our car was missing. My eyes slammed across the water, searching for Booth Island by the light of the crescent moon. It felt as though someone had unhinged my universe, floating the planets and stars about the Milky Way in disarray. Penny put an arm around my shoulders.

"Is it Dad?" I asked as Meg turned away.

"No, Roy. Roy's gone," Mom whispered.

"Where?" I asked.

"He drowned." Mom stared at the white knuckles of her clasped hands. "They found him floating. Mike, Brad, and..."

"How possibly?" I asked.

My mother shook her head, clasping her hands against her stomach.

"Roy fell on the boulders at New Landing. He hit his head," Dred responded over my shoulder.

I checked the sky. The sliver of moon was gone. The lake ink black. Wind rippled. On nights like this, reflected light undulated shadows that shapeshifted the rocks and water, making the known dangerous. A rock became water, and water, rock. Distances changed. But, Roy, Roy was an otter, a sturgeon, a beaver, water was his element.

None of it mattered. Roy was dead.

The Lower Bay people rallied round. Roy was cremated. Dad scattered Roy's ashes over the island and the waves of Lower Bay. Mom insisted we each contribute one thing that fit into a clean Christmas cookie tin found on the top shelf in the kitchen. No one peeked to see what the other had offered with a whispered prayer. Then, my bonnie brother was gone, my buddy, and my protector.

Life took a different trajectory. My father ran off with Misty Lapp from across Lapp Strait. My mother stayed put, raised me, then flew away. We promised each other that we would open Roy's tin on the twentieth anniversary of his death. That was before Dad defected with Misty and Mom with her movie star. Now, there was just me, Roy's tin, Roy, and my fractured life.

I was in good company. That summer, Mike Gagne worked at a resort in Upper Bay. The general consensus of opinion was that he had peaked at seventeen. With his lifeguard-perfect physic and meager intelligence, he seemed destined to be the Lower Bay handyman. But I never believed the talk. I knew Mike loved astronomy; I knew he had dreams. Instead, he fell into the natural rhythm of the lake. He was good with his hands. Everyone said so, especially the girls. By contrast, Brad Dixon finished high school, immigrated to Australia, and disappeared into a cattle station in Queensland. And now, he was back.

That night, Mike and Brad found Roy floating, his body pounding against the back of the island. They identified Finn Sturdevant as the person seen stroking across Beaver Course. They swore under oath that Mike jumped to shore and dragged Roy onto land, tried chest compressions, relying on his lifeguard skills to bring my brother gasping back. When that failed, Mike ran to our cabin for help, leaving Brad to continue resuscitation. No matter what anyone tried, Roy was dead.

In a matter of hours, the OPP brought Finn Sturdevant in for questioning. Finn admitted lying in wait for Roy, but only to punk him, as though somehow that mattered. It offended me that the last thing my brother saw was Finn Sturdevant watching him bounce off rocks into the lake. While drowning, Roy may have watched Sturdevant dive in and stroke away.

Though Sturdevant insisted he brought Roy ashore, Mike and Brad swore otherwise. No one believed Sturdevant. There were too many reasons not to, including suspicions about his part in his own father's death. The judgment of malicious mischief included an order restraining him from contact with our family for twenty years and a choice of juvenile detention or the U.S. Marines. He chose the Marines. He was seventeen.

Roy would have liked to have had the same choice, well, not actually that choice, but a choice. Instead, Sturdevant denied my brother all the opportunities that stretched out before him. Forever.

The morning after Roy's memorial, if you could call it that, I rowed our wooden skiff from Old Landing on Beaver Course to New Landing on Upper Bay. Back then, New Landing was wooden decking that hung six feet out over and parallel to the glacial boulders upon which our island sits. Nothing fancy. It provided enough dockage for one boat on calm days and was unusable when the water was rough.

I oared further along the shore, checking every rock for a dark spot that might be dried blood. Obsessed. Even falling, how could Roy have miscalculated the rocks then drowned? We were fish. We not only swam Beaver Course; we swam the third-mile across Lapp Strait to Lapp's Beach for something to do. Little did we know Dad rowed our skiff across the same waters to woo Misty or bonk her, in my mother's vernacular.

No blood-stained rocks dotted the shoreline. I did spy one rock seven feet above the waterline with a rusty splotch on it. It was surrounded by ruts like a heel or hooves of an animal who grazed itself while skidding downhill for water. It was too far from New Landing to be Roy's blood. I rowed back, catching my mother scrambling over the rocks by the dock. Searching for anything, as I had from my seat in the rowboat.

A little further around, I found a scrap of cloth clinging to a birch branch near shore. That night, I pressed the fabric between the pages of a Nevil Shute book stacked on the reading shelves in the front room.

The remnants of our family stayed through that summer. Whenever Dad mentioned packing up, Mom would say no, the night sounds will frighten Roy. Mom must have meant the night sounds in the ground, bugs, nightcrawlers, even ground squirrels. My Roy was afraid of nothing. Like me, the loons sang to him, the bees announced morning. The wind soughed his lullaby. Besides, he was ashes and small chunks of bone either cast or captured in the leather pouch that Dad contributed to the tin. Yes, I sneaked a peek.

I tapped the pencil eraser on the open notebook. Someone, probably Tim, had filed the pads from the intervening years on the same shelf as the other seventy or so years of reminiscences.

I would read them. Just not tonight. I stood. My ankle was grumpy, a bruise wove up my foot from my big toe. I hobbled into the bedroom, changed into my shorty pajamas, and lay on the old horsehair mattress. After a moment, I sat up and stared out the window.

Normally, I left the thin batiste panels open, inviting in the night breeze, the soft buzz of the woods, and the rays of the morning sun. Tonight, I drew the sheer panels. Worried, I suppose, about the note and my left-handed visitor.

Boo!

Day 2

v

MY REGULAR ISLAND ROUTINE, perfected over the three years that Mom and I summered on the island after Roy's death, was to rise, take a swim in Beaver Course, then sprawl on Roy's Deck to dry. Not today. I limped to the kitchen on my twisted ankle, my body stiff from the unforgiving vintage horsehair mattress.

I plunked my shorty pajama-clad body in an aluminum chair on a flower-print plastic seat cushion within reach of my single-cup coffeemaker. Then I inserted a pod selected from a variety pack, placed a mug under the nozzle, and flipped the switch. It was pure luxury: the one negative, no coffee grounds, which was quite inconsiderate of me. The island's nightcrawlers had been feasting on coffee grounds for over a hundred years and poached for bait as long. I eased my conscience, knowing the worms had survived quite well without fresh grounds for nine years.

Coffee brewing, I returned to the bedroom, opened my knapsack, and pulled out a pair of cotton shorts and a red-and-white striped camp shirt. I slipped them on, then my feet back into my sandals, returning to the kitchen as the coffee stopped dripping. I had packed in eggs, the essentials for breakfast, and about five dinners. Nothing for lunch. And toilet paper.

The outhouse, about twenty feet downslope from the kitchen door, was still de rigueur, yellowjackets, and all. We had détente. I wouldn't bother them if they didn't buzz under my naked, seated bottom. It was a tenuous agreement.

I set one place for breakfast. A melamine plate covered in orange poppies and silverware from a plastic box, knife, fork, and spoon washed thoroughly before use. Sitting in the straight-backed aluminum chair, I munched toast, sipped coffee, and idly smoothed the oilcloth covering the kitchen table. The soft rustles of morning sifting through the screen door kept me company, birds in the grass and trees, bugs scratching and buzzing, lazy, lulling sounds as the day warmed.

When I finished, I stretched my arms over my head then brewed a fresh cup of coffee. Cup in hand, I rattled out the backdoor, down the ridgeback of the island for my first chat with Roy. The sun spangled the ground through the dense green of the leaves on interlocking branches overhead. Blue periwinkles and white lady's slippers flowered under the shade of the canopy, fluffing in the morning upswell off the lake.

At my level, the air was still. Bugs danced in the rising sunshine. I stopped, stretched my arms out from my sides, and twirled in pure joy. A small mammal crunched through the undergrowth. I peered, hoping for a sighting. No luck. A soft gray grosbeak with a yellow wash and black and white wings cocked its head, then sang a warning that the bush ahead was occupied. A spider flew by on a slender spindle of thread anchoring it to the lower branches of a buckeye bush. Then the spider reversed direction, spinning as it climbed its sun dazzled webbing.

My coffee, meant to share with Roy, was half gone by the time I sauntered up the path to the tip of the promontory. I came first to a cement bench, hauled in pieces across the water by my father, then wrangled and assembled in the shade of an alder. Since I had last been here, the trees, their leaves, ash thin to maple thick, hued in the darkest to lightest greens, had formed a sort of cathedral over Roy's bench and marker.

It was meant to be a contemplative, peaceful place to sit with my brother. Now I stared dumbstruck at the jagged edges where Roy's tombstone had been cleaved in two, glad for Penny's warning. I slid the heavy pieces together. They fit well enough; no chunks were missing.

Roy's epitaph was challenging to read, both broken apart and worn by twelve years of rain and snow. His name was legible, Roy Andrew Treader, the beginning and end dates still visible, but the words etched by my father in wet cement with an ash twig were nearly unreadable. I rubbed dirt into the concrete until the letters emerged. Not for the first time, I wondered what my father was thinking as he wrote: *What the loon calls.*

"Boo!"

My coffee cup landed in the heaved dirt at my feet. A nightcrawler, the size of my little finger, wiggled toward the coffee spilling from the mouthpiece. I grabbed the mug, uttering inanely enough, as I stood, "Mike Gagne, you scared me!"

His smile made me smile. "You look great, Boo. I like your hair shorter." I swiped stray hair over my left ear and, I think, blushed. He tucked a finger under my chin and raised my face. "You're limping?"

"Tripped on the way to the john last night. I guess I don't have my island legs yet," I lied, not sure why besides being embarrassed to be found out chasing a phantom.

Mike had grown into an uncompromisingly handsome man. Dark hair, light eyes, a scar over his right eye descending through the eyebrow, as though he had been dueling, masculine mouth, a daring chin. That wasn't all of it, he was broad-shouldered with hands that looked as though they could mend anything, thick fingered and scarred. I felt a jolt deep in my stomach.

"You were communing with Roy, and I've disturbed you," he said.

"I planned to but found myself wondering at nature's force instead." I pointed to Roy's split marker.

Mike raised his dark eyebrows with a shrug. "I'm here at Tim's bidding. He asked me to fix Roy's stone." Mike produced a trowel and bag of pre-mixed cement. "Though, I suspect Tim hoped I'd have it done before you saw it." Mike knelt, fingering the two halves of the marker. "Looks like someone took a sledgehammer to it."

I saw the round scar on the stone before he pointed it out.

"Maybe a bait hunter with a bad aim. One good thump on the ground and the worms rise to the surface," he said.

"Spoken like a true bait poacher," I joked.

"Still, I keep expecting to see Roy hanging by his knees from one of the branches."

When and how, possibly, had I forgotten that Roy hung upside down like a bat, whenever and wherever he could.

"Being here is harder than I imagined for me as well. Roy scaled the rocks where he supposedly died almost every day to dive off that stupid platform of his. All you guys used it. He knew this island from one end to the other, he shinnied up the trees, he walked around the base of the island once, it took him hours. Roy hitting his head and drowning has always been hard to accept. It just has. Even harder to believe that Finn Sturdevant made no attempt to rescue him. How devoid of humanity do you have to be to do something like that? I don't care how scared you are."

"Remember how the OPP, sorry provincial police, worked Brad and me over, off and on for about a month. Dad drove me in, left me. Brad's dad, too. Like they thought we were responsible, like we could have breathed life into Roy's lifeless body. It wasn't like we didn't feel awful enough." A slight shake of his dark head and downward curve of his mouth sold me. "I've never thought malicious mischief was the right call. In my book, Sturdevant murdered Roy. That simple. And for what?" Mike prepared the marker, then the cement, and deftly healed the stone's wound, somehow matching up my father's scrawled words. "There. Fixed."

"Good as new," I responded, mindlessly.

Mike stood, wiping his hands. "You know, I always thought we had a chance, you and me. Right up until I saw your dad's face as I tore into the cabin, yelling that Roy was on the dock, that Brad was trying CPR."

"Nothing could have brought him back. He was already gone." I squeezed Mike's right hand. Years of wondering slipping away. Back then, I liked Mike, like a fifteen-year-old dotes on an older boy, an older, handsome, high-spirited boy who enjoyed showing off. The memory of Mike diving into the lake then powering back onto the dock, giving a shake of his wet, dark hair, and a self-conscious smile overwhelmed me.

He smiled that smile now. A flowering buckeye stalk fell where Mike had just troweled. He swiped it off with the toes of his boot. Another flower landed on his head, draping him in white blossoms. He lifted it and placed it on Roy's bench, as another one tumbled next to it.

"We did have a chance, didn't we?" he asked, as though it mattered, as though he hadn't married, been widowed, had children, and didn't make his few dollars as the Lower Bay welder. He worked for Penny's Joe, installing and fixing docks. That smile again, a row of perfect white teeth showing between his masculine lips. My mind tunneled back to the sight of him sitting on the dock at Dixon Landing. His elbows rested on his thighs, one hand holding a cloth over his bloody forehead, his eyes red-rimmed from crying. That night, he stared woefully at me. I felt our future, his future, sliding away. Now, I reached up and touched the scar over his right eye.

He covered my hand with his. "Your father. When I told him about Roy, he picked up the heaviest object he could find."

I raised my eyebrows.

"The Triathlon trophy Roy won two weeks before."

"I'm sorry," I muttered without thinking.

"Roy's dead, Boo. We've both had to live with it...try to find a way to deal with it. At least Brad Dixon made a life for himself down under. I've bungled everything. And here you are, eh?"

I started to object but said, instead, "It must seem

weird Brad being back home after all this time."

Mike snorted. "Not very. Brad strode in like he never left. Meg has been by to see Penny more in the last two days than in the previous month. Joe is a bit testy about it. Meg is not his favorite."

"Meg always thought her father favored Brad."

Mike nodded, glancing at his watch. "I promised Tim I would check in on the Sturdevant property on my way out. Tim keeps the grounds and chases off trespassers. What with the ruins of the bottling shed rusting in, big scraps of sharp metal on the ground, and the toxins from whatever the heck was being brewed over there, Tim's worried someone will get hurt or worse. He swears there is a new squatter on the property, saw smoke, lights bobbing, the usual eerie doings last night. As much as I love Sturdevant Beach, the minute I step into the trees, every hair on my head stands on end. But I told Tim I would check it out, so off I go."

"Oooh, smoke, lights--"

Mike bucked his head then slung the remainders of an eighty-four-pound bag of cement over his left shoulder like it was a bag of cotton balls. "Since you're so fearless, do you mind keeping an eye on Sturdevant Beach and sending a message if you see anyone using it you don't recognize? That would be a big help. Then Tim and I can concentrate on patrolling the acreage on Tim's ATV."

"Not at all."

Mike brushed my left cheek with his lips, then trotted off toward New Landing.

I touched my cheek, remembering Mike and another stolen kiss. The summer I was fifteen, the summer Roy died, Mike and I walked hand in hand to this promontory under the light of a full moon. He swung me into his arms and kissed me on the lips. My first real boy kiss, well, semi-man kiss. It has defined romance for me ever since.

That night, Roy ruined the moment by clearing his throat to let Mike know he was approaching. Mike ran off. Roy swung me by the arm toward the cabin, uttering a brotherly warning. Mike had a reputation. I misinterpreted it to mean '*be careful*' when what Roy meant was people will talk. So, Mike and I gave people something to talk about. Dad scolded me. Roy signaled I told you so with a hunch of his shoulders.

A movement in the brush brought me back to the present. Without a thought, I pivoted toward the wavering shadow, caught my toe on a root, and crashed in a heap. From the floor of the woods, the shadow resolved itself into a sapling. Under questioning, I would have sworn it was Roy busily warning me away from Mike a second time.

Laying on my back in the leaves, feeling every sort of fool, I stared at the wispy clouds clustering in the cerulean sky. I blamed the shadow, and Mike's attentions, for distracting me from the obvious. There were only two reasons to use a sledgehammer on Roy's tombstone. One to deface it, the other to unearth the cookie tin.

Standing, I limped back to Roy's stone. I knelt beside the healing marker, digging under it at an angle to avoid the setting cement. When my fingers bumped the sides of the tin, I disinterred it. The lid's metal collar was rusted to the tin, the contents of the still brightly gay Christmas decorations undisturbed. I jammed the round can back into the hole, smoothed the ground over it, then sprinkled leaves and twigs liberally on the bare spot to mask my digging.

vi

I WASHED THE DIRT from my hands in the kitchen sink then signaled Meg Dixon with the Aldis Lamp, screwed to the prow of Roy's Deck, that I was on my way for a visit. No need to worry about Meg decoding my message. She would either be home or not; after all, we had the whole summer to chat. But I suspected she would be standing by with coffee, her homemade jams, and scones.

I grabbed my knapsack, checked that my purse, car keys, and laptop were inside, then limped out the backdoor, down the ridge of the island to the dock. The new motorboat was fast enough to get me to Dixon Landing in about seven minutes from push-off to tie-up, half the time of the old skiff. I untied the prow, idled the engine, then pulled the stern rope from a metal eye on the jetty. The lake water was still high from the spring melt, so I motored out through Beaver Course, a quicker run than around the island and through Lapp Strait.

The boat's wake lapped on both sides of the narrow channel. The *No Trespassing* signs posted on the Sturdevant property twelve years ago now hung rusting and lopsided from rotting posts and tree trunks. No one walked, ran, or sat on Sturdevant Beach, nothing to report there. On the island side, someone had cleared the path from Old Landing to the cabin. Tim hadn't mentioned doing it, nor had Mike. Meg would know who and when, I would ask her.

As I cleared the island, the wind tangled my

chestnut hair into knots. The sun brought out the red highlights, making me feel like some glamorous wannabe. I liked me. My shoulders were broad, my chest just enough, and my hips lean but still hips. Like my brother, I was built to live in the water. Or maybe our lives in the water shaped us.

The day was silky warm. The blowback from the slapping boat splashed and dried, leaving cooled spots on my exposed arms and legs. The minute I throttled down for my approach to Dixon Landing, heat descended. Water bugs skittered across the surface of the sheltered cove while minnows dashed to and fro in the swaying seaweed. Leaves rustled overhead and in the brush. These late spring days, filled with the buzz of bugs, were spangled in light and froth. I had missed them these last nine years.

I tied off, hefted my knapsack onto my back, and climbed onto the wooden pier. Ashore, I dropped my knapsack off at my aging SUV then trudged up the bumpy tire-track road to the Dixon farmhouse. Meg watched me. The rutted dirt road was a quarter-mile long at a fifteen-degree grade; climbing it took forever on my gimpy ankle.

Meg's grin showed the gap between her two front teeth. Her blue eyes, flat on the bottom, round on the top, gleamed happily. She was an inch shorter than me, and she was minimally ten pounds heavier. Her hair was professionally coiffed, her natural ash brown was streaked with a coppery color. The shaggy chin-length cut became her. She had been to a manicurist, too, her fingernails were perfectly lacquered, and I thought extended. She wore a becoming sundress. Pineapples and strawberries splashed across the retro-print fabric. The neck, cuffs of the cap sleeves, and pocket fold were all piped in red. Her sandals had small heels, kicky red straps, and open toes. Her toenails were polished red.

I wondered if she was using one of those online shopping sites that offered personal shoppers. My Meg would have met me in cut-off jeans and a tank top, not unlike what I currently wore. Meg had definitely upped her game. Tim must agree with her or being a councilwoman did or both. Penny reported that Meg was the terror of the Township, which Tim had confirmed last night. The difference was, Penny thought Meg let her elected position go to her head, but Tim touted her accomplishments. Jealousy versus genuine affection?

Meg held me out at arm's length, shaking her head. "What happened?"

"After Tim left me last night, I stumbled on my way to the outhouse. Too many Labatts and too embarrassing."

Two kittens tumbled past, a gray one and a calico. They scampered under a lilac bush then out the other side to continue their roughhousing among summer green blades of grass that danced in the breeze. The same breeze ruffled a red and white checked tablecloth spread over a picnic table shaded by two thick black walnut trees.

Meg pointed me toward the table. A thermos pot of coffee, two teacups with a pink peony design, and a plate of assorted cookies held the tablecloth down. Meg sat opposite me, her elbows on the table. I folded mine in my lap.

"Brad's home," Meg said.

"Tim told me. You need to be extra nice to Tim. I don't think he likes being displaced."

"Brad brought his kids for the summer. His wife

stayed in Cairns."

"So, quite the surprise, how's the visit going?"

"It's good to see him after all these years. But a surprise. We both got a bit of a start when the body and the dead beaver showed up at Booth Island. You know, after...well, after everything." She patted my arm. "I was checking a few properties on Lower Bay at the Land Records Office after the last Township Council. The Township is hoping to acquire Sturdevant Peninsula for a park. It has that lovely beach. While I was at it, I sneaked a look at your property as well. I was surprised to see that your mother was the sole owner of Booth Island and deeded it to you."

"Oh, grandfather gave Mom the island and the house in Gettysburg and Uncle Nick everything else when he retired and moved to Arizona."

"So now that the island is officially yours, what are your plans? I mean other than upgrading the old dance floor."

Now, in context, her advice over the phone regarding lakefront access made sense. And, yes, Mom and I had requested permission from the Council to repair the rotting Prohibition dance floor. "Well, as you well know, I am unable to sell without access. But I'm not sure that I want to either. If I can work here successfully this summer, I'll likely keep the island and continue using Dixon Landing. If you agree. And, of course, Roy's there."

Meg poured two cups of coffee. "I thought Roy's ashes were distributed over the lake?"

"Dad kept some for the cookie tin. So, besides dead men and beavers, what's going on in the neighborhood?"

Meg stuffed one of her delicious homemade

oatmeal chocolate chip cookies in her mouth, took a slurp of coffee, brushed the crumbs from her hands, and laughed, "Much!"

"I saw Mike Gagne this morning," I said as a starter.

"Gorgeous, widowed, and dumb. Twenty-nine and a welder. Lost his shop in Tichbourne two years ago. Never could keep his hands on a penny, not if there were women around. He has two kids, lives off the kindness of his sister. His second wife died in a car accident in Smith Falls. She was one of us." Meg meant a Lower Bay person. "Donna Pence."

The Pences lived farther up Lower Bay Road. The house always seemed in need of paint. When I was a kid, the yard looked like a toy store, littered with bikes, balls, badminton nets, a trampoline, and an above ground pool. I could see the yard from where I sat in Meg's side yard. No kids. No bikes. No pool. Same paint peeling.

"How did Mike take her death?"

"Shook it off. Mike works with and for Joe Withers. I wonder about that; Mike takes a lot of managing. He has a short attention span. His two kids run with Penny's mob. The good news is Mike's available if you're in the market for a handsome deadbeat."

"Tim sent Mike up to patch Roy's stone. Mike claims someone used a sledgehammer on it, complete with round marks to prove it."

"Doubtful, a couple of nights ago, branches were flying everywhere."

"Mike and I talked for a few minutes. He brought up being questioned by the OPP after Roy's death. How Brad and Mike both felt deserted, especially Mike."

"Brad left the country if that's a hint. Brad's home

for a visit," Meg repeated.

"I saw his kids playing on the rope swing last night."

"A boy and a girl, they're enjoying the lake life. Tim took them swimming this morning while Brad went into town. Lots of noise. I am planning a welcome to the lake picnic a week from Saturday. You will come, of course. Everyone is dying to see you all grown up."

"Of course, I will. Just being invited brings back fond memories of picnics on this lawn. Which reminds me, as I cruised through Beaver Course, I noticed that someone had cleared the path up from New Landing."

"People climb up that island all the time. Always have. Tim does his best to keep an eye on the place, Boo. Still, I wonder if you should be out there alone after that body washed ashore. Think about it, what if you had been the one to find it?"

"I'm fine, Meg. For heaven's sake, I feel safe enough. After all, you're all looking out for me."

"A kayak cruised around the island late last week. I got my trusty binoculars out. The rower came from around the bay behind the Thumb." The Thumb: the O'Dell house, the one Tim grew up in, sits on a thumb-shaped piece of land that juts into Lower Bay. Meg swiped a fly from the sugar and slurped her coffee. "Boo, I'm not kidding. Seeing the kayak snooping around and now hearing that someone cleared the Old Landing trail worries me.

"I'll check in this year's guest book to see if any of the regular visitors saw anyone or thing unusual on the island."

Meg sucked air in through the crack between her two front teeth. She could whistle, too. I had spent a good part of one summer trying to mimic her and failed. "Boo, I'm serious. Tim's not given to worry. But he is worried about you up there alone, no cellphone, no internet, just the old signal light. What if someone comes up Old Landing, anyone could, what if something happened?"

"Ooh, I'm all a shiver. Are you trying to scare me? Huh, Meg, are you?" I kidded. "Besides, Mike already warned me, asked me to keep an eye out."

It must have been something in my voice or my lack of worry because Meg gave me a hard stare. As long as the shaded in *Boo* in the notebook intrigued more than worried me, Roy and I could watch out for each other. Meg cocked her head to give me more time to voice any concerns. When none were forthcoming, she added, "Of course, not."

"Good, because it's not working." I poured more coffee. "What other gossip is there?"

Meg started with the Gagnes and worked her way around the Lower Bay until coming to a full stop with a story about Pences' new puppy. There had been deaths, births, runaways, new kittens, marriages, new dogs, old illnesses, and new joys. I oohed and aahed at her gossip for a good hour before begging off.

vii

TIM DOCKED IN MEG'S boat as I hobbled downhill to my car. I waved. He waved back, looped the bow rope over a stanchion, then stood, a flour sack in one hand and a shovel in the other. Nightcrawlers! A flour bag full of the juicy, thick nightcrawlers that aerated the dense loam around the outhouse and Roy's marker went for a tasty Canadian Loony or two at the bait shop.

Some things never change.

Tim stood in a white T-shirt and wet cut-offs, knee-deep in swaying grasses, watching as I climbed into my car, a speculative look on his face. A moment later, he looked uphill. Meg must have waved. He grinned and walked toward the lane.

As I climbed into my car, a twinge from my ankle reminded me that there was a charming little apothecary in Westport, the nearest real town. I could buy an ankle brace there, which was good because my ankle screamed for more support than the athletic tape from the first aid kit provided. And I could replenish the first aid kit while I was at it.

I drove out New Road, a dirt lane plowed through the thick timber fifty years ago, thus new, without thought to the grading of corners or smoothing of the rills. The track was narrow, bumpy, deeply rutted, and harrowing in parts, but was a direct cut to Westport Road. The alternative route, Upper Bay Road, though scenic, wound north around the lake until it reached the ghost of a small town and exited onto the highway.

I reached Westport Road, thoroughly jostled, with the past as my backseat passenger. Every turn in the road revealed some family memory. Our car broke down on one corner, steam pouring out of the radiator. Dad found a beach bucket in the trunk and took off walking. He filled it at the first lake he came to, hiked back, and filled the radiator enough to get us to that lake and so on until we reached a little auto garage on the outskirts of Westport.

A bump joggled loose memories of a barbecue at a small community church. I danced with all the boys, including Roy, and especially Mike Gagne. It was also the first time any of us laid eyes on the boy who changed our lives. Finn Sturdevant, tall, dark-haired, dark-eyed, strolled through the crowd as though he belonged wherever he happened to be. Weaving in and out of people, he snapped candid photographs with a fancy camera.

Sturdevant took a photo of Brad Dixon kissing some girl. Brad shoved him into the brush, landing Sturdevant on his butt, his camera still snapping. When Sturdevant gave Brad a look of utter contempt, Brad spat ineffectually in Sturdevant's direction. Unphased, Sturdevant snapped another photo. And, so, by the end of the evening, we not only knew his name but that he disdained us.

Our past, Roy's past, departed the car when The Beer Store signaled the outskirts of Westport, a village of Victorian-era houses built along a curve of Upper Rideau Lake. The lake is part of the Rideau Canal system, constructed by Colonel By to keep the supply channel open from Ottawa to Kingston during the War of 1812. The War was well over before the canal was completed. Now the Rideau Canal provided a recreation venue for boaters from all over North America with its narrow winding channels and lakes connected via a system of picturesque locks.

Driving into Westport is a step back in time. Pastries are sold out of a home one block from the main street, deadly delicious, buttery pastries. The far end of the village is dominated by a bed and breakfast hotel, consisting of two Victorian-era buildings on opposite corners of the road to the lovely town of Perth. Small shops built in various eras peddle keepsakes or geegaws for tourists depending on one's point of view. An LCBO store is snuggled in the corner of a modern building for those who need liquor harder than The

Beer Store sells.

The village has all one needs, including a grocery store, gas stations, a chip truck, and the café from which I hoped to work. It was just luck that the coffeehouse also boasted an ice cream counter scooping Tiger Tail ice cream. Anyone who has ever been to Ontario knows that the orange and licorice ice cream is the pièce de résistance of all ice creams on a hot summer day.

I found a parking space near the apothecary, bought the ankle brace, then limped down to the café tucked in a brick building on the corner of two of Westport's main streets. The Westport Post, to which my Gettysburg mail was being forwarded bi-weekly, was across the street.

I installed myself at a round wooden table tucked in a bay window at the front of the cafe, unloaded my computer, and dug out my wallet. Under a mural of a pair of nesting loons in moonlit rushes, I ordered two scoops of Tiger Tail from the teen working the ice cream side of the long wood and glass counter. The non-ice cream side of the counter sold sandwiches, pastries, and coffees, including lattes.

The store was crowded with chatty locals and tourists. Flyers were taped to the walls extolling all of the upcoming picnics, art showings, and tasting parties. Copies of the local free newspaper fluttered when the entrance door opened and closed. Conversations salted the air. It was altogether a wonderfully comfortable place to set up my editing business.

I sat at my table, spooning Tiger Tail from a plastic dish, and availed myself of the café's internet. Two manuscripts awaited me, one a romance, one a vampire thriller. I accepted both and provided delivery dates. I emailed an edited manuscript back to its author after ensuring that my invoice was paid and then transferred the online money to my checking account. I was in business.

One of Westport's two real estate offices occupied the brownstone next door. When Meg first reminded me that I would need lakefront access to sell, I ordered a Land Office map that provided the owners, liens, and property identification information. At home, I studied the map for parcels that met my needs, planning to call a few owners during the summer. From time to time, I checked online listings for properties on the lake, the whole lake, not just Upper and Lower Bay, and watched prices rise as summer neared.

Though I said nothing to Meg, my research settled me on the abandoned Sturdevant property across Beaver Course from Booth Island. Just as Meg had, despite it not being for sale. According to the satellite map, the property was over eighteen U.S. acres. Only the Dixons and O'Dells held more acreage. Salivating at the lake access the Peninsula offered, I got lost in the weeds of research trying to identify the current owner. Praying it wasn't Finn Sturdevant.

I started my hunt with what I knew. My great-great- George Booth, talked up Lower Bay so delightfully that the Sturdevant and other Pennsylvania families surged into Ontario to buy lake properties. Booth Island was considered a must-visit during the Roaring Twenties. Rumors swirled. Alcohol flowed. U.S. citizens rumbled across the border to avoid Prohibition summers.

When the party flag flew, everyone was welcome onto our three acres of heaven. It sounded delightful to me, wasted Gatsby summers, booze, and dames flowing, drunken rows by moonlight. No doubt, there was a dark side to it but, if there was, I hadn't heard it.

Until digging through the Land Records, I discovered that an Ardyss Sturdevant purchased the Peninsula in 1912. The deed was transferred in 1933 to a Lyle Sturdevant. A little more research coughed up an article in the *Detroit Free Press* accompanied by a grisly photo of Ardyss' body after a shoot-out with federal agents in front of a Detroit speak-easy. Prohibition ended five months later.

Ardyss' obituary was brief; Lyle Sturdevant of Harrisburg, Pennsylvania, was given as her next of kin. I searched on Lyle Sturdevant of said city. Yep, he mowed down the hood who mowed down his sister. Lyle was sentenced to life in a Michigan prison for murder. He was stabbed and killed in the penitentiary in 1936. The article noted that his wife, Rebecca, missed his burial because she was in labor with their only child, a son. The line and the deed descended from there to the current owner, Finn Sturdevant, a killer himself. I guess that apple did not fall far from the tree. And, frankly, it disturbed me that he had survived the Marines.

I ordered another two scoops of Tiger Tail ice cream in a cup, then picked up my research. The Sturdevant property, with its half-mile of shoreline, was gorgeous, heavily timbered, rocky coast with an actual beach.

No wonder Meg wanted it for a Township park. Maybe we could cut a deal that would provide me the access I needed and Meg her darned park. I considered paying $9.99 for one of those spook sites to get the scoop on Sturdevant. What I really wanted was a photo of Finn Sturdevant's gravestone.

"Hey," Penny Gagne Withers said, scooting in next to me. Sundresses must be in. Penny's dress tied around her neck and left her untanned back exposed to below her shoulder blades. She glanced at the screen of my computer as she shoveled some of my ice cream onto my spoon and ate it. "Finn Sturdevant. What would possess you to spend time searching for *him*?"

Penny's short strawberry blond to red hair was in a bob this summer. It curled around her ears. Bubbly, happy with her stocky frame, Penny effervesced as she always had. She poked me in the ribs for her answer.

"Good to see you, too!"

"I was going to come by the island but saw you motor by to Meg's."

"And that's my greeting after nine years!"

"And a few dozen video chats! But look at you, Boo, you look wonderful!" She slung an arm over my shoulders, gave me a hug and a kiss. "Better?"

I butted my head against hers as my answer.

"Okay, now, why Sturdevant?"

"You know I'm looking for lake access. In fact, you probably spread the news."

Penny produced a toothy grin. "Yes, I do. And, no, I did not. If you had access, all your own, you could sell. I am not for that. But I do think, as rumored, you should start your mother's Friday night bashes back up. Those were the best. If having your own ramp at lakeshore would make that possible, I'm all for you having a dock on the land side of the lake."

"What are you doing in town?"

Penny wiggled her feet, which never touched the floor no matter how short or tall a chair was. "Groceries. Joe forgot the eggs of all things." She dangled a bag. "I guess Sturdevant Peninsula would be Finn's. I wonder if he is still in the Marines. You know, I liked him from the start. I can't believe I was so wrong about him."

"You like everybody, Pen. The signs were all there, you know the whole *he was always a quiet boy* thing, his contempt for us, all the crazy photography, the thefts. Too sullen, by half."

"He kept to himself for sure. On the other hand, the gang of three was pretty mean to him. Did Meg tell you Brad was visiting? It's been a long time; must mean he feels safe."

"Meg told me, twice. She seemed a bit distracted. Safe?"

Penny scooped some more of my Tiger Tail then sucked it off the spoon. For a natural gossip, it was a telling halt in the conversation.

"What?" I asked.

"Meg is not thrilled Brad's here is all. They never got along. Her father assumed Brad would get the farm, and Meg would get a man. Instead, her Dad died, her brother took a hike, and Meg got the farm, a man, and stuck on Lower Bay. She makes the best of it. Remember, Meg always wanted to go up north and run a guide service or move to Great Britain."

"Sibling stuff."

Another nod. "Like Mike and me. Losing Donna set Mike back for sure. At least, Joe can keep him employed. Joe says Mike can weld anything. Now that summer is here, business is booming, so we are afloat in cash, which is always nice. If you are serious about starting the parties up, you should talk to Mom and Aunt Lou. Mom tells some great tales from days of yore. By the way, she lives in town now, just around the corner, helps Aunt Lou bake. They'll chat your ear off, but you'll get some great party tips, maybe even an offer to cater."

"Wait! Your aunt owns the bakery?"

"Auntie Lou, yep. Her husband died of a heart attack last winter. Wonder why? She cooks the way she bakes. It is all luscious. Anyway, Mom was tired of the Lower Bay, had been for years, just up to her ears, not happy with the goings-on. So, when Auntie Lou hinted that she would like the company and help, Mom was all over it. Joe was, too. It's nice to be on our own after eight years of marriage and two kids."

"Do you think your mom and aunt would mind if I stopped in?"

Penny shrugged. "They will probably tamp pastries down your throat until you weigh what I do. Did Meg warn you about the mysterious kayaker?"

I nodded.

"Poor Tim," Penny said, shaking her head as she stood. "I better get back. I take it you're okay with boating back in the dark?"

"I like it. Moon on the lake. Ghost kayakers."

"Missed you, girl." Penny swung through the door then walked up the hill toward the municipal parking lot.

I finished my second ice cream, logged-off my computer, and left, limping uphill toward the bakery. Penny's mother, Mary Gagne, was sitting in a lawn chair in the dappled shade of a hickory tree drinking something that looked suspiciously like a gin tonic. Her sister, Lou, sat next to her. Both wore jeans, tunics, and aprons. Their feet were bare, as were their arms, their reddish hair grayed at the temples, and their smiles infectious.

Mary waved as I walked up the sidewalk. Lou stood and unfolded another lawn chair before disappearing into the house. I sat next to Mary. Lou returned with a Labatt beer.

"Too late for sweets, time for an adult beverage," Lou said, handing me the can. "Don't try to say no."

"You must have run into Penny in town," Mary said, patting my knee. "So nice to see you."

"Penny thinks I should revive the Friday night dances. She suggested that you could give me tips," I commented, lacing my ankle into the recently bought ankle brace.

"The dances started during your Prohibition," Lou said. "But you must know that. The parties were free, the booze was not. Alcohol sales were through the roof. From the gossip, anything went."

"I don't think I'd charge for the alcohol. But I thought it might be nice to have everyone from Lower Bay up on the island for a fling or two. Though I was so young when Mom threw the parties, I don't know who she asked, what she served, who she got for entertainment, even where everyone's boats docked. I want it to be spectacular."

"You will need to be careful with your invite list," Lou commented, with a raise of her eyebrows.

"Why?"

"There's always some spat going on. Check with Meg, she'll have the latest on who is in or out."

"Would that include anyone involved in the latest doings?"

"Dead fisherman, dead beaver, those doings?" Mary laughed.

Lou swatted her sister. "You know as well as I do the fisherman was way over the limit. They found enough beer bottles at the bottom of his boat to stock The Beer Store. And he was likely the one who gutted the beaver with his motor. The whole town's been a twitter."

"Besides, all the murderous drownings stopped when they shanghaied Finn Sturdevant into the Marine Corps. Nothing crazy in twelve years." Mary added.

"Except Josh Dixon's death, Donna's death, and the beaver," Lou answered, lumping Meg's father and Mike's wife in with the gutted beaver. "Guess, that's not funny, like just uttering the name Finn Sturdevant isn't."

"Finn waltzed in here with his big boots on, you know the stranger comes into town and changes everyone's life forever. Especially the impressionable young women." Mary caught my eyes, blushed, and added, "The other boys shied away from him. So, we had the threatening photos and the escalating thefts."

"His dead father, my dead brother," I added.

"Your brother and Brad gave Finn a hard time. I took it for boys trying out their testosterone, but it was rough stuff. I mentioned it to Mike. Mike said Finn weirded them out. Still, I told your father I was worried." Mary shook her head, "Wasn't long after that Finn's dad died."

"Alcohol is the only cure for sore feet!" Lou lifted her glass and disappeared up the stairs into the house.

"Seems odd Brad is back for a visit. I swear all those boys got their heads screwed on sideways that summer. Even the Sturdevant boy. Finn had that fancy camera. Used the thing all the time, too. Snap, snap, snap. No matter where you were or what you were doing, he had that darn camera out. It felt desperate, sad to me," Mary continued.

"Remember, Pen, Meg and I were at a social the night Roy died. When Dred got us back, everyone was going every which way. I felt useless, lost, and more than a wee bit invisible. Dad had already left with Roy's body. I regret that I never got to see Roy one last time. Then I am glad because, in my memories, he's Roy as Roy was."

"Your hero," Mary patted my knee and sighed. "We better change the subject before Lou gets back. Her tolerance for Lower Bay gossip is so low it is subterranean."

"How's this? I didn't know you were from Lower Bay."

"Born and bred. Mary and Lou O'Dell at your service," she answered.

"Then, Tim is?"

"Our nephew."

"This is the first time I've had much to do with Tim. He has a nice way about him."

"Tim is Meg's guy, you know."

"I do—end of that subject. Besides, I am so not in the market. But I was hoping you could help me. I have been researching the Sturdevant property. They were a tough, wild crowd."

"Bootleggers," Mary spewed as Lou rejoined us with fresh drinks all around.

"Must be talking about the Sturdevants and the Booths," Lou chortled, "Oh, the stories our parents used to tell. Booth Island was the favored place for rendezvous. That was the term the Lower and Upper Bay people used. Rendezvous. Thursday through Saturday nights, partygoers swarmed in and drank. Nothing illegal about it in Canada, but that booze didn't stay here; it went across the border by boat. Some say a secret route through the Thousand Islands, others through Windsor to Detroit, until everything became legal. Of course, everything we know about back then is hearsay, and you know how tales grow."

"Speaking of which," Mary said, "Penny tells me you're interested in purchasing lakefront access. Could that be why all the interest in the Peninsula? If so, it might be smarter to focus on another property. Maybe on the east side of the bay. I'm aware of several owners over there who might deed someone access."

"Meg?" I asked. Mary nodded. "No harm in dreaming, is there? I just need a strip of land."

Mary bobbled her head.

"Okay, new subject, again! Tell me Prohibition lore about the Sturdevants that I don't know?"

Lou cackled, "The Sturdevants made wads of money during Prohibition, as did your family." By the gleam in her eye, Lou loved this. "Every Monday, either Lyle Sturdevant or George Booth deposited their profits in a secret safe hidden on the Sturdevant property. The rumor was that Ardyss Sturdevant ran speakeasies in Detroit that brought in millions. Lyle smuggled the booze made in the old warehouse to her. None of the money ever surfaced, nor did the safe."

"Oh, Lou, not that pack of bologna," Mary scoffed, taking a sip of her drink.

"Some of it checks out," I commented. "According to the Sturdevants' obituaries, Ardyss was definitely involved in speakeasies and Lyle in rumrunning."

"So, when Don Sturdevant shows up with his son, rumors fly that they've come to dig up the Bootlegger's Take," Lou said.

I laughed. "People have a name for it! That's too rich!"

"Don and his family used to summer here when he was a boy. They were the first Sturdevants to visit Lower Bay since the 1950s. In between, the place was abandoned to fortune hunters, vagrants, and horse-eating fishers."

"Plus, the Booth clan and all the Lower Bay families who availed themselves of Sturdevant Beach. I assume all that time some Sturdevant or other paid a groundskeeper like Tim is now."

Mary slapped Lou's leg, "Too right! Every year like clockwork, an envelope came addressed first to our father, then our brother, with a check for the next year. Except for the one."

"The year Don drowned, and his seventeen-year-old son got hauled back to the States and enlisted in the Marines for killing my brother?" I asked. "And the whole restraining order thing. I never did understand in what world knifing a photo of me floating face down in the lake to his bedroom wall, *Hey, Boo,* scrawled on the back, made any sense."

Mary patted my knee. "It doesn't, didn't have to, did the job. Didn't it?"

I was still mulling Mary's comment as I steered the motorboat across the lake from Dixon Landing to Booth Island.

viii

BY THE TIME I reached our dock, the sun had set, leaving its shimmering signature on the softly undulating lake. A barely-there breeze ruffled leaves in passing. Crickets rubbed their legs. A frog dove into the water, another harrumphed from a knot on a mossy log, as a dog's barked carried across the water.

A loon gave its first haunting call, another answered. The breath I took reached the bottom of my lungs. I tied up the boat and sat on the lowest step of the staircase, looking out over the reach of Upper Bay, miles and miles of it.

Like a fort, Booth Island, perched at the entrance to Lower Bay, only lacking a cannon emplacement to fire across the bow of any invader attempting to enter our little corner of paradise. North of us, Upper Bay, was a fisherman, hunter, and pleasure-seekers' delight. From the summer homes lining the lake, families waterskied, plied watercraft, fished, swam, sailed, did anything one did in the water.

I waved at a pontoon boat headed for my dock. The vessel turned back up the lake without an answering wave as another bark sounded from the distant dog. I took my leave of the dusky lake and climbed the stairs, the solar lights shining on the trail carefully marked by small white rocks. As I approached the back of the cabin, the kitchen light blinked off. Something or someone rustled off to my left. The hairs on my arms stood on end at the furtiveness of the quaking leaves. I hurried up the slope as best I could in my ankle brace.

A movement to my right drew my eyes to the shadows. Someone stood still as a tree. Tall. The next moment the breeze of sunset hit. The scene shapeshifted in the dance of shadowed leaves stirred by the last susurration of the day. I waited where I stood, staring into the dense undergrowth atop the island. I heard a splash to the east of New Landing. Fish jumped in the channel. The Beaver Course beaver, his den at island's edge, worked his wiles on the thin-barked birch. A frisson wove its way up my spine as Roy's presence invaded me.

I slammed in the backdoor of the cabin, making noise just in case. I flipped on the kitchen light and relaxed until it hit me that the generator was on and humming. A beer bottle decorated the picnic table on Roy's Deck. All the talk about digging, wild parties, and strange boats must have given me the jitters, or I would have assumed the obvious--Tim.

Having eaten dinner in Westport and filled to the gills with Tiger Tail ice cream, I raided the refrigerator for an ice-cold Labatt Blue beer. I opened a self-sealing bag of pretzels, filled a bowl, then plopped at the front room table. Comfortable, I flipped open this year's notebook to the first entry.

The Gale family summered towards the north end of Upper Bay. For as long as I could remember, Sue Gale documented their exploits down to the amount of dish soap they used. And ended each missive: "Sorry, thanks." Meaning, sorry we used the dish soap and every other thing, and thanks for letting us.

She brought her daughters to the island for a picnic this spring. They were growing up. Sue noted that her oldest had guided their pontoon boat up to New Landing. They tied off on the aluminum jetty despite the raised pier. Though I had never met Sue, I felt as though I had from her many missives. She met her husband at a resort on Upper Bay one summer, they married at the same resort a few years later. All documented in the binders shelved behind me.

The writing on the next page in the tablet was an angry diatribe about the raised pier, undeterred the old-time visitor had motored into the channel. Then docked his boat at Old Landing as he always had and availed himself of the island's offerings. He, too, was from Upper Bay.

A quick note from Penny followed. Her clan had come up Old Landing and barbecued on Roy's Deck the first day of May. Apparently, the lake had barely thawed. The day grew so cold that they moved their picnic inside. They lit a fire in the Franklin stove at the bedroom end of the front room and ate by candlelight, explaining the new pack of utility candles on the top bookshelf. Penny noted that someone had been sleeping in the bedroom and that no knives and ketchup were involved. It was a Booth family tradition to leave an age-worn sleeping bag and pillow out in case one of our visitors got stuck for the night. Tim must have continued the tradition.

The overnighters could have come from anywhere. The lake is an expanse of nearly 8,000 acres. Booth Island is one of 120 islands in the large, octopus-armed lake with hundreds of miles of shoreline. The shore consists of sheer outcroppings of Canadian Shield, the ancient layers cascading forty feet to the water, grassy lawns, marsh, and rarely, beach.

A variety of inlets, stump bogs, and marshes harbor large and smallmouth bass, lake trout, walleye, pike, and assorted panfish. Dad took us to the tiptop of Upper Bay for fun once. It took the day. Not a lake that you strike out across in the dark unless your boat has running lights and plenty of fuel. Or you might very well end up spending the night in a little cabin at the top of a granite island.

A realtor left the next note. Alice Cornish, real estate agent, heard I was looking for lakeshore property. I copied her contact information into my telephone and continued reading.

Most visitors extoll the virtues of the view from

Roy's Deck. Generally, they apologize for using the water, the deck, napping in the bed, taking in the vistas, and fishing off the boulders that make up the point.

One family got caught atop during a heavy thunderstorm. They slept in the bedroom and on the couch, cleaning and sweeping before they left. Their son borrowed a book from the bookcase. He was unable to finish it before leaving despite draining the batteries of their one flashlight. They took the book with the promise to return it next time they came. I checked the bookcase. It was one of the Max Brand westerns dating back to the days when paperback books cost a whole quarter.

I could have saved time by turning the page. A note in a young hand read: Brought your book back. I really liked it. Thank you for letting me borrow it.

With a flip of the page, I reread last night's note. *Boo!*

Careful, you're being watched was scrawled beneath. I stared at the letters, my pulse pounding. Someone had been here. In this room! Again!

A breeze rattled the front door. I jumped two feet straight up out of the chair—what a stupid note, what a foolish reaction. Tim was watching out for me. Meg had her scope out most nights to catch any signals I sent. Of course, I was being watched.

I checked the time by the battery-powered clock nailed to the wall above the threadbare horsehair couch ferried over the ice by horse and cart when my great-grandfather was a boy. Tim must have refreshed the clock battery for my arrival; the sweep-hand ticked into the silence. The cabin had always been a noisy place, filled with voices, games, joy... I reached for the binder of visitors' notes from the year Roy died.

Before we arrived that summer, Sue Gale and her sisters had partied on the island with a boatload of other teens. It had turned a bit wild. Sue and her sisters stayed the night to clean up the mess the next day. Still, when we arrived, we found a bag of empty beer bottles sitting outside the kitchen door, and the outhouse rocked back on its foundation. Roy and Dad set the shed straight and reinforced the back foundation, plugging a few holes with new rocks and cement.

That summer, Sue's sister Trisha had a crush on Roy. She motored over regularly when we were in residence to ogle him. And why not, Roy was darling with his droopy, dark forelock and sparkling blue eyes. He had this way of smiling, his eyes scrunched, his mouth lopsided that reduced females to whimpering twits. He wasn't fully formed yet, but he would have been broad-shouldered and above average in height.

I turned the page in the binder. An oft visitor had noted: Ran into that boy Finn again. He was hanging around down by the landing. I told him it was Booth Island. And shooed him off.

Not a boy really, a junior man, even at seventeen. Us girls, Meg, Penny, and me, giggled over Sturdevant's nice tight butt and broad shoulders. We were fifteen and stupid. He caught our eyes from time to time with his shy smile. After his father's death, Sturdevant seemed bruised to me. I wasn't into bruised. I was into sunny. Because of him, I have been bruised ever since.

Enough of that. I grabbed my Star Wars lunchbox and took it with me to the bedroom. At least, Roy and I could share the room as we had for years.

I tossed, then turned in bed, then trundled into the front room and checked Nevil Shute's *On the Beach* for the scrap of Roy's shirt pressed between the pages – the bit of torn cloth I'd found and hid, made fragile by time. As I fingered the rotting threads, one more piece of Roy unraveled.

That summer, Roy packed sparingly, leading me to wonder if he had intended to stay the whole season. He cajoled Dad to enroll him in summer classes toward his goal of attending Yale, as though ready to move on from his Booth Island friends. Or maybe to avoid them. Dad egged Roy into coming, reminding him it might be his last full summer with the other two members of the gang of three.

Roy packed four shirts meant to impress the summer girls and his personal items. All four shirts were white. None were seersucker like the fragment from the bush, nor were the shirts that wintered-over in the cedar chest chained to the bedroom floor. The scrap wasn't from a shirt of Roy's at all.

Dad had a classic light blue and white striped seersucker shirt that he adored. The fragment was pale red and white, pink, really, like the pink seersucker shirt Finn Sturdevant had worn to a Lower Bay picnic. I remembered it because Meg Dixon was hanging on his left forearm, looking sheepish, her eyes on the grass between her feet. Meg raised her eyes. Her brother, Brad, roared across the grassy expanse of lawn from the lake. She dropped Sturdevant's forearm and teased Brad, claiming that Sturdevant had taken her behind a bush and kissed her.

Sturdevant melted into the crowd around the watermelon table, his soft pink shirt melding with red dresses and polo shirts. I saw him trot across the grass toward a small outboard. A moment later, he was on the open water. The next day a photograph of Brad necking with some girl, his hands where they ought not to have been, was taped to the Dixon farmhouse door.

The boys, Roy, Brad, Mike, roared through the summer day to day, prank to prank, girl to girl, Sturdevant stalking them with his camera. The fragment of cloth was insignificant now, despite seeming horribly so then. I returned the fabric to its rightful place, the book to the shelf, and yawned, knowing it could have been waving on that bush for weeks before I found it.

Still, sleep refused me. Loon calls ricocheted across the lake like lost lovers. The wind came up, rattling doors, windows, and moaning as though Roy beseeched me to join him. I thought of Dad pouring the concrete to keep Roy's cookie tin deep in the earth as if the devil might seek it out. Another loon beckoned his mate.

What the loon calls. Woe?

Dad adored his son. They not only shared a similar scholar's mind, but they were near twins. I remembered Mary's comment as she patted my knee: *did the job. Didn't it?* I had never questioned my brother's death or Finn Sturdevant's resulting punishment. Roy was just gone. Forever. Except here. He was everywhere here.

No matter what part of my brain I used, or how many times I spelled relax, *careful you're being watched* swam before my eyes. Someone had been in the kitchen, helped themselves to a beer, and fired up my generator as though home.

A hissed *Boo* wove through the window screen into the bedroom. I brushed back a curtain panel. Yellow eyes stared back: *hoo, hoo.*

Day 3

ix

I FOLDED MY ARMS under the pillow where I lay on the old horsehair mattress in the cabin's bedroom, listening to the morning bugs droning industriously about. Sun glinted from the back window across the foot of the bed. I sighed, wiggled my toes, and rose.

A mug of steaming, freshly brewed coffee in hand, I sat at the front room table. Uneasy and troubled, my mind groped through the past, trying to find truth in a shirt fragment as a means to overcome my guilt at living and Roy's disquiet with death. Roy should be here. He should have a wife and kids like Brad Dixon. My brother would have a degree from Yale, learned from his mistakes, become a gentle, upstanding man. He had so much potential. Not just because I am his sister but because he did.

Boy, did I need to get out of my head and off the island.

I loaded my backpack with a steno pad, my computer and wallet purse, intending to eat in town. That thought buoyed me. Backpack over my left shoulder, I stepped out the kitchen door with a happy smile.

At the dock, lake water lapped softly against the boat's hull, sucking it away from the pier, then urging it back. I set the knapsack on the seat, climbed in, and started the motor. A reflected mirror-like light bounced off the metal seat of the boat. I shaded my eyes with my right hand and checked Sturdevant Beach. Nothing. I rounded the island into Lower Bay. A boat towing a waving water skier roared past.

A few minutes later, Tim grabbed the aft rope as I nudged into Dixon Landing. He wrapped the line around a cleat and put a hand down to help me out. All appreciated.

"Oh, hey, I brought some stuff to the island, started the generator, and flipped on the kitchen light last night. It wasn't until I was tying up that it hit me how stupid it was not to leave a note. I hope it didn't scare you." He cocked his head for my reaction. All I could summon was the memory of the kitchen going dark and finding the scribbled note. Which meant I had two visitors last night.

"Hey, did you have a beer on the deck while you were on the island?"

Tim shook his head no, so my second visitor was both mysterious and cheeky. I smiled, shading my eyes with my hands. "Mike asked me to tell you if I saw anything or anyone on the Sturdevant property. I just did."

"And?"

"Someone out for a hike with a camera or binoculars is my guess."

"I'll keep my eyes open. I braced a squatter over there the day you arrived. He moved on. You headed back into town, eh?"

"I am. Still researching my options for lake access."

"Good luck with that," Tim said, stepping into his boat.

The drive to Westport includes the shores of two lakes, beautiful marsh wildflowers, and miles of fertile farmland pockmarked with picture-perfect brick houses and red barns. Today, I was treated to the intense green of uncut alfalfa and two women placing fresh flowers taken from the back of a van at each grave in a shady churchyard cemetery. The markers were upright, some listing, some new, in the welcoming cool of death, real, lasting, well-tended memorials to those who had passed. If I ever sold the island, I might move Roy's tin here where I could provide him a proper headstone.

I passed The Beer Store, turned left down the main street, and found parallel parking next to the café and in front of Alice Cornish's real estate office. I grabbed my wallet from my knapsack, hung it over my left shoulder by its narrow strap, trotted up a flight of stairs, and through a glass door. The receptionist seemed bored enough until I introduced myself. She pushed a red button with a coral-polished fingernail. Announcing me when a woman answered the buzz.

A moment later, the realtor slid out of her office, her right hand extended.

"Miss Treader," she said.

"Ms. Cornish," I acknowledged, "I saw the note you left in the Booth Island notebook."

"Alice, please. I thought I left my telephone number?"

"Is this a bad time?"

Alice shook her head hard enough to free her overdyed blond hair from its bun. "No. Goodness, no, sorry if I gave you that impression. I heard that you are interested in buying lakefront property or acquiring deeded access to the lake. I have several clients, one whose property would provide excellent access. I can't divulge names, though."

"Are any of the properties on Lower Bay?"

The realtor's hazel eyes narrowed. "Just one. It is quite a large piece of land, nearly eighteen acres, and the asking price seems high."

I told Ms. Cornish what I could afford, having had the presence of mind to obtain a prequalifying letter from a US bank, just in case Roy was willing to sell. At eighteen acres, the property was the right size and place to be Sturdevant Peninsula. Odd that neither Penny nor Meg had mentioned that the Peninsula was for sale, only that Meg wanted it for her park.

"The price is in Canadian dollars, estimate approximately twenty-five percent less in US dollars." Alice tapped a number into her calculator, cocked her head, and reported, "The acreage is still considerably beyond your budget. There are other less expensive properties to the north in Upper Bay that may meet your needs."

"Is the Lower Bay offering open to negotiation?" I asked.

"There is a little wiggle room. I think. But…"

"Can we drive out to see it?"

I could swim across the channel and hike the Peninsula on any given day. But with Alice as a chaperone, I wouldn't be trespassing, and I wouldn't be alone. The flash from the beach this morning, the squatter, my memories, nothing was appealing about being on Sturdevant Peninsula without moral support.

Alice strode away from her desk, lifting her purse from where it hung by a strap on a coatrack. "Of course."

"As a US citizen, if I am unable to acquire lakefront access, can they force me off my island?" I asked, following her.

"No. But without deeded access, you can only sell to a Canadian citizen. And if you die without lake access, the island must be left to an immediate relative. Otherwise, it is considered a sale, and ownership of Booth Island would revert to the Township through the Province. The Township could auction it or retain it. I should inform you that the Township is interested in the property we are going to see. Given Booth Island's proximity to the acreage for sale, I feel certain the Council would entertain purchasing both. And deeded access is not required to sell to the Township, as I am sure you are aware."

It was news to me, as was death as a method of Provincial acquisition. Of course, if I died, the Township would only get the island over Liza Booth's dead body. That alone might cause my feisty mother to live forever.

Alice led me to a big black sedan parked at the curb then waited while I settled and buckled my seatbelt. "If you do consider selling, the Township is required to purchase properties at market value. How much might you ask for Booth Island?"

Though I had no intention of selling, not without my dead brother's permission, I asked, "How much would you recommend?"

"With lake access, you could easily ask $400,000 Canadian of a private party. Without access, your market is limited to Canadian citizens. Of course, the island's history might add or subtract depending on the buyer. There are families around here who would bid it up to make sure what's buried there stays buried."

I laughed as Alice pulled out into what passed for Westport traffic. She returned to the lake the way I had come into town. We followed Lower Bay Road, past the Dixon farm and the Pence place, to a tarmac lane. The lane wove up a long, wooded peninsula that divided Upper and Lower Bay from the lake's main body to the west. At a sign reading S 1-10, Alice turned up a dirt road then made a right-hand turn at a tree with a handmade wooden sign. We bumped down the rutted, washed-out road for another quarter mile, deep grass rubbing the undercarriage of the car.

The trees grew thicker, the understory denser, and the bugs more aggressive the closer we came to the lake. The tire-track lane stopped at a rusting metal building. One side of the structure curled down, another up with jagged edges, two walls were intact, held upright at their shared corner. A tall, gangly tree, several buckeye bushes, and waving grasses heavy with seed heads grew within the ragged walls. A ten-foot circle, perhaps two inches deep, so toxic it was unable to sustain life, dominated the near center of what had been a floor of planks over dirt.

"The storage barn," Alice waved a manicured hand in the direction of the crumbling building. It was a heap of metal that needed hauling off, including the rusting machinery lining its peeling walls.

Alice led me down a dirt path. I could smell lake water and hear lapping waves. We emerged onto the soft pebbly curve of Sturdevant Beach. She pointed south. I turned.

Twelve years ago, Roy had waved to me from here, his bare feet planted on the minuscule ground up rocks that stood in for sand, urging me to swim over from

New Landing, watching me as I did. Sometimes we stuffed towels, drinks, magazines into waterproof duffle bags strapped on our backs and spent the day in the sun or shade depending on the state of our skin. We stayed until called for dinner.

My spine prickled as my memory rioted. A dark-haired boy's powerful, clean crawl plying the water of Upper Bay, then rolling to his back, floating. Alone. Not alone. A dog. A fluffy, curly-haired goof of a dog, the size of a retriever, danced up and down the shore, barking and snorting until the boy swam ashore. The dog pranced. The boy, not a boy, an elegant, long-limbed teen, threw a ball into the water. The dog roared in and back.

"Well, what do you think?" Alice asked, startling me back to the present.

"The warehouse will have to be torn down."

"There may be some environmental concerns, as well," Alice added. "The building was a distillery during your Prohibition. There are two cabins on the property. The nearest is unlivable. The raccoons, pigeons, and rats moved in years ago. It once was quite nice, but it was never other than a summer place. The other structure is about a kilometer north, either through the woods or past the rocky end of the beach."

"I wish I could afford this property, for the beach alone, and as you said, the proximity." I pointed to New Landing.

"Just as well," Alice said, "Frankly, I don't like bringing clients out. There is just...well. Something."

"Have you given many showings?"

"The Township Council. Meg Dixon asked me to arrange for a showing last month before the property was listed. When contacted, the owner gave his permission as long as Tim O'Dell, the groundskeeper, accompanied the Council. I think the Council's tour helped the owner decide to sell. I received a call a week or so later. Even so, with the paperwork zipping back and forth, the property was only officially listed two days ago."

A twig snapped to my right. As I pivoted towards the sound, Alice smoothed down the hairs on her left arm. Careful, I thought, *you're being watched.* My mind slid back to the flash of light as I left the island this morning. It may have come from near here.

"Any reason other than the general state of disrepair?"

There. A hushed step.

Alice checked the nearby tree line. "Just that the owner is the one—the teen arrested for killing your brother. The boy whose dead father was found bobbing in the stump bog north of the Peninsula. Everyone still believes the boy killed his father. We all knew Don Sturdevant beat his son and, of course, what his son did to your brother and the threat to you. You can feel what happened. It's in the air."

Alice shook her head and turned back toward her car. I stayed. When she was a hundred feet ahead, footsteps shushed in the deep undergrowth. I shaded my eyes against the dappled sun, hoping to see movement or form within the shadows.

Nothing.

The moment I took a step towards Alice's car, I was paced by our stalker. Pivoting, I bolted into the woods. A shadow slid behind the trees. I ran further, my twisted ankle twanging its displeasure. Panting, my hands on my knees, I listened. The mood of the timber lifted; what or whoever dogged us was gone. I caught up with Alice at the car, scanning the brush every few seconds like a surveillance camera.

The moment I appeared, Alice ducked into the car, started the engine, and motioned for me to hurry. She babbled on about other unsuitable but available properties until The Beer Store appeared on our right. Once parked and out of the car, Alice smoothed her skirt, muttering, "That's it. I will not show that property again. I'm handing it over to a male associate. He can show it. I'll take a cut."

I cocked my head.

"You felt him, didn't you? The killer? Stalking us?" Alice asked, tucking the loose hairs from her bun back into place. When I only humphed, she huffed, "Well, if you're interested at all in pursuing the property, call me."

My mind was made up. One way or another, I wanted Sturdevant Beach. For me, for Roy, for posterity, for revenge, no matter how many bodies, how much evil, how much damnation occupied that land. If having the beach meant owning the Peninsula, I would find a way to buy it out from under Meg Dixon and her Township Council.

"Next opportunity, ask the owner if he is willing to take this offer." I wrote a number on a piece of paper and handed it to Alice. "For access from the road to the beach and the entire beach. I would deed eleven feet of beach access to the main property, enough for a boat landing."

After providing my cell phone number, I turned for the café. Before I took a step, someone grabbed my left arm. When I jumped, Penny laughed happily.

In all the summers spent on Lower Bay, no one ever went to town two days in a row. Never. Westport was far enough away that neighbors offered to buy in-between things for each other. The Lower Bay version of knocking on the door for sugar. Maybe it had been Penny who scrawled the second note; she was certainly watching over me.

I humphed.

Penny took it as what it was, disbelief. "I saw you leave Dixon Landing and followed. It has been a long wait. Where did you go? We need to talk."

I strode toward the coffeehouse and Tiger Tail ice cream. From the sound of Penny's voice, it was at least a three-scoop conversation, two for the first two sentences alone. I ordered a bowl of ice cream. Penny ordered a mocha latte.

We wandered to a table on a mini-patio between the coffeehouse and Alice Cornish's office building. Penny slurped her drink in the shade of a red umbrella. I scraped the soft ice cream with my white plastic spoon then licked it. Stress rimmed Penny's eyes. Her strawberry hair was everywhere but up in the quickly spun and jaw-clamped twist that her bob barely accommodated.

"I'm all ears," I said.

Penny fiddled with the plastic lid on her latte. "I feel so stupid now that I don't know where to start or even how."

"Start with whatever made you run out your door to follow me, even better whatever it was that brought out the binoculars. You had to have been watching for my boat."

"Mike."

"Mike? Your brother, Mike?"

"Don't get involved with him. Mike is a mess. And, for the record, I wasn't watching you. I was keeping an eye on Mike. I think he thinks you two have a future. He was out there on the island yesterday, right? He came home whistling. He hasn't whistled since Donna died."

"Is that so bad?" I asked, seeing Mike's smile, feeling his hand.

"Yes! Yes, absolutely. Oh, Boo, no! Just no!"

"Why?"

Instead of answering, she fumbled her drink, the plastic lid popped off, and latte splashed my blouse. Penny rubbed the splatters into the fabric with a napkin grabbed from the dispenser on the table.

"Answer me!" I said, covering her busy hands with mine.

Penny burst into tears then blew her nose into her napkin. I spooned ice cream into my mouth as she sobbed, listening to some small colorful bird warbling.

"Sorry," Penny muttered through the napkin. "This was a colossally bad idea. Joe tried to stop me."

"You're here now, Pen. Come on. Mike?"

"He's all sorts of crazy. After Roy, Mike went to college, got on drugs, married an addict. She overdosed. Mike got clean, married Donna, had two kids. She died. Now he is a full-time father, only I am raising his kids and ours. Joe thinks Mike is taking advantage of me. Worse still, most days, Mike's exercise or relaxation is to swim from our place to Booth Island and back. Crazy as it is, he seems driven to do it, obsessed, and now you're there. You're forewarned."

"That is crazy!"

"And dangerous."

"I get that Mike's never gotten over what happened to Roy. How could he?"

"But, Boo, Mike went wackadoodle. Brad emigrated for criminy sakes. Does that seem normal to you?"

"At the time, it did. For years, really. I ran, too, I guess. And now that I am back, memories are playing havoc with me, frankly, making me want to run again. For instance, I remember Dad chastising Roy for hanging around with Mike and Brad. He said they were bad influences, that they would get Roy into serious trouble, then desert him. But Dad all but coerced Roy into coming with us that summer. When Mike tore into the cabin for Dad's help, Dad threw Roy's trophy at Mike. Dad was furious with Mike and Brad. I missed that, all these years, how? How did I?"

Penny cocked her head, took a sip of what remained of her latte before answering me. "The guys used to play this stupid game. They would start from a point in the lake that was equidistant from several points ashore. Each had to steal something from their assigned leg as proof they had been there. The first one to reach the third point of the triangle won. Mike called Friday night game night."

"So, you're saying Booth Island was the appointed destination the night Roy died?"

Penny shook her head. "Always. It always was."

"Always?"

"Always. Fast forward twelve years. Now, Mike takes one look at you and thinks if I can get my first girl back and give her the island access she needs, she'll forgive me for any part I played in her brother's death. He needs you to absolve him. Don't get hooked up with him, Boo. Please, he'll make you miserable."

"I'm pretty miserable as it is." I eyed Penny over a spoon of ice cream. "Alice, the realtor, took me to see

Sturdevant Peninsula. I want the beach Roy and I played on every summer of his life. And, to spite Sturdevant, I want it cheap. No one is going to buy it for what he is asking. No one."

"I don't think you should have gone to Alice. She went out to your island right after the Council toured the Sturdevant property. She is up to something. I'm sure Canadian Loonies are involved."

"She's a realtor, of course, Loonies are involved."

"Look. Boo, on my way here, I swear I saw Finn Sturdevant leaving the Land Office. If not, it should have been him. I know it has been twelve years, Boo, but remember...remember how he moved? And there is only one reason for him to be here, to sell. Which means Alice is the reason he is in town, she contacted him, she brought him here!"

"Penny, I'm not sure Mike's the only Gagne that's nuts. Twelve years ago, Finn Sturdevant could have passed for half the teen boys in the province. Besides, Alice just told me he contacted her, as in by telephone. He doesn't have to come up here to sell. It is all managed online anymore."

"It struck me, is all," Penny said, ringing her teary napkin. "Whatever happened to his dog? Remember Finn's dog?"

"Actually, I did while I was touring the Peninsula. He gave it to the family renting the next cabin up. He couldn't take it with him, not into the Marines."

"Then his father goes fishing and ends up floating in the stump bog in the cusp of their peninsula."

"Other way around. Dad dies. Roy dies. Finn gives the dog away."

"That must have been so hard! Remember them romping in the water? Besides, the dog was the last touchstone to his father, to life as he knew it, really."

I stroked Penny's near arm, her sleeveless seersucker blouse was rumpled, her shorts had absorbed some of her latte, her eyes were red, she was a wreck.

"What did Alice say?" Penny asked, shutting her eyes to relax.

"The problem is best solved if both my mother and I are dead," I chuckled. "Then and only then, the island reverts to the Township."

"Not funny!"

"Have you been on the Sturdevant Peninsula in the last few days?"

Penny nodded then shook her head, more hair slipped out of the jaw clip. "With Joe's dog, he likes to run, but I never let him off the beach."

"As Alice and I were leaving, I heard footsteps that were neither Alice's nor mine. And someone, other than you, watched from the beach as I left the island this morning. Alice is convinced the Peninsula is inhabited by evil. Evil feels a little over the top; fraught might be a better word. Still, I love the beach. Such good memories."

"Can you afford it? And can you afford to anger Meg? The park is all she talks about. I think she sees it as something she can leave the Township, a sort of legacy. It wouldn't be much of a park without the beach."

"I asked Alice to place my offer for an eleven-foot wide access strip from the road to the beach and the whole beach. In turn, I would deed eleven-feet of beach access to the remainder of the acreage, though it really isn't necessary. There's plenty of lakefront on the Peninsula that isn't beach. I guess since Sturdevant is in town, I should ask him myself," I joked.

"Funny, Boo." Penny managed a smile, minus her usual cackle of enjoyment. I guess she wasn't ready to be kidded about Finn Sturdevant. Like me, I suppose she never would be.

"Tell me this, Pen, tell me about Sturdevant."

Penny tipped her head, gazing into my eyes for a minute. "Then or now? Kidding. Honest. He seemed pretty hoity-toity compared to the gang of three." She hesitated, seeking the past, then said, "He listened to me and was always quiet-spoken and gentlemanly when we were together. He was a good dancer, too, like you imagine someone who had dance lessons might be. Still, the evidence against him was so strong.

"For instance, the night I danced with him, Meg sent Brad to cut in. Finn let him. Gentlemanly, eh? A few hours later, a photograph of Roy and me was taped face-in to the outside of our kitchen window. Roy was giving me a peck. Mom threw a fit, yelling I was too young and forbade me from being alone with Roy for the rest of the summer."

Penny shrugged, then continued, "It wasn't just the photos, though, was it, Boo? Two deaths that we know of and the robberies, not kids' toys like our brothers took, but precious things like my grandmother's diamonds."

"That's a lot for one boy." I filled my spoon, speculating on what had just slipped my lips.

"Yes." Penny twisted her hanky so hard I expected it to rent in two. "What was it like to walk on his land, really?"

"I felt the same way on that property as I do at some locations on the Gettysburg Battlefield. A weight, a thousand voices. Something more happened there than we know."

"Oh ho, who's crazy now?"

I hugged Penny. It was the least I could do because she was right, I did sound Bedlam ready.

"One thing you should know, Boo, if you're going to start up the Friday bashes. Mike and Brad do not mix. The whole OPP thing did it. Neither one has ever gotten over the pressure of the interviews. I think they were terrified one or the other of them would say something stupid about what they were doing out on the lake that night."

"Brad's off the list." I made a checkmark with my hand.

"And don't get any ideas about Mike, okay?" Penny asked, her eyes wide, pleading me to say yes.

Instead of answering, I said, "I was on my way to see your mom and aunt when you waylaid me. Now that I've been on the Peninsula, I have more questions for them about the old days. Come with me. Who knows, we might run into Sturdevant on the way."

X

AT THE BAKERY, LOU was elbow deep in dough, her apron sheeted with flour. She took out her current frustrations, whatever they were, on a lump of dough, beating it soundly before rolling it into a ball.

Lou waved Penny and me onto the front lawn. We sat in the dappled shade of the hickory trees eating cookies from a bowl Lou thrust at us as we passed. A breeze ruffled the narrow leaves. Clouds banked over Big Rideau Lake, sending broad shadows over the earth.

"Back so soon," Lou said, joining us after a half-hour, with a pitcher of milk and more cookies.

"Prohibition," I responded.

"Why?"

"I took a tour of the Sturdevant property today."

"I haven't been out there in years. When I was a girl, we would swim to their beach, then over to Booth Island for drinks. It was like the two properties were one. Your mom would remember. She had a crush on one of the Sturdevants for a few summers."

It was possible. Mom rarely spoke to me about her summers on the island, just smiled a Mona Lisa smile, maybe that was why.

"Alice Cornish. The rotting, rusting distillery intrigued me. Alice implied...forget it." I bit into a cookie, embarrassed. "Who is the best source of information about Lower Bay and Prohibition?"

"Dred Dixon lives on Lake Opinicon with her mother," Lou offered in what seemed a non sequitur but was a suggestion. Dred would be in her seventies now, which meant her mother must be in her late nineties, within range of first- or second-generation memories of Prohibition.

"Coming?" I asked Penny.

"Nope. I need to get home before Joe sends the OPP in search of his bubbly little wife."

"Come visit tomorrow if you can. I'll be home all day editing and planning my imitation Liza Booth island party."

Penny waved me to my car. Following Lou's direction to Dred's home on Lake Opinicon, I stopped at tree-shaded Chaffey's Lock on the Rideau Canal for a cup of coffee. I sat at a picnic table shaded by a stand of maple trees and studied the boats waiting their turn to enter the lock. Then watched them ride up or down, depending on whether they were traveling from Ottawa to Kingston or vice versa. I felt like that, up and down, swiveling in any direction.

Chasing down Prohibition history made no sense. I knew it, just as I knew Roy sending me postcards of his exploits was impossible, but the cards weren't any less real for it. A hand brushed my shoulder. I batted it away, not a human hand, a twig fallen in the light breeze.

With a sigh, I got back on the road, following it to a neat little white clapboard house with a mowed green lawn that sloped gently down to a covered dock and the sweep of Lake Opinicon. I knocked on the front door. Dred answered it.

When had she gotten so old? I was starting to get a feel for the answer, my guess, it began one night twelve years ago. The word fraught came back to mind. Burdened, laden, beset, charged, heavy with mystery where none should have been.

"Boothe Treader!" Dred announced, loud enough to wake Roy.

"Don't know her," came from somewhere in the house.

"Liza Booth's daughter," Dred called.

"Little Liza's girl?"

"We're coming, Momma. You will recognize Boothe the minute you see her. She looks just like Madge." Madge was my maternal grandmother, of the blond hair, blue eyes, and Fifty's screen legend smile. Had Dred lost her senses while she was shrinking?

I followed Dred onto a screened-in porch. A tiny, wrinkled woman occupied a rocking chair that faced out onto the lake, her legs swathed in her knitting.

Glasses hung on her button nose from memory. Her eyes were a faded blue, the color of her pull up fake denim pants. She watched me enter, knitting without looking at her work. I hated her for that. I couldn't weave a potholder with a loom to guide me.

Dred gestured toward a chair. As soon as I sat, lemonade appeared at my elbow, freshly squeezed from the taste of it. "I was surprised to hear that you changed lakes," I said.

"Needed to let the next generation have the old Dixon farmhouse is all. And Momma needed caring for. I always liked this lake even though it has a few skeletons of its own."

"I asked Lou, at the bakery, who the Prohibition historians were. She suggested I talk to you."

"Ah. All that was so long ago. Right, Momma?"

Momma just kept knitting.

"Off subject then, do you remember the night my brother Roy died?"

Two sets of eyes shot up and locked on mine. I took that as a yes.

"Did anything strike you that night?"

"Damn Sturdevant kid lurking around," Momma snarled and kept knitting. "Wherever they turn up, somebody dies. That's what!"

"Sturdevants aren't popular up here, and that summer only reinforced the opinion, eh? That boy. His photos. Killing your brother." Dred added with a shrug. "We don't talk about it, not anymore. But Prohibition, Momma came along after but is no stranger to the tales."

"Tell me some?"

Momma laid her knitting on an end table, freeing a hand for her lemonade. "My grandmother would dress in a beaded chemise. Grandfather in a tux. Can you imagine? The Gagnes had a flat decked boat that they taxied from dock to dock, picking people up and ferrying them over to the party. There was a party every Thursday through Saturday night. The island twinkled with swaying lanterns hung from every third tree. If you were still, you could hear the sounds of the merrymaking clear across the lake."

"Momma's family lived in the clapboard on the Thumb. She is an O'Dell; I am a Pence. Lou and Mary are Momma's great-nieces. Just to get you oriented. Momma's grandparents, Rusty and Clair O'Dell, died when the bridge across Beaver Course collapsed. There isn't a spot of it remaining."

"Too many people on the bridge dancing, they said," Momma added. "Some say it was murder, that someone killed the many to hide a crime."

"Oh, Momma," Dred admonished. Momma stuck her tongue out at her daughter and humphed. I laughed, listening to the two irascible knitting ladies weaving mysteries out of thin memory.

"Where did the party boats dock?" I asked.

"On the Sturdevant side. At a landing in Upper Bay near the stump bog where they found Don Sturdevant's body. The guests walked a promenade through an arbor to the bridge. The arbor was lit by lantern light on the nights the island was open." Dred cocked her head, waiting for Momma to correct her.

"The boats, loaded with partygoers, circled the island through Lapp Strait and rounded to the dock. The bridge over Beaver Course was too low for anything but a rowboat to cross under. Drivers parked under a grove of trees at the crest of the hill near the tin-sided warehouse. Not much of the warehouse left, not after the raid."

"Was it a big booze operation?" I asked.

After another sip of lemonade, Dred replied, "Huge. Sturdevants bootlegged, and the Booths threw the parties, handled the gambling take, and Lordy knows what else. Money flowed. The revelers bought booze, gambled, paid for dances, paid...paid...paid. Right through the crash until the Depression deepened and the visitors slowed. I tell you, everyone knew to stay away from the island when the lights were out because it was then that the real business was afoot."

At least now I knew from whom my mother got her party chops; it was in her DNA.

"All I know," Momma said, "is George Booth brought Prohibition lawlessness to Lower Bay, ran the operation right from that island."

I thought my eyebrows would never lower. "What happened?"

"The Feds, OPP in tow, raided the warehouse operation. The Sturdevants were gunned down or knifed. Deserved it, too. Prohibition ended. Everyone prettied up and pretended like nothing ever happened. Money disappeared, people disappeared, one whole payroll shipment, poof, gone. Lots of folks on both bays went without because of it. Rumors got around that the money was buried on the island. People been prospecting for it out there ever since, eh? Bait poaching, my knitting needle!"

"No, they haven't. If anyone is prospecting for gold, it is the island they're after?" I responded.

Dred glanced at Momma, who kept knitting. Dred waited. When nothing came out of Momma's mouth, Dred said, "The way we hear it, you're looking to either buy access or sell. Mostly buy, hoping to make the island party central again. Since you arrived, old crud is floating up from the bottom of the lake like it was a water treatment plant. Watch yourself, Boo."

"Thanks, thanks for the warning. It's just that being here, by myself as an adult, everything is so new."

"Nothing's new up here, Boo, nothing," Dred said, walking me to the door. She patted my right shoulder.

I turned back with a smile. Her eyes were a million miles away.

"Dred? That night?"

"I just remember the confusion. People jumbling up with each other. Everyone wondering how it could have happened. Who knows the why of it? I don't." She patted my arm. "Don't let it ruin your summer. Now is now. Truly. Time to move past it all."

"But...you...said old..."

She squeezed my arm. "I meant that, too."

xi

MY POOR GOSSIP SOAKED brain came to a hard stop at Momma's comment that George Booth brought Prohibition lawlessness to Lower Bay. I was brought up to believe I descended from a very respectable colonial Pennsylvania family. One that had given succor to soldiers from both sides at our farm during the Battle of Gettysburg.

I shook my head to clear it—a fat lot of good that did. I drove to Davis Lock at the tip of Lake Opinicon and roosted at a picnic table in the shade of one of the tall bushes dotting the green expanse of lawn beside the lock. I popped the top on a can of soda water, opened a sandwich purchased at the Hotel Opinicon, and made a picnic of it. Using my smartphone, I accessed the 18th Amendment, which began Prohibition. It read:

> **Section 1.** *After one year from the ratification of this article the manufacture, sale, or transportation of intoxicating liquors within, the importation thereof into, or the exportation thereof from the United States and all the territory subject to the jurisdiction thereof for beverage purposes is hereby prohibited.*

The amendment did not ban the consumption of alcohol or home brewing in your basement, bathtub, or barn for your own enjoyment. But it was illegal to make it for sale, sell it, or ship it anywhere, especially across state or national boundaries.

Our family myth was that George made stellar basement beer. But the truth was a bit uglier. George Booth and Lyle Sturdevant were either inspired to rum run from Lower Bay by Prohibition or, by necessity, moved an extant booze operation to Canada then bootlegged it across Lake Ontario.

George, having spread the word about Lower Bay, brought the Sturdevants to Ontario. He trusted the Sturdevant family implicitly with his scheme and likely supplied the fermenting casks via Booth Milling, the family furniture business. A connection I just made. George made them rich. And, in two cases, dead. In other words, my great-great George was on par with the worst offenders of Prohibition. I wondered if he paid taxes on any of his ill-gotten gains.

There had been a bridge.

Wooden?

People died. The Westport newspaper would have covered a story as big as a deadly bridge collapse. Sitting at my picnic bench, I called Vintage Westport at the contact number on its website. I asked the woman who answered if their archives went back to the 1920s. I had a scan of the article ten minutes later.

There were two photographs. The first shot was of a simple suspension bridge with wooden decking strung over Beaver Course. It would have swayed wonderfully as you crossed it. Bobbed hair fluffing in the breeze, skirt billowing as you stepped carefully between the boards and squealed to the delight of your escort.

The path to the top of the island dazzled with lights as people streamed up the hill to our modest cabin. I counted the partygoers in the photo. There were twenty either waiting, crossing the bridge, or climbing the stairs from Old Landing.

Every step of the trail was still recognizable. Few of the rock stairs were left now, just random flat rocks on the steep hill and three steps at the apex of the path. And, yet here was photographic proof that stairs, railings, and landings with benches had existed. In the photo, a couple canoodled on a wooden seat, wrapped in each other's arms, encircled by the branches of a bushy hawthorn.

I wanted to be there. I wanted to know these people. I wanted to hang out with George Booth and his rumrunning buddies, my hair bobbed, my knifed-pleated skirt shimmering in the light, and my lipstick red. I felt cheated.

George Booth, recognizable from old family pictures, was greeting the arriving partiers as they stepped from the bridge to the base of the stairs. A shadowy man stood to George's left, his right hand in his coat. Whoever he was, he was secure in his strength, able to throw down on any miscreants or Feds. His mouth quirked as he checked out the arriving visitors. He may have been the island's bouncer before fading into the shadows of time.

The second photo, taken on a different occasion, was a nightmare caught in the incandescence of an old flashbulb. The suspension ropes hung free of the deck, lights dangling. Bodies splashed or floated in the lake. Others were being dragged to shore.

George Booth wore waist-pleated flannels, and a casual tropical shirt splashed with hibiscus blossoms. His dark-haired shadow was missing. But another tall, lithe, dark-haired man stood on the opposite bank, dressed casually like George, a long-handled object in his left hand. It could have been anything from a cane to an ax.

According to the article, a group of partiers formed a rhumba line as they crossed the bridge, their night of debauchery over. The bridge swayed in time to their coordinated movements. A line snapped, or one of the trees gave, or... Five people drowned, including Momma's grandparents.

There was an inquest. The judge ruled it an accident. The parties continued until George Booth left the island for good a few months after Lyle Sturdevant was knifed. Prohibition was over by then. George lived in the house I was raised in until his death. His descendants resumed summering on the island after World War II. George was gone by then, as were two of his sons.

Now, here I was, idly watching a group of kayakers gathering within Davis lock to descend and continue their paddle. Dred's words replayed in my head — *Sturdevants aren't popular up here*, forcing me to wonder why Booths were. Was it possible that some of the old crud killed Roy?

xii

ON MY WAY BACK to Lower Bay, I stopped at a chip wagon we had favored as teens. The small, well-vented trailer had been parked at the same dirt pull-out at the same four-corner intersection for as long as I could remember. It was a thrill to find it still pumping the aroma of frying chips into the Ontario air. I ordered poutine ladled over hand-cut potato fries cresting the biggest take-out basket offered.

The aroma of chips, cheddar cheese curds, and beef gravy accompanied me as the boat plowed across Lower Bay. I tied up at the dock in the dark, climbed the stairs on my gimpy ankle, and followed the solar lights to the cabin.

As I did, I wondered why I never questioned how my mother put me through Columbia University without a scholarship, student loan, or part-time job. She never worked, ever, and my father never paid child support, nor did my mother ask for it. The day's research provided the answer. Mom came from money, as in George Booth invested his Prohibition dollars wisely and possibly offshore.

I stepped into a hole—the same ankle, pain hit me like lightning. I rubbed my ankle and cursed Tim's sideline bait business. The area around the outhouse was laced with newly dug holes.

A breeze caught a branch and raked it against the outhouse. One of the solar lights blinked out, darkening a corner of the path. I ran, well, trotted as best I could for the kitchen door. I plunked my butt in one of the kitchen chairs and pulled the ankle brace from my knapsack. A moment later, I realized the generator was humming, and the cabin lights were ablaze.

My eyes scanned the kitchen for anything amiss. My breakfast dishes had been done. Tim or Mike? A shadow swept across the floor. I stood. The chair tipped back, hit the screen door, and slid to the aged linoleum.

Like Penny, I would have known him anywhere.

"Alice Cornish says that you are interested in buying the Peninsula," Finn Sturdevant said, setting my chair upright before motioning me to sit.

I backed toward the door. "Can't afford it, though I might be able to buy the beach with an access road through the rest of the property," I said. The man responsible for my brother's and possibly his father's death held a chair out for me. I sat.

"Eleven feet wide to the water and all of the beach?" Sturdevant smiled a snake's smile. Nothing, no warnings from Dred, Meg, or Penny, prepared me to face Roy's killer, alone, atop this island.

Tim would find my body in the morning. Where was Tim? Penny? Anyone, for that matter?

"Except for eleven-feet of beach deeded to the remainder of the property for a dock," I responded, trying to keep him engaged. Thinking. Planning my escape. If I ran out the backdoor then around to Roy's Deck, I could get off one SOS on the Aldis Lamp before Sturdevant took me down as he had threatened twelve-years ago. It was my only hope.

Sturdevant's eyes roved over my shirt and down my shorts to my sandals. Meanwhile, I studied the jagged scar over his left eye that continued into his hairline. It was new since he was cuffed and taken into custody, as were the glasses he now wore. Horn-rims. The left lens was as thick as my little finger. His black hair was shorn short on the sides, unmasking a thickly scarred depression above his left ear. Dark stubble stained his strong jawline and accented the hard lines of his mouth.

"Need me to strap that on? I have some field experience." Beneath the black horn-rims, his eyes, noir, schwarz, beltza, svart, black in any language absorbed the light in the room. He kneeled next to me, took my ankle in his hands, checked it over, then strapped on the brace. "Boo, they call you Boo, right? Relax. I'm not here to hurt you." His silky baritone belied his claim.

"What about the gifts you left me, the fisherman's body, the beaver, what about them!" I snarled then slapped his right shoulder for good measure. "It was you watching Alice and me, following us, listening."

He grinned. A hank of the long, wavy hair that topped his head fell over his forehead. He was in swim trunks, a swim shirt, and water shoes. His abdominal muscles made a nice six-pack, and his long legs were draw-me masculine with a fine silt of black hair.

"You swam?" I asked, my eyes traveling back to his. He quirked his mouth, knowingly, enjoying himself far too much.

"You and your brother used to do that distance every day."

"You watched us?"

"You've got watching on your brain. Sometimes, I hung around the beach, hoping to be asked to join you. I wasn't. Your brother acted like he was the leader of the pack. You were just cute, especially in your madras swimsuit. You'd kind of prance whenever you had it on like you knew how adorable you were."

His eyes unlocked from mine and drifted down my seated frame. My mind raced back to the photo of me floating face down in the lake in my madras two-piece knifed to his bedroom wall.

He leveraged himself up using the table, then turned his back on me. He had broad shoulders and the same tight bottom Penny, Meg, and I had swooned over. I followed him into the front room. This year's notebook lay open on the table.

"Did you think to bring me dinner?" Sturdevant asked, walking his fingers across the open pages.

"How'd you get the scar?" I responded, tapping my left temple.

"IED. Took out my vehicle, my buddies, and chunks of me. When I could walk again, I got duty at a training command as a reward for nearly dying. When my second hitch was up, I got out. Wandered. Tried to find a modicum of peace. Didn't. Went home. A few days ago, the *Detroit Free Press* published an article providing explicit detail from my presumably sealed juvenile record. Publicly branding me. How do you think that made me feel?" The fingers on his left hand thrummed his thigh as he spoke. He jangled.

"I'm sorry," I mumbled.

"Sorry?" he swung toward me, trapping me against the only empty space on the front room wall. I stared out the picture windows. The unlit lights on Roy's Deck swayed in the night breeze. "I have a brief period during which to clear my name and to get the *Free Press* to print a retraction," he snarled. "I assumed sealed meant sealed, that if I kept my mouth shut, it would all end. Go away. Drain like time in a bottle. I guess I was wrong."

"It wasn't me," I protested.

Sturdevant bucked his head. I ducked to clear his right arm. He blocked me with a rock-hard bicep. My heart raced. I could swear those black eyes were amused, taunting me to make another move.

"I brought some chips drowned in poutine?" Maybe if I fed him, it would postpone the inevitable. He could kill me in an instant. That much was obvious. Every part of him was coiled.

"Are you offering?" His head bobbed.

"Look, whatever you may think, no one in my family is responsible for your current predicament."

"I haven't had poutine in twelve years. Has to be pretty nasty cold, though." I couldn't quantify why his comment was so off, but it was.

"I can heat it up," I said, squirming under his arm, around the corner into the kitchen where I had a straight shot out the backdoor to the dock and the boat. I pocketed the keyring, with keys to my car and boat. No purse. Nothing to give my next move away.

"You're not going to run from me, are you? I'm not sure I can catch you being a wounded veteran and all." Like I believed that body of his couldn't make a pretzel out of mine, take a selfie with me in it, and tape the picture on Penny's front door before I hit the floor.

I held up the greasy bag. Sturdevant watched me turn the dial on the oven to 165 C. "I have some Labatt beers chilling in the refrigerator."

He opened the refrigerator door and unscrewed the tops from two bottles. I grabbed two forks, asking, "Did you do the dishes?"

"Your boyfriend did," he answered.

"Mike?"

"Yeah, Mike," he eyed me with his disconcerting

eyes.

"Did you smash Roy's marker?" I asked, emptying the box of chips and poutine into a casserole dish. Keeping the chips on the bottom and the poutine on the top was difficult enough without an animal of prey watching. I slid the pan into the oven.

"No. It seems a petty and pointless waste of time. Roy didn't send my juvenile records to the *Detroit Free Press*, so why mess with him?"

I popped my head into the front room. He sat in one of the dining chairs, left leg over right, hands clasped behind his head, all sorts of comfortable. Too comfortable. He cocked his head so that his unscarred ear was up--compensating. Advantage, me.

I edged toward the back door. Sturdevant slammed an open hand against the frame. That fast from chair to door. I raised my chin and stared into his emotionless eyes.

"What am I missing?" I asked, appalled by the quaver in my voice.

"About every damn thing, I'd say. Starting with the truth."

I pulled the chips and poutine from the oven and placed the hot casserole on the dining room table, my hands shaking. The smell filled the room, my stomach growled, his echoed it.

Sturdevant fingered the blue cover of this year's spiral notebook. It was open to one of Sue Gale's notes. I recognized the handwriting and the spacing. He saw me and closed it, smoothing down the pages so that it was impossible to tell how far he had read.

"Tell me about the Marines."

"Like I said. I went through basic, got shipped overseas, got blown up, finished college while I was recovering, went to a training command, got out, didn't look back."

His elegant fingers played with the edge of the poutine dish. His agility was evident in every move he made. He could kill me in a heartbeat. My heart, having hit 120 some time ago, still pounded away. I was beginning to wonder how long it could keep beating. Maybe that was his plan.

"Must have, looked back, I mean."

He quirked his mouth, "Eh?"

"Why else would you be here?"

"Same reason you are?"

"I own this place."

"Roy owns you. Owns me. That's the real reason you're here. Don't lie, not now."

"Never did, never lied. And unlike you, I never lurked taking pictures. Never used them for blackmail. Never killed anyone," I snarled, angry now, having tried flight.

He wrenched my arm behind my back and looked murder into my eyes. Footsteps thundered up the hill from Old Landing. I yelled. Sturdevant dropped my arm. Mike Gagne slammed in the back door.

"What the hell!" Mike took two long steps into the front room, where I stood rubbing my right wrist. Mike grabbed my hands, asking, "Who was here?"

He pushed me aside and tore out the front door. I followed. Mike ran to Roy's Deck. At a splash, Mike leaned over the rail, then scrambled down the hill. A few minutes later, he bounded back up.

"Dammit! Are you really okay, Boo, are you?"

"Fine. I was just warming some poutine. Join me?" I asked, leading him back into the cabin. He lagged, checking over his shoulder, before joining me at the table.

"Two forks?" he asked, fingering one.

I offered Mike one of the offending forks. "Lucky for you, I stopped at the chip wagon on the way back from Davis Lock. Remember that one, how good the chips and poutine were? I got the jumbo size. Come on, you know you want to dig in."

"Not before you tell me why you screamed."

"I yelled Mike. I heard you coming."

He checked my eyes for the lie, then sat and dug in, demolishing the poutine. Finished eating, we lit a fire in the pit on Roy's Deck and gazed overhead as the gazillion stars of the Milky Way formed an ocean current overhead. When he checked his watch, I walked him down to Old Landing. His motorboat, a fourteen-foot metal boat with an outboard, rocked gently in the water. I untied the stern line while he fingered out the knot on the bow.

Rope in hand, he turned, took me in his arms, and pulled me in for a kiss. It felt familiar. Comfortable. Penny's warnings whistling away on the night air. He had rushed to my rescue; it never crossed my mind to ask how he knew I needed rescuing. But he dashed in expecting to do hand-to-hand combat. It was just south of darling.

"Sorry, I burst in, Boo. I worry about you," he muttered between kisses. One of his strong welder's hands splayed between my shoulder blades held me close. He nuzzled my neck. "You're shivering."

Call it the Sturdevant effect. I considered asking Mike up for the night. Instead, I said, "I'm fine, Mike. Why worry?"

"Penny claims she saw Finn Sturdevant in Westport."

I shook my head, concerned that we were being observed from across Beaver Course. Something splashed a few feet to my right, near the beaver house.

"No?" Mike asked.

I shook my head again.

"I suppose you're right. Even if Sturdevant were here, he would have to be stupid to try to hurt us—you. That whole summer was a colossal screwup. Talk about wishing you had taken your mother's advice. My mom was off Brad and Roy that summer. I didn't listen to her. All I know is, testosterone became my mother's favorite word. I admit there was a lot of macho floating on the lake."

"Flexing?"

"King of the mountain. Sturdevant waltzed into a game he knew nothing about. Things changed, got rough."

"How could he have challenged the three of you? You were such good friends. Some new adventure every day."

Mike shook his head like a dog, his hangy hair swaying in the breeze. "You weren't looking."

"Au contraire, we all looked."

"You're not a guy. Sturdevant strolled in like he had some provenance because he was a Sturdevant, like eighteen acres made him one of us."

"He had the same provenance as Roy." Across the water, Sturdevant emerged from behind a tree trunk two feet above the waterline. He leaned there, listening. I swear he was smiling. I shivered, so Mike hugged me tighter.

"No, not the same as Roy. Roy grew up on Lower Bay. Sturdevant acted like all he had to do was swagger in and best us." The shaggy head shook again. The hand between my shoulder blades stretched then slid around my shoulders. I admonished myself for categorizing Mike as slow; he wasn't. He was as damaged as me.

"Look, Mike, it's late. And, though no white knights were needed, it's been great."

"You want to go on a real date?" he smiled as he turned. Sturdevant slipped up the hillside. A rock loosed by his foot tumbled into the water with a quick splash. Mike checked the opposite slope. Nothing. Though I swore someone or thing trod the path above us.

I heard Penny's warning to stay away from Mike as though a bullhorn blared it on the night air. I stared into Mike's blue eyes. He kissed me. I must have stiffened because Mike strong-armed me against his chest.

"Answer?"

"Meg is having her usual welcome to the island picnic; we could meet there?" I offered.

"It's a date." Mike gave me a quick kiss, then climbed into his boat, took the ropes from my hands, and growled off home, one hand on the tiller.

I climbed the dangerous curves up the path from Old Landing, taking care on the sloped stairs leftover from Prohibition. I pictured myself one arm draped over the strong forearm of a handsome, dark-haired man, my beaded skimmer dazzling in the moonlight. We would drink until we were tipsy and dance until the boat left.

The string lights ringing Roy's Deck bobbed, casting wavering shadows. The fire Mike lit snaked skyward from the firepit, dancing in the night breeze. I thought I heard the splash of a clean dive followed by the rhythm of swift strokes through the water. Voices rose from a boat anchored at the spit off the southeastern corner of the island. The splash was nothing more ominous than their oars dipping into the water.

Still, I wrapped myself in my arms, chilled by the clouds scudding across the setting quarter moon. I grabbed the fire rake and a coffee can of water kept in a box by the deck for such emergencies. I put out the fire, raking until I was satisfied that all the embers were out. As I replaced the rake and water, I noticed the moon had sunk another inch toward the lake. I pretended to hold the moon in my hands, sighed, then turned for the cabin.

Roy's favorite madras shirt hung over the porch rail, fluttering in the evening breeze. The last time I had seen it, Roy had been wearing it.

"Roy...Roy!" I yelled. The fishermen called up from the point, asking if I was okay. I lied, then ran to New Landing.

"Roy, please!" I called. My fluty voice floated across the water, wavering with the ripples at the shoreline. I saw him then, across the water, sitting in the tumbled boulders at the top of Sturdevant Beach.

Sturdevant was free to watch me, stalk me, come for me at any moment. With my eyes locked on the form across the water, I called for Roy one more time.

Sturdevant waved.

I ran up the stairs to the cabin and onto the porch. The shirt still hung on the railing fluttering in the breeze. With my feet grounded on familiar dirt, I held the shirt to my nose, rocking until the moon sank.

Day 4

xiii

I HADN'T SLEPT, COULDN'T sleep, even with Roy's shirt cuddled to my chest. I was afraid to close my eyes, worried that when I opened them, Roy would be at the end of my bed with Finn Sturdevant lurking behind, his hands wrapped around Roy's throat. Sometime in the night, I snuggled under Roy's shirt, his smell comforting me. Of course, it made no sense that the shirt still smelled of Roy, unless...

I lay clutching the shirt to my nose until the slanting sun grazed the floor. I stretched, rolled over, and pulled the pillow over my head, waking sometime later to hammer blows and the whistle of a saw blade.

The curtains fluffed in the late morning breeze. I yanked them shut and changed out of my pajamas. Unable to part with Roy's shirt, I threw it on over a blue tank top and slipped on a pair of white shorts.

I walked through the cabin to the vanity trees, my hair in knots, my eyes bagged, and my shorts unbuttoned. I kept my eyes on the ground stewing over whether to tell Tim O'Dell about Roy's shirt and Sturdevant's unnerving visit.

The shirt wasn't a photograph of someone's secret taped to a window, but it was meant to cause me pain.

Someone had been on the island, someone fanned the embers in the firepit, perhaps not, but someone left the shirt...it hadn't wafted in on the night breeze. I brushed the knots out of my hair with undue vigor, sawing and hammering for background music.

I twirled my hair in a twist and jammed a jaw clip in to hold it as unwanted memories wormed their way through my mind. For instance, the compromising photo of Brad taped to the Dixons' front window. Another photo of me with Mike thumbtacked to the outhouse door. Back then, I showed it to Roy, not wanting Mom and Dad to know that I had snuck into Mike Gagne's room to short-sheet him.

Roy tore the photo up and snarled that he would take care of it. Later that day, I saw him brace Sturdevant on the beach then shove him away. Sturdevant stalked off. Roy said something to Mike, who laughed and waved at me across Beaver Course. Today, I gave myself a brave smile, reflected in the spotted mirror desilvered from years in the weather.

Unraveled. The word of the day. An odd word to pop into my head, untangle, resolve, disentangle.

Breakfast was eggs, bacon, and toast. Coffee would involve lots and lots of waste, three or four of those disposable filter cups. I planned to hunker down on the island and work. I had three manuscripts, one due on Friday, three days from now. I needed to work night and day to make the promised delivery date.

The moment I began to fry eggs, Mike Gagne and Tim O'Dell showed up. I added four more eggs to the pan, blushing when Tim caught the look Mike threw my way. Meg would know by the end of the day, Penny shortly after that something was cooking between Mike and me. Mike grinned like Finn Sturdevant's pup, a golden retriever cum mutt. I stared at my plate, wondering why Sturdevant continued to invade my thoughts.

"There are fresh ashes in the firepit on Roy's Deck," Tim noted.

Here was the perfect opportunity to rat out Sturdevant. "It's nothing. A flareup as the breeze freshened. I put it out."

"When?" Mike asked. Tim recognized the question as an admission that Mike had been on the island late last night.

"What difference does it make?" Maybe discomfort was a better choice for word of the day.

Two sets of eyes met mine, convincing me something else had happened. With a shake of his golden head, Tim stuffed a forkful of fried eggs in his mouth. Mike continued to stare at me.

"Some fisherman reported hearing a woman calling out for someone," Tim added, chewing.

"Boo, maybe you should move over to our place. Penny and Joe have plenty of room," Mike suggested. His eyes narrowed. "Roy had a shirt like that, you didn't..."

"No, I didn't drag it out of the summer chest. I'm fine." I swirled my fork through the yolk of one of my eggs, mixing in the whites.

Mike reached across the table and patted my right shoulder. I wanted to slug him. Oddly enough, Tim looked like he wanted to as well.

I needed a diversion. "Okay, what's going on? What are you pounding and sawing? Then tell me whatever else has your knickers in a twist. I have work to do. I don't just dawdle around here waiting for Roy to flit in."

It was supposed to be self-deprecating. Instead, Mike covered my right hand with his. Tim finished chewing a second mouthful of eggs, pursed his lips, and played with his napkin. He could not have been more uncomfortable if he had been sitting across from me naked or me, him.

Instead of telling me how pathetic it was to wear my dead brother's shirt, Tim said, "Your request to update the old dance floor was approved by the Council. The dance floor is in such bad shape the sooner we fix it, the better. When it is completed, it will have to be tested. A few Friday night parties should do it."

"Who is paying for the work?"

"Liza Booth?" Tim reached into his front pocket, unfolded an 8½-by-11 sheet of paper, and slid it across the oilcloth covered table. It was the plan Mom and I had roughed out before she dodged down to the Caribbean and left me the island.

The original dance floor was cantilevered over the water, so the new design required steel trusses under the decking, new top decking, electricity, screens, and a metal roof. Mom's handwriting was all over the page, her little arrows, lengths, widths, numbers of lights.

"The money cleared?" I asked, unable to keep suspicion out of my voice.

"Cha-ching, it landed in my business account this morning," Tim pretended to count bills.

"Mom and I drew up these plans, but I had no idea they were approved or that my mother had paid for the work. Until I double-check with her on the dollars, cease and desist your building spree, okay? Out of curiosity, does Meg know?"

"Sure, the Council had to approve the plans. It was

on the agenda at the last meeting. Meg really championed it as a favor to your mother. She wants something fun on Lower Bay to get people out enjoying themselves again, like your mother's parties did."

"They did that. But I'm not sure I have the skills required to pull off a Liza Booth dance party."

Tim grinned. Mike laughed at some memory.

"Really. On the other hand, the parties are my legacy, as I learned from Dred Dixon and Momma yesterday. There have been parties on the island since Prohibition, dames, dances, booze, and murder. In short, gangsta's gone wild."

"What?" Mike guffawed.

"You know, infinite treasure, bodies, and sloe gin buried all over this hill. It's a wonder you didn't unearth a skeleton or two while sinking the pylons for Roy's Deck."

Tim quirked his mouth and shot a look at me that Mike caught. "Heck, no," Tim said, "Too stony. But up where Roy is, now that's got enough topsoil to hide a few corpses."

"Or by the outhouse," I offered.

"Oh, wouldn't that be rich," Tim chuckled. "The outhouse must have been moved sometime over the last one hundred years. Especially with all those party-goers. That's a lot of..."

"Poop," Mike said, grinning.

"You guys okay taking a few days off until I can contact my mom?"

Tim swung an arm over Mike's shoulders. "Looks like we got a free day, wanna go fishing?"

And off they went, leaving me wondering why I hadn't told Tim or Mike about Sturdevant. With a single word from me, the OPP would snap cuffs on Finn

Sturdevant's wrists and haul him away for good. Because as I burrowed under Roy's shirt, I knew he was right.

Roy owns you. Owns me.

xiv

ALONE ON A PERFECT June day, I set up my computer on Roy's Deck, ready to edit until dusk. Working on Booth Island this summer was something I hoped to repeat year after year. I needed to prove to myself that I could work surrounded by Roy (if he refused to leave), the glory of the land, water, and puffy clouds.

I stared at what remained of the hammock Roy had designed strung high above my head. Roy leaned over the edge, grinned, and pinged green nuts at me. A nut bounced. I fiddled with the green husk's bumpy surface. A deer fly, with its black-striped wings, walked across the tabletop. A fisherman coughed in his boat anchored off the slide. The waves lapped at the base of the island. Every object, every sound brought Roy to roaring life; who needed his smelly old shirt? A laugh rippled from somewhere nearby. Someone or something scrambled through the undergrowth, a bird trilled, then it was silent.

I wrote my start time in ink, in a ratty old composition book. One of my gigs was a historical romance. I knew the author's work and anticipated the fun of her Regency Era damsel's romantic entanglements. It was a delight as advertised. I grinned while editing and nearly swooned once.

The sun moved across the sky until the glare on my computer screen made it impossible to work. The afternoon breeze came up as a shadow fell over my shoulder.

Sturdevant, in swim trunks and shirt, made himself comfortable on the bench seat across from me. The web of birch branches at his back kept him strategically out of sight of any binoculars that might be trained on Roy's Deck.

He had shaved, though bristle still stubbled his jaw. In the sun, his hair was a lustrous deep brown. Longer on the top, it flopped over his forehead and ruffled in the breeze. While editing, I learned that human eyes are never genuinely black but can be of the darkest brown, the pupil barely visible. It must be the dimming daylight because Sturdevant's eyes were as black and emotionless as they had been in the front room last night.

My eyes tracked a scar through the left corner of his lips to a depression in his jaw. He drummed the wooden table with his left hand, head cocked, watching me. I pretended to ignore him and got back to work.

"You and Mike Gagne have fun last night?"

"You were watching. What do you think?"

"You didn't tell your darling friend about us," he scoffed. "That is what you girls always said about Gagne, that he was darling, right?"

"What do you want?"

He flicked the bruise on my right wrist. The one he left. I swatted his hand away. As I reached across the table to finger his jaw, he grabbed my hand, splaying it on the table. I left it there, unsure what else to do. I did know keeping him off balance was my sole weapon. It seemed to have worked last night.

"The scar?"

He thrummed the tabletop, one leg bounced up and

down, jostling the table legs. "I don't remember. I remember the blast. I remember the heat of the road, dust between my fingers. I remember the vehicle rising and the tires, doors, engine falling, bouncing. I still have no memory of being injured or anything else for a few months. The doctors told me I might never regain my memory. When I did, it was as though losing my new memories enhanced the old and wrapped them in thunder."

A breeze twanged branches against the deck railing. As Finn glanced over his shoulder, Roy ducked behind a tree trunk, pulsing out a blast of warm air. The hand holding mine stiffened, then relaxed.

Sturdevant chose to go on, as though it mattered, as though somehow, he could gain my sympathy. "I couldn't walk at first, nothing wrong with my spine, I just couldn't remember how. Physical therapy was the worst of it. Every day when the therapist would come, it was a reminder of how much I had lost. How my life had changed.

"I am legally blind in my left eye, though I can discern shapes and shadows. The glasses help sharpen what I can see. And I lost most of the hearing in that ear, as well. I still get these brain-bending headaches. Blinding. Things were edging toward normal when the first article appeared in the *Detroit Free Press*. Now, I have national news media camped outside my home."

"Do you remember killing Roy, or are you going to claim amnesia?" I asked, wondering what he considered normal.

"Roy was a piece of work. Mean." I started to object. He threw his hand up, palm out, stopping me. I did, not because of the gesture, but because of the look in his eyes. "Roy tried to apologize once for screwing with me.

I suspect your Dad put him up to it."

"For what?"

"I got that Brad and Roy spent all their summers together, that I was an interloper. They made it clear they were happy with the way things had always been, including their use of Sturdevant Beach. I tried to stay off their radar. I did. But they went out of their way to bully me, spread lies. I made plenty of mistakes of my own trying to be accepted, bumbling around, thinking as Pop did that I'd just fit in with the crowd. I take responsibility for my missteps. Being on the outside was new to me. Making friends had always come easy."

"You had a nasty black eye once."

"Roy. I was on our beach with my dog, Rory, goofing around. Roy wanted me off. My own beach!"

"So, you got even by ruining...wait...everything, like our lives?"

Those black eyes studied me until I was compelled to avoid them. He drummed the tabletop and bounced his left leg. I waited.

"Hardly. Lower Bay is a beautiful place, this island, you must have noticed, maybe not, maybe it is all too familiar, but not to me. My Dad gave me a camera, a good one, better than I deserved. I cherished it, and I wanted to make him proud. I took pictures pretending I was a famous photojournalist, sometimes a war photographer. I documented what I saw, life on the lake. Even that was taken from me."

His response seemed so boyish, it almost worked. "Where's your camera now?"

"The last time I saw it was the night Roy died."

"The night you killed him, you mean. Roy would go out in the boat at night with his Nikon and take wonderful photographs of loons."

"I got up my nerve once and tried to talk to him about his camera and technique. Roy shrugged and walked off. Brad was watching, though." Sturdevant shrugged, now. "Is the photo in the front room one of Roy's?"

I nodded. "Mom had it developed and framed after the fact."

"Not your dad?"

"He met Misty Lapp at one of Mom's parties. Mom didn't know, I didn't know. Dad left us after Roy died."

"Roy knew."

I raised my eyebrow into my bangs. "How would you know what Roy knew? How?"

"I was on the rocks on Sturdevant Beach. Roy was taking photos from New Landing. Your dad waved from your boat as he passed and called out that he was ferrying Misty home. It was after one of your mother's parties. Even I could tell it wasn't innocent, not the way Misty was dangling her hand in the water. Roy jumped in the rowboat and rowed to Gagne's. Mike and Brad were waiting for him. It was a Friday night." Finn continued thrumming. "They stole, Boo. It was their gig."

"Little things, worthless things."

"They stole my camera."

"So, you killed Roy?"

Sturdevant bolted to standing and ran a hand over his scarred temple. "Believe me, Boo, I paid for everything that happened that night. Now, I am paying again. Is that fair?"

In my book, fairness was Sturdevant being sent to prison for life. So, no, it wasn't fair.

"Did you ever get your camera back?" I asked, rather than answer his question, hoping his answer might explain the photoshopped pictures of Roy.

"No. It was a Nikon, like Roy's, better model, I guess from something Roy sniped at me. When the gang stole my camera, they set me up. Worse, Gagne and Dixon told lies to the OPP that made me into some sort of immoral monster, and Lower Bay lined up behind them. I still don't understand what generated all their fear."

I pictured Roy with his shaggy hair, tall, broad-shouldered the way natural swimmers are, blue-blue eyes, loopy smile. If someone had hung his pheromones out, every girl in the township would have been glued to him. Finn Sturdevant pushed people away with every move he made or word he uttered. But I know Meg, Penny, me, and every other girl were attracted to the angry bad boy Finn was selling.

"I can't let that summer define me or destroy my future."

"You shouldn't have stood," I said, gaining my feet. "Someone's coming."

Sturdevant waved, walked down the slope disappearing into the undergrowth to the left of Roy's Deck. As soon as the oncoming boat passed into Beaver Course, I heard his ripple, neat, likely no wave, a 9 or 10 on the diver's scale. Last night's splash from whoever fanned the firepit and left Roy's shirt had been no different.

I took a deep, cleansing breath, all before I realized Sturdevant hadn't recognized or, if he had, hadn't remarked on Roy's shirt. The shirt Roy wore the night Sturdevant killed him.

Sturdevant kept it all these years. He knew what it meant to me when he draped it on the porch. And with that thought, Sturdevant's departing words became a threat.

XV

BY THE TIME MIKE tied his boat up and reached the cabin, I had a beer, chips, and bottled salsa waiting and was hard at work editing the romance novel. He strode across the lawn to where I perched, put a hand on my left shoulder, and peered at the print on the screen.

When I ignored him, he asked, "Sorry, do you want me to leave?"

I shook my head. He sat next to me, sipped my beer, and scooped a chip. He smelled good, well better than he had in the morning. He took another slug of beer, continuing to read over my shoulder. At a particularly lurid passage, he stood and lifted his shirt, rippled his abdominal muscles then went for more beer. "Your two-four is getting low," he called back.

First *two-four* I had heard, assuring me I was back in Canada where a case of beer, twenty-four cans or bottles was a two-four. I would pick up another case or two when I went to town to call my mother about the deck plans and money to build.

"What brought you here?" I asked, knowing Mike's arrival was way too coincidental.

He shrugged. "Your company. Quit ignoring me. You know you can't resist my Canadian charms."

"Sorry." That cracked him up as I hoped it would.

"Eh?" He joked back. "Any more poutine?"

"Nope."

"What's for dinner then?"

"Are you kidding me?"

He bit my ear, nuzzled his nose in my hair, and ran

his hand into the back of my shorts. I slapped it. He laughed. It struck me then that it was all too easy; I was too easy. I had the cure for the growing familiarity. "Tell me about the robberies."

Mike sputtered beer across the surface of the table, wiped it off with his shirt, and cleared his throat before answering. "We gave everything back."

"Really?"

"Hey, what happened to your wrist."

I flicked his hand away as I had Sturdevant's. He raised his eyebrows.

"I gave everything back," he corrected. "I can't speak for Roy or Brad."

"Yes, you can."

"Really, I can't. I don't know if Roy and Brad did or not."

"Then, you suspect one or both didn't."

He ducked his head and fiddled with his beer. "My mom inherited a necklace from her mother. It dated back to your Prohibition. Art Deco, I think it is called. It had a big chunk of diamond held in place by a stylized hand on a gold beaded chain. When we started our Friday forays, we agreed not to take anything of value from our own families. When Mom found the necklace gone, she just stared at me. I remember the look. I asked Brad about it; he blew up and fingered Sturdevant." Mike huffed. Twelve years later, he radiated disquiet.

"Tell me about game night?"

"Penny?" he asked.

I nodded.

Mike went on, "Every Friday night of summer for four years, the three of us would go fishing. We grabbed our rods, climbed in a boat, and headed out. The folks were never the wiser because we always caught enough fish for one family's breakfast. The first two years, we swam a quarter-mile out, quarter-mile back; we each nicked something to show we swam the distance."

"So, you'd swim out, steal the item, and swim back to the boat?"

"Yes and no. We'd steal the item and swim back to Booth Island."

Just as Penny had said.

"You didn't think it was wrong?"

"Kids beach buckets, a jelly donut, an empty can of beer? No. Anything that wasn't food turned back up."

"Except for your mother's necklace. Other things were stolen as well, Mike. My Mom's engagement ring disappeared. Penny, Meg, and I searched all over the island for it."

"Really?" His surprise seemed genuine enough.

"At what point did the fun start to wear thin?"

"Around the time that Penny started hounding me to befriend Sturdevant. She insisted that he would quit blackmailing us with those darn pictures if we were nicer to him. She blamed us for his actions, said we were too mean. The thing was, we all knew he had worse pictures...especially of Brad and Roy. I was pretty steady with you."

"Pretty?"

"I was lifeguarding, remember?"

"And stealing a kiss, here and there?"

"Girls threw themselves at me. I...well...Penny talked me into asking Sturdevant to go fishing. Roy and Brad found out, beat Sturdevant until he hit the sand, and bullied me back into line. After a few unpleasant days, Penny and I had a huge fight. She called me gutless. She was right; it was a defining moment for me.

Next thing I knew, Mom's necklace was gone."

"I found this shirt on the porch railing last night," I blurted out.

"I knew it was Roy's. He loved that thing." Worry washed over Mike's open face.

I closed my computer. No more work tonight. "I have two nice thick pork loin chops. How are you at barbecuing?"

"Got anything to pour all over them?"

"The ingredients for a barn barbecue sauce."

Mike showed me some barn dance moves on his way to the porch. He really was utterly adorable, still as giddily sweet as I remembered. As I went into the kitchen, Mike positioned the grill and began the rhumba that ends in the perfect charcoal fire. I slathered barn barbecue sauce involving a considerable amount of applesauce, brown sugar, and ketchup over the loins. I carried the chops to the porch for Mike. Returning to the kitchen, I made two salads and wrapped two potatoes in foil.

Over dinner, we reminisced about our summers spent circling ever closer to each other. Mike clearly regretted waiting to make a move, especially given the tragedy that ultimately defined our young lives.

Now we snuggled on the bench on Roy's Deck. The Milky Way blanketed the sky. The North Star dazzled like a beacon. I thought about a sequence in the romance I was editing where the heroine is cuddled by a man planning her death. I wondered what it would be like to be snuggled by Finn Sturdevant.

I shivered. Mike drew me closer, kissing the top of my head. It felt luxurious and a wee bit dangerous, perhaps as it had for the flappers as they drank and danced.

Around ten, Mike and I walked hand in hand to New Landing.

Day 5

xvi

I TUMBLED ALL NIGHT. When I did sleep, every chirp, rustle and shush woke me. By early morning, I was a wreck. I lay in bed, my arms under my head, watching flies hang onto the outside of the window screen. Rain was on its way. At a minimum, high humidity. The air was stagnant, another sign of a coming storm. The bay water was still, indicating inches of rain brewing. I considered what I might wear on a threatening, hot, muggy day.

On a similar day twelve years ago, Roy and I sat side by side on the rocks to the right of New Landing. We waggled our feet in the glassy water, watching the fish pop up for bugs, leaving water rings behind. Our metal boat bobbed against the dock thumping the wood with a clink of the oarlocks. A flock of mallards swam past, in their familiar vee, the teal blue head and white neck slash of the males bright against the dull near-gray of the water as the clouds lowered.

"Breakfast," Dad called from the path above. Mom was frying up the fish Roy and his buddies caught the night before. We stood and hiked up to join Dad. As we passed, Dad grabbed Roy by the crook of the elbow and snapped, "Don't follow that boy around. Think. Think before you act!"

That boy. Sturdevant.

Roy shook Dad off and charged up the hill. Dad didn't snap at people. Not that he didn't have the chops for it. Roy got his agility and strength from Dad, his looks too, except for his smile, that was all Mom. Still, it was surprising to see Dad so upset.

Roy vanished while the rest of us ate breakfast. He stormed out to the promontory, dove into the bay, and swam off. Later, I saw him romping with Mike, Brad, and a bevy of girls on Sturdevant Beach. Sturdevant watched from a rocky outcropping at the upper end of the beach. His arms hugged his knees, and a bruise colored his ribs. Sturdevant's dad walked around the point, tapped his son on the shoulder, urging his son to follow him up the hill.

I shook my head to empty it of memories then counted the current number of flies on the screen. Three. The gang of three. The humidity and my memories weighed me down until I wanted to stay safely tucked under the sheet, Roy's shirt against my right cheek.

A cumulus cloud let loose with a great rumble of thunder. Lightning cracked. The lake began to tumble against and over the rocks with the rising wind.

The call to my mother would have to wait another day; it was no day to take a metal boat across open water. Lightning slammed into the water. The cabin shook it off. A wobbly lightning rod attached to the roof and grounded to the left of the front porch would attract and deflect any island strikes. Which suited me fine. The storm would keep everyone away, leaving me a day to commune with Roy and work without interruption. That joyous thought got me out of bed before the sun was fully up.

I threw on a pair of cut-off jeans, a favorite turquoise sleeveless shirt, and red canvas shoes. I looked in the cracked mirror hanging on the back of the bedroom door. Yep, I was dressed like my fifteen-year-old self. Mike residue, I suspected.

I unlatched and opened the wooden front door, letting the freshening breeze riot through the screen. As I did, a quarter-inch crack between the frame and the door screamed open me with a penknife. Anyone could break into the cabin in five seconds and be settled in the kitchen brewing a cup of my precious coffee before I made it from the bedroom. Nerves. The lightning and thunder were making me jumpy.

I peered out the screen door before taking a hesitant step onto the porch. No surprises, no random pieces of Roy's clothing, no fire in the firepit. No Sturdevant. No Mike. Just me and the lake water booming onto the rocks and white-tipped waves rushing toward Dixon Landing ahead of the coming rain.

By 8:00 a.m., rain drummed on the cabin's tin roof. I checked the gas in the generator, half-full, flicked it on, then made a cup of coffee. The guys had finished off my eggs, so I filled a bowl with cereal, cut up some strawberries, and poured half-and-half over the whole.

Afterward, I propped my computer up on the front room table with paperbacks until the screen was at eye level, then adjusted the backlit display to compensate for the dreary day. My favorite stylus was to the left of the screen, my coffee cup to the right of the computer. I rolled a towel to make a ramp for my wrists and hands.

All set up for the day, I ran for the outhouse. My

ankle felt good, if not healed. The wooden door, swollen from the rain, was stuck shut. The facilities also stank, which happened when the humidity was high. I grabbed the metal handle, put my back into the pull, and yanked. I settled in for a good pee. A yellowjacket buzzed away, a spider watched me as the trees moaned in the wind.

No.

I sat perfectly still. Another moan. I peered around the outhouse door. A groan. Perhaps my name. The path to Old Landing crested five feet to the right of where I stood. I eased around the plywood shed, listening.

"Boo," someone whispered, "Boo."

A clawed hand clung to the riser of the last stair. Mike Gagne's dark head lay on one of the remaining Prohibition stairs, the other hand flung to his side. His body tumbled below like a broken rag doll.

"Mike?" I kneeled beside him.

"Mike!" I said more sharply.

He rolled onto his right side and opened his eyes. His forehead was a bloody pulp, his left eye black, his nose had bled. He had taken a header face-first onto the rough, chipped cement, bruising his ribs on a lower stair in the fall. Sitting, I lifted his head onto my lap and dabbed his forehead with the hem of my turquoise blouse.

"You're hurt," I said, stupidly.

"Beaver Course," he gasped, stopped, took two ragged breaths. "Someone climbing Old Landing. I ran up. A shadow. Warn you. Fell. My head hurts. Everything is in twos."

"You've been out here all night, like this? Oh, Mike!" I felt his forehead. He was quivering with chills.

"You need out of the rain and warming up." I tried lifting him without any luck. "Can you get to your knees? We're not far from the cabin?"

He rolled off my lap and pushed himself, awkwardly up, ready to crawl. I guided him toward the back stoop of the cabin, my hand on the top of his head. He stopped every few feet to breathe. When we reached the back door, I managed him to sitting on the porch under the overhang, barely out of the rain.

Mike was pale to ashen and wet to the skin. Rain-thinned blood coursed down his face. I fingered hair out of the wound on his forehead. He must have been roaring up the hill when he lost his footing.

After propping Mike against the cabin wall, I went inside to round up the items needed, towels and a blanket, one to dry him, the other to warm him, and the first aid kit. I rummaged through the bag for a large bandage. Finding none, I went through my clothes for a clean T-shirt.

Returning, I grabbed the oilskin off the kitchen table as I passed, then rough-dried him with a bath towel and bundled him in the oilskin tablecloth to keep him dry. When some color returned to Mike's face, I tore the T-shirt in strips and wound it around his head turban style, his blue eyes unfocused beneath.

You hear stories, read them in the newspaper about head wounds left unattended that result in death. I leaned Mike against the exterior wall and ran to Roy's Deck. I flicked out S-O-S on the Aldis Lamp. Once. Twice.

No answering flashes!

I signaled again.

Nothing.

I grabbed my binoculars, checking for movement

at Dixon Landing. Nothing. I rapped out the dots, dashes, and dots again. There it was! A flash from the picture window. I referred to the code on the side of the lamp and signaled: *man down.*

Within minutes, two men slid as much as ran down the tire track road from the farmhouse to the landing. One carried several wooden rods and a blanket for a litter. Though, it was hard to be certain at this distance and through binoculars.

Word spread. A boat roared to life at Gagnes' dock. Red hair let me know Penny was on her way. The boat with the men growled out from Dixon Landing. Meg signaled that help was on its way, or something similar. I flashed an R, letting her know the message had been received.

I jogged back to Mike, fallen sideways off the stoop, his head in the wash of rainwater flowing around the corner of the cabin. I felt for his pulse. It was light and fast. I ran into the cabin, yanked the blanket off the bed, wrapped him in it then the oilcloth over it. By the time I scrambled down to New Landing, Penny was tying up.

"It's Mike," I gasped.

She stood on her toes then ran for the stairs.

"I'll wait for Tim and Brad," I yelled as she passed, "He'll be fine, Pen, he will."

With a look of anguish, Penny tore up the hill to her brother, her bobbed hair dripping rain, wet to the skin in bare feet. Had she known it was Mike, or should I be flattered that she had rushed to help me without a thought for herself?

Though I hadn't seen Brad in years, I recognized him the moment Tim and he arrived on Meg's pontoon boat. Tim steered it in, Brad tied it up, while I called out Mike's condition. Brad took the aluminum stairs two at a time. Tim gathered up the boards and blanket then followed me. When we arrived, Penny had Mike's bound head in her lap and held his left hand, tears galloping down her face.

As Tim assembled the litter, Mike struggled to upright, arguing that he was fine. Brad loomed over him. Mike peered up then meekly laid on the litter. The two guys carried him down to the pontoon boat and loaded him aboard.

"He's fine, Penny," Brad reassured her.

"I am," Mike agreed. "I don't need to be hauled to Westport Clinic."

"Well, you're going," Brad snapped. "What were you thinking?"

"Saw someone," he muttered.

For a second time, Mike had rushed to my imagined rescue. It was endearingly stupid. I wanted to hug him. Instead, I croaked, "I'm coming."

All three men chorused, "No!"

I sat on the top stair at the dock until the float-boat rounded Lapp Strait for Dixon Landing. Penny sat beside me.

"Tim warned me that you two had a thing going," she said flatly. "I told him no, then I saw Mike and you at New Landing last night. Joe and I were out walking the dog."

I sighed. "Sorry."

"I told you to stay away from Mike. I blame you for what happened. Sorry, Boo, but I do." Penny bolted to standing. "I've got to get home to the kids. Joe's in town at the lumber store."

"You can't stay?" I whined.

"So, you can ignore everything I tell you." Penny slammed her hands to her ample hips. "I'll tell you this,

Boo Treader. You've got it all wrong."

With a flip of her sopping bob, she thundered down the stairs to her boat and gurgled off, leaving me wet to the skin and deserted. Rather than wait for Meg to signal that the guys made Westport and Mike was okay, I decided to ignore the storm and head into town. I knew the clinic where they would take Mike. I could check on his condition then call Mom about the dance floor.

First, though, I checked the area where Mike had fallen for footprints or broken branches. I descended the narrow path then wove my way back up—nothing out of place. I picked up a fallen branch at the base of the old stairs and thwacked it against my shoe. I studied the path, toe-deep impressions dug into the loam where I had found the limb.

Mike must have tripped on the limb, then flailed, enough to slow the fall, or he would be dead. The distinct imprint of a knee set me straight. Mike had slammed onto his left knee before pitching forward. I checked for footprints at the top of the path and saw only my own. Whoever he had followed had disappeared, leaving no footprints or disturbance of any kind.

Mike's baseball hat lay in the leaves, just off the path. I picked the cap up and slapped the branch against my thigh as I walked up to the kitchen. I jammed the offending limb under the vanity in the fork of the tree. The kitchen screen door slapped in the rising wind. I caught it on an outswing and entered, half-expecting Finn Sturdevant to greet me.

The room was empty, as was the cabin: no ghostly footsteps, no shadows, just the brushing, thumping, and thunder of the storm. I set Mike's hat on the kitchen table. As I did, my fingers found the Pittsburgh Steelers' sparks applique on the front and an old stain on the bill, one left twelve years ago by Roy's oily fingers.

I thumped into a kitchen chair and stared at Roy's hat. Chilled. I hung the cap from a hook by the door, palmed the boat keys hanging from the next hook over, grabbed my purse, and locked the door with its hundred-year-old keylock pickable by a four-year-old with a paperclip.

xvii

THE BOAT BOUNCED AROUND in the wind-driven water as I zigzagged my way toward Dixon Landing. Halfway there, I realized I had left the generator running. At the worst, it would burn through the gas and cycle off. Still, it left me uneasy.

The boat slammed into the pier at Dixon Landing, rattling the wood all the way to shore. Meg, standing near the waterline, rode out the jarring motion, her feet planted shoulder-width apart, an umbrella shielding her head and shoulders. I was wet down to my underwear, my hair clung in lank hanks to my neck from the rain and slapping of the boat across waves. Meg handed me an umbrella. I shrugged it off.

"Saw your boat. Come up to the house. We can wait for Tim to call with an update on Mike. I bet you didn't bring any dry clothes. If we have to go to town, you can borrow some from me."

That was a joke. I was taller, thinner, and broader in the shoulders. Meg had softened over time until she looked every inch a Councilperson. And she lived with big, handsome, straight out of a romance novel, Tim. Everything about her was lighter and happier now.

In a show of her common sense, Meg had driven her car to the dock. I climbed into the passenger seat, dry for the first time in hours as we jostled up the farmhouse lane. She dropped me off at the back door. I let myself in as I had since I was six years old and proclaimed an honorary Dixon.

Papers were scattered across the dining room table. A newspaper, the *Kingston Whig-Standard*, was spread out on the davenport. The TV was blaring, tuned to the CBC news station. Tim, Brad, and Meg had dropped everything as soon as the Aldis had flashed. A flush of gratitude warmed me.

Meg wiped her feet on the doormat before disappearing through a door on the right into the kitchen. I stood in the entry, dripping. Returning, Meg offered me a clean, dry dishtowel with a circular drying motion.

"I know the rain is warm, but the breeze is cool, and you've been out in it for hours. Dry off before you get sick."

I wound the towel around my hair. Meg dodged down the hall off the living room to the bathroom for a bath towel. I wrapped the deep cotton loops of the emerald green luxury towel around the rest of me. She moved the newspaper from the couch. I sat in the cleared spot offered, as Meg settled in catty-corner from me in a lounge chair. We stared at each other, not knowing where to begin.

"Alice Cornish called," Meg offered, "She said you'd been on a tour of the Sturdevant property. Any thoughts?"

I shrugged, surprised she hadn't asked why Mike

was on the island. "I asked Ms. Cornish to get me in contact with the seller, but I've been out of cell range since then. I don't have sufficient pre-approval currently to buy the whole property, so I hope to wangle the beach and access to it from the road."

"I'm sure Alice will call Sturdevant; she's very efficient. One thought, if the Township purchased or acquired the property, the Council might allow you to buy a wedge of beach north of Old Landing for easy island access. Or better still deed you access for less."

"Has the Township made an offer on the property?"

From her remarks, Meg seemed ready to counter any offer made and had sufficient influence to make it stick.

She shook her head. "It would make a wonderful park, though. Don't you think?"

"The Township might have to pay for hazardous waste cleanup at the abandoned warehouse."

The phone in the kitchen rang. Meg rushed to answer it. I stayed where I was in case it was a private call. Her voice seemed calm, which slowed the jump in my heartbeat. For whatever reason, I glanced out the picture window. Jumpy. Nothing out there in the storm.

Turning back, I noticed a framed photograph of Brad and Mike in their swim trunks, each with an arm thrown over the other's shoulders. Roy must have taken it. Brad was grinning, and Mike stared into the camera, as though he expected Brad to pinch him at any moment. Why not? Everyone knew that the gang of three pranked each other. Occasionally the pranks escalated past the boundaries of good sense. Though never reaching the level Sturdevant's had, jumping out from the bushes, and literally scaring my brother to his death.

"Good news," Meg said, rounding the kitchen doorframe. "Mike's fine. Nasty abrasion on his forehead, a gash on his right shin, which needed stitches. And a concussion. Nothing permanent if he takes it easy for a few days. Joe turned up at home, so Penny is driving to town to be at Mike's beck and call. Tim and Brad are on their way back."

"Mike was following someone up the path from Old Landing. It was late. He rushed up the hill to save me." It was out of my mouth before I realized it. Soon everyone would know Mike had barbecued my dinner, as well. I was equally sure I knew who he'd followed. What game was Sturdevant playing? First the shirt, now Roy's Pittsburg Steelers hat?

"Mike, the hero," Meg scoffed.

"Mike's a good guy." It was a mindless thing to say, but her words put me on the defensive. "Since I'm off the island anyway, I should drive into town and call my mother about the dance floor funding."

"Use our landline," Meg offered.

"She's in the Caribbean, so it will be expensive."

"Don't be silly. Call your mom."

Meg led me down the hall to a study cum office. The room was dark and, today, dank. The wood-paneled walls were walnut or cherry. Photographs hung everywhere above eye level. I recognized a photo of the bridge dangling across Beaver Course, another of the Prohibition dance floor, and a third of George Booth and his shadowy friend. Meg must belong to Vintage Westport.

I sat in a swivel chair facing the photos, my back to the living room door, and dialed. The aroma of baking bread wafted through an open archway on my right into the kitchen. Meg puttered preparing a late lunch, pans clanked, cutlery clinked.

My mother answered her office phone on the second ring. I asked if she knew the Township Council had approved our plans for the old dance floor.

She guffawed over the line. "Of course, Boo."

"Did you post funds to Tim O'Dell?"

"I did. But if you do need more money, I'd be glad to send it to you. Have you set a date for your first party?" Questions tumbled out of her mouth.

"First, Mom, how are you?" I needed to slow her down. It even crossed my mind that she had been drinking despite the early hour.

"Great!" She meant it. "Our guests are happy, sending referrals our way. We're booked until the cows come home! So, come on, what's up, Boo? Seen Roy?" she laughed.

"Well, remember Roy's Pittsburgh Steelers hat?"

"That old thing. Sure. Roy bounced out the cabin door in his swim trunks and that hat every day, right up until he didn't. Why?"

"It's turned up is all and in the most unlikely spot. The last time I saw it was the day he died. If you don't know what became of his hat, how about his Nikon?"

Mom sighed. I waited, noticing a Canon camera gathering dust on a ledge over the door. Like everyone else, I took all my photos with my phone now.

"I found Roy's camera in the rocks near New Landing the morning after his death. The lens was cracked. I put it in a shoebox and stuffed the box deep in the bedroom closet shelf. I thought we could use it when we opened the cookie tin. Then, to be honest, I forgot it in the ensuing ruckus, until now."

I swiveled the chair toward the door and asked in a

hushed voice, "Outside of your engagement ring, was anything else of value ever stolen from the cabin."

"Jack's father's watch. It was gold."

"When?" I fiddled with a photo in a simple black frame. Roy, in a swimsuit, his left arm thrown over Meg's shoulders, his fingers brushing the strap of Meg's one-piece swimming suit adorned with various sized polka dots. Meg grinned ear to ear at the camera, the gap in her front teeth on full display.

"Who knows! Who even knows why Jack had it with him? Who takes a gold watch on vacation?"

"Did it disappear the summer Roy died?"

"Yes. I am sure of that. I caught that boy in the timber behind the house. I wanted to call the OPP, Jack told me to leave the boy alone. I made Jack check his valuables. He was sheepish when the watch was gone. Course, that boy was gone, too."

Mom began calling my father Jack the moment he left her for Misty. Jack. Just Jack. Sometimes Treader. I thought it odd that she never referred to him as Dad when talking to me. But then she had been left for a younger woman and stranded on an island in Canada with a teen daughter weeks after her son's death. Who was I to judge?

"Mom," I said, "That boy had a name. Finn Sturdevant."

"That boy was responsible for your brother's death, Boo. No matter what he achieves in life, he will always be *that boy* to me."

"Did Dad's watch disappear on a Friday night?"

"Boo, have you lost your mind! How would I remember something like that? I do remember it was dusk. The fishermen were lining up at the rockslide, the loons were tuning up. I remember that. So, probably not a Friday. Fridays were party night."

Not true, there had been no party the Friday Roy died. "Where was Roy during all this?"

"Off with Brad and Mike, as always." By the edge in her voice, Mom was getting bored.

"Can you think of anything that happened that summer that you and Dad kept from Roy and me?"

"Outside of Jack's cheating? Sorry. Just this, Jack floated the theory that someone murdered Don Sturdevant. He even went to the OPP. They investigated, but there was no evidence, nor did Jack have anything other than a hunch."

"What was his hunch?"

"I never knew. Jack spent that whole summer with a guilty conscience because he hooked up with Misty Lapp. It colored everything. Jack set a horrible example for a seventeen-year-old boy. Roy knew something was going on. I was past caring, ready to move on. Misty introduced Jack into a different circle of friends; maybe one of them convinced him or made an argument Jack could subscribe to just to annoy me."

The Lapps lived on Lapp Strait on the east side of the bay. Our friends all lined the western lakeshore for no other reason than the boat ride was shorter and the shoreline more welcoming than the stacked cliffs opposite.

"I should talk to Dad, then."

"Good luck with that. Jack and Misty are off with the heir and a spare on some romantic vacation. God forbid, they spawn again."

"I think I should try, though. Thanks for being my mom and try to be good."

"Me? Of the Prohibition Booths!"

"Hey..." The phone went dead. I had meant to ask

Mom about the bridge, the deaths, the booze factory on the Sturdevant property, and, in the interest of full disclosure, from whom George Booth had purchased the island. Of course, I could go to the Land Office next time I was in town. Still, asking Mom would have been quicker and easier.

I studied the photo of Meg and Roy, wondering who had snapped it. I doubted it was taken by Sturdevant. As I remembered, his photos were sharp and detailed, too detailed. I stretched then strolled into Meg's living room to find Meg and Brad seated, chatting on the couch.

"Mike's fine, Boo," Brad stood and motioned to a chair.

Brad was maybe 5' 10" and loose-limbed. His sandy hair was still damp, his pant legs wet to the knees. Meg's long nose was a better fit for Brad's face. His lips were thin, his long upper lip turned down at the corners. His eyes were the same color as Meg's but seemed close together. Like Meg, there was a gap between his two front teeth.

At some point, I realized Brad expected me to walk into his arms. So, I did. He gave me a brisk hug. "There," he said stiffly.

"Thanks for everything. You guys were wonderful and so efficient. Lucky for me, someone was watching," I said, glancing out the window. "It looks like the storm is worsening. I better head across the lake."

I shoved my feet into my sodden tennis shoes set on a mat by the backdoor. Meg stood to drive me to Dixon Landing. After she dropped me off, the car continued toward Upper Bay Road.

The sky unleashed a torrent of water that thundered on the cabin's tin roof. Before entering, I topped off the gas in the generator, started it, then, once inside, lit all three electric lights.

It did little to brighten my day.

xviii

MY COMPUTER WAS STILL running on its nearly depleted battery. Admittedly stupid, but I assumed everything would just shut off when the generator ran out of gas. Only, the tank had been half full.

Someone had been in the cabin.

I checked the *Recent* file section on my computer's directory. My visitor had scrolled through my photos, then read a sample of the book I was editing. Nothing had been deleted or harmed, though a comment was inserted next to the description of a beefy man unlacing the feisty heroine's bodice. *Too funny*.

Sturdevant. No one else. He had taken advantage of Mike's injury to search the cabin and run his long fingers over my things.

One Labatt, a thousand glances at Roy's hat, and hours later, I signed out of the book's file. Drops of rain sprinkled the roof. The wind blasted the logs as the storm blew itself out. Feeling a bit silly, I locked myself in again, knowing the door latches were useless. Front and back.

I opened my last Labatt and carried the notebook from the year Roy died to my seat between the refrigerator and the corner of the cabin, with windows on two sides. One window provided a view of the porch and Roy's Deck beyond; the other looked over the summit of the Old Landing path where Mike had fallen. All the better to see anyone coming.

Instead of opening the notebook, I stared at Roy's hat alone on a peg in the kitchen. I went into the bedroom for his shirt and hung it beneath the cap on the same hook.

On the day Roy died, he had jumped up from the kitchen table and flipped his black hat on with flourish before slapping out the door, his madras shirt open and billowing. By nightfall, he had changed into his swim trunks, a red bandanna, and a white T-shirt, his madras shirt over it. Now the hat and shirt were back.

I trotted into the bedroom to check the chest where we kept our summer clothes between visits. Both locks, one key, one combination, and the wire through the pin were still in place, dusty, rusty, and untouched for nine years. I looked at my handprints left in the layers of dust, sighed, and returned to my seat at the table.

No matter what I wished or wanted to believe, no matter how many pieces of Roy's clothing mysteriously reappeared. My brother was still dead.

Sturdevant killed him. Roy, dashing, swashbuckling Roy, would not allow Sturdevant entrée into the gang of three. So, Sturdevant laid in wait, jumped out from a rock, scared Roy, who lost his footing, dropped his camera, fell, hit his head on a boulder, then rolled into the lake where he drowned.

"That's not how it happened," Sturdevant said, twirling the stick he had used to raise the latch on the kitchen door.

I stood, pointed my finger, and yelled, "Get out of here! Get out! You tripped Mike, you broke in here, then looked at all my photos! What is the matter with you? What!" I scuttled around the table and grabbed the hatchet used to trim wood for the Franklin stove from a copper bucket near the front door.

"What's the matter with me!" Sturdevant took two steps and snatched the hatchet from my hand. "I admit I watched the parade leaving the island, then came over for a little look-see."

I reached for the hatchet. He tucked it behind his back. I poked his chest, screaming, "Did you find what you were looking for? Huh? Did you? Well?"

He gave a sharp twitch of his head. I held my hand out for the hatchet. He brushed me out of the way, opened the front door, and threw it. It thwacked into a birch tree fringing Roy's Deck. "Now?"

I ran out the door, off the stairs toward the tree. Sturdevant grabbed me around the waist. Set me on my feet and yelled, "Stop it! I am not here to hurt you. Frankly, you are as screwed up as I am. The shirt, the hat, what the…"

"Leave me alone. The minute I contact the OPP, your gone. Out of my life. Gone!"

"But you haven't. You could have called the OPP from Dixons. You didn't."

"So!"

"My and we're mature, too."

"You threatened me and killed my brother. Exactly, what is there to be mature about! What?" I stamped my foot.

His dark eyes lit, laughter lightened the planes of his face. When he turned, I took the advantage and ran for the birch tree.

"If you pull that hatchet out of that tree and come for me, I'll put you over my knee. I can. I'm bigger than you, and I'm trained."

I stopped. "Which means…what?"

"Boo Treader, I could have killed you six times in the last two days if I wanted."

"You're watching me. You wrote the second note!" I crossed my arms.

He quirked his mouth. "Look, I'm not clairvoyant. You were muttering when I came in and before you tried to ax me." Sturdevant leaned against a porch post. "I'd like to explain what happened between Roy and me. Are you settled down enough to listen, are you?"

I bobbled my head, brushing the hair on my arms flat, thinking, one spin and a grab, and I could have the hatchet in hand. One perfectly timed move and...no one would blame me. No one!

"It was supposed to be a prank. And you are right, I did want to belong. Not much of an excuse. My final rite for entrée into the gang of three was to scare the first swimmer ashore that night. So, I did. It was Roy. He lost his footing, fell, hit his head, tumbled into the water. I went in after him, swam him to the dock, then pulled him onto it. I gave him artificial respiration until he spewed water and gasped. When Mike showed up with Brad not far behind, I swam off thinking Roy was okay."

"So, his best friends killed him? Then lied over and over and over to the OPP?"

"I didn't say that. It was wrong to run. But..."

"Which excuses you, how? My brother's been dead twelve years, and here you are leaning and breathing."

"My father was murdered, Boothe."

"Give me a break. Is that your excuse? Or are you accusing someone in my family of killing your father? My mother? Roy? That it?" It would be a cold day in hell when I told Sturdevant that my father shared the belief. "And who are you to come and go?"

"Your conscience. I'm not what you're afraid of— you're afraid of your brother's ghost. You are! Now that we've settled that, how about a beer?"

"No." I snarled, "You guys cleaned me out."

"Come on, you're a bootlegger's great-great-granddaughter!"

"I bought some Jim Beam at the Duty Free as a gift for Joe Withers, Penny's husband. It's in a box on the floor under the kitchen table."

"Are you planning to use the hatchet on my back while I'm on my knees?"

I strode past him into the cabin.

"Glasses?" he asked as I passed.

"Top shelf." Conflicted, the word of the day. Confused, inconsistent feelings, a discord of action.

Run. Where?

He had already shown he could beat me to any door in the cabin or disarm me with a sleight of hand. And, tonight, there was no Mike Gagne to rush to my rescue. As I closed down my computer, Sturdevant slapped through the screen door and into the kitchen.

I heard the clink of cheap glasses followed by a thump as Sturdevant placed them on the kitchen table. The shush of a cardboard box pulled across the bubbled, cheap linoleum followed. He lifted the flaps. At a sharp oath, I ran into the kitchen. On his knees, Sturdevant reached into the box and pulled out a stained red bandanna. Roy's. I took the scarf and held it drooping from my fingers, draping it over a chair back in the dining room.

Sturdevant joined me, tapping his left foot until the floorboards bounced. The scar on his temple was white and shiny, his skin pallid. Moisture rimmed the nascent mustache on his upper lip even though the night had cooled. He wore little, just drenched swim trunks and an equally wringing wet cotton shirt, not

Pima cotton, but cotton lawn. Who wears a hundred-dollar shirt to swim a channel? Or to kill, for that matter.

"I could use that drink," he said flatly.

In the kitchen, kneeling, staring in the box, both madness and hurt had flashed across his black eyes. I hardly knew what to think or how to breathe.

"Drink," he said, fingering the bandanna, tracing the outline of the stain.

"Ice?" I asked, wrapping a towel over his shoulders for warmth.

"Neat," Sturdevant answered. I turned. He was reading from the notebook I had set out, the bandanna around his neck, the towel beneath, his left foot pounding away. I snatched the kerchief from his shoulders and draped it over Roy's baseball cap.

Returning to the front room, I nudged Sturdevant over so I could open the refrigerator door and reach into the freezer for the ice tray. I took the ice to the kitchen, filling a glass with ice for me, leaving the other empty, then walked them into the front room with the booze.

I plunked the bourbon bottle and glasses down in front of him. He poured. No fingers were involved in measurement. When our drink glasses were full, he went on reading. I returned the ice tray to the freezer then joined him.

After a while, I said, "Tell me."

"Roy's head was bleeding. The bandanna was around his neck. It was all I had to stanch the flow of blood. I found a sock hanging on a boat line at the dock and put it over the wound, then used the bandanna to keep it in place."

"How?"

He shot his empty black eyes at me. "Did it get in the box? Why are you asking me? Oh, I put it in, then acted all surprised? Is Gagne okay?"

"You watched. When Mike started back, you ran ahead. When he roared up, you flanked him then hit him with that branch—the one I found. You left him unconscious in the rain, Roy's hat beside him. Where do you watch from? The woods? The beach? You weren't on the beach. I would have seen you."

"I admit watching him kiss you goodbye last night then motor up Beaver Course. He throttled back at a movement in the bushes, could have been your beaver for all I know. Next thing, he's charging up the hill. Something or someone made the first corner in the path before he did, by seconds."

"Who was it?"

"Honestly, I don't know, blurry."

"Roy?"

"If I had to go with an impression and if I believed in that sort of thing, I'd say possibly."

"Lots of equivocation there, eh?"

"Maybe." He said lightly, then with a buck of his head, added, "Gagne?"

"He's okay." I sipped my drink from the glass held in my shaking hand, waiting for the goosebumps on my arms to diminish. "I found Roy's madras shirt two nights ago, hanging on the porch railing. Someone fanned the fire in the fire pit. I heard the splash as they left. When I checked where Mike fell, I found Roy's hat."

He pointed through the kitchen door to the growing shrine. I nodded.

"Maybe Roy is trying to communicate with me? Is he? What does he want me to know or do?" I blushed, embarrassed by how hopeful my questions sounded.

"Doubtful. Did anyone stop by the day the shirt reappeared?"

"Mike. You. Tim."

"After I left here this afternoon, I swam over to the beach, planning to check out the property markers for the realtor and against the plotlines. As I dressed, I noticed a male sitting on the rocks, my rocks, you know the ones. When he saw me, he dove into the lake and swam toward the island. He never emerged from the water." Finn cleared his throat, took a sip of bourbon, replenished his glass though it was far from empty. "I shook it off, picked up my stakes, and hiked the south side of the property."

"Roy's dead. Right? We agree on that?"

"The person I watched seemed short, but twelve years ago, I was three inches shorter. Dead, I don't know...last I saw Roy, he was breathing."

"The coroner, my father, the crematorium. Dead."

"You called out for him two nights ago."

"The fire...his shirt. It still smelled of Roy, I swear."

"Maybe Roy keeps it in a plastic bag when he isn't wafting about in it."

"Fine. I get it! You don't feel Roy, see him, or care any more than you did when you killed him. So, did you kill your father?"

His eyes narrowed and, impossibly, darkened as he sipped. "No. I was here, stalking your brother. Can't be two places at one time."

"Is that supposed to be humorous?"

"No, just feeding into your contempt."

"I'm asking?"

"I was in the shower when I heard Pop sneak out and leave me. We always went fishing together. I took photos. Pop fished. I dried off, threw on some shorts, grabbed my camera, and ran after him to the dock. The boat was gone. I sat on my rocks and waited...forever, listening to the party on the island.

"Eventually, I ran over to O'Dells. Farley and your dad got a search party going. I should have participated, I know that. It stoked the rumor mill. The next thing I knew, it was all over the lake that I was some sort of unfeeling monster. That night, I decided to stay at the lake, to be near Pop for the rest of the summer, maybe find out why he went fishing without me. I was totally complicit in destroying myself. Totally."

He refilled his glass, threw the bourbon back, then refilled the glass with a clink of the bottle on the neck.

"Why should I believe you? For all I know, you stuffed the kerchief in the box while you were in the kitchen and draped Roy's shirt over the railing." I sniped. "And wore the hat so poor Mike would think it was Roy running up from Old Landing."

"Of course, why not?" Sturdevant shrugged. It seemed impossible his eyes could narrow further, but they did.

"Next, an incriminating photo will show up on someone's door. By the way, did you enjoy your trip through my photos?"

Ignoring me, he turned a page in the twelve-year-old notebook, then flipped it back and reread it.

He slid the pad to me, pointing. The scrawled words were difficult to read. Some of the letters were unformed, others wobbling either in anger or from some other stimulus, my guess, booze. *Jack,* it read, *went to the bastard, told him like you said. The old boy's scared of something. His eyes just rolled. Liked to lose it. Nothing came of it, damn it.* The note was unsigned.

"That's my father's writing," Sturdevant said. "I whined to Pop about Brad and Roy. He kept giving me ideas about how I might befriend them. When my efforts made things worse, Pop talked to your dad. Roy seemed to back off for a few days, but not Brad. He sucker-punched me, knocked me flat on my own beach, then stood over me, waving his arms and screaming that if I wanted in, I needed to learn to take it, not go tattling to my daddy. Done, he helped me to my feet and challenged me to ask Meg out."

"Did you?"

"Yes, to one of those youth dances up lake, she accepted. We had a decent time, not great, but okay. Next thing I know, she told everyone I pinned her in a corner and forced myself on her. The next morning, a photo of a girl trying to ward off Brad's advances was taped to Dixon's backdoor. Brad used it as an excuse to beat the hell out of me. Brad set me up, and Meg, too. He used both of us. As far as I am concerned, the photo was justice served."

"Your way of getting even seems like it backfired." I cocked my head. He tilted his. I rolled the bottom edge of my glass in circles on the table. He drank. I would need another bottle of bourbon for Joe before the night was over. If I survived.

"I asked Roy what was going on, he corked me in the bicep then warned me to stay away from Meg. I whined to Pop, he went to see Mr. Dixon and was dead two weeks later."

"You can't think your father's death had anything to do with his visit to Mr. Dixon."

"I do. I've had plenty of time to think about it."

Sturdevant topped off the glass again. The clink of the bottle on the drinking glass rang around the room.

"You didn't know Mr. Dixon. Nothing riled him. He was always on an even keel. He had this great laugh. Half the time, he had a kitten crawling on him. He would sit at the picnic table under the walnut trees and hold court, telling stories about the old days on Lower Bay. No one, absolutely no one had a bad word to say about him."

"He died about five years after Roy, didn't he?" Sturdevant asked.

"How would you know?"

"I hear things, heard things." Which meant his source could have told him I was expected at the island for the summer.

"Natural causes, in his sleep. Meg found him when she went to wake him. Erase any other theories from the slate."

"Pop's note proves that Mr. Dixon had little control over Brad."

I sighed. Without thinking, I reached over and squeezed Sturdevant's left hand. "I'm sorry about your dad. It must have been awful to lose him and be orphaned so young."

"You think it threw me for a loop so big that I killed your brother?" he huffed, "I told you it was an initiation prank!"

I stood and stepped away. "Don't get angry. It's just..."

"I didn't sneak around leaving damning photos in my wake. I didn't. I was set up. Do you think I don't know who is responsible for the photographs, the rumors, killing my father, killing Roy? Do you think I don't know why it all happened? Do you!" He roared to his feet.

I ran for the bedroom. Sturdevant took two steps, caught me, and dragged me by the elbow to an empty spot along the wall. He slammed me against the plasterboard hard enough to rattle the propane sconces and held both of my hands to my sides. I scrunched my eyes closed, waiting for a hand to encircle my neck, and nodded, yes, to save my life.

He was faster than me, and the hands clamping mine had killed. I knew that. I opened my eyes, ready to drop to my knees, break his hold, then scramble out the front door. With the hatchet, I might stand a chance. He tilted his head to the right, his right eye studying me.

He took his hand from my right wrist, blood rushed into my fingers. His free hand under my chin, he turned my face to his. His lips met mine, his stubble sanding my chin. I squirmed. He held me against the wall with his body. My toes curled, and my arches cramped.

Eventually, I sputtered for air. Sturdevant quit the kiss and ducked, attempting to see into my lowered eyes. In the end, he placed two fingers under my chin and gently raised it until our eyes met.

"Please, believe me, Boo," he whispered, searching for my lips.

We fumbled. His right hand cupped the back of my head. He draped my left hand over his shoulders with his free hand, then slid it to the small of my back. I felt our hearts struggling to match beats, a syncopated mess, mine fast, his slow and even. I tucked my head against his chest, ashamed of the warmth I felt. This was my brother's killer.

"Who? Who set you up?" I asked.

"That's for me to prove." He took my hand and led

me into the bedroom, then kissed me on the brow, saying, "By the way, I have a mother and, as of the last count, five half-siblings on the West Coast."

I heard the latch go down on the front door and, after some fiddling, the same in the back. I hardly knew what to believe. I did know sleep was gone. I waited, then carrying the damp towel last over Sturdevant's shoulders, walked the backbone of the island to the stairs down to the new pier.

The stars blazed like LED lights through pinholes in black paper. A loon called. What *does* a loon call, Roy? Eternity.

I sat, wrapped in the towel, feet dangling in the waves, and stared across at the Peninsula. Hoping, I suppose, that he was watching me. Seeing nothing, I made finger binoculars to help me focus. There, a soft light flashed on just off the beach near the trees.

A rock bounced down the stairs. I twisted to see who was there. A shadowy figure lurked amongst the bushes at the top of the hill. A stiff breeze rattled the trees, the shadow slipped into the dark beyond the reach of the solar light.

When another rock bounced to my left, I stood and waved across the water, in case the light on the beach was Sturdevant training his binoculars on New Landing. At another rush of wind, another snapped twig, another thrown rock, I jogged to the cabin.

Tucked in bed, worthless latches, latched, I thought I would never sleep. But I did, as though I were being watched.

Over, that is.

Day 6

xix

IT ALTERNATELY BLEW CLEAR or clotted up with rain all night. Towards morning, a clap of thunder woke me. I lay in bed, analyzing what had driven me to follow Sturdevant to the dock and, later, why my brother skipped rocks at me. When light dusted the horizon and a loon called morning, I dozed, waking to an azure blue sky, horizon to horizon.

I slipped my feet into a pair of black skimmers, then ran out the backdoor to the john in my shorty-pajamas. The shed door flapped in the wind. I eased onto one of the two holes. My mom always said *you know you're amongst 'em when you have a two-holer.* I had no idea what it meant, only that a two-holer was wasted on a brother and sister once one of them reached the age of three.

When footsteps padded up the pathway, I stared at the dangling latch on the outhouse door. A moment later, Tim O'Dell opened the door, blushed, mumbled sorry, and turned his back. Red roared up the back of his neck.

"Second," I said, pulling up my shorty shorts, then burst out of the john and up the hill into the cabin and through to the bedroom.

By the time I dressed, Tim had bread in the toaster and two cups of coffee on the dining room table. He even poured a little pitcher of half-and-half for anyone who wanted creamer. It was a wee comfortable for me.

"Meg said you talked to your mother yesterday. Anything to report?" Tim asked, blowing on his coffee to cool it.

"She admitted to the deed."

"The plans are approved, and the money has cleared. Not much wrong that I can figure, eh? What do you say we start on the dance floor?"

I put my elbows on the table and my chin in my hands. My mother wanted this for me just for the fun of it. It had been a dour, dark twelve years without Roy, without Dad at times.

Honestly, my father's infidelity left me wary of all men, Roy's death of loss, and Mom's bouts of frivolity, suspicious of joy. People who smiled too often scared me like clowns do some people.

At twenty-seven, my life was built of persistent memories. First joyful, then hurtful. Mom wanted me to live in the moment, to adventure out, to really fall wackadoodle knee-rattling head over heels in love. She didn't care with whom. Not true, she *would* care if it were that boy, the toe curler, Finn Sturdevant.

"Sure. Yes, let's do it! Set a date, and I'll throw a real honest to god George Booth Prohibition blast. Lights, booze, dames, dancing, and canapes!"

"Any maracas?" Tim kidded.

"There are some in the bedroom! ¡Olé!"

"No," he scoffed, "Not really." It was a good bluff, but Tim knew. He likely had picnicked here with Meg and danced a few tangos in the front room before adjourning to the old horsehair mattress. "Brad's going to help me build until Mike is back in action. Send out the invitations for two weeks from Friday."

"You'll have the wiring strung by then? The floor solid? I don't want a repeat of the bridge disaster."

"We'll put in a few extra piers to ensure nothing tilts."

"With audio speakers on each pole!"

"Gonna dance the night away. I volunteer to ferry the booze and broads." Tim gave me one of his blazing smiles as he slurped coffee. I thrummed the tabletop with my right hand, thinking Tim and Meg.

"Okay, this is great! Do you think Mom's money will be enough?"

"Yep," Tim said, with a final slurp. "Need to get to work, got an important deadline to meet."

Me, too. As a result of my talk with Mom and evening with Sturdevant, my urge to talk to Dad was so great that I would have driven the three and a half hours to Montreal for a private chat. Mom saved me the trip when she told me he was out of town. Wherever he was, Dad would answer a call from me as long as it originated from planet earth.

If I remembered, I would ask him from whom George Booth purchased the island. If he knew, it would save me a trip to the Land Office. Meg would know in a heartbeat, then the rest of Lower Bay. After I called Dad from the café, I would take advantage of being in town and check my email, my gigs, do some editing, and replenish my stores. I whistled as I slid my wallet and computer into my knapsack and headed out.

I waved to Tim and Brad, happily measuring away. Meg's pontoon boat had been converted from ambulance to barge. Tim must have been confident I would give the go-ahead because the boat was packed to the gills with steel girders and wood for the dance floor. I glanced across the water to Sturdevant Beach. No binocular flash this morning. In fact, there was no sign of life.

The boat ride to Dixon Landing and the drive to town passed without incident. I stopped by to see Alice Cornish, asking her if she had spoken to Mr. Sturdevant about my offer. She reported that she had tendered my offer but hadn't heard back. So, I asked if there were any other nibbles. She blushed. I urged her to negotiate the beach and access for me from either the owner or any potential buyer, then went next door to the café to set up shop.

I called Dad via the internet. It had been a while since we had seen each other, and the talk we needed seemed better-accomplished face to face. I texted him as I drove into town, giving him a time for the call. I checked for his response before I dialed. None, but his face popped up on my telephone screen as soon as my phone signaled his. He had been waiting.

He waved. I waved back. Dad had a pleasantly masculine face that was aging well. A few lines edged his mouth, smile lines. Roy would have had the same character in his face, and gentleness in his blue eyes, given a chance. A sprinkling of gray hair salted Dad's currently sun-streaked dark hair. He wore a red shirt decorated with macaws and may have been naked below for all I could see.

"So, where are you guys?" I asked through the microphone on my earbuds. Wherever it was, it was sunny, hot, and sandy. In the background, someone dangled from a striped parachute attached to a motorboat.

"Costa Rica," he answered, echoing a bit. "What's up?"

"I am up at Booth Island for the summer. Mom deeded it to me. Remember, I told you."

He nodded.

"I might have a chance at lake access."

"The old Sturdevant place?" Dad asked. "It belongs to Finn since Don's death."

"I know. Promise you won't tell, but Finn Sturdevant is here, now."

"Still a hunk," Dad laughed.

"He's okay, pretty banged up." My cheeks warmed, feeling Finn's arms around me. If Dad noticed, he ignored it.

"Finn's been through a lot, BG. Sounds like he's coming out the other side okay. Is he why you're calling? The restraining order is still in effect."

"No. I was talking to Mom. Mom sent Tim O'Dell, Meg's live-in, enough money to refurbish the dance floor, adding a roof, electricity, and removable screens. The thing is, Mom failed to tell me, so I stopped construction until I could talk to her. Once we cleared that up, our conversation took a left turn to the summer Roy died. She said you lost your father's gold watch and never found it."

"It was stolen, as was your mother's engagement ring. I always suspected your brother. I think if Roy had survived, both items would have shown up. Those boys kept getting progressively wilder. I knew about the crazy game of theirs. I put the hammer down on Roy, to no effect. It was as though he was afraid to opt-out. What got me was the vendetta directed at Finn."

"That's a rough word, vendetta?" I asked, hoping to hear a version different from those offered by Penny,

Mike, and Sturdevant.

"Pushing, shoving, name-calling, telling lies to the girls so Finn couldn't get a date, using Sturdevant Beach without permission. Don came to me. Like I said, I told Roy to cease and desist. Instead, he upped his game, if you will. I even accused Roy of taking and delivering the compromising photos. He swore up and down he hadn't." Dad bobbled his head. "Don went to Mr. Dixon. Nothing happened, well, not true, Brad whaled on Finn. Don worried a lot; he said his boy had a pretty hot temper. Then Don went fishing."

"Mom says that you think Don Sturdevant was murdered. Why?"

"You probably don't remember the gossip that circulated about Don. It made the rounds on the adult drum. Trust me, I didn't know Don well, but I knew what was being said was construed, and I had a fairly good idea who started the talk. Gossip on the lake always flowed in one of two directions; this was counterclockwise."

He sipped a drink, something tropical looking. "Don loved his boy. Finn even called him Pop, so the rumors that Don beat Finn were just that. Mean spirited. I never saw Don drunk, sure he drank the occasional beer or two, but that was it. The man who came to me for help was sincerely concerned about his son. And, the one thing that always bugged me, still does, is that Don always took Finn fishing with him. He never went alone. Don would fish, and Finn would take photos."

Sturdevant had said the same at the front room table the night before.

"To Finn's embarrassment, Don had a bunch of Finn's photos matted then took them to one of the gift shops in Westport. They sold like hotcakes. One of Finn's best is right in front of you, BG, if you're at the Westport café."

I looked across the room. A mural made from a black and white photograph of a pair of loons on a windy moonlit lake adorned the wall behind the ice cream cooler.

Dad must have heard me suck in my breath. "Something, isn't it? Now, BG, you tell me, could that kid have done the things they claim he did."

"I don't know, Dad." I stuttered, thinking of those fierce black eyes penetrating me as I sat. And of the amused curl of his lip when I tried to hatchet him. "Do you remember what became of Roy's red bandanna?"

"Hmmm. You checked the clothes' locker?"

"I did. You don't suppose?"

"I don't. Roy's gone, BG."

"I know, it's just..."

"Time to move on."

I almost screamed *like you and Mom did without a second thought*. Instead, I nodded. Dad grinned, adding, "Misty is on a beach chair, her legs crossed, her head cocked to one side listening. No, wait, she wants to say *hi*, or something."

Dad handed his smartphone to Misty, who wore her golden tan well, her streaked hair piled high on her head. "I was listening, Boo. I hope you don't mind. There is something I want to share that seems pertinent. I saw Finn and Roy get into it at one of your mother's parties. Neither Finn nor Roy was backing down until Meg walked over. Finn threw his hands in the air and stalked off. He forgot his camera. Meg picked it up and fiddled with it before running after Finn. Still, it struck me as odd that a kid with Finn's physical prowess would cower from Roy or Brad, but he did. I thought I should mention it."

In the background, Dad said, "Cower is a bit too strong. I thought Finn showed good sense."

"You heard Jack, right?" Misty asked.

"I did. Thanks, guys. Thanks for your insight. One more thing. Dad, do you know from whom George Booth bought the island? It would save me a trip to the Land Office."

"Your mother would know?" I bobbled my head. He answered with a knowing smile, "As I recall, the Dixons homesteaded the entire west side of Lower Bay in the early 1800s. All of it. Not our island, but all the land. The island was a bone of contention between the Dixons and the Lapps, Misty's family." Over Dad's shoulder, Misty nodded her agreement. "Ultimately, George paid the Lapps for the island. Lots and lots of bad blood between the Dixons and the Lapps over it. Apparently, all the fuss stopped when the Land Office recognized the sale and recorded the deed."

"The Sturdevants bought from the Dixons?" I asked.

Dad humphed, adding, "It's all a bit hinky, but, yes, according to the land records. Misty, anything you want to add?"

She shook her head.

"Thanks, Dad. You were lots of help. Bye, Misty." They both waved as we disengaged.

I stared at the mural made from Finn Sturdevant's photograph. It reminded me of the one hanging in the front room of the cabin. Had Roy stolen then taken credit for Finn's photos? If so, no wonder Finn pushed back when the gang of three refused him entrée. I chastised myself for excusing my brother's killer, then wondered when Sturdevant had morphed into Finn, and finally, how had I missed so much that summer. And, not necessarily in that order.

Meg and Penny were the answer to the first question. We were the second gang of three, maybe a lower-case gang of three, but we went everywhere together. Penny bounced from boyfriend to boyfriend, pudgily cute in her two-piece swimsuits. According to Finn, I was watchable. And, Meg, the mother hen ensured we stayed out of trouble and, if we did get in it, extricated us via the capitalized gang of three, our brothers.

She called them into action more than once, even when we really weren't interested in being extricated at all. A vision of an angry Penny sniping at Meg for the rumors Meg spread about Finn occupied me for a second. Counterclockwise. The first grumbling complaints about Finn were voiced by Meg. It was later that she claimed he had taken advantage of her.

I gave up on checking my email or getting any work done, deciding to visit Mike instead. I folded up my computer just as Penny and her mother, Mary, strolled into the café arm in arm. I waved and motioned to my table. They ordered and joined me. It didn't take a seer to divine that Penny was still miffed at me. Mary shoved Penny's arm, her motherly way of signaling Penny to behave.

"How's Mike," I asked.

"Fine," Penny mumbled, "No thanks to you!"

"I didn't trip him!" I protested.

Penny plunked a photo on the table of Mike and me kissing at Old Landing the night of his accident. "I found it taped onto the outside of the kitchen window, picture side in. This, after I asked, no begged you to leave Mike alone. Well, one thing, it proves Finn Sturdevant is in town and up to his old tricks. What did you do to tick him off, eh? You better be careful because that's more than playing with fire!"

"Oh, grow up, the pair of you," Mary intervened. "Let me buy you some Tiger Tail, Boo. I know how you adore the stuff. Penny, one scoop or two? And, girls, don't fight while I'm standing in line."

"Taped to your window. Just like old times?"

Penny thumped the picture with her index finger.

"Someone is trying to drive us apart, Pen. You and me. Not me and Mike. Who? That is the real question."

"No, it isn't. The real question is why you ignored my worry."

"No, *it* isn't."

Penny scoffed, "Well, we know Mike didn't tape it to the window."

"Do you know that Finn took the photo used in that mural? The one over the counter." Even to me, I sounded more than familiar with the photographer.

"Finn?" Penny asked, catching my tone. "I get it now. Mike saw Sturdevant climbing up from Old Landing, got on his white charger, mounted the hill, tripped on his face, that is what happened. It is, isn't it? How could you!"

"Is not!" I snapped, never mind that I had already accused Sturdevant of the same. "Mike charged up the hill, but it wasn't Sturdevant he was following."

"You'd tell me if Sturdevant was bothering you, wouldn't you? Oh, Boo!"

"I'm fine."

Penny pursed her lips and tried to read the back of my mind. "Mike told me how great you were when you found him. He is embarrassed beyond words. Don't expect him to darken your doorstep for a few days. Besides, Mom insists he stay with her and Aunt Lou until his noggin heals. Does the term to spoil rotten mean anything to you?"

I laughed. As far as I was concerned, Joe Withers had won the lottery when he wooed and married Penny.

Mary arrived balancing three dishes of varying amounts of Tiger Tail. She plumped down across from me. "Any more thought about buying Sturdevant Beach?"

"Are there no secrets?"

Mary shook her head. "None at all. Meg told Dred, Dred told Lou, Lou told me and around and around it goes."

Counterclockwise, I thought.

"I was talking to my Dad about Don Sturdevant."

Mary licked the ice cream off her spoon, her eyes on me as she did. Penny ignored us, plowing through her two scoops.

"Dad told me he went to the OPP; he was so sure that Don was murdered." I scraped melting ice cream from my scoops and sucked it off the spoon.

Mary nodded. "The OPP listened to everyone else instead; drunk, a child beater, et cetera, et cetera. Don died on an island party night. As I motored over to the island, I passed him going out fishing. He usually took Finn, but not that night. At first, I thought his passenger was Brad, but Brad and Roy were greeting people that night. And you girls were all in attendance. I told your dad about seeing Don in his boat, but not until after they found Don's body."

"Where? Where did they find him--exactly?"

"In Upper Bay in the marsh, you know how the

Sturdevant Peninsula curves away from Upper Bay creating an arm, the marsh is in the armpit. Don was found in the stumps near the shore. Had he been conscious, he could have crawled out."

I humphed.

Mary responded, "My sentiments exactly."

"Still," Penny said, "Mr. Sturdevant's boat was found in Upper Bay floating upside down as though it had flipped. Right?" She checked to see if we agreed. When we ignored her, she shook her head and concentrated on her ice cream.

"Don was athletic like his son. It is hard to believe he drowned. Despite a few peculiarities, the OPP called it a boating accident and stuck by their guns. I'm glad your dad hasn't given up." Mary finished her one scoop.

"Peculiarities?"

"Though he struck his head on a stump hard enough to kill him, his back was bruised. The coroner found the bruises consistent with losing his balance in the boat and hitting the gunnel as he fell. The real mystery was why his boat floated upside down into Upper Bay while his body stayed in the stump bog. Makes no sense."

"Why?"

"The water in the bog is stagnant. It evaporates, and that is about it. There is no current that could have carried Don's body into the stumps, except during a major storm. The water was placid that night, all over the lake."

"Ah?"

"As in the boat should have been there, too. But it was over a mile into Upper Bay bobbing in another stagnant bay."

"That is peculiar."

"That is everything. The only explanation the OPP put forward was that Don got drunk, fell out of the boat, started swimming for shore, got into the bog, and..."

"Which doesn't match his injuries. I get it. I'm glad my dad's in Costa Rica. I'd rather he not be the next victim."

Mary gathered my right hand in hers. "Oh, Boo. It is old history, isn't it? No one is in danger. Best leave those old dogs to lie."

"I worry that's just what they did...lie...lots of lies." I studied Finn's photograph plastered on a ten-foot-wide wall. The background was the stump bog, where his father's body had been found. Penny hugged me. I hugged her back. "Love you, Pen. You're the best."

"If that were true, Joe and I would be rich as rich."

"You are."

Mary grinned, "You bet you are. Great guy, great kids, not much else matters, Penny."

Penny threw her other arm around her mother and kissed us each on a cheek. "Joe is bringing the kids, ours, and Mike's to Lou's house. We're going to have some beef on a bun." Penny raised a questioning eyebrow as an invitation.

"Sounds like fun. But I want to be in the cabin before dark." I licked my spoon, a thought sparked. "Mary, did your family buy their property from the Dixons?"

"Everybody on the westside of Lower Bay did."

"Even the Sturdevants?"

"Well," Mary's head bobbled. "Lyle Sturdevant not only ran rum, but he was a hell of a poker player. If that answers your question."

It did.

Oblivious, Penny bubbled, "It must be weirdly

quiet on the island without your mom."

"Not really," I laughed as they stood. I made a stop by The Beer Store on my way out of town to resupply for my workmen and ethereal visitor. I bought two two-fours of Labatt Blue Label, then circled back to the LCBO for some locally brewed bourbon.

I read my way down the shelves until I came to a highly recommended Canadian bourbon named Lower Bay. According to the handwritten sign, voted the best Canadian rye whiskey. The label was a hoot. The company established in the U.S. moved to Ontario to escape Prohibition and stayed. The writeup touted that over 100 years later, the whiskey was still made to George Booth's exacting standards. There was no buried treasure on Booth Island; this was it. The brewing company: Sturdevant Distillers in Windsor, Ontario. A bridge away from Detroit city.

I circled back to town, parked in front of the café, went to my favorite table, booted up my computer, and did the research. Sturdevant Distillers was privately held by the Sturdevant and Booth families from 1910 to 1947. From 1920-1925, it operated unlicensed out of a facility in southwestern Ontario, for instance, a tin-sided warehouse in Lower Bay.

Sturdevant Distillers licensed as a Canadian producer in 1926, no doubt to make it easier to smuggle hooch across the river to family-operated speakeasies in Detroit. In 1947, the then Sturdevant bought out George Booth, who returned to the family furniture business and Booth Brewing Company in Pittsburgh. Finn Sturdevant was listed as the current Chief Executive Officer of Sturdevant Distillers. I dialed my mother's cellphone.

"Really?" I started. "I've been bourbon shopping."

"Ooops. Read the label, did the research?"

"That's it?"

"Pretty much."

"Did you ever get the impression that the locals wanted their lakefront back?"

"Oh, sure. Exactly why I always threw parties, ensured you kids buddied with their kids, and left the island and cabin open for use. It seemed to be working until Roy's death."

"Is there any connection between the Sturdevant owned and Booth owned companies now?"

"No, not anymore. It all started because George made great beer and better aging barrels. When Lyle and Ardyss were murdered, it took the gilt off the fun. George stayed with the Distillery until 1947, feeling he owed it to Lyle's widow, then went back to making furniture and beer. Now, Uncle Nick runs the furniture business. Booth Brewing was sold to Budweiser when George died."

"Do the Lower Bay folks know anything about Sturdevant Distillers?"

"Of course, the Sturdevants offered each Lower Bay family five-percent of the distillery, I think. When Sturdevant Distillers licensed, the Gagnes and O'Dells took them up on the offer. The O'Dells sold their shares after the Second World War and bought more land."

"From the Dixons?"

"No. Can't remember who they bought from, but it wasn't the Dixons. The O'Dells did buy their original property from the Dixons in the late 1800s, I think."

"Gagnes?"

"As far as I know, they kept and still have their shares. Maybe more, I think they were offered the O'Dell shares when the O'Dells sold."

"Cripes! And the Dixons?"

"Everyone was offered the same deal. The then Mr. Dixon called the OPP. The warehouse was raided. Ripped apart is more like it. The OPP call led to Ardyss' death, then Lyle's, of course."

"No hard feelings?"

"Not from the Pennsylvania side of the street."

"Seems like some hard feelings on the Dixon side."

I could almost see Mom shrug. "Most of what happened was forgotten or forgiven over time or became apocryphal stories about money and bodies buried on the two properties."

"Did Lyle Sturdevant cheat the then Mr. Dixon out of the peninsula in a poker game?"

"According to the Dixons, yes."

"Anything else I should know?"

"Not that I know of." I could tell by the giggle in her voice my mother was enjoying the heck out of this. "Of course, you never know."

"Mom?" Her laugh echoed across the miles as she hung up.

Sturdevant Distillers. The best Canadian Rye Whiskey was Finn Sturdevant's to lose. For fun, I searched the online *Detroit Free Press*. The day's headline blared, *CEO Teen Killer!* Of course, I read the article.

I docked the boat at New Landing just before 8:00 pm. A radiant sunset blazed, then hushed, then disappeared. In my absence, Brad and Tim had demolished the rotting dance floor, the salvageable wood was set to one side, the dirt below was exposed. I used the rolling cart to carry the beer and booze to the kitchen.

I lowered the cart with a thud onto the tongue at

the kitchen door. A bloody, long-fingered handprint decorated the doorframe as though some kindergartener had painted his hand red and pressed it on wood as a gift.

XX

I SLAPPED THROUGH THE kitchen door, making as much racket as I could. "I brought two cases of beer!"

"Any food, or are we drinking our meal again tonight?" Finn asked, his voice drifting in from the front room.

"What did you do to your hand?".

"I've been going through the notebooks year by year. Nothing. Well, except two angry non-sensical notes claiming you're a rat, well, and a part of the female anatomy that I will not repeat."

"That summer?" I unpacked my few groceries and set the Rye bottle on the kitchen table.

"No, that's why I marked the pages in the notebooks."

"I could use some help. I hauled the beer up from the dock. It's outside in the cart."

Finn appeared in the doorframe in his swim trunks. His left hand was wrapped in what was left of the T-shirt used to bandage Mike's head. Undaunted, he retrieved the beer from the wagon. He opened one case and took out six beers, then slid both boxes under the table. He handed the beers up to me, I walked them to the refrigerator.

"Food?" he muttered, looking way too sleek for pity.

"I'll start the barbecue out on the porch and broil

some hamburgers."

"I see you stopped at the LCBO for a bottle of the best, Lower Bay. Who needs Jim Beam, eh?"

"Your great-great ended up being shived in prison because of his distilling acumen."

"I suppose."

"I didn't know about Sturdevant Distillers until today. I just assumed the rumrunning was a Prohibition thing resolved by the 21st Amendment."

"I'm surprised at that. George Booth made a bundle, invested it well, and grew it into a fortune. Plenty of money on your side. And Booth Brewing reaped some serious swag when it sold in the 1960s."

"I never knew. I mean, I knew about the family furniture business. Mom's brother runs it, but not that we were wealthy. I think Mom wanted Roy and me to have normal childhoods with normal friends, so she made sure we had the best of what we needed but never told us we were rolling in dough. I suspect she wanted all us kids to be on an even footing."

He opened a warm beer and sipped. "Interesting, that."

"Tell me about your hand, then about the notes."

"I gashed it climbing out of the water. A piece of serrated tin, raw edge up, must have washed in and lodged in the rocks in the storm. Hurts. I washed it out then found some hydrogen peroxide in the kitchen. Rinsed it with that."

I noticed a bloodstain at the edge of the shelf that housed a few first aid items. I wiped the shelf and doorframe clean as Sturdevant watched with those eyes from where he leaned.

"Sorry for the mess. I was bleeding like a stuck pig. As for the notes, apparently, you were quite the rat eighteen years ago. Anything you can think of that happened on the lake that year that would make someone anxious?"

I would have been nine. I passed Sturdevant and sat in my favorite place between the refrigerator and the wall. Finn added my choice of the seat to his mental portrait of me as he handed me an open beer. I sipped while working my way back in time.

"Nine? A baby raccoon. I found it because I was the first one in the cabin. Dad said it got caught inside and starved, but I knew he was lying. There was an unopened box of cereal on a low shelf. And all the windows were closed. So how had it gotten in at all, much less locked in?

"There was just something about the way the raccoon was laying like it was on display, I would say now. Of course, then, it just looked odd. Dad scooped the little guy up in a rag and buried it by the outhouse where the ground is soft. But I told everyone about finding it, laying there, it's little paws...still bothers me."

"Anything else happen that summer?"

I cocked my head. "Meg asked about the raccoon. I asked her how she knew. She told me she and Penny had come up to the island expecting to find us, but we hadn't docked yet. They must have come from Penny's, a much closer run. Anyway, they peered in the front window and saw the raccoon's body. I checked it out with Penny, who broke into tears."

Finn shrugged, clearly unsatisfied with my response. "There's another note left five years later calling you a whore and a--well--" He blushed as he flipped back through the pages to show me. Square printed letters gave no clue as to the writer's sex or age.

"This reads like something an angry young male might write, hoping to ruin your reputation. Something happened when you were thirteen to provoke the writer." A gust of wind tore across the top of the island. Branches banged on the tin roof and rattled the walls. We both looked up.

Fourteen years ago, two years before Finn came into our lives. The first thing that came to mind was that I started my period on Sturdevant Beach. Penny was the first to notice. I left Penny and Meg on the shore, jumped in the water, and swam to the island. Brad, Mike, and Roy met me. If embarrassment needed a photo, I was it. I slammed my hands to the stain in my crotch and screamed for my mother.

Mom, as moms often are, was totally prepared, having been expecting it. I hid for five days as though I had been sent to the red tent. The three guys avoided me. Penny was all advice, and Meg was all questions, not having started her cycles yet. In limbo, I only knew that I had passed from my childhood. Nothing else changed.

"Not really. It was the last summer that Penny, Meg, and I were all girls." I checked to see if he understood. His gentle smile reassured me. "The guys started checking us out. Penny was all curves, like now. One thing, though, the next year before we arrived, someone poured ketchup in a puddle on the mattress and jammed a butcher knife through it."

Finn moved closer, sitting at the corner nearest me, blocking me in behind the refrigerator, his right hand against my left. So much anger, so few words spent to shame me. Anyone reading the notes would be influenced by what they read. And plenty did. I thought of today's headline in the *Detroit Free Press*, the ugliness of it ate into me.

Finn lifted several strands of stray hair over my left ear then kissed the ear. I came undone. He squeezed past the refrigerator and took me in his arms, resting his chin on the top of my head. His breathing was rock steady, but his hands were shaking. We were a pair.

I took a deep breath that caught beneath my ribs. Finn lifted my face to his, his injured left hand hot on my back.

"Let me look at your hand," I said, slipping out of his grasp, around him, past the refrigerator, and into the kitchen. "I need your hand in here."

"Can I come with it?" he asked.

"I'm sorry, I just suddenly felt trapped. I didn't mean to be so abrupt." But I had.

I pulled one of the two aluminum-framed kitchen chairs out for him. He sat. I unwrapped the T-shirt used as a dressing. A gasp slipped my lips.

"You need to work on your bedside manner," he said, staring at a jagged wound that ran the width of his palm. The torn edges were rimmed in red, muscle visible beneath.

"I think you need stitches. We should find whatever did this. It might be rusty."

He squeezed my right arm. It did little to reassure me. "My shots are up to date. I'm not worried about tetanus."

"You should be worried about this!"

"I've seen worse."

"That's not the point. You need to go to the clinic right now!"

"Whoa. No. Fix me up as best you can. I'll go in the morning."

"Where have you been coming ashore? We need to

find what did this." I insisted. "You've got to find whatever it is. Finn, you do!"

"It's balanced on the generator. I brought it up with me. I think you'll find it interesting."

He was right, I did. It was a rusty chunk from one of the *No Trespassing* signs that decorated the Sturdevant Peninsula. The edge was like a saw blade.

"A message," I said, plunking it on the table.

"If so, it worked. I got it." He fingered the sign, "First, Mike, now, me."

No, first Finn, then Mike, then Finn, again. The article in the *Detroit Free Press* swam in my head. It contained facts about my brother's death that were new to me. Over and over, I imagined Roy bouncing against thick boulders, splashing face down in the roiling water, forced in then out, out then in, each time shredded by the glacial rocks. Alone. Conscious of what was happening. Unable to save himself. Sturdevant watching. Unmoving. Waiting for Roy's death. Mike and Brad finding him.

The coroner's report was reprinted on page two. We all believed Roy struck his head, bounced into the water, and drowned. He hadn't. There was too little lake water in Roy's lungs. I mulled the idea that Finn pled guilty to malicious mischief because, in fact, he had murdered Roy. The lesser charge.

Or had he pulled Roy to shore, saved his life, then swum away, assuming Roy was okay, as he claimed?

I changed the subject, afraid to bring up the article. It was damning, career-ending, and ugly. A chill grabbed hold of me and wrestled with my reason.

Finn saw me recoil; it shone in his dark, empty eyes. Safety fled. He could have cut his own hand, trying to gain my sympathy, distracting me from the possibility that he tripped Mike and left him exposed in the rain, staging Roy's hat to scare me.

I gasped out, "Did you snap the picture hanging in the next room, the photo of the loons taking flight? How about the one taped to Penny's door yesterday? Did you?" The question sounded reckless, worse stupid.

"The loons, yes, Penny, no. But somebody took a picture of the bloody mattress. I saw it in your lunchbox with Roy holding the knife."

Hydrogen Peroxide bubbled pink in the wound. It had to be painful. When the bubbling stopped, I applied an old salve that had been a staple on the island likely since Prohibition. It was greasy, oily, and brown and, by the wad of air Finn sucked in, stung. I tore up another T-shirt and bound the wound.

"I can't believe you snooped in my lunchbox."

Finn raised his eyebrows. "It was on the table. Who wouldn't?"

"Normal people who respected other's privacy, that's who."

Finn waited until he had my attention. "Does anyone else know about the pictures?"

"The envelopes were addressed to me, so no. The six photos you saw were sent anonymously over five years from a processing house in California. I called. The only name they had was Roy Treader."

"Can I see the photos again?"

I shook my head. "You pawed through them once. That's enough."

"It's just that there is a possibility the shots of Roy are all from one of my SD cards. One night, after I showed Dad my pictures from the day, I ejected the SD card, placed it on the end table next to the Adirondack chairs, and put in a new one. When we went in for the night, the card was on the table. I went back for it, but it was gone. Someone had been on our screen porch. The latch on the porch door was dangling."

"Look, I know the photos of Roy are photoshopped--I know that. I don't need some wannabe photographer to tell me that! Even I can photoshop! I saw your work, the photo of me floating!"

"Not mine. Never was."

"Not true. The OPP knew it was. You meant it as a threat. You swam back and killed my brother, and you were going to kill me." It tumbled out then, "I saw it in the article in today's *Detroit Free Press*. It's in your juvenile records."

He grabbed my wrist with his right hand. I slapped him as hard as I could. He bolted to standing, pushing off with his left. Blood oozed from under the bandage. "I'm out of here."

"Run, why not. You're good at that. You swam away from my brother--you let him die!"

He bucked his head. I thought he would strike me. Instead, he turned away, his hands in fists. "I swam away from Brad and Mike, not Roy! They—I gave my youth up for Roy. I—I thought..."

"What, that you'd charm me into forgetting?"

"No. Who could? Someone's gaslighting you, Boothe, and someone is still framing me. Again. Who has that much to lose?"

"You weren't framed. You jumped out of those bushes."

His shoulders hunched. "I guess that's it then."

"You can't row, not like that." I pointed at his hand.

Finn humphed, "You can't take me. Your boat lights up like a Christmas display. Besides, why would you, why would you choose to be alone with me in a boat on the water?"

"Sit. I need to rebandage your hand." He sat. "Swear you'll get your hand taken care of tomorrow."

"If you promise not to come to town. No matter what happens or what you hear. Please?"

"Why?" I asked, tying the two ends of fresh cotton together, extra tight from Finn's pained eyes and squinched mouth. He deserved it. My brain was wracked. Worse, the minute I touched him, I believed him. Not the facts. Him.

"You can't keep a thing off that face of yours. Don't look at me like that! You can't, never could. If we met, even by accident..."

I stopped him. "I get it."

"I'm not sure," he said, wrapping his uninjured hand around my neck and kissing me. "Now?"

I wanted to hate Sturdevant. I never wanted anything so much as I wanted him gone, out of my life. Or in. I blushed at my thinking. "I'm going down to the dock to float the canoe. Give me fifteen minutes."

"What about dinner?" he whined, holding out his bandaged hand like a puppy with a hurt paw.

I barbecued the hamburgers and roasted a couple ears of corn on the cob. We washed it down with Lower Bay whiskey, which seemed to solve most of our problems. Finn's hand quit hurting, and I didn't care.

Two hours later, I tottered out the kitchen door. Leaves rustled on every tree. Branches quaked, leaving pterodactyl shadows in their wake. I could hear the monster birds squawking overhead, readying their long talons to dive in, grasp me, and carry me away.

I followed the path to the dock, my eyes on the ground, avoiding the frightening shapes overhead. The solar lights faded as the day's charge wore down. I dragged the rolling cart behind me, pretending I came down for the rest of my shopping.

A beam of light danced through the trees across Beaver Course. I expected a splash, none came. Instead, a shadowy figure appeared on Sturdevant Beach.

A dog barked and danced as Finn's Rory had that summer. The dog wouldn't be alone. I rummaged in the motorboat and found enough loose jumble to make it look like a load, filled the lift, mounted the stairs, and emptied the random goods into the rolling cart.

Finn appeared out of the ether. Couldn't he make a noise? A rattle, a soft footfall, just any old mousey sound to give me fair warning. I shook my head. He saw the dog.

Leaning down, he whispered, "To the left off the beach, beside the fallen tree."

I saw her then. Her form was unmistakable. I shoved Finn further into the shadows and emerged at the top of the stairs. Penny walked onto the beach. Her retriever, Dusty, pawed and pranced at the waves. Penny flashed her flashlight on and off twice, called to Dusty, and started for home. I waved and walked onto the dock.

Dusty raised a ruckus barking at turtles, loons, fish, and anything else that moved. Penny followed him, her flashlight bobbing along the shore, weaving her way to the Gagnes' dock. Dusty got a paw in the water, whimpered, and darted for the house. Penny turned and signaled bye-bye in Morse code.

Meg, Penny, and I had learned the strange dots and dashes when we were eight, using a card Meg found in her father's study. We practiced with flashlights then messaged each other all summer. Now, I used oars to awkwardly return the message in semaphore, learned the same summer. Penny raised the light and flashed the beam over her head before turning for home.

I waited fifteen minutes before easing the wooden canoe into the water. Finn appeared. I rowed. He held his bandaged hand at the wrist to his chest with the other. The only words spoken were directions.

He was staying at a rental cottage no more than a quarter-mile from his property. I ran the canoe aground. He clambered out.

"Why did you come tonight?" I asked. He leaned over and kissed me. I suppose that was an answer. "It's just--promise me you'll get your hand tended to?"

He nodded and disappeared into the trees. I paddled around the island, rounding Lapp Strait then around through Beaver Course to New Landing, where I shipped the canoe on the jetty.

The moon rippled across the soft waves, the loons echoed each other's call, reminding me that nothing was as it seemed. The picture on the front room wall that Dad was so proud of was Finn's. I hardly knew what or whom to believe. I only knew that Roy ushered me to the cabin, a shadow dancing from tree to tree.

What the loon calls, was it sorrow?

Day 7

xxi

SUN POURED THROUGH THE bedroom window and across the foot of the bed. It was late. I was late. After delivering Finn and returning to the cabin, sleep eluded me. I wished I had saved the article from the *Detroit Free Press* to my hard-drive, had I, I could be rereading it now. Instead, my mind went up, down, and around the damning phrase in the coroner's report, comparing it to Finn's claims that he had resuscitated Roy after swimming him to safety.

I tried warm milk, cold milk, a bologna sandwich with ketchup, pretzels, an apple, and Lower Bay rye. Nothing worked, nor should it have. Indigestion drove me to the front room table. I edited the romance novel until four in the morning, seeing a fierce-eyed, dark-haired man in the hero's part, despite the hero of the book being tall, blond, and well-muscled—more Tim than Finn. In the end, the thought of Meg romancing Tim on a picnic table in the woods like the heroine in the book got me to sleep.

Tim and Brad shouting at each other woke me. I leaned out the bedroom window to see what all the fuss was. Tim held a 12-foot pole upright on a cement pier while Brad pounded nails into a metal cuff. The pole was going to fall over the minute Tim let loose. I yelled as much out the window.

Tim waved me off, which meant letting go of the pole. It teetered. He managed it erect with a toothy, happy smile. Neither of them wore shirts. It was as good a display of pure machismo as I was likely to see all summer. Brad's chest rivaled the hero of the romance novel, while Tim's was movie-star perfect, which provided a five-star recommendation for farming. No matter how I tried, it was a struggle to picture sturdy, brown Meg in bed with Tim O'Dell.

I dressed then went into the kitchen to start breakfast for three, never doubting the guys would join me. Last seen, the jagged *No Trespassing* sign had been on the kitchen table. Now, it hung by a nail just inside the kitchen door, above the hook that held Roy's shirt, hat, and bandanna.

Tim or Brad?

I noticed the empty beer bottles in the trash and threw a few more into the refrigerator. As I did, I wondered if Finn had followed through on his promise to drive into the clinic. I was tempted to go to town, as well, if only to reread yesterday's *Free Press* article and see what was printed today.

The minute the bacon sizzled, the guys knocked on the door. Knocked. Odd, but polite. Tim entered first. Brad followed, making a show of covering his chest with his arm. Funny boys.

"How's it going?" I asked.

"We got the I-beams in place and the first post up, second soon," Brad answered.

"Be careful and don't get beaned; one head wound is strictly my limit," I joked, flipping the bacon. I moved it aside and cracked five eggs on the griddle. "Do either of you know how that chunk of metal ended up hanging on the doorframe?"

Brad raised his hand. "I came in for a glass of water, saw it on the table. It must have gotten wet because it left some rusty stains on the oilcloth. I hung it up. Problem?"

"Not at all. Over easy or hard?" I asked, then flipped the eggs based on the answer.

"I did wonder how a Sturdevant Beach *No Trespassing* sign got in your kitchen," Brad commented.

"I found it floating at the dock last night, fished it out so no one would hurt themselves. It's really sharp," I lied again, serving each guy two eggs and wads of bacon.

"That explains the rusty stain," Brad said between bites. Well, not so much bites as swallows. Nothing got chewed, it just went down Brad's gullet.

Tim glanced at the trashcan. Three bloody wadded paper towels mingled with the beer cans.

"Hey, my dad said that Lyle Sturdevant won the Peninsula in a poker game. True or false?"

"False." Brad snapped, then softened his response, "Well, true. It depends on whose story you buy. The Booth version or the Dixon version. Let me say with either lots and lots of alcohol was involved and few witnesses. I'm not sure George Booth counts as a reliable witness in a four-man poker game."

"Who was the fourth?"

"Lyle's sister, Ardyss."

"Wow, bootleggers and rumrunners, can't beat the company your great-great kept," I laughed.

"Nobody knew Sturdevant was a card sharp in addition to his other credentials, not until it was too late," Brad commented between gigantic swallows.

Tim smiled, "Crazy times and hot flappers."

"And a long, long time ago, lots of peace-loving citizens since then," I joked.

"Some," Brad grunted and changed the subject. "Are you still thinking about buying Sturdevant Beach?"

Tim's glance, accompanied by the butterflies in my stomach, was disconcerting.

"I just want lake access. As far as I am concerned, the Township can have the majority of the Peninsula." I swallowed.

Tim and Brad peered at me over their eggs. With a shake of his head, Tim stood. "We better get back to work. Got our deadline. I haven't seen any invitations going out, Boo." He clapped his hands. "Hop to it!"

"Hey, why invitations, Mom just announced the date, and you all showed up!" I squawked.

"True enough, come on, Brad. I swear you're slower than Mike."

"God forbid," Brad said, standing. He wiped his mouth and smacked the *No Trespassing* sign with his right hand as he left. The sign bounced off the wall and clattered to the floor.

I stayed seated. Sick to my stomach. Last night, something had worried Penny enough that she walked Joe's dog to Sturdevant Beach to check on me. Had she seen someone at shoreline earlier fiddling with the signs? If so, I knew she was standing in for Mike, who would have been on that beach dog-less if not for his injury. Instead, Penny may have seen Finn with me and, if she had, anyone else on Lower Bay could have or might know by now.

I brewed a cup of coffee and stared at the rehung

No Trespassing sign. After a while, I went out to visit Roy. I sat on the bench Dad built and stared at Roy's mended marker. When I opened the computer on my lap, a single sheet of paper drifted to the ground. I closed the laptop, set it on the bench, and reached for the paper. A photo of Finn pinning me against the great room wall, my arm slung around his neck, my back to the wall, his to the window, his elegant lines enfolding me. I stared at it, at us, as flies buzzed me, and ants paraded at my feet. Roy shook a finger and laughed at me from his perch overhead in a hemlock tree.

With Roy egging me on, I realized that Sturdevant's promise to go to the Westport Clinic meant his cabin was empty. The opportunity to wade through his things and his life enticed me.

I ran to the dock, pushed the canoe into the water, and rowed up Sturdevant Peninsula. I made a left hook at the stump bog then drifted in toward the jetty where I had deposited Finn the night before, all in twenty sweaty minutes.

xxii

I BEACHED THE CANOE on the steep grassy slope that led to a comfortable little clapboard house with a broad front porch. I mounted the stairs and knocked on the screen door. A lie ready, after all, Finn had told me not to follow him, and here I was at his door in full sight of New Landing. When he answered, everyone would know he was here and that I knew it. On the other hand, we had already been spied together. I had the photo to prove it.

A young woman in shorts and a halter top opened

the front door then the screen. I must have had the same look on my face that she did. A blush rose up from my neck to my cheeks.

She asked, a hand on one hip, "Can I help you?"

"No. Sorry, I met this guy last night, and he said he was staying here. Well, he was..."

Was this his wife? Did Finn have three kids and a dog? I heard one yapping at the back of the cabin.

"Not anyone here," she answered. "Sorry. We rented the cabin for the week and checked in last night. It is perfect for us, we're really pleased. I hope you didn't come all the way down lake to meet your mystery guy."

I shook my head. "I'm sorry to have disturbed you. I'm summering as well. Nearby." I waved in the general direction of Upper Bay.

"Sorry," she said again, closing the door and going back to whatever was wafting the luscious smells from the kitchen.

I turned, tripping in my rush to the canoe, my emotions vacillating between distrust and fury. Why had Sturdevant lied? Why did he do anything? I shoved the canoe into the water, scrambled in, and paddled.

I wanted Mike Gagne. Right now. I wanted to feel his strong, capable hands holding mine, to see his soft blue eyes and crazy Gagne grin. I wanted to be enfolded in his goodness, but Mike was still in Westport at his mother's and all bunged up. The next thing I knew, I had beached on the rocky north point of Sturdevant Beach. I threw the rope around a pointy boulder, yanking to make sure it would hold. Then realized I should have swum over as Sturdevant did to hide his comings and goings. On the other hand, I had nothing to hide.

I sat in the rocks, surveying the woods, looking for a path from the beach to the cabin. Readying to stand, I noticed that someone used these rocks as a refuge. The loose pebbles were scuffed, a black windbreaker had been forgotten, and a scrap of paper was balled into a wad.

I smoothed the paper on a flat rock. It was that photo, the one of me floating face down in the water in my madras two-piece, ripped from a newspaper. A hand-rolled cigarette stub was jammed between a crevice made by three small rocks.

I searched the jacket's pockets, a disposable lighter, lens caps for binoculars, two AAA batteries, and a few shiny black shale rocks. I held the windbreaker up for size. A stain marred the front. I rinsed it in the lake; the spot ran in a rusty brown streak—blood, no more than a few hours old. I knew more about Sturdevant now than I did from all of his nocturnal visits. He must have torn the photograph of me from the *Detroit Free Press*, then spied on me through binoculars while he smoked. And what? Stroked the picture, planning how he would kill me?

All while his hand bled.

Nothing could stop me from searching his cabin now, not Tim and Brad pounding atop the island, not the boat bouncing down Upper Bay, not Roy watching from New Landing, nothing. I jogged up a narrow, grass and bush choked path from the beach. It might lead me anywhere, but it was the only break in the undergrowth I saw.

The cabin when I came to it had two flights of stairs leading to a raised screened-in porch. I mounted the stairs and called, "Sturdevant."

When no one responded, I entered. The rough

cedar of the cabin was whitewashed on the interior of the porch, even the floorboards. Two Adirondack chairs sat at angles, a table between them. An ashtray, filled to brimming, sat on the table, along with a rolled-up newspaper. A trashcan near the table held the remains of other newspapers. Several articles had been cut out with a pair of scissors, now weighing them down.

Both chairs had comfy cushions and footrests. I sat in the one nearest the door. It had an uninterrupted view of New Landing. A telescope on a tripod, the long lens against the screen beckoned me to look. I stood and put an eye to it. The backdoor of the cabin on Booth Island popped into view. I tracked the path to New Landing, then to Old, then returned the lens to the original position to cover my tracks.

Discovering that Sturdevant smoked, his legs up, a newspaper on his lap as he spied on me, revulsed me. I picked up the snipped articles. Not articles, but headlines, as bad as or worse than the one I had read the day before. I grabbed the bottom clipping and read. Finn Sturdevant had been raised in Grosse Pointe Shores, Michigan, a rich kid in an affluent town on an estate cut out of the Ford Estate. His home was a Cotswold Cottage designed by an imminent architect for Lyle Sturdevant's wife.

Sturdevant was captain of his private high school's swim team. He had been given the nod to try out for the Olympic team and a full scholarship to the University of Michigan though only a high-school junior. Sturdevant was the captain of the basketball team and Jr. Prom King. He made the Dean's List every year he attended. Yes, the fancy school he went to had a Dean of Students.

Penny's comment about Sturdevant's dancing bounced around in my head. He was everything we were not. And everything he said he was.

He was also known to be a hell-raiser with his buddies back home. Boyish pranks, one woman was quoted as saying. Another quote was: He was a good kid, straight up. I can't imagine what happened to make him go bad. Maybe Don's death, perhaps that, but I can't imagine. They were such good friends; I see him honoring his father, not revenging him.

Revenge? On my seventeen-year-old brother? Revenge? Not once had I considered revenge. Revenge or not, all of Finn's privilege was denied then stripped away by six lake kids. Now, he was back.

I slipped the article back into the stack. Leaving the others for later, I stuck my head through the cabin's unlocked front door. A photograph of nesting loons stopped me in the doorframe. The male's neck was wrapped over the females. The moon glowed over them, highlighting each dot of white on their wings. Her eyes were closed, his open and watchful. Grasses and cattails cosseted them. How did the high-spirited boy with everything and the poignancy and delicacy of this photo merge?

A beat-up leather couch occupied the wall under the photo. End tables with table lamps and clutter stood at either end. A footrest in some Middle Eastern style was to the right end of the couch and bore the indentations of two legs. Two well-used leather armchairs faced the sofa. A colorful hook rug covered the whitewashed floorboards, starting beneath the couch and encompassing the chairs. A traveling blanket was slung haphazardly over the arm of one of the chairs. A stone fireplace of stacked slabs of

Canadian Shield occupied one end of the room. Cozy and warm, the two words leaped to mind. Two doors were near the hearth, one for each bedroom.

Sturdevant was using the larger of the two bedrooms. The old mattress on the bed dipped in the middle. Because it was a corner room, there was a window on two walls. Light filtered by the surrounding trees drifted patterns across the floor. A light blanket, streaked with blood, tumbled at the end of the bed, a nightstand held an ashtray filled with hand-rolled stubs.

A photograph of Mike holding me at Old Landing was tacked to the backside of the door. Beneath, it was another of me, alone, sitting at New Landing, waggling my feet in the water. Sturdevant had taken both. There must be a printer somewhere. Not somewhere, but in the other bedroom. A computer as well.

For the first time in my life, I felt overexposed, like that old dream in which you're naked in a room full of clothed people. At that moment, in Sturdevant's upscale cabin, I never hated anyone as much as I did Finn Sturdevant. He had taken my brother from me and now stalked me day and night.

I bound his wound last night. I listened to his version of my brother's death, the lie he told himself to make living possible.

Rummaging through a pile of clothes in the spare room, I uncovered a gun—a revolver. I don't know caliber; I do know loaded. I sat with a thump on the desk chair. Sturdevant had held me, kissed me, and wooed me into believing that the wounds he had suffered were his debt paid to me. He had a gun.

Worse, he smoked.

I booted up his computer. It required a password. I

tried versions of his name, his father's name, Booth Island, everything that might make sense. Then, as a last resort, I typed the date of my brother's death. When the welcome screen opened to a photograph of Roy and me lolling on an old inner tube roped to New Landing, I slammed the laptop closed and hit the off button.

Back in his bedroom, I rifled through the clothes he had with him, a pair of dress slacks, next to an empty hanger, five short sleeve shirts, a sweater, and the windbreaker in the rocks. A swim shirt, four pairs of swim trunks, water shoes, flip-flops, netted running shoes. I pulled down a shoebox from the closet shelf and sat at the end of the bed. I held it, hesitating to open it, worried about what I might find within.

I lifted the lid. Enough marijuana to start a store.

I closed the box and slid it in place on the shelf. I selected a butt from the ashtray. The smell was distinct.

The picture that emerged horrified me. I stared at New Landing, my fingers in knots. The sound of a car engine galvanized me. I tore through the house and out the screen door then through the trees without looking back. On the beach, I heard a man greet a woman, followed by a car door slamming. Taking a deep breath, I floated the canoe and paddled to New Landing, chastising myself with each stroke for both the search and my resulting fear.

Squeamish about being caught inside the cabin, I took my computer out to Roy's Deck and got to work. At any knocking sound, a ping, anything, my eyes left the computer screen. I simply could not concentrate for more than two minutes at a time, especially with Roy trying to catch my attention by tossing catkins from his perch in the branches overhead. I found it unsettling that he appeared undisturbed that his killer relentlessly stalked us...me.

Brad and Tim worked until dusk on the corner posts, preparatory to cementing and bolting them in place. I continued to work as well, though I was forced inside to avoid the man-eating mosquitos. I swear I could hear them ramming their nasty proboscises against the screens.

Tim came by to tell me they were leaving for the night. His torso, every muscle glistening with sweat, was a vision. Tim caught me looking, so I pretended to swoon in the doorframe.

He shook his head. "You okay on the island by yourself? Not to worry you, but you are exposed out here."

"Tim, if there is something or someone you believe wishes to do me harm, tell me who, please!"

"Well, I feel a whole lot better now that the family who rented the cabin up from Sturdevant Peninsula checked in...I keep the key for the owner."

"Why?" I stuttered, "Why do you feel better?"

"Same old same. I worry about the properties under my protection. I was about to search the Peninsula for another squatter when Sturdevant left a voicemail that he had rented out the one decent cabin to a friend. I got close enough to see lights and a Land Rover parked out front. Sturdevant asked me to give the guy space, so I am. I'll clean up after him when he leaves if any cleaning needs to be done. Frankly, with all the work right now, I'm glad to have the Peninsula off my worry plate."

"Oh..." I mustered. "Glad to have a neighbor, so, see, I'm fine," I lied. "Besides, I've got the mighty Aldis Lamp."

"I'll be sure Meg leaves the drapes open on the front window. Tomorrow is supposed to be hot, so Brad and I want to get an earlier than usual start, say 7:00. Mike may come if that helps convince you the deck will be done in time for the party."

"It does. Thanks, Tim. I can't believe the progress you guys made today."

"Like I said, got a party to throw!" With a wave, Tim loped down the path to Brad, waiting at the top of the dock stairs. They each carried a wooden tool bucket, the oblong kind with a handle that extends from end to end. In their dirty jeans and bare chests, they could have been from any era.

When I heard the pontoon boat exit Beaver Course, I opened a pack of hot dogs and grabbed a box of macaroni and cheese. I chopped two hot dogs, stirred them into the macaroni, then took the saucepan, a fork, and a hot pad to the front room table. I set the pan next to my computer, scrolled to the next torrid page as the villain pinned our heroine against one post of her four-poster and...

All night.

Day 8

xxiii

WHEN I DID SHUT MY eyes, Sturdevant was watching, a joint attached to his lower lip and a revolver in one hand. Around five, as the sun cusped the horizon, I went out to sit with Roy. We were joined by ten-thousand, six-hundred one mosquitos and black flies.

At seven, I heard pounding. I waved to Tim, Brad, and Mike as I hiked across the island's crest toward the cabin. At eight, they all showed up for breakfast, Mike smiling that smile. A two-by-three-inch bandage covering the right side of his forehead complemented by a black eye the likes of which I had never seen. His nose was pulpy, as well. I suspected they all wore their shirts to the table at Tim's urging. Darn.

I stared at the *No Trespassing* sign dangling from the nail.

Tim caught it. "Joe said he saw your canoe up by Peninsula point yesterday morning."

Was someone spying on me every second of every day?

"Just curious," I answered. "Worried a bit, too. You know, a beaver, a body, a...., Mike, the rusty sign. It was my first time on Sturdevant Beach, not counting the tour with the realtor."

Tim, no dummy, caught the hesitation. "Nothing's happened, though? Have you had a problem with the renter? When Sturdevant called to tell me the place was rented, he said he made sure the guy knew that we all used the beach."

The renter, the watcher, the stalker, the killer trampled through my thoughts like a line from a malevolent nursery rhyme. I went for distraction. "Are you guys hanging around building under some weird chivalrous impulse to keep me safe?"

Mike downed his eggs, oblivious to the tension whanging around the room.

"We better get back to work." Tim wiped his mouth with a napkin and stood. The others followed suit. "Hey, Boo, thanks for the food."

Brad ducked out the door. Mike waited until Tim was well down the path before pecking me on the cheek and squeezing my right hand.

"It's so good to see you," I muttered, tucking my bowed head against his chest. "I've been worried."

"I'm fine, Boo. I am." Mike kept my hand in his. "You look like you had a rough night."

"I didn't sleep at all. An article I read upset me. And I heard new sounds from the Sturdevant side of the lake. A yippy dog. A deep voice. So, I worked. I'm editing a romance thriller in which the heroine is about to run off with the villain, I think."

"That's so not me!"

"Gagne!" Tim called.

Mike raised his eyebrows until it hurt. "I'm being paged. Dinner tonight?"

I froze. Mike waited. "Seven, okay?" I stuttered.

"Great," he leaned in for a kiss. His full lips met mine, he backed me up until my butt rested on the range. The burners were still hot enough to singe through the cotton of my shorts. I jumped into his arms, laughing. "There for a minute, I thought I'd gotten you all hot and bothered!" he joked, kissing me again.

"Gagne, no kidding," Tim said, through the screen door. "Get your butt out here. I need your help."

xxiv

I GRILLED CHICKEN. MIKE brought a bottle of white wine. I whipped up a green bean casserole in his honor, baked a couple of potatoes, and made two salads. We ate at the table in the front room. Mostly I listened to his excitement about the new dance floor. In his happy head, the parties had already begun; we greeted partiers, ate, danced, and cleaned up together. What wasn't there to like about the guy?

Leaning against the refrigerator, I asked, "The other day, someone asked me if I remembered anything out of the ordinary that happened when I was nine. You and Roy would have been eleven. Does anything come to mind for you?"

Mike scooted his chair from the table. The remainders of our feast, chicken bones and potato skins littered our plates. He reached for the wine bottle and refilled our glasses. I settled into my usual place, having refrigerated the remainder of the bean casserole and the butter.

Mike pursed his lips, then laced his hands behind his head, winced having forgotten his stitches, then settled for his hands locked on the top of the table. His index fingers thrummed. "Penny showed me the picture of us at Old Landing."

"Any idea who took the photo?"

"If Penny's right, Sturdevant is around, despite what Tim thinks. He's a nasty piece of work."

Perhaps, but someone else had taken the photo of Sturdevant and me. No one was that gymnastic unless Sturdevant set a timer. No. Just no. Sturdevant swam over, in tight swimming shorts. Not only no room for a phone, but no way to keep it dry. But then how much did the marijuana affect his judgment?

"Eighteen years ago?" I urged.

"Wasn't that the year of the baby raccoon?"

I nodded.

"Thing is Boo. You and Roy came for the summer. We lived here year-round. For us, the highlight of the year was Booth Island springing to life. We looked forward to it from the minute you left until the minute you arrived. The other nine months of the year were filled with school and winter. Not much happened. Sometimes it did.

"The winter, when I was eleven, was fierce. The lake iced over early and stayed that way. Brad, Tim, and I just hung out, Meg and Penny in tow some of the time. I guess what I am getting at is that your memories are more vivid because coming here was a big deal for you. For us, things happened, but they were part of a continuum. Seasons came and went."

"I get it. The year went by, then we arrived."

"No, Boo, the year went by, then you and Roy arrived!" Mike hesitated, then continued, choosing his words carefully, not wanting to hurt me, but wanting me to understand. "You see everything through blinders aimed at June, July, and August."

"What happened, Mike. Something?"

"My dad died."

My right hand flew to my mouth. I stuttered, "Oh. Oh, of course."

"Your Dad asked mine to bring a new stove over if he found one. He was doing that, dragging a travois with a stove on it when it broke through the ice. The snowmobile, travois, and stove are still at the bottom of the lake. A diver went in after Dad, found him. We buried him. My mother let your folks know. Ever since, we've had enough to get by even without Dad. I figure because it was your stove that took him down that your folks paid my mom off. All in all, I'd rather have had my dad."

"I can see how it would seem to you that my folks felt guilty, but, no, Mike," I held up one finger, scooted out of my corner, and grabbed the bottle of whiskey I'd purchased at the LCBO. I set it on the table in front of Mike then turned the label to face him. I pointed to the pertinent fact.

"Lyle Sturdevant offered everyone on Lower Bay shares in Sturdevant Distillers. Your great-great took him up on it. O'Dell's did, too. The difference is Tim's family sold their shares to buy more land for farming. Your family kept their shares. I suspect the quarterly dividend checks gave your mom the freedom to stay at home and be a full-time mom."

"I'll be damned," Mike grinned. "Still?"

I laughed at his choice of words, still, indeed. "Losing your dad had to be tough for you and Penny, then we show up all shiny-faced. I am so sorry if we hurt you guys. We were kids."

He nodded. "But that is my point, Boo. It was the same every year."

"So, we arrived all giggly oblivious to the currents

flowing in and out of Lower Bay."

It hit me then that as a child and teenager, I felt irrepressible, joyous, and able to slay dragons only on Booth Island. Denied the island these last years, I had withered, become dour. I lived for summer as had Roy. We still did. I could feel my brother in this room at this moment, sitting next to Mike.

"Tell me. Tell me anything you think I should know?"

Mike reached over and played with my hand, thoughtfully, then said, "Be careful who you invite to your dances. Dixons rule the roost. Always have. They decide who gets land, who gets access, who doesn't. Even ice fishermen from Upper Bay know to pay homage.

"Everyone loved Josh Dixon, Mr. Dixon, and hated his wife, Silvie. Brad and Meg's mother. Do you remember her?"

"Not well, but yes."

"Well, Silvie stalked around the Lower Bay shoreline, dropping in at everyone's house, telling them how to run their affairs. It went on for years. She spread the rumor that I was so stupid I was barely functional. That woman had so much influence that I was placed in a track for slow learners at ten and funneled into trade school at fourteen, though Silvie was dead by then."

"Oh, Mike, oh, but your mother knew better!"

"She did. Thank heavens. Silvie and Mom were oil and water. They just stared hate at each other at functions."

"What became of Silvie Dixon? I just remember her being here then not."

"One day mid-October, I was ten, so nineteen years

ago, I guess, seems so long ago but not, if you get my drift. Silvie made her usual rounds, stopping at our house then at O'Dell's. By dusk, she hadn't returned to the farmhouse, so Mr. Dixon sent Meg and Brad out to look for her. They knocked on doors until a sort of posse formed. Meg found her mother, like rubble, in the rocks at the peak of Sturdevant Peninsula. Everyone has a theory."

"Poor Meg, she was only eight, right?"

Mike nodded, folding my fingers, then unfolding them. "According to my mom, it was a particularly gruesome sight."

"Was it an accident? If not, who did, I mean, who do people suspect?"

Mike laughed, "Lyle Sturdevant, George Booth, ghosts, fishers, madness. That whole autumn, before Silvie Dixon disappeared, someone was squatting on the Peninsula. Reports of lights bobbing in the woods, smoke rising above the trees, fires on the beach late at night. Mom made us swear not to go near the Sturdevant property. It was a hardship for us kids, but we obeyed."

"Anything else?"

"After Silvie's death, Dred moved into the farmhouse to help Mr. Dixon raise Brad and Meg. That's about it, except Mr. Dixon remained enthroned as a benevolent dictator."

"I always wondered why my parents referred to the Dixons as Mr. and Mrs. Now, I know." I cocked my head, studying where Mike's dark hair had been shaved to accommodate the bandage. "Do you think Silvie Dixon was using her visitations to cover up some other activity?"

"That's a grownup thing. You'd have to ask my

mother or Aunt Lou."

"Tragedy seems to stalk this small place on earth," I mused.

Mike guffawed. "What the heck you been reading? Wait, I know the answer to that...romance novels. No, it doesn't. About a hundred families live in the vicinity, not counting the summer people. Five people have died. Spread over twelve years. Though two drownings in one summer is a bit much, eh?"

"Eh? Especially since, according to my dad, Don Sturdevant complained to Mr. Dixon about you guys bullying Finn and demanded that Roy apologize to Finn. Two for two.

Mike squirmed where he sat. "Throw in the photographs, and none of us were safe."

"Brad?"

Mike quirked his mouth and shook his head. "Not a chance."

"You're sure?" It wasn't an idle question.

He nodded and checked his watch. "I would be glad to stay the night. Tim told me about the guy renting Sturdevant's cabin, the useable one. He said he regretted not greeting the renter because, according to Tim, the screen porch has a clear view of New Landing and a partial of Old Landing. Which means of you."

I let that sink in. If Tim was so worried, why didn't he call the OPP? Did he suspect it was Sturdevant? Even more reason to call the OPP. Then why hadn't he? I held one of Mike's hands as I stood. When his eyes lit, I let his hand go.

"No, Mike, it would be all over the lake by morning. I'll be fine."

He pecked my right cheek. "You're right. My kids think I'm a case as it is, and I'm sure the photo of their dad kissing the mysterious island lady wasn't helpful."

"I'll have to meet them one of these days. Maybe a picnic when the dance floor is done. How about that? In the meantime, Mike, thanks, thanks for being you."

He leaned down and kissed me. It took a while. I held his sweet face between my hands, worried that I was hurting him, wondering who would find the photograph of this moment taped to their door. A thought cruised by.... cruised as in came and went. Whatever it had been, it left me jangly.

I walked Mike down to New Landing and made him swear that no matter how many shadows he saw climbing the island, he would let them run amok rather than chase them. I patted the back of his head as a reminder.

He kissed me again, muttering, "You were great the other day. I haven't thanked you, at least not while I was of sound mind."

"I was lucky Tim saw my signal."

He shrugged. "Tim told me it was Meg who saw it. That she got all prickly when the storm came up as though she had a premonition something might happen."

"Something bad this way comes," I misquoted, "Well, she was right."

Mike started the motor on his skiff and was soon a silhouette on the sparkling, undulating water. When the engine faded away, I was left with the lapping of water on the rocks, a breeze strong enough to ruffle leaves, and my thoughts. Or rather, one thought.

Sturdevant.

XXV

I KEPT WATCH OUT the window as I washed the dishes. A branch crashed to the ground pinging the roof as it fell. I jumped.

Mike's soft recollections had left me hopped up and jumpy. The island was shapeshifting into something violent and unexpected. It had always been there, floating below the surface tension of the water, but I had been a child thrilled to see my summer friends as Mike so carefully pointed out.

What had Dred said? Old crud is floating up from the bottom of the lake like it was a water treatment plant. I plunked into my favorite chair at the table. From there, I could see the photo of loons that wasn't Roy's and his newly minted shrine of the hat, shirt, and bandana.

I studied them, the brushing, clapping, smacking, and roaring outside the cabin setting the mood. I had come here to resolve whatever caused Roy to haunt me, hoping to free us both from that summer so long ago. Instead, others had been hurt. Perhaps because of me. What was I missing?

That thought reminded me to punch a note into my phone to ask Mary Gagne about Silvie Dixon's death. The adult version.

A branch twanged against the window to my back. That was enough. I turned off the lights, reached outside the kitchen door, and turned off the generator. I locked the outer kitchen door, latched the screen door then repeated the process at the front door. The knowledge that Sturdevant stalked me, coupled with Tim's concern, impelled me.

A wedge of moon glowed outside, enough to light my way to the outhouse. Just then, the wind whipped a branch on the roof. In response, I tucked the old chamber pot on the left side of the bed, where I could squat unseen from either window.

The soughing wind and soft ticking of the windup clock kept in the cedar chest between island visits wooed me to sleep. I dreamed I drowned. The spangled water tangled me in seaweed, the light of the sky visible dancing on the water overhead. If I stroked upward, I could live.

Instead, I grappled for something beneath me, something hidden by the murky undulating waters at the bottom of the lake. I swam down, my arms outstretched. My hands clasping the item dearer than life. I turned, ready for the surface. The light, once visible, had disappeared. I began to sink, refusing to drop the object that weighed me down. I sat bolt upright on the horsehair mattress, the sheet tangled around my feet, gasping for air, my hands clutching the square clock.

Outside the bedroom window, the moon was down. Wind-whipped clouds scudded across the black sky, their underbellies deadening any ambient light tossed their way. The denizens of the night were active; an owl hooted, a loon called, while a sly raccoon clawed in the dirt for grubs or nightcrawlers. Beneath all the soothing sounds, a stealthy hand worked the front door latch.

With visions of my photo knifed to Sturdevant's wall, I tiptoed to the bedroom door and jammed it shut with a chair. I eased the bedroom windows open and removed the screens, ready to leap out and run for the boat.

The threshold creaked.

I curled into the corner, the chamber pot to my side, one hand gripping the rim, ready to use it as a weapon. A moment later, the door handle jiggled; the chair rattled but held, not for long, not with the pressure being applied. I scurried out the back window, my knees hit the soft woodland loam as the chair hit the floor, and the bedroom door swung open.

I grabbed the nearest weapon I could find, a chunk of trimmed two-by-four from the dance floor construction, then rushed to the front of the cabin, roared in the unlatched front door, and swung.

An arm blocked the swing, grabbed the board, and tossed it to the floor. I turned to run. Sturdevant grabbed me around the waist and plunked me on the couch. I kicked. He yelped. I cursed.

"Boo, damn it."

"That's for scaring me." I punched him again, proving I *could* hit harder. "What were you doing sneaking in here? For all I knew, you could be armed with a loaded revolver."

"Where have you been hanging out?" he asked softly.

"I...I..."

"Searched my cabin." The idea seemed to amuse him.

"You watch me! You sit on that porch, and you watch me! I can't even dangle my feet in the water, sharing time with my brother without you spying. I..." My voice choked with emotion. My elbows on my knees, I covered my eyes with my hands.

Finn sat next to me, lowering my head to his shoulder. "Is that what you think?"

"You told Tim someone rented your cabin!"

"Of course, first the Dixons then the OPP then jail, why would I do otherwise?"

I pulled away, angling on the couch to see him. His right hand was professionally bandaged, wrist to palm. "Why do you have a gun?" I asked.

"Oh, for Pete's sake," Finn laughed. "This is the greeting I get for following your advice. I spent the night in the clinic. The on-duty doctor insisted I stay the remainder of the night. That fast, the cut got infected. Antibiotics all around, fever gone by noon, stitches, bandages, and release."

"Wow."

"Wow? It hurts like hell."

"Sorry, sorry, it hurts. You were using the rental cabin as a decoy?"

"Yes. But it is rented now. Nice people." He cocked his head. "The clinic dropped the news on the OPP that Finn Sturdevant stumbled in with a bloody hand. An Officer Callahan stormed into my room. Next thing, he reminded me of the restraining order noting all it would take was one word from you to lock me up. In case he asks, I told him you gave me much needed first aid before boating me home. Callahan shook his head, snapped his notebook closed, and left."

"Why did the clinic call the OPP?"

His eyebrows shot down in a vee, "Come on, Boo. Someone warned the clinic to watch out for me. You're the only one who knew I would be there." His voice had taken on a quiet hardness that rankled and worried me.

I shook my head.

"If not you, who then, eh? Come on, Boothe, don't bother to lie. You make me crazy." He swung those laser dark eyes on me and grabbed my upper arm in his vice grip.

"Me? You with your telescope and binoculars!" Sturdevant spied on me day and night. He watched me come and go, knew who was on the island and timed his visits. "You're stalking me! Admit it!"

"Stop it, Boo," he scolded, giving me a sharp shake.

"How dare you snap at me," I muttered, angry that I sounded so submissive.

How could I be so confused? Sweet, dear Mike Gagne had been in this room no more than two hours ago. And now, Sturdevant was here. Distrust and hurt bounced off the walls and swirled around us. I wanted Finn to pin me to the wall. I wanted him to leave me alone. I wanted him to kiss me. I...

"You're a mess," Finn said, dusting dirt and leaves from my exposed knees. I pulled on the cuffs of my shorts to mid-thigh and adjusted the T-shirt I wore to bed.

"I had a bad dream, that's all. I was drowning. Still, I dove for something at the bottom of the lake. I grabbed it. When I turned for the surface, I sank deeper. Then the latch lifted on the front door and..."

Finn sucked in his breath. "And here you are covered in leaves." He ran a finger down my right thigh. "Like you, I have a recurring dream. In it, I locate the one thing that will clear me of Roy's death. I have since that night. I wake up screaming, holding nothing."

I stood and crossed to the table. "Hold this." I handed him the photo of us, my back against the wall, his lips seeking mine.

He humphed as he rotated it in his fingers. "When was it left?"

"After you were hurt."

"Like Penny found the photo of you and Mike after Mike's fall?"

"Someone's counting coup," I blurted out the thought that had jangled me as Mike left. "Just like Roy's summer, those photos, your photos hurt all of us girls. All of us. They literally changed our lives. I would be with Mike, and the cabin would be our summer home. And Penny with Roy. Now, this!"

"I didn't take this photo, and I didn't take the others! I don't know, maybe, maybe I did, but not to use against anyone. Remember the SD chip that was stolen off our porch? I always thought Roy snatched it. Most of the pictures that you girls found tapped to your windows were on the stolen chip. Anyone could have used the chip, but Roy had the same make of camera. Your brother, no other, snatched it and used it against me. It wasn't until I saw my photo framed on your wall that I knew. Those are my loons, my nesting pair." He pointed at the picture Roy had framed for my folks. "That picture was on the stolen chip."

My right hand flew to my mouth.

"Don't look at me like that! Don't!" He shoved me away and strode to the table. He slammed his right hand on the surface so hard the table jumped. I backed away. He grabbed my arm, becoming the horned creature of my dream.

He bucked his head, his eyes slid away, his grip loosened. "My camera's here, isn't it? You or your mom found it. Hid it. Come on, Boo, where is it?"

Without bidding, my eyes drifted to the bedroom door. Finn brushed past me, bouncing me off the edge of the table.

"It's Roy's," I yelled to his back. Or so my mother said. By the time I ran through the door of the bedroom, Finn had emptied the chest of drawers. He held a palm out for the key to the cedar chest.

Angry now, I folded my arms. Finn snorted and opened the closet door.

In my rush to stop him, I stumbled over the corner of the bed and went down in a heap. He tossed all the clothes, emptying the boxes onto the floor at my feet, then started on the shelf. Ignoring my pleas to stop, he reached into the deepest corner of the top shelf. The box made a shushing sound as he pulled it along the board.

I remained on the floor, sick to my stomach. Sturdevant strode into the front room with the box.

Something hard hit the floor.

The front door slammed shut, the screen door quaked in the aftermath. I sat shaking.

When I could, I scrambled to my feet and rounded the doorframe. The box with the camera was on the floor. Sturdevant was a rigid silhouette on Roy's Deck, as though cut from construction paper. Then the wind-tossed his hair. The white of the bandage on his hand blared in the dark. I struggled into an anorak jacket kept by the door. The length of it covered my thighs. I slipped my feet into a pair of flip-flops and stepped onto the porch.

A boat rocked at the outcropping below Roy's Deck, oar locks clinking. Finn's uninjured hand opened. I crossed to him and took it.

"Sorry. I'll clean up my mess."

"If you had given me a minute, I would have told you where Mom hid it and why. It is Roy's, right?"

"Yes." I squeezed his hand. He pulled away and bucked his head in frustration. "Where's my damn camera?"

"Let's sit," I led him to a bench. "Tell me again. Tell me what happened the might Roy died. No editing this time. Please."

We sat side by side. Finn worked the fingers of his undamaged hand between mine, meanwhile holding the bandaged one at his waist. The stitches were seeping; a thin line of blood stained the palm of the gauze.

"Here goes," he started. "Brad convinced me that all I had to do was scare Roy as he climbed the hill. I did. Roy tumbled into the water. When I saw he was unconscious, I dove in after him and swam him to New Landing. It was a struggle to heft him onto the dock. Once I did, I started artificial respiration, Roy sputtered. I turned his head to clear his throat. When he was breathing, I dressed his wound with the bandanna and sock from the line. Mike swam up, yelling. Brad maybe six strokes behind him. I realized how it looked to them, dove in, and swam.

"While I was waiting at Booth Island for Roy, someone broke into our cabin and stole my camera. When the OPP searched the cabin for evidence, they demanded my camera, claiming that witnesses had seen me delivering obscene photos with the intent to do harm. And, of course, they found the picture of you knifed to the wall with my pocketknife.

"Boo, my camera was the only thing I had left of any real value, that and my last photos of Pop captured on the discs. With the OPP watching my every move, I went to the shelf where I kept it. The camera was gone. I remember staring at the empty shelf, knowing I'd been set up." Sturdevant ran his bandaged hand through his hair. Then picked at the gauze as though reminded it was there. "Don't you see how perfectly I was played?"

I shook my head.

"Everyone knew what that camera meant to me, that I would do anything to keep it, find it, whatever. At first, I thought if I told the OPP my camera was stolen, it would corroborate my version of what happened. Then I realized it would only make it all look worse, make me look guilty as hell. I was seventeen and alone; I gave myself up instead. After I did, the OPP told me Roy was dead. I remember being relieved that I hadn't squawked about the camera. I would have been charged with murder."

"What about your mother?"

"When they told her the options, she thought joining the Marines was the best. The OPP presented a solid case, and I'd pled guilty."

"You had no one on your side?"

He took a deep, uneven breath. It shuddered through his body. "Mike and Brad swore to the OPP and your father that Roy was dead when they found him. Your dad and Farley O'Dell were the only ones who stood by me. I never understood how they could, especially your father, given everyone's belief that I'd killed his son."

"You did kill my brother. Roy died from the head injury. You caused that when you scared him, and he fell."

"No, Boo. No, the head wound was bloody, maybe a concussion, but not life-threatening."

"Now, you're a doctor?"

"I know what I saw. Especially after being in battle. Roy didn't die of a head wound any more than my father drowned."

"But your father *did* drown."

Finn shook his head, his frustration with me apparent. "For the last time, Roy was alive when I left him. Alive—period.”

“Question then. Did your father ever come up to Lower Bay without you? Even to check on the property?” I asked, my mind racing, trying to weave that potholder without a loom.

Finn cocked his head, swiping at his eyes with his bandaged hand. My heart lurched. “No. Most summers, we stayed near home. I was on a local swim team. My mom ran off with a technology tycoon when I was five, exchanging Pop’s millions for billions. It was a good move. Mom’s happier, and so was Pop, which meant I was happier and spoiled because everyone felt guilty, at least until my stepbrothers and stepsisters were born.

“Pop was determined to raise me as something resembling a gentleman. He brought in an au pair from a different country every two years. As a result, I was fluent in French, Italian, and German by my eleventh birthday.” I squeezed his unbandaged hand. “Pop crossed the bridge to the Distillers in Windsor weekdays. I lived the Grosse Pointe Shores life. Bringing me to Lower Bay was a huge mistake. It cost him his life. Cost me, my father. My life.”

We stared over the water. The wind tearing at our clothes. The waves rumbling beneath us. I knew from the clippings what Sturdevant told me about his childhood was true.

“Why? Why did he bring you up that summer?”

“To meet you and Roy. Pop summered here as a kid and loved it. He told me stories about his Lower Bay friends, especially one of the O’Dells and your Uncle Nick. Pop ran the family business and bought aging kegs from your uncle. Your Uncle Nick runs the furniture business, right?”

I nodded.

"Pop thought the world of your mother, uncle, and your dad after he met him. He had it in his head that Roy, you, and I would be great friends like Pop was with your Uncle Nick and your mom. In Pop's mind, Tim, Mike, and Brad, who were all near my age, would bond for life like they had with Roy."

I gazed into his dark eyes, now red-rimmed with hurt. "But you stayed on after your father's death. Why?"

"Pop. I was so sure that he would never go fishing without me that I was determined to find out who killed him. Not the smartest move I ever made. But, Boo, it made sense at the time. Now, I wake up every morning, knowing if I had stayed with Roy, he would be here with us."

Finn kissed my fingers enfolded in his. A branch dipped, grazing his right shoulder. Finn grabbed onto it for just a second before freeing the leaves to dance in the night air. He turned his hand palm-side up then down, puzzled.

"Do you think your father's murderer set you up? If he was murdered." I hesitated. "Mary Gagne saw someone on the boat with your dad that night. She thought it was Brad, but all of us kids were on the island that Friday. Mary saw us there." Finn huddled me to his side, shielding my bare legs from the wind. I kissed his unbandaged knuckles one by one. "That's a thoughtful, yes?"

After a while, Finn asked, "Mike Gagne. What's that all about?"

"You need to sleep."

"Not a very subtle goodbye. I guess I was just leaving."

"No, no, Finn. That's not what I meant. One question, the marijuana?"

He checked his watch. "Your buddies will be back building in three hours. I better go."

"I'll give you a lift if you answer my questions."

"I boated over."

"Finn?" He shook his head. "The gun?"

"Drop it, Boo."

I did. We walked single file down the path to Old Landing. A camouflage duckie was tucked in the trees. I floated it and held it steady as Finn clambered into it, ungainly with one fully operable hand. One hand, one oar, he rowed across Beaver Course. He grounded the duckie on the opposite shore, then pulled it up into the bushes and waved goodbye.

I sat at Old Landing, watching for the watchers. The hurt and anger from that summer so long ago crawled inside me. A tumble of earth broke free of the hill, small pebbles splashed in Beaver Course, followed by a thick limb. Our beaver began to pull the branch toward his house, sending more scrabble into the channel. Finn stood across from me, the white bandage on his hand a beacon in the dark. When Roy sat next to me, Finn walked the shore to Sturdevant Beach.

"Well?" I asked the shadow beside me. The night breeze sent a twig tumbling onto my naked thigh. It spread out like a hand, soothing me.

For days, Roy had thrown rocks and tossed limbs peevishly. Now, this. I shivered. The air around me grew warm. I leaned back against a tree trunk as I had leaned against my brother and tried to unscramble what I knew.

It remained a jumble.

Day 9

xxvi

UNABLE TO SLEEP, I spent the night waiting for Roy to provide the kernel of wisdom that would free us both. All I knew was that Finn Sturdevant had me by the toes, and Roy seemed okay with it after their handshake on the deck.

By morning, the knots in my hair had knots. The bedroom floor was covered in clothes and whatever else Finn had emptied from the drawers and closet. I found a pair of capri pants slung in one of the heaps on the floor. A peasant blouse topped a second pile. I changed into them then rushed to clean up the bedroom and have breakfast on the griddle when the guys showed up.

"Bacon," Tim uttered, taking in the kitchen aromas as he stepped through the door. "It's not everywhere you get fed *and* paid."

I smiled at him. Warmth descended wherever he chose to be. I shook my head. Tim O'Dell could have had any woman he wanted in the township; he had Meg. And Meg had upped her game for him producing one of those rare romantic win-wins. Every time I saw Tim, I was happier for Meg.

"Any more news about anything?" I asked, trying

my best to make it sound like an innocent question.

"Nope," Mike answered, pulling a chair up next to Tim's. "Well, at the new renters, the woman claims some gal, she said gal, dropped by yesterday looking for a man she met. The renter thought her visitor was from up lake. But she only went as far as the rocks on Sturdevant Beach where she sat for some time."

"Good thing the guy renting that cabin was out," Brad added, gulping his way through a biscuit before he sat.

Yes, I made biscuits. I suppose I hoped fresh biscuits would loosen their tongues. It turned out to be a waste of flour and propane. My work crew came chatty.

"Sturdevant is definitely around. A friend of mine said he checked into the clinic night before last with a bad gash on his hand." Tim glanced at the dangling *No Trespassing* sign and the trashcan, now empty except for breakfast garbage. "The OPP talked to him. From what my friend said, the Officer gave Sturdevant a pretty stern warning."

"Really?" I asked. "What, because he should have checked in with them like a sex offender?"

"Murderer?" Brad scoffed. He pointed to the sign hanging on the wall. "Oh, come on, Boo!"

Mike's bright blue eyes studied the puffy bags beneath mine. "You don't suppose Sturdevant's renter is Sturdevant?" Mike checked with Tim and Brad, who shook their heads at Mike's innocence.

"Well, that explains what happened to Mike," Brad said, shoveling in an egg. "Bastard isn't welcome around here. He killed Roy and blackmailed us with those pictures. I don't care how many honorable discharges Sturdevant got, he's back, and he's not an amateur anymore."

Mike scoffed.

"Not funny, Mike," Brad snarled, stuffing more food in his mouth.

"I found a tree branch near where Mike fell. Sturdevant, right?" I tossed out, processing that Brad, who lived in Australia, knew Finn had been honorably discharged from the Marines when I had not.

"Sure, why not?" Brad quipped, cocking his right eyebrow. I cocked my left, giving Tim and Mike a good laugh.

"I'm heading into town. Are there any supplies I can get you guys? I'm out of eggs, milk, toast, bacon, beer...again...and did I say beer."

"You need to find yourself a new class of friends," Tim grinned.

As soon as they had eaten every scrap of food prepared, Tim stood, the others followed suit, and off they went to work.

"Be careful. Okay? Promise?" I called out the door as they left.

A minute later, I heard them joking and pounding. It all sounded so convivial it made me jumpy.

xxvii

AS I GUIDED THE boat to Dixon Landing, my eyes locked on the sky, gray with the signature dip of mammatus clouds. I would tune into the weather station on the way to town. But even a motorboat sailor knew the clouds indicated rough sailing ahead sometime tomorrow.

Because I insisted that he get medical attention,

Finn's trip to the clinic was already a tattoo on the lake drum. The list of people who knew he was here included Penny and her mother, Mary. Mary was the reason I was headed into Westport. We needed a chat, followed by a telephone call to my mom and maybe Dad, too.

The green of the trees and grasses grew deeper in hue as the sky clotted with clouds. The wind picked up, buffeting my car. I parked in front of Lou's Bakery, walked up the tree-lined sidewalk to the bakery door in the shed-roofed add-on to the right side of the house, and knocked.

Lou was helping a customer, so I studied the day's loaves of bread. I selected a loaf of dense rye bread and held it up until Lou nodded and pointed to a rack of paper bags. I bagged the loaf and returned to the display.

Lou rang a call bell. Mary stepped down from the house into the add-on. Seeing it was me, a wide grin spread across her face. Mike was her boy, no kidding. Mary gestured with her head for me to follow. I set my bag on the counter so Lou could ring it up and stepped into the house after Mary. She sat me at an oaken table in the kitchen.

A tall window framed an array of hollyhocks on the lawn. The tall stalks bore single, double, and triple petaled flowers in every color from yellow through a purple so deep it looked a velvety black. The stalks waved in the freshening breeze; their hues intensified by the bumpy clouds.

"The hollyhock blossoms would make gorgeous sugar plum dancers," I commented, then kidded, "I don't suppose you have any toothpicks handy?"

"The hollyhocks are Lou's pet project. She literally

clucks over them. How about some tea and scones?" Mary poured with my nod. "What's up?"

"Mike and I had a long talk." Like Penny, Mary balked, but unlike Penny, no warning followed. "What can you tell me about Silvie Dixon?"

"Silvie?" Mary uttered and sat. "Nastiest woman I ever knew! I have no idea how Josh, Mr. Dixon, found her, but he did. She was from somewhere near Montreal. Quebecois." Mary gurgled the word as though she were clearing phlegm.

"Mike suggested Silvie was murdered."

"Shoved maybe. Hard. Really hard. By someone who sincerely did not like her. Which means almost everyone on Lower Bay."

"Why would anyone kill her. I mean, there are plenty of nasty women in the world, but they aren't generally murdered?"

"True. Here is the tale, you decide. Silvie was having an affair and using the neighbors for cover. By neighbors, I mean Pences, Gagnes, and O'Dells. She just kept coming around, knocking on our doors, checking up on the kids, she said.

"She would meet her lover in the older of the two cabins on the Sturdevant Peninsula. It was the only place guaranteed to be unpopulated, except by vermin. I still find it hard to believe anyone could love Sylvie. I never thought Josh did. One day Silvie came around but never returned home. Meg found her mother's body heaped on the rocks at the point of the Peninsula."

She died on the same rocks where Finn Sturdevant now smoked pot and focused his binoculars on Booth Island.

"Does anyone know who Silvie's lover was?"

"Lou!" Mary yelled. "Lou told me she saw Silvie and a tall young man on the beach then asked around the summer people along the lakeshore until she got a hit. The family staying at the rental just up from Sturdevant's ran into the guy on the beach. Lou never told me who Sylvie's paramour was, but it hardly mattered. The OPP ruled that Silvie lost her footing, crossing the pitched rocks. It seemed a fair enough finding."

It struck me then that the folks of Lower Bay preferred fair, if not factual. Particularly if the facts had to do with the Dixons.

Lou hustled into the kitchen, wiping her hands on a flour-shaded apron, my bag of bread in one hand.

"What?" Lou asked, handing me my loaf. I reached for my wallet; Lou waved me off.

"Silvie Dixon's love interest?"

"Oh," Lou sat. "Some Alberta cowboy she picked up at a bar down in Kingston. Nice looking man. Just a fling. She had no intention of leaving Josh. Being the queen of Lower Bay was a big step up for a salesclerk from the wrong end of Montreal. Whoever the cowboy was, he evaporated after Silvie's death. He's probably still running in his high-heeled cowboy boots."

"Do you think he killed her?" I asked.

Both Mary and Lou shrugged.

"Finn Sturdevant was at the Westport clinic night before last," Mary offered.

"Really? He wasn't anywhere near the lake twenty years ago." I quipped, to avoid a detour down that road. The sisters tandem shrugged again, so I asked, "How did Meg react to her mother's death?"

"She was just a little girl. Josh sent her to a therapist. That was that," Lou answered. "Meg withdrew for a while, wouldn't play with Penny, took a few heads off her own dolls and an arm or two from Penny's Barbie. Right, Mary?"

"How about Brad?"

"He got a little rougher is all I noticed," Mary answered. "That's about the time Tim quit hanging out with him. Not Mike, though, Mike was all in. And, of course, Brad blossomed whenever Roy showed up."

"And Mr. Dixon, Josh?"

"To be honest, he seemed a bit relieved that Silvie was gone. She was pushier than Mr. Dixon would have liked. She ran Lower Bay with an iron fist. Decided who got to be friends, when and where events occurred, who played with her kids, who got the best cuts of meat at the picnics," Lou said

"According to Mike, she spread the rumor that Mike was..."

"Bitch," Mary said, summing it all up. "I blame that woman for what happened to Mike after Roy's accident. Mike had trouble at school, got on drugs, married, married again, had his babies, and ended up widowed--again. Made a mess of his life. He is a good guy and a marvelous artist. You should go to Joe's workshop and see Mike's work. He does things with junk metal you can't imagine."

"I'd like that and to meet his daughters, too."

"No, Boo, please. You'll just break his heart." Mary patted my hand.

"One more thing. The photo left on Penny's door, the one of Mike and me, reminded me of the one of Penny and Roy that summer. I never saw it but heard it upset you. Do you mind if I ask why?"

"For the same reason that the photo of you and Mike canoodling on Sturdevant Beach upset the applecart back then. You were all teens, not kids. Your mother and I decided to nip it in the bud. You were from different worlds and on different trajectories."

I wanted to argue but knew it was true, I would break Mike's heart now, as I would have then. But Mary and Mom had no right to make us feel so guilty; we would have made the same discovery ourselves. And, if left to our own devices, maybe things would have turned out differently.

They might even have been wrong.

xxviii

I SAID MY GOODBYES, my head reeling with disconnected thoughts. All I knew was that I needed two scoops of Tiger Tail, and I needed them now. The ice cream would keep me company while I contemplated what I had learned in the last twenty-four hours from Mike, Finn, and the O'Dell sisters.

I purchased the ice cream in a bowl this time, outran a mother with two children to my favorite table, felt like a dog, apologized, moved to the table in the bay window, and dialed my mother. She answered on the first ring. She was worried.

"Jack called," she said.

"Ah, he's worried, so you're answering your phone. Everything is okay," I said. I slurped Tiger Tail off my spoon. "So, question, Silvie Dixon?"

"Wow! There is a name from the past. Rumor has it ol' Silvie kept a boyfriend hidden on the Sturdevant property. She would make the rounds to all the neighbors, meet him, bonk, go home. Then one day, she stayed gone. Meg found her. It wasn't until the searchers found Meg that they found Silvie."

"Doesn't that strike you as odd?" It also struck me as odd that Mary and Lou had left me the impression that Meg found her mother and sounded the alarm, not that Meg had stood guard over her mother's body until they were found.

"Not really. Meg was in shock. She just stared at Silvie's body. As soon as Josh came into view, Meg ran into his arms and was inconsolable. Josh sent her to a therapist. Dred moved in and mothered her."

"On another subject. Finn Sturdevant is a Grosse Pointe Shores rich kid. All the manners in the world. How come you let me believe he was trash?"

"He is. He killed your brother."

"On the books, but you knew better, you knew his dad, you knew Finn's background but trash-talked him from the start. Roy took his cue from you, I did, everyone did. Why didn't you come clean when the bullying started?"

"Jack was supposed to take care of that with Roy. Instead, everything whirled out of control. Tell me that boy is not up there, please?"

"He's not up here." The thought that my mother was implicated in my brother's death by her omissions took root in my mind.

"Oh, don't lie to me. I'm telling you, Boo, honest to dirt, don't get mixed up with something you can't finish."

"How did you know the Nikon camera you found in the rocks by New Landing was Roy's?"

"What did I just tell you? What? Did that boy tell you some lie? Of course, the camera was Roy's. It had a gouge on the bottom. Roy did that in the boat. He showed it to me, trying to avoid a Dad lecture. He got the lecture anyway. I'm sure it's Roy's."

"Roy stole Finn's camera, a Nikon just like Roy's, and presumably swam it to the island. When Finn scared him, it clattered from Roy's hands into the rocks," I fabricated, hoping for the information I got.

"No, baby. I found Roy's camera by the dock. Nowhere near where that boy said Roy fell."

My heart tumbled, searching for a beat. I raced back to the dark hours of this morning. Truth or lie, Roy stole Finn's camera?

"Boo?"

"Nothing, Mom." But it was everything. "Did you take an SD card from Roy's camera? Did you?"

"I told you I did. I put it in Roy's cookie tin, Boo. Why else would we need his camera? SD cards are already old hat. I hid the camera so that twenty years on when we met, no matter what the current technology was, we would be able to view Roy's last photos."

"Thing is, Mom, Finn's camera was gone when the OPP came for him."

"That's why he killed your brother? His damn camera?"

"No, Finn never told anyone it was stolen, afraid they would jump to the same conclusion. You sure you didn't find another camera in a case and destroy or hide it to protect Roy?"

"Finn? You lied, flat out lied. That boy is up there, why?" she snapped.

"Someone sent his juvenile files, newspaper clippings, whatever to the *Detroit Free Press*. The newspaper did the research and printed damning articles. I read two. Someone is trying to destroy him, as though having been nearly killed by an IED was insufficient. Finn needs to rebut the articles to save his good name, his future, and possibly stay out of jail."

"Nothing can exonerate him, Boo. Your brother is dead because of Finn Sturdevant." For a brief moment, the idea that Mom had provided Finn's records to the *Free Press* occupied my thoughts.

"I know, but..."

"Boo, don't go there, don't dive into that water. Please!"

Chills roared up my spine.

"All those dance parties you threw didn't protect you, did they?" I sniped.

She hung up. I hit redial, her phone rang unanswered. I texted her a one-word message, then finished my Tiger Tail as I considered whether to call Dad or pack out of Booth Island. I glanced at the photo of the loons plastered over the ice cream counter.

All I saw now was Finn. It scared me, worried me, it felt as though I was losing Roy. It felt like treason. Roy needed me, had always needed me. We were a team, right up until that summer. I tried to identify what had come between us. Whatever it was, it was lost in the morass of my memories. I loved my brother, and he protected me. Ah, there it was! From what? From whom?

Finn Sturdevant?

I thought not. But, somehow, Finn's arrival at the lake had triggered violence then as it had now. Well, it was my turn to protect Roy; it had been for twelve years.

The door to the realtor's office swung open, catching my attention and thoughts. At Meg's urging, the Township planned to make a public beach and park on Sturdevant Peninsula. If Finn died, the property would revert to the Township. But it need never come to that because Finn would sell it in a heartbeat to the Township, to me, to anyone who made an acceptable offer.

Would that acquisition alleviate the Dixons' long-standing grudge over losing the Peninsula in a poker game more than a hundred years ago?

I licked my spoon, wondering what sort of person holds a hundred-year grudge.

xxix

NO ONE WAS POUNDING, yelling encouragement, or generally making noise when I docked at the island. So, it was no surprise when I topped the stairs to find Tim, Mike, and Brad sitting in the shade of the trees staring at a dirty, rusted safe. I waved at them.

Tim made a sweeping movement toward the iron box then beckoned me over.

"Where?" They all pointed to the corner of the dance floor closest to the cabin, about fifty feet to the northwest. I crossed to the hole. The three men were stabilizing the corner pole when they struck the safe, apparently used as part of the original post's foundation.

"Should we blow it open?" Tim asked.

I took him seriously until I saw the twinkle in his eyes. Visions of money floating over a blown-out safe made me grin. "I saw that movie. I wonder who would know what the combination of the safe is? Likely no one living. We may *have* to blow it."

Mike stood, wielding a crowbar. "The hinges are corroded from the rust. We might be able to crack it with this." He brandished the bar over his head like an ape with a femur.

"Give it a try." I leaned against a tree, never believing it would work. But with both Mike and Tim leveraging the bar, the hinges popped enough for them to shine a flashlight into the dark. Mike took a turn, then Tim.

"Well?" I asked.

Tim stood disarmingly, stuffing his hands in his pockets, and toeing the dirt. "Anyone in your family been missing for say--a hundred years or so?"

I joined Tim. "Can I look?"

On my knees, I directed the flashlight beam through the chink in the door. A man had been stuffed in the safe. At the time of the stuffing, he wore a suit and patent leather oxford shoes. The suit had thin stripes woven vertically through the fabric. In the pre-Beaver Course bridge collapse photo from Vintage Westport, the shadowy man to my great-great George Booth's left had been similarly dressed as the two men greeted partiers stepping from the bridge to the island.

The intact skull provided no clues other than the man had good teeth. If George's shadow were in the safe, the man in the photo with George, whom I assumed was his partner in crime, Lyle Sturdevant, couldn't have been. So, who was he?

"Well, what do you think?" Mike asked. I checked Brad. He chewed on the sweet end of a grass blade, lost in thought.

"I asked for some photos of the bridge disaster from Vintage Westport. The scanned newspaper article they sent had several pictures of the general partying on Booth Island. Let's take a look."

I trotted up to the cabin. The guys trooped in

behind me. By the time they arrived, I had the downloaded pictures displayed on the screen. I pointed to the man in the pinstripe suit lurking in the shadows behind the man I knew to be George Booth.

"Any of you know who he is?"

Brad cleared his throat. Tim leaned in so close he left a nose smudge on the screen. I keyed in on the shadow and zoomed in on the face, which only served to make it a blur of ancient pixels. I went into the photo edit function and worked on the image for a few minutes.

The editing clarified the face enough so that an everyman emerged. The shadow of his nose made it seem unusually long, his cheekbones flat, his eyes submerged under dark brow ridges. I returned the photo to its original size leaving the edits in place.

Mike and Brad stared at Tim. What the heck, I stared at Tim. "Anyone in your family been missing for say a hundred years?" Mike teased Tim.

Tim humphed, which was an answer of sorts. I thought the same. Humph?

"Don't you think we should call the OPP?" Brad asked. "They have a forensic anthropologist on staff, and if theirs is out, there is one in Montreal."

Tim started for the dock. "I'll head to the farmhouse and call it in. It needs to be reported, though it is likely one for the files. And I'll call my aunts, Mary and Lou. One of them might know something."

"Or Dred Dixon," I added.

Tim acknowledged me with a wave of his hand. Halfway down the path, he called. "Shouldn't take long. What say you guys finish the remaining corners of the dance floor so we can pour the cement for all four when I get back."

Mike and Brad returned to the building site to follow Tim's orders. I stayed, peering at each of the photos one by one, enhancing each. People had tumbled toward the center of the swaying bridge as it fell, piling in on the two people who were dead center when it collapsed. A woman's shoe floated up, a man's pinstripe clad leg, skirts, hats, tangled limbs.

I saved the enlargement. Brad and Mike pounded away. I sat in my corner, confident that finding the safe was nothing more than a distraction. Unless...

Unless what? Unless Prohibition molded the Lower Bay community, influenced what became of Don and Roy, and now threatened Finn. I knew better, and I knew there were nothing in Roy's tin but memories. Still. I liberated a paring knife from the kitchen then took a circuitous route to the promontory rather than tromp past the guys happily joking and driving nails. Reaching my destination undiscovered, I dug beneath Roy's marker.

Cookie tin in hand, I ran the point of the knife where the collar of the lid met the base. Rust flaked off. The top still refused to loosen, so I pressured the blade under the collar until the knife tip hit the lid. I turned the tin over. Finding a handy rock, I pounded the handle of the knife.

The top popped. I lifted the tin letting the contents fall onto the cover. Roy's SD card was jumbled in with the other strange tidbits preserved by his family, including a curled photo of Finn shoving Roy, not off the island but on Sturdevant Beach, and, of all things, my grandfather's missing gold watch. I gathered up the card, photo, and watch, returning the other items to the tin.

As I pressed the lid back in place, my fingers

detected other pry marks dimpling the rusting lid. With a little more study, I noticed that the Christmas elves on the tin's side were still colorful; only the bottom lip showed any sign of rust. Which meant that whoever deposited the watch had dampened the collar to promote rust and cover their tracks. It had worked well until now.

I jammed the top onto the tin and returned the can and contents, minus the SD card, the watch, and the picture, to the hole under Roy's marker. After backfilling, I patted the dirt down to cover my diggings then disguised the tamped earth with loam, going so far as to place fresh moss over the topsoil as though I were sodding. I worked the moss tight to the stone, noticing that Mike's patch job was almost cured and would soon be indistinguishable from the old cement.

Good as new, eh, Roy? A berry bounced off my forehead. "What?" I asked. Another berry ricocheted off the stone.

Tim patted my left shoulder. I jumped a mile. His laugh made me grin as I slipped the found objects into the pocket of my pants.

Tim gave me a hand up. We walked side by side to the safe. More prepared than we had been, three OPP officers managed to take the pins out of the corroded iron door and remove it from the safe. The body remained within as it had for a hundred years. The police photographer got to work snapping pictures.

One of the officers talked to the three guys. I waited on the top landing for Meg's pontoon boat to appear. The OPP planned to use the barge-like boat to get the heavy safe to a stake-bed truck idling at Dixon Landing.

My fingers twiddled with the SD card in the pocket of my capri pants. I was itching to have a look at the photos. These were Roy's last images. How could I not want to see the world through his eyes? I once had a brother with hangy-down hair, one who loved and protected me. Even now, he watched me from behind the nearest buckeye bush.

Meg rounded the corner from Lapp Strait at the helm of the pontoon boat, easing expertly up to the new dock. She jumped onto the pier and tied off. Her hair was in wind knots, and her lips pursed until they nearly disappeared—not a good look for her. Plus, Meg's carefully extended, manicured, and polished fingernails were chipping. A hiss wove through the air. Meg looked over my shoulder toward the top of the hill. A rock, not quite a boulder, bounded down the hillside, splashing into the water, wetting Meg's deck shoes.

She shook her feet, then trotted up the stairs. "Found a body? In a safe? Tim claims the safe has been in the ground since Prohibition. Wow!"

"Any ideas?"

"Not a one," Meg shook her head until I was worried it might pop loose like one of those dolls' heads the O'Dell sisters claimed Meg detached from her Barbie. "All Dixons are accounted for from the year 1815 on. If you think not, check the graveyard next lake over."

We climbed the stairs to join the investigation if it could be called one. The OPP officers closed the safe door and readied a sling to position it on a dolly for a ride down the lift to the dock.

"You'll let us know?" Tim called as the officers rolled their cargo to the top of the stairs.

They transferred the safe to Joe's lift, which creaked and groaned as it descended on the rail. Meg joined them on the dock. Once the safe was loaded aboard, she piloted the pontoon boat around the promontory into Lapp Strait then toward Dixon Landing.

"Well?" we all asked.

Tim put an arm over my shoulders. "The aunts were a bust."

"But not Dred!" I cheered.

"Right you are, Ms. Treader. And who is it, old miss smarty pants?" Tim tickled my side. Mike cut Tim a disapproving look to which Tim responded with a shake of his head.

"Rusty O'Dell, the very O'Dell who invested in Sturdevant Distillers!" I crowed. Three sets of eyes snapped to mine. Mike knew. I had shown him the bottle. Tim had to know, didn't he? Brad?

"Spot on. Rusty worked security at the warehouse on the Sturdevant property. He was on the bridge when it collapsed. His body was never recovered. The investigators assumed he floated away, maybe got tangled in all the wood. They searched the lake for him for days. Then waited for years for him to pop up with the spring thaw."

"So, how did old Rusty get from the water to the safe, and why?"

"Maybe we should have searched his clothes before we called the OPP," Mike speculated.

"According to Dred, someone stole the payroll for the warehouse employees, and Lyle got out his six-shooters," Tim joked.

"So Rusty was involved in the theft and fell afoul of George and Lyle?"

"Well, there would be some sense to that, you know, you steal from the safe, and you end up in it. Sturdevant justice," Brad quipped.

I held my tongue. Poor Rusty. If he drowned, why stuff him in the safe and bury the whole package. The answer was obvious, so he would never be found. Why a sentence of forever?

"What do you mean by Sturdevant justice?" Tim asked Brad for me. Mike used his left foot to mess with the dirt beneath his feet, clearly uncomfortable with the question.

"Man steals your land in a poker game then offers you shares in some cockamamie homegrown distilling company as though that evens the score. Man tells his kid to be your friend then kills your best friend. Sturdevant justice."

Mike cleared his throat. "That is not fair, Brad. You know it. I know it. We all paid for that night. Sturdevant most of all. The rub is I liked Finn. I think I'd like him now if I ever got the chance to meet him," Mike's eyes locked on mine. In all my years at the lake, Mike had never challenged Brad. He just had.

Brad shoved Mike's right shoulder. Tim stepped between them.

"Horsepucky," Brad said, bulling past Mike.

Tim raised his eyebrows and grinned, "Guess we're done working for today. You think you guys can get along well enough to work together tomorrow?"

With a shrug of his shoulders, Brad gave a humph, Mike grunted in response. Tim seemed okay with the man-language. "We'll start at seven."

Tim led his troops to the dock. When Brad's right foot rolled on a step, he grabbed the stair rail and growled at Mike. Mike picked up a round metal pike welded to replace the broken plastic one from a solar light at the top of the stairs. He lodged the rod between the railing and a rock as a reminder for the morning,

Brad grumbling at him.

I shuffled through the leaves to the cabin, my fingers working Roy's SD card, my brain another problem. The answer was Mike. Mike had opened the cookie tin to return Dad's watch. It had to be.

XXX

I STARTED THE COALS in the barbecue. Rummaged in the freezer for a fat T-bone steak purchased in Watertown. Corn on the cob and a salad finished off the menu. I set my spot at the table. Plugged in my computer and slipped the card from Roy's tin into the SD slot. By then, the coals were ready.

Overhead, clouds fluffed in great heaps, rising then falling, first brilliant white then purple-gray as though unable to make up their minds. I knew how they felt.

The medium-rare T-bone on my plate, my corn buttered, and dressing on my salad, I forked a bite of meat and opened the first picture on the SD card. With one look, I spewed a chunk of half-chewed T-bone across the table.

A deep breath later, I peeked at the screen with one eye as though it might change the picture. I slammed my computer shut. Ran to the bedroom, banged the door shut behind me, threw myself across the bed, and sobbed. At some point in my sobbing, the door rattled. I ignored it. Another rattle was followed by quick strides across the worn plank floor.

A hand stroked the small of my back until the sobs slowed. I rolled over. This was the first time I had seen Sturdevant in anything other than swim trunks. He wore tan slacks and a pale blue shirt with his initials over the pocket. He cleaned up good though stubble still shadowed his jaw. Unable to find a paper tissue, he handed me a roll of toilet paper. I took the hint and blew my nose.

"Tell me?" he asked.

"I found Roy's SD card. I thought maybe something Roy photographed would help. Honest. I looked, I wanted to...I guess...I wanted to show off. Oh, Finn?" I wailed.

"Oh, Boo?" he mimicked, collecting me in his arms as he sat on the bed. "Nothing can be that bad, can it?"

"Well, we found Rusty O'Dell today, missing since 1934. I found out the Dixons have a thing called Sturdevant justice. Apparently, Rusty fell victim to it when he was suspected of stealing the payroll from the safe and ended up *in* the safe, now in the OPP's hands. Poor old Rusty."

"That's not what the tears are about."

"No." I snuffled.

"Tell me."

"I better show you." I rolled onto the edge of the bed, my legs hanging over, my bare toes stroking the old wood planking polished by the oils of a thousand bare feet.

Finn offered me a hand then followed me into the front room. "Would a beer help?" he asked, already head deep in the refrigerator. He poured two Labatts into a pair of pilsner glasses from the perpetually undusted head high shelves in the dining corner of the cabin. He handed me one, ordering, "Sip."

I did. I lifted the screen of my computer as though hell would slip out the crack. Those black, black eyes assessed my every move. I slammed the screen closed, took another slug, asking, "Where have you been all dressed up?"

"OPP and the clinic." He raised his left hand. It had been bandaged anew.

"Why the OPP?"

He shook his head. My questions were getting me nowhere.

"Show me," he said.

I ceded my seat to Finn before raising my computer screen. Finn whistled at the image but, unlike me, scrolled to the next picture. With one look, his eyes blackened. He scrolled again, glanced at me, then sucked in his breath. "Bugger," he said, viewing the next photo.

"Surely, not," I quipped, staring out the window at Roy's Deck, anywhere but at the photos.

"When?"

"Then--that summer, maybe, before, I guess. I don't know, how could I!" I wailed.

Finn's father and my mother. Don and Liza. Roy had photographed them making love. It was love; it showed in their eyes. And it wasn't new. It was something brilliant, rare, like a perfect blue diamond. Mary had mentioned that my mother had a teen crush. If so, it had either lasted or been rekindled?

"Did you know?"

Finn shook his head. "Something Pop said once left me with the impression that they had a thing one summer in their teens, yes. But this--this is not a casual romp with an old flame. Look at them."

"I did. I can't, not now. My father must have been devastated."

"He took these pictures, Boo. This is Roy's SD card, five pictures of your mother and my father, then it is filled with loons and the gang of three rough-housing."

As we talked, he clicked through Roy's pictures stopping every now and then to review one.

A hand over my mouth, my cheeks burning, I stuttered, "Roy knew Dad spied. That is why there was so much tension between Dad and him. It explains why Roy became so belligerent, not with Mom or me, but with Dad. And Roy kept it from me, protected me from it!"

Finn shrugged. "How did your mother react when Pop's body was found?"

I struggled to find the memory. Everything I thought I knew had just been reordered; the Ls were filed before the Ds—nothing made sense anymore. I gazed at my reflection in the front window and crawled back to the summer of Don Sturdevant's death. Clawed, really. New images fluttered at the fringes of my mind like demons dancing.

"Mom threw one of her parties. It was a Friday night. No one knew about your dad until the next morning when the news hit the lake. Mom ran down to New Landing. She dove into the lake in her shorts and halter top and swam to Sturdevant Beach. She ran up the beach toward the bog where they found your dad. My dad followed her in the boat. He must have caught up with Mom because they came back together. Mom was crying as Roy helped her onto the dock.

"Oh, Finn! Roy scoffed at her. Dad snapped at him, so Roy shoved Dad. I thought they were going to throw punches. Mom ordered me to the cabin then insinuated herself between Roy and Dad. When the three reappeared, they seemed fine. Mom went into the bedroom and changed, saying something about cleaning up the mess from the party. All very civilized. Dad offered to help. But Roy was fuming. Where were you that night?"

"I told you, waiting for Pop on the beach most of the night, except for rowing to the island to see if he was at the dance. Once I saw he wasn't there, I went back to the beach."

"You really didn't know that my mom and your dad were having an affair?"

"I knew Pop had a woman friend that he saw once or twice a month. A local woman, I thought, someone he liked but not seriously. I suppose if I had been more astute, I would have noticed more. Sorry. One thing, when I was fourteen, about then, he became a huge fan of the Pittsburgh Steelers, he started going to the home games." I snuck a peek at Roy's Steeler's hat. Booth Furniture was headquartered in Pittsburgh. Mom was on the Board.

"Do you think your father came up here to break it off with her, and she turned on him?"

"No." He stroked the scar on his temple.

"How can you be so sure?"

"The .jpg date on those photos is the day Pop died. And those aren't the eyes of a woman breaking up a relationship, nor are his."

My hand covered my mouth again. "Did Roy kill your father?"

"We need to reason this out. The photos are too crude to be Roy's work. Roy had a great eye. Say Roy was out with Mike and Brad all day, came home, and took his camera to the Friday party to snap a few pictures."

Finn forwarded through the pictures, showing me a few to make his point. "Next morning, Roy reviews them. He starts at the beginning of the SD chip and sees the first photos. By the time they found Pop's body, Roy knew about the affair, but not before."

"And, if Roy had taken the pictures, he would have been furious with your father, not mine," I added.

"Someone borrowed Roy's camera, hoping to expose Pop and your mom. Why?"

Devastated, today's word: shattered, shocked, stunned, gobsmacked.

"Once Roy saw those pictures, why didn't he erase them. All he had to do was hit delete six times."

"At a guess, blind with anger, Roy showed your dad the photos and accused him of taking them. Your dad denies it. Roy removes the chip and slaps it in your father's hand. Your dad keeps the chip, if for no other reason than as evidence of your mother's infidelity. Your dad must have known something was up. Pop did with my mom."

"So, somehow, someone exchanged this chip for the one Mom put in Roy's tin, but why? Why do it?"

"To hurt you and your family--you, to hurt you. Who's been in the tin?"

I shook my head, suggesting in a small voice, "Maybe you should talk to Mike?"

"Gagne? Are you certain it was Mike? What else did you find in the box?"

I reached over my head to the top bookshelf and handed Finn the photo of Roy and him. "And Dad's gold watch."

Finn flipped the photo checking for a print date. "You can buy this photo paper at any drug store. It wasn't done professionally."

He scrolled through the remainder of Roy's disk. The printed photo was among the last on the chip. Someone other than Roy had snapped it because Finn was shoving Roy into the bushes as it was taken. Finn raised his eyebrows.

"Anyone could have picked up the camera and taken the picture, Boo. Brad, Mike, and Roy were always together."

"Do you remember the confrontation?"

Finn nodded. "When I checked to see if Pop was at your mother's party, I asked Roy if you ever mentioned me."

I ducked my head as a blush crept into my cheeks. I hadn't blushed so much since Roy's death ended his brotherly teasing. "I guess from the looks on both your faces, Roy said no?"

"From the color of your cheeks, I'd guess he was wrong."

"Penny, Meg, and I secretly swooned. We thought you were some sort of bad boy. We had never met or even seen an overly educated, multi-lingual rich boy, so we had nothing to use for comparison. You've seen our stock. We enjoyed watching you move. Penny and I still do if that matters."

Finn ruffled my hair with his good hand then tickled my armpit, running his graceful fingers down my arm until I started giggling. His eyes lit, he shook his head, his mouth quirked. Understanding rushed me. This was the reason my mother glowed at Don Sturdevant in those photos.

Finn cleared his throat. I eeled out of the corner. He rose, swiveled me toward him, then danced me backward until my shoulders met the refrigerator. He ran his right hand from my armpit to my hip. I giggled.

"I'll talk to Mike tomorrow," he said, his voice husky. "What if Roy was sent for my camera but refused, and Brad or Mike did the deed? If that is true, *my* camera might still be somewhere in the case with the SD cards in it. Not that it will help prove anything, just...maybe..." He took a deep, raspy breath. He rubbed the scar over his ear, wove his way to the couch, and sat. "Sorry."

When he shut his eyes, I ran my fingers over his scar, asking, "So what if the *Free Press* dissed you. So what? Why is it so important? What is there left to print?"

Black, pained eyes flashed at me. "It's not a small thing. It's everything I am or have. The *Free Press* needs to print a retraction, the truth, something that sets the record straight. If they don't, whenever I'm offered a position on a Board of Directors or volunteer to coach a swim team, I'll be judged by the trash they printed. Which is that I killed a summer friend, that I slunk about delivering incriminating photographs, that my father drowned under mysterious circumstances.

"Then, I took all those skills to the military, where I beat a fellow Marine senseless, never mind he deserved it, and spent time in the brig for it. That, to this day, everyone on Lower Bay thinks I got off easy. In short, I am an unpredictable menace. The Board will oust me. Sure, I'll still be the owner, but I won't have any real control. I will be branded as ruined, damaged goods. And may still be charged with Roy's murder if any new evidence floats up."

I massaged his temple, knowing he thought I was involved in his pain.

"I didn't kill Roy, Boo, I didn't." His eyes opened to mine, naked with hurt. He grabbed my fingers and held them away from his head, his eyes eating holes into me that I might never be able to fill.

"Then, who, Finn? You admitted you saw Roy fall that he wasn't breathing and was bleeding—badly.

Sure, you claim he was alive when you left him. Why wouldn't you? All I have is your word for it. It doesn't matter that he didn't drown. It's worse, in fact. Both Mike and Brad swore Roy was dead. To any decent investigator, that just means you swam back as soon as Brad left and murdered Roy over a camera! I only have your word that you didn't know about the camera when you jumped out of those bushes. So, don't expect me to believe that the punishment you received is sufficient for denying me my brother for the rest of my life? Roy is dead because of you. No one else. Roy's dead. Dead. Dead. Dead."

"And I'm not."

"Tell me again, tell me what happened that night. Make me believe you." He pinned my fingers together until they ached. I pulled them out of his grasp.

He put his own hand back to his temple, then behind his ear, pushing in, leaving finger marks. "Being here brought back memories I thought had been blasted out of my head, Boo. Every time I swim to the island and use Roy's platform, something new comes back.

"Brad told me Roy would come ashore at New Landing. I waited there. In the end, I had to run across the promontory to intercept him. Roy clambered from the water and up that hill as though being chased by a shark. He kept looking over his shoulder, clawing his way up the rocks. I called Roy's name. Roy bolted upright, lost his footing, and fell. I didn't jump out of the bushes; I called his name. He looked scared, Boo. I had forgotten how scared. Someone or thing was after him."

"Someone who knew the boys were stealing. Someone like Dad?"

"Boo, your father is the only level head in all of this, no, just no! Your father didn't kill Pop, and he wasn't chasing Roy."

I was staring into his jet-black eyes when a scream shattered the night. One of those screams. The kind that hits you right in your fight or flight response. Finn bolted to his feet. He seemed disoriented for a moment, his head cocked, his eyes shut, then he strode toward the kitchen door.

Scrambling, I ran after him. He was going to slip away from me into the night, leaving me to deal with whatever this was. That is what he did. He dove into the water and swam away from the chaos he created.

"No, don't!" I entreated as Finn took off for New Landing at the run. Stars came and went between tree branches fluttering in the night breeze. The nocturnal bugs held their breath. The water lapped. Somewhere a boat oar creaked.

Finn dropped to his knees at the top of the dock stairs. He tore off his shirt. The moment I was within sight, he snapped, "Get on the Aldis Lamp now! Send an SOS. Rotate it up and down Lower Bay until someone responds. I'll do my best here."

"Who? Who is it?" I gasped.

"Go, Boo! Get help. It's bad."

"Tell me, someone may ask."

"O'Dell." I ran to the front of the cabin and blinked S-O-S straight at Dixons' front window. Then rotated the lamp toward Penny and Joe's, then back again. It was late. These were working people. They were sleeping. I kept going. S-O-S.

S-O-S

A light flicked on at Penny's. Then the porch light, then the dock. Voices carried across the water. A boat thrummed to life at Gagnes'. Mike ran across the open lawn between the two houses and climbed aboard with Joe. Joe hit the throttle, and they tore up Lower Bay. I ran to join Finn.

Two men fishing off the point had intercepted my signals and were the first to arrive. Finn was barking out orders. One of the fishermen ran back to their boat and got on the radio. Mike and Joe roared in rocking the fishing boat against the pier. The fisherman, mic to his mouth, gave them the finger but kept talking. Mike patted the fisherman's shoulder as the two men passed.

Joe thought to bring a spotlight which he aimed at Finn. Tim's blond head rested on Finn's lap. Finn's hands were covered in blood. His shirt jammed under Tim's back wicked blood into the dirt. Finn glanced at me with woeful eyes. I wanted to comfort him but knew he was Tim's best hope. This was a combat veteran, wounded himself.

The whooping of a big boat rumbled toward us. Mike and one of the fishermen ran down the stairs to move their motorboats aside. An emergency unit slid across the pier. The man at the tiller held it in position as two men walked onto the dock then trounced up the stairs.

They ordered everyone to stand back. Finn refused, speaking softly, his voice subdued but calm. The medical technicians acknowledged his advice and acted on it. It was only when they lifted Tim that it became evident that Tim had tripped and fallen on the welded metal spike for the top solar light. The force of his fall had driven the spike through his chest.

Mike walked up to me. "Has anyone notified Meg?"

"I signaled, but there was no response." I grabbed Mike's right forearm. "What if something happened at

Dixons? What if Tim was trying to warn me?"

Mike shook his head. "Penny was phoning them when we took off. The kids were in an uproar, both sets."

"Look," I pointed. "The yard light is on now."

The light at Dixon Landing blazed out onto the water. An ambulance, lights flashing, skidded around the bend in the road near the Pence place then backed up at Brad's direction into the parking area. Brad walked out to the end of the pier as the boat with Tim aboard left our dock, throttled down through Beaver Course, then roared the moment the water deepened.

Finn stayed on his knees, unmoving. His slacks were soaked in blood, as were his hands up to his wrists. His face was the color of wet ash. Slow, steady respiration rippled down his back. Joe knelt beside him. He waved his hand in front of Finn's face. Finn moved so fast Joe barely had time to whimper, his hand blanching above Finn's grip.

"Say something," I whispered to Joe.

Instead, Joe carefully lifted each of Finn's fingers from his wrist. "The medical technicians were impressed. They told me you saved Tim. Fast thinking, but I guess you have been in similar situations. Finn Sturdevant, right?" Joe held out his right hand. "I'm Joe Withers. My wife, Penny, speaks highly of you. Well, lowly, something about your butt."

Finn glanced at Joe. It was the first break in the trauma he had just relived.

"I'd like to help," Joe whispered, touching Finn's right leg. Finn gasped. Joe kept his hand where it was and squeezed. "Speak to me."

Finn lowered his head until his chin rested on his heaving chest. As I approached, Joe waved a hand to stop me while whispering softly to Finn, his calm catching. No wonder Penny loved this man.

Joe fingered Mike over. Mike ran to the cabin returning with a pan of water and towels. Joe dipped a cloth in the water and washed Finn's hands. When he came to the bandaged left, Joe showed it to Mike.

"The *No Trespassing* sign?" Mike checked with me. I nodded.

"What's going on, Mike?" Joe asked.

"Whatever it is, it's all about Boo. I have had a crush on her since we were kids. I got beaned. Finn—you just said the girls had the hots for him. He nearly loses a hand. And, today, Tim was mouthing off about how funny Boo is. Brad's ears were set like a retriever's waiting for a gunshot." Mike raised up on his toes. The big engine had stopped. A moment later, sirens howled down Lower Bay road. "I hope Meg's with him."

"Boo, do you know what happened?" Joe asked.

I shook my head. "We heard a scream. Finn ran out. By the time I got here, everything was a tableau. Finn sent me out front to signal. When I returned, there was blood everywhere. Finn... Finn, he..."

Joe swiped his hand over Finn's scarred temple. "Come on, man."

"Boo? Where's Boo?" Finn managed.

"I'm here." I walked up next to Joe and ruffled the top of Finn's black hair. He reached up for my hand. "Sorry."

"For what, exactly?" I asked as calmly as I could.

He took a breath that filled his lungs. "I don't know. I don't know. I..."

"Tim O'Dell," Joe said, his voice more strident now because sympathy wasn't working.

"O'Dell?" Finn muttered, renting his hands so hard

he winced, reopening his own wound. "I need a new bandage."

"Let's get you to the cabin. Everything we need is up there," I said, trying to sound stern.

Joe urged Finn to his feet. I gasped at the sight of Finn's blood-soaked slacks, instantly wondering if someone could lose that much blood and live. Joe shook his head at me. I colored with guilt as I led them along the path to the kitchen.

Joe settled Finn in a chair. As I gathered my first aide items, Mike used soap and water on Finn's hands, concentrating on the left. When he was satisfied, I applied the traditional family ointment and placed a pad over the wound, then held it all in place with a gauze strip. As I worked, Finn watched my hands, his square shoulders rounded heaps.

"Tim O'Dell?" Joe asked again.

"In and out." Finn started. "Spike went in here." He pointed with his right hand to a mid-point in his left pectoral muscle. Joe followed the line to a spot on Finn's back.

"And out here?" Joe asked.

Finn nodded. "So much damage."

"Did you hear anything other than his scream?" Joe asked.

Finn jerked his head up. Mike jumped. "A boat. Old Landing. Small. Maybe the fishermen."

Mike started for the door then stopped. The fishermen left without leaving their names or even the number from their boat. But the OPP would have both.

"Tim was."

Joe lifted his eyebrows in question.

Finn responded, "Conscious."

"Did he say anything?"

"*Meg?* I shook my head. *You, Finn?* I nodded that I was. Whatever he fell on nipped or collapsed a lung. He was gurgling. I don't know, I don't know if he can make it."

"Like I said," Joe calmed, "The medical technicians made it clear Tim had a chance because of your quick action. They asked me how you knew what to do. I hope you don't mind that I guessed, because of the scarring over your ear, that you'd been on the receiving end of an IED blast."

Finn nodded. "Was."

Mike rummaged in the refrigerator. "Beers?"

I followed Mike in and whispered, "Did you dig up Roy's cookie tin and return my Dad's gold watch?"

Color flashed across Mike's cheeks. "Years ago, Boo. I knew you guys planned to open it someday."

"There was a photo of Roy and Finn in the tin. Did you put it in with the watch?"

Mike shook his head no. I stared at his black and blue eye and scarred forehead.

"Did you exchange the SD card in it with another?"

Mike shook his head.

"Who, then?" I asked.

I waited. Mike squinted at me over the beer he slurped. I pinned him against the refrigerator, not easy; he was taller and outweighed me. "Mike, come on, come clean. Don't you think it's time?"

Mike finished the beer then started on the one he had gotten for me. He sipped, checked in the kitchen, and whispered, "Roy was the best swimmer of the three of us until Sturdevant showed up. It drove Brad nuts. How could a city boy swim like that? As the dumb hanger-on, Brad had no issue with my swimming, plus he knew I worked as a lifeguard. I was slower, but I could have dragged a whale out of that lake.

"Brad just wanted to win once. Roy knew it, too. Brad suggested we swim further. He thought he could beat Roy at a distance. Roy suggested we draw lots, and the loser had to steal one thing of real value. They got into one of those arguments that end with everyone's chest puffed out. We tried it Roy's way; your grandfather's watch was the target. I lost the draw. Afterward, I put my foot down. They put pressure on me to keep my mouth shut. Finn heard it all, probably got photos. All of a sudden, Brad's making overtures to Finn like he's going to let him join our gang."

I continued for him, "Brad gave Finn two tasks that I know of the first was to ask Meg to a dance. And the night Roy died, Brad sent Roy to steal Finn's camera then asked Finn to scare Roy, you know that, right?"

Mike bobbled his head. I was unsure what the bobble meant, yes, I think, confirming that Roy stole Finn's camera.

I tried a new tack. "It was quite the setup. The OPP had Finn dead to rights. No matter what Finn told them, it was clear that Finn scared Roy because Roy stole his camera. Easy-peasy. Except they were wrong. And I suspect, after the lies you and Brad told to save yourselves, nothing Finn said would have mattered. Not one of you mentioned the camera, did you? Not you and Brad, not Finn."

Mike shook his head, drained the beer in his hand, and reached into the refrigerator for another. Mike had lied to himself, the OPP, his family, my family for twelve years, so I asked, "Did you break Roy's grave marker or go fishing in the tin again. Did you plant the photo?"

"No." Mike tried to get around me. I put a hand on

the refrigerator. He leaned against the refrigerator door, looking toward the kitchen for rescue. Joe's head bobbed up from tending Finn. I waved my finger to let Joe know Mike was unavailable. Mike twisted open a new beer, keeping his back against the refrigerator door.

"Come on, you thought Roy was alive when you went for my dad, didn't you?"

Mike bobbled his head.

"Come on, Mike! Brad killed Roy, you knew it then, you know it now."

"Sturdevant did. He swam back and did it," Mike charged with another nod and slurp of beer.

"Whose idea was it to steal Finn's camera?"

Mike laughed. "All of us. With what was on his SD chip, he could have blackmailed us for eternity. I mean, girl kisses. You and me, for instance. But not just us kids, adults, too. It was like he was making a documentary of all the Lower Bay doings."

"But Brad instigated it and challenged Roy and Finn, one to steal and one to scare?"

"That is the thing, Boo, it was complicated. The camera was kind of an insurance policy, you know. It wasn't the camera, and it wasn't jealousy on Roy's side. It was survival. If we had the camera, Finn couldn't lord the damn photos over us or Roy, particularly Roy."

"What about us girls. What about the pictures taken of us?"

Mike shook his head. "The pictures he snapped were full-on wicked. You know...he caught us in all sorts of incriminating circumstances."

"Did you see an SD card when you stole Dad's watch?"

"I just reached into the saucer where your dad kept

the watch and scooped. I kept the watch, intending to return it. Brad called me stupid and took the SD card. I never saw the card again."

"I found it and the watch when I opened Roy's tin today."

"Like I said, I put the watch in the tin. Brad snatched the SD card from me. I swear."

"You've sworn to a warrant full of lies, Gagne," Finn growled from the kitchen. "I didn't kill Roy Treader. End of story."

"Ah," Joe said, "He's back among us. Here is my guess. Brad was tired of being second. Finn wanted to belong. Brad used the promise of acceptance into the gang of three to coerce Finn into scaring Roy. It was a win-win for Brad, but the rest was all bad luck. Finn scared Roy, who lost his balance and hit his head. Finn went in after him and swam him to the dock, just as Mike and Brad showed up. Finn took off, a better swimmer than Roy, Mike, and Brad put together. Mike went for help, but Roy was dying. Roy's death was an accident, a horrible one, but nothing more. About right, Sturdevant?"

"Maybe. Except Roy responded quickly and was breathing when I dove in, and something drove Roy out of the water. I'm sure of it." Finn picked at the fresh bandage on his injured hand.

The four of us stared at each other until a sharp knock on the screen door broke it up. I crossed behind Joe and Finn to open the door. An OPP officer stood hat in hand on the stoop.

"Officer Milburn," the policeman entered. "O'Dell is in critical condition, but the doctors say he has a fair to good chance of making it. They asked me to make a point of thanking the dark-haired guy." He inclined his head toward Finn. Not because he was the only dark-haired guy, but because he was both dark-haired and covered in blood. "Quick thinking. I need a statement from each of you. Did anyone witness the accident?"

We shook our heads.

It was three a.m. before the officer finished. Nothing new emerged. Well, not true. Tim had been delivering gas. The cage was open, and one five-gallon jerrycan was missing. The fishermen had seen a 17-foot motorboat emerge from Beaver Course just after Tim screamed. The boat continued north into Upper Bay. They were unable to get the boat's numbers. Once the craft's pilot hit the bay waters, the throttle opened, and the motorboat tore out. The wake had been rough enough to pitch the fishermen's boat against a rock. They weren't sure if the boater came from the island or heard the scream and tore out in fear.

"Go home, Joe," Finn urged, "Go to Penny and your kids. I'm okay."

Joe shot a worried look my way then squeezed Finn's left shoulder as he stood. I ushered Mike and Joe through the kitchen door. "Thank you. I'll make Finn a bed in the front room for the night."

Joe nodded. Mike took my hand. Something in the way he played with my fingers signaled his understanding.

Finn showered Tim's blood off under the water tanks, a plastic bag wrapped over his injured hand, returning in a pair of white skivvies and nothing else. I made up the horsehair couch for him. He snuggled down in a folded bedsheet. I covered him with a thin, flannel blanket.

A moment later, a soft snore humanized the silent, blood-filled night.

Day 10

xxxi

I ROAMED THE REMAINDER of the night, keeping watch over Finn. He slept on the couch, his back to the door, snuggled deep in the blue and pink dancing sheep woven into the blanket flannel that covered him.

I mulled over Mike's belief that all the hurt had to do with me. Maybe now, though, I doubted it, but not then. Then events were driven by jealousy, pure and simple. Roy swam faster than Brad, and Finn faster than both. Finn's photos were better than Roy's, so much better Roy took credit for Finn's work.

Sure, it was an over-simplification; there was more to it than swimming and photos. Mix in competition for the local girls and the fear of the outsider, and you had a toxic brew. Still, I was missing something, something essential.

The night that Roy died, Brad stayed with Roy while Mike ran to the cabin for my father. Dad hurled Roy's trophy at Mike, scarring and scaring him for life, then outran Mike to the dock. If Roy was alive when Mike left, he was dead when Mike returned. I needed to know what Jack Treader saw the moment he arrived on the dock. I would call Dad while Finn's hand was being rebandaged at the clinic. Maybe my father, who, according to Finn, stayed in Finn's corner, had the answer.

I sat in my spot between the window and refrigerator. I loved the corner chair because I could see out onto Roy's Deck and now, in the half-light of morning, watch over Finn. His black hair curled on a flowery pillow cover, the scar on his temple a webbed slash, the missing tip of his left ear exposed. He moaned and pedaled his legs as he slept. Last night, he had saved another life.

In my Sturdevant research, I found an article from a past *New York Times* describing an incident in a war zone. It detailed how Sergeant F. Sturdevant dragged his men, smothered their flaming limbs, and tended to the wounded after an IED destroyed their armored vehicle. The rescue unit found the unconscious Sergeant, his skull fractured, leaning against a burned-out armored personnel carrier. The only member of his unit that he was unable to save cradled in his lap.

Finn's black eyelashes fluttered on his cheeks. His nose was straight, his mouth flawed by the puckered scar at the left corner. A thin line in the ever-present stubble indicated that the healed wound continued to the depression in his jaw. Another scar cut through his left eyebrow. It was the face of a man, not a movie star, not a grownup boy, a man. A face you could gaze at thirty years on and still find it pleasing and filled with character.

I thought of Mike and his stubborn allegiance to Brad. His belief that this all had to do with me. That I was the incendiary agent applied to an inert substance.

I ran over the incidents that were piling up. Mike tripped in the dark and fell headfirst onto the carefully fitted rocks and pitted concrete of the Prohibition stairs. Finn jammed the jagged edge of a *No Trespassing* sign floated in from his own property into his hand while sneaking ashore. Now, Tim. I am not stupid. I got the obvious connection. Me. All three men were misguidedly protecting me. From what? The shadow that climbed the hill, swam the channels, and lit fires. So, Mike from Finn, Finn from Mike, and Tim? I suspected from both Mike and Finn. I saw that summer playing out again but now between adults and with dreadful results. And then there was Roy.

Last night, he was beside me as I signaled for help. He watched Finn save Tim from the tree line, a wavering shade still as death, waiting... My mind flew back to Finn, his hands putting pressure on Tim's wound, stanching the flow of blood, suddenly shifting his eyes to his right. He gulped in air, shook his head, and returned his attention to Tim. When next I looked, Roy had left his vigil.

The sun breached the horizon as I shook the memory off. A soft mist rose from the waters. The air chilled as it does in the early hours of the morning. I brewed myself a cup of coffee and wandered out to Roy's Deck. A boat drifted into the point, oars clacked, whispered voices reassured me that fishermen were paying homage to the goddess of bass, trout, and crappie.

Sturdevant justice. The term popped to mind. The long-held myth that the Sturdevants were the slime of the earth, villains, and gangsters was just that, a myth with the possible exception of the infamous poker game. But in return for any misconceptions, the Lower Bay families had been offered shares in Sturdevant Distillers. The O'Dells and Gagnes bought in, the O'Dells sold their share, the Dixons had refused the offer out of pique. Ardyss was murdered. Lyle knifed in prison. Rusty O'Dell perhaps set up for a robbery he did not commit then stuffed in the safe he had not robbed. The litany gave a whole new face to Sturdevant justice.

It had been Lyle standing in the shadows across Beaver Course the night the bridge fell. I recognized him now. I liked Lyle's face. His great-great-great-grandson, framed in the doorway lit by the morning light, wore it well. Deep purple bags emphasized his black, black eyes. He held his injured hand against his chest, clearly in pain. I scuffed across the open ground from Roy's Deck to the porch.

"Thinking?" he asked.

"Trying."

I eased past him into the kitchen. We had some oversized, square cotton towels for dish drying. I folded one in half and tied the ends behind his neck. He slid his bandaged hand into the makeshift sling.

"Sorry to be such a wimp," he sighed.

"We need to get you into the clinic. I have a phone call or two to make while you're being seen. If that's okay?"

"Fine with me. Tim?"

"Nothing new." I brewed coffee for us. The old percolator sat unused on a shelf by the stove, not for long. Brewing a cup at a time wasn't working, and, further, the waste was useless even to the worms.

Finn sipped coffee while I scrambled eggs with chopped ham and onion. He picked out the onions as we ate, making a neat pile on his napkin. Good to know.

"Out of curiosity, did you ever snub Brad Dixon?" Finn asked as I washed the dishes. It was not an idle question.

I shook my head. Brad was the catch of the lake.

The heir of a respected, powerful family with roots that went back to the War of 1812. A good-looking boy with his dusty-blond hair and farmer's physique muscled by his penchant for swimming. Every teen girl's dream. With the possible exception of the tall, slender, broad-shouldered stranger currently sitting at my breakfast table and Roy.

"Mary Gagne commented the other day that your arrival changed the dynamic on Lower Bay. The women all acted up. Including the female version of the gang of three who kept their eyes on you."

"You, Penny, and Meg?"

I nodded. "I remember Meg snatching Roy's camera to take a picture of you. We were all at Sturdevant Beach. Roy grabbed the camera, but she got the shot first."

"What happened next?"

"You smiled at us. Penny skipped over to you. You ruffled the hair on the top of her head. She left it unwashed for a week. Then you checked me over, top to bottom, and gave me a low wave. Meg waved, you waved back and dove into the water. It was a moment. We talked about it for days. Roy warned me to stay away from you. Mike paid me more attention than ever before. Brad grabbed Meg by the arm and hauled her to their boat. Not necessarily in that order. The next time you were on the beach, Meg pretended to trip over something and landed in your arms."

Finn shook his head.

"Don't remember it, eh? Meg did. She bragged that you felt her butt."

"She claimed much worse later," Finn said, fiddling with the knot in the towel where it rubbed the back of his neck. "I need to change out of these clothes; maybe you can motor me over to the beach. I can't go into town covered in blood."

"Or without a hit on your weed?"

"It dulls my physical pain, Boo. It keeps me from using the gun to end it. When I smoke, I relax, sleep, even eat."

"Oh," I blushed sharply. "Then, let me see what's in the cedar trunk."

I left him in the kitchen while I rummaged through the trunk in the bedroom. I came back with my prizes, a pair of khaki shorts, and a batik print shirt, both of which were my father's. The shorts were a brainstorm since Finn was a couple of inches taller than Dad. Finn made a squinch mouth.

"Not stylish enough?" I asked.

He showed me one sock and loafer clad foot.

"Ditch the socks," I suggested.

He took the clothes into the bedroom. When he emerged, he looked like a Boston technology nerd on vacation. He put his arm back in the sling. It only amplified the effect.

We skirted the dark splotch of dirt at the top of the dock stairs. Finn relied on the railing down to the pier and meekly allowed me to help him into the boat. He sat with an ungraceful thud and fiddled with his borrowed shirt.

The lake was rough. We bounced our way through Lapp Strait toward Dixon Landing. When I saw a crowd gathered, I diverted to Gagnes'.

Penny forced coffee on us while Joe walked the half-mile to Dixon Landing for my car. Like me, Penny had not slept; her sad, sleepy eyes made me hug her. She whispered, "We need to talk--soon."

I squeezed her arm, promising to stop in for that

chat on my way back to the island. Joe entered the kitchen, poured a cup of coffee, reporting that the crowd was no more fearsome than the Township Council's quarterly retreat. Joe squeezed Finn's left shoulder; Finn produced a small smile.

xxxii

FINN SLEPT MOST OF the way to Westport. I drove straight to the clinic. He was so feverish by then that I asked for a wheelchair. Though there were people lined up, he was beelined into a treatment room. Instead of leaving as planned, I stayed with him.

They reopened the wound, cleaned it, glued it closed before rebandaging his palm, and then shot him up with more penicillin. A young doctor fingered me into the hall.

"First, let me introduce myself. I'm Greg O'Dell, Tim's brother. The OPP was pretty clear that Sturdevant saved my brother's life last night. I'm guessing you're Boo Treader, all grown up."

I shook his hand. Greg had his brother's way about him; it glowed in his smile.

"Mr. Sturdevant needs to stay overnight or until the fever breaks. We expect the results of an earlier blood sample first thing tomorrow. Meantime, we will take good care of him. He needs to take it easy and give his hand a chance to heal. Sorry to ask if this is too personal, but does he suffer from Post-Traumatic Stress?"

"Yes," I answered, hearing Joe cajoling Finn back from the edge. "Finn had contact with a considerable amount of blood last night other than his own. I don't know if that is a matter of concern."

"Not at all. Mr. Sturdevant will be fine, barring any surprises in his blood sample. Honestly, I suspect a good night's sleep is all he needs. By the way, Tim was airlifted to Ottawa this morning. Arrived in good shape. Surgery is scheduled for tomorrow to repair the damage. He hasn't regained consciousness, but the doctors are confident he will. Your guy was amazing. Everyone says so."

I started to walk away. My guy? I turned back. "Greg, twelve years ago..."

"I can tell you this. Tim got all tangled up in that mess. It was and is like a gill net. No matter how he struggles, he can't find his way out. I don't know what happened, who saw what, who knows what, but everyone's life changed and not for the better."

"Penny Gagne?"

"She claims you were her salvation. If true, she's the only one involved with Sturdevant that isn't still strangling in the net. Oh, and if you are spending the night on the island, plan to pick up Mr. Sturdevant tomorrow around noon. If there is a change, we can talk about it then."

I stepped out of the clinic then walked down the block and around the corner to the café. I ordered a cup of coffee and a sticky bun dripping with frosting, oozing cinnamon and filled with nuts. I sat in the bay window, in my second favorite but more private location. The table offered a clear view of the stairs to Alice Cornish's realty office and down the town's main sidewalk.

A slight breeze ruffled the leaves on the trees as tourists roamed up and down the street. A little boy clutched a stuffed black and white loon and ran circles around his parents. Locals chatted each other up mid-sidewalk. I dialed my father while promising myself a scoop or three of Tiger Tail before I left.

Misty answered the ring, all peppy, I didn't mind. She made my father happy. He deserved that. I didn't even blink at my change of heart. A moment later, Dad was on the line, sounding rushed, "What's going on, Boo?"

"Mike Gagne returned your grandfather's watch by way of Roy's cookie tin. I thought you might want to know," I started.

"Thanks, not sure it warrants a call to Costa Rica, though." I could tell by the noises on the phone that he had settled onto a comfortable chair. Now, with the phone an inch from his ear, he would listen to me, taking in every nuance like the trained field anthropologist he was. "We promised the boys we would take them snorkeling. Sorry to say, I've only got fifteen minutes."

"Jack Treader, you are a great guy." I had been so unfair to him. He needed to know that I loved him. I needed him to hear it and hoped he would internalize it. Given the time constraint, I plunged in, "Dad, I know about Mom and Don Sturdevant. How can you have been so gracious with Mom and still be trying to prove that Don was murdered?"

"Because I love you, Boo. It made being gracious easy. And, because Don *was* murdered. I made myself go in and look at the body. The OPP let me. Someone walloped him between the shoulder blades. He went overboard, hit his head on a stump, fell into the water, and drowned. The bruise on his back was too high and too wide for the gunnel. But I never could get any traction with them."

"Any ideas why?"

"No weapon, no witnesses, no anything."

"Okay then, the night Roy died, first impressions, you ran down the hill to New Landing and saw what?"

"Brad Dixon white as a sheet at the top of the hill come to meet us. Roy below him on the deck dead. I hear a small boat off Old Landing. Roy's camera is on the dock. I run my index finger in a pool of blood under Roy's head, see his right knee is scraped. The moon is waning but shining bright enough to light our boat floating into Upper Bay."

"Was Roy's head bandaged with his red bandanna when you arrived at the deck?"

"No," He hesitated, then asked, "How did you find out about your mother?"

"Roy's SD card. The pictures you took. Mom told me she put the card from Roy's camera in the tin for later. Oh, Daddy!"

"The SD card your mother put in Roy's tin was filled with pictures of loons, girls, and the guys. Your mother and I looked at the pictures together. Someone must have switched the SD cards later. I took the card you now have from Roy the day after Don was murdered. I stashed it in a safe place. The last thing I wanted was for the photos of your mother and Don to be seen by outsiders, especially the OPP. What would they think? The obvious being that I had killed Don in a rage."

"Roy accused you of snapping the pictures, right?"

"He did. I saw those pictures for the first time when Roy shoved the camera under my nose. Nothing would convince him. He screamed that I had been seen sneaking around peeping in windows, then threw his Nikon to the ground. It ricocheted off a rock. Your brother and I had words about the damage done to the camera box. It kinked our relationship. Mind you, Roy, and I would have worked it out if there had been time."

My mother had lied to me about the damage to Roy's camera, about Finn, about what else? "What happened to the SD card you kept?"

"It went missing with my watch. I assumed Roy snatched both. The last thing I expected was for it to turn up again, BG."

I humphed. Mike had been telling the truth about grabbing the SD card when he stole Dad's watch. I changed the subject. "Tim O'Dell was nearly killed in a grisly accident on Booth Island last night. Finn saved him. Oh, Tim, Mike, and Brad, the new gang of three, turned up Rusty O'Dell's body stuffed in a safe previously used to buttress one corner of the dance floor. Brad called it Sturdevant justice like it was a thing people knew about. Also, Silvie Dixon was rendezvousing with someone on Sturdevant Peninsula when she was murdered."

"Wow!" Jack Treader, my dad, laughed. I snorted. People stared at me over their coffees and ice creams. I glanced up in time to see Meg Dixon climb the stairs to the realty office.

The Council met at the Dixon farm this morning, now Meg was at Alice Cornish's office. Busy bee considering Tim was in critical condition an hour and a half away in Ottawa. My thoughts sounded catty even to me.

"Boo?" Dad queried, my silence.

"I just saw Meg Dixon go into a realty office by the café."

Dad chuckled again. "Damn Dixons, probably still angling to get their famously stolen property back. What a hoot! And what a grudge! When your mom and

I first married, I was fascinated with the history of Lower Bay. I researched the Prohibition period, the bridge, the disappearances, and oral history."

"Really?" Not unlike me, but probably much more thorough research than I had done.

"I thought I'd died and gone to tribal heaven. Josh Dixon was the chief. They had their own creation myth, beginning with the dirty rotten, low-down poker playing Sturdevants. It seemed ludicrous and funny until I got tired of it and all the stupid rules and games."

"And Mom."

"She was a victim. She kept trying to win their approval with her parties. In the Dixon myth, George Booth bought the island under false though legal pretenses from the Lapps, cheating the Dixons out of the land and the money. Then George introduced Mr. Dixon to Lyle Sturdevant, and wham Sturdevant gets Mr. Dixon drunk and cheats him out of eighteen prime acres. Which left poor old Mr. Dixon owner of most of the arable land and lakefront property around Lower Bay."

Dad took a deep breath as though questioning whether to continue, then did, "Wanting revenge, Dixon ratted out Ardyss Sturdevant then called the Feds. The Feds burned Sturdevant Distillers' peninsula warehouse with help from the OPP. When Lyle was knifed, Dixon made a play for Lyle's property. Lyle's wife, an O'Dell, by the way, produced Lyle's son, nipping the land reversion in the bud. Fearing for her life, she fled to Grosse Pointe Shores. She asked George Booth for protection and help with the distillery business, then ingratiated herself to the Fords who rewarded her with a Cotswold Cottage and surrounding acreage on the Ford estate. The rest is history."

"Her brother was Rusty O'Dell?"

"Yes, he was. He disappeared when the bridge collapsed. Dred's Momma always believed that the bridge collapse was to cover Rusty's murder. The thing is, Rusty's wife died, too. Her body was found, but not Rusty."

"Why Rusty?"

"Mythology is he stole the payroll from the safe. None of the locals were paid for a week. A hardship for many of them, it was not only Prohibition in the States, but the Depression everywhere. Here is the rest. Lyle never killed anyone. Period. He didn't gun down Ardyss' killers, and he didn't whack Rusty. Those murders or deaths and the payroll theft fall right at the Dixon doorstep. The Lower Bay people know it, too, and have toed the line ever since. The Dixons run roughshod over the Township. To me, they're the gangsters and always have been."

"Holy crap!" Faces popped up all over the coffee shop to stare agape at me. "Oh, sorry. Sorry." I apologized to all and sundry for my outburst.

"Sorry?"

"Not in the least. I bet Misty has a perspective, too."

"She has never been south of New Road. The old Lapp family joke is north of New Road is Lapp-land, everything else is below the Maison Dixon line." Dad enjoyed my laugh.

"Whoa! What would you say if I told you that Brad is home visiting Meg? That his visit caught her off guard. That she lives with Tim O'Dell."

"Now Tim's in critical condition. And Sturdevant is there."

"Finn wants to clear his name. Someone sent his

sealed documents to the *Detroit Free Press*. I don't know the truth of it, but he says you stood by him."

"Of course, I did. At worst, it was a prank gone bad. Still, Roy died because of Finn's actions. He has to live with that, but it shouldn't be allowed to ruin the rest of his life. So, BG, channel your old Dad, then start thinking like a field anthropologist, and you'll find the answer."

"Daddy?"

"You know enough now to do that. If you can, you'll save your fella."

"Oh, Dad, that's just so archaic and chauvinist and..."

Jack Treader started laughing and couldn't stop. I waited. "BG, one thing that continues to make you special is how oblivious you are to the motives of mankind. Think like a sought-after editor of romance novels, wasting away on an island in the middle of a Canadian lake while mooning over her long-dead brother. How's that."

"Don't laugh at me, Dad."

"I'm not laughing, Boothe. Figure out whatever is bothering you, then give me a call so I can quit worrying."

We said our goodbyes. I ordered two scoops of Tiger Tail and returned to my table in time to see Meg Dixon leave the realty company. I finished my ice cream, then, spurred on by Dad's words, went to visit Alice Cornish.

xxxiii

ALICE CAME OUT TO greet me in a straight skirt so tight

she had to tip to walk. Her blouse was sleeveless and as brilliantly white as her teeth when she smiled. At a guess, both had been bleached. I shook her hand, and she whisked me into her office. "You just missed Ms. Dixon," Alice said with a brittle smile.

"Really?" I asked.

"It's too bad, really. I think we might have been able to solve your problem with Booth Island. Meg seemed certain the Township would acquire Sturdevant Peninsula within the week. She showed me the Council's plans for the park."

Alice tapped landscape drawings unrolled across her desk. I'm not good at reading upside down, but I did my best to remember the details.

"It will be a great attraction, boat ramp, wedding chapel, dancing over the weekend. There are even plans to rebuild and repurpose the bottling facility for public rental, family reunions, company retreats, that sort of thing. Oh, my, it will be grand. Even grander if you sell Booth Island to the Township."

"I want the beach and access through the Peninsula. I asked you days ago to speak to Mr. Sturdevant about selling it."

"Sturdevant will sell to the Township before he does to you. So, it is in your best interest to negotiate with the Council."

"No negotiation and no sale. Booth Island is not for sale. Won't be for sale. Ever, not as long as I draw breath," I said coolly, though my armpits produced sweat enough for two.

Alice's mouth dropped open, displaying all thirty-two of her shiny white teeth and a few fillings. She stuttered, finally choking out, "I'll let the Township Council know."

I pivoted as well as one can in sandals and made a beeline for the door. I could almost hear Alice dialing Meg's telephone number. Two steps later, I regretted my pique.

I hiked back to the two-story U-shaped red brick building that housed the clinic. At the reception desk, I asked for Mr. Sturdevant's room number. Greg O'Dell met me and led me to the room Finn shared with a teen who had broken his leg.

Finn, in the bed nearest the window, smiled as I entered. The boy was intent on a hockey game blaring from the one TV. Finn still had not shaved but must have slept because most of his color had returned. I sat on the edge of the bed and fumbled for his right hand.

"Sorry, I think they drugged me," he slurred, proof enough he was right.

I squeezed the hand I held. "I'm heading back to the island. I will pick you up early tomorrow afternoon. Considering how much better you look, I'm sure they'll let you out!"

"I would prefer it if you stayed in town," Finn said. All I could see were the black curls at the top of his head.

"Ah, you're worried about me," I kidded. "I'll be fine. I am not a guy. And I am not a guy interested in me. And, as such, I'm doubly protected by my very Booness."

"See, that scares me."

"It shouldn't. I talked to my Dad. I think I have enough information to resolve everything and help Roy over. I just need a pad of paper, a lonely island, and maybe a blowy, dark, angry storm."

I reached over and urged his face towards mine. He quirked his lips in disapproval. I ran my free hand over his lengthening stubble; the softness of it caught me off guard.

He checked the next bed, and, in a move I still have to figure out, he dropped my hand, got one of his behind my head, and pulled me in for a kiss. I hoped the teen was taking notes.

Finally, he said, "I keep thinking that we are--I'm missing some essential detail. For instance, jealousy never crossed my mind, but it factors between Brad and Roy, possibly with your mother and father. It ripples through, doesn't it? And, with me stuck in the clinic, no one has your back. No one."

"Mike and Penny. They do."

Finn shook his head. "Joe, Joe maybe, but he's not going to risk Penny or his kids. Mike's got kids to raise, too. Remember, he is a single father. No, Boo, it is just you. You and me."

Finn's use of *you and me* caught me off guard, especially since I hadn't forgiven him. I couldn't until I was certain Roy had. Heaven knows, there was enough culpability to go around the island several times. I felt the weight of the accidents that had befallen Mike, Finn, and Tim, for starters. And I was more than a little peeved that Finn thought me so helpless that I needed backup.

"I'm fine for the night. Don't even think of leaving this clinic. I will be here in the morning. Concentrate on healing. Can you do that!" I stood so fast it jarred his bed. "And, for criminy sakes, just sell me your stupid peninsula!"

That caught his attention, his eyes stopped me in my tracks. Even the boy with his broken leg became jittery.

"Why would I do that, Boo. Why?"

"So, no one kills you while I'm not here to save you. That's why!"

"You're angry. What happened? Tell me!"

"You. Underestimating me. Alice Cornish. I popped off at her. She keeps assuming Booth Island can be purchased. It can't. Not while Roy's...."

"Roy's what?" Finn's cocked head. I dropped his hand and fled.

Confused, the word of the day. Bewildered. Bemused. Chaotic. Muddled. I had a familiar ring to it as though I had declared it before.

xxxiv

I STEERED MY SUV down the main road, not tempting New Road in the descending dark, then took Lower Bay Road to Gagne Lane. Proof enough, the Gagnes were part of the Lower Bay community. I parked in the circular drive at the front of Penny's house.

The newest house in the Gagne compound had been built in the 1970s and still had the vibe. Penny leaned in the kitchen doorframe, watching as I walked towards her. We texted, Penny reminded me to stop, I reminded her my boat was at her dock. She texted back a laughing face.

Dressed in shorts, sandals, and a sleeveless knit shirt, Penny ushered me into her recently remodeled kitchen. Last year, Penny won her campaign to have the kitchen redesigned, including removing anything in any shade of avocado. Which meant reflooring since the linoleum had green flecks. The floor was now an indestructible tile that looked like hardwood.

The counters, formerly oak chopping block

patterned Formica, were a soft coffee-colored stone, all the better to disguise splashes. The cabinets matched in a deep brown with nickel handles. The appliances were stainless steel, and the best money could buy. Under Penny's sharp eyes, not a smidge of green remained. At one time, I would have wondered where they found the money. No more. I knew the answer, Mary via Sturdevant Distillers' dividend checks.

The tour included tutelage on all of Penny's new gadgets. Including a single cup coffeemaker that made mine look like a cheap knockoff. The redesign had not stopped with the kitchen, so Penny gave me the grand tour of the updated house.

The tour ended at a breakfast bar between the kitchen and a great room of dynastic proportions encompassing the features of a dining room, living room, and recreation room. She had furnished the area with patio furniture, rattan chairs, couches, and an ottoman with bright cushions. The whole place made me smile, as did the myriad toys flung helter-skelter on furniture, on the floor, and, in one case, on a lamp.

"The minute Mom moved into town with Lou, Joe and I went to work. It was a wonderful opportunity to get rid of all the old furniture, knickknacks, and general clutter. I love it," Penny responded to my grin.

"Joe did all this?" I sipped a hand-squeezed lemonade Penny had made, especially for my visit. The lemon bars she made were my favorites, too.

"You betcha he did."

"He's a great guy, Pen. You're super fortunate."

"So, are you Boo. Joe told me everything, tells me everything. He says there is something big going on between you and Finn."

"I don't know. Big? Maybe?"

"Joe's taken the kids to his folks. They go every Friday night. It's a thing. The kids get spoiled rotten, I get a night of my own, and so does Joe. Honestly, I think he meets his old bachelor buddies down at the pub and ties one on. It's good for him. He works so hard."

"He was so amazing with Finn. I don't know how Joe knew what to do. Kind, gentle, thoughtful."

Penny beamed. "Is Finn going to be okay?"

"He's fine. We will deal with his PTSD. I don't know anything about it, but I can read up."

"I heard *we*, Boo. Plans already?"

"Finn makes my toes curl. Though he is a bit bossy. And Pen..."

Penny laughed. "Joe made me go all weird in the stomach. Every time I saw him, I got butterflies like the night I sang at the dance."

The night of Roy's death, Penny took a Karaoke challenge and won. How had I forgotten? I had egged her into it. I could tell she wanted to from the blush on her cheeks. She bloomed right in front of my eyes. It was shortly after Penny accepted her award with an encore and a curtsy that Meg found a ride home, claiming she had cramps.

Penny's next words caught me off guard. "Weird, when I remember that night, I see the three of us riding home in Dred's big old car. But it was just us, you and me, wasn't it?"

"Meg wasn't having much fun that night. Then you upstaged her with your version of *Raindrops Keep Falling on My Head*. You were so adorable in your shorts and ruffles. I remember being skeptical about Meg's whole cramp claim from the start. We had to cajole her into coming, and once there, she seemed determined to have a rotten time." I shrugged, "Still, Meg was at Dixon Landing and at the passenger door the moment Dred stopped the car."

Penny cocked her head, "The guys were sitting on the dock, their feet dangling. Mike's head was bleeding. Brad stared aimlessly into the water at nothing. Your Dad had already left for Westport with Roy's body. The only thing that seemed to move was your mother, who ran up to us. Oh, I don't know, Boo, I've tried so hard to forget."

"I can't. The minute I relax, my brother comes to me. I need to exorcise him, or help him cross over, or whatever the mediums would say. If not, I'll never be happy."

"I prescribe two servings of Finn Sturdevant with a side of Tiger Tail." Penny hugged me. "Poor Boo. Is there a Ouija Board stashed on Booth Island?"

I wiggled my eyebrows.

"I miss Roy, too. Sometimes, and this is a secret between us, I swear, I see him on the island. In the shadow of the trees, just beyond my reach. He likes Joe." Penny stopped, then shared, "Once, we were picnicking on the island with Mike and Donna. Everything went wrong. Joe's only comment was *Roy is upset about something.* It was a joke, but it wasn't. Your brother had a way about him. He did. Thank heavens Joe came along, or I might still be pining. I loved to watch Roy move like you did Finn."

"Six months, Pen. Finn was hospitalized for six months. He had to learn how to walk again."

Penny's blue eyes teared up. I pulled Penny into my arms for a hug, feeling a shift away from Roy toward something new.

"How about a sleepover, Boo. Come on, you know

you want to!" Penny laughed. "We can Ouija it up!"

"Grab a few things for the night. We'll double up in the old bed, the mattress is as horrible as ever, but we will just talk the night away. You can help me decide how best to throw the dance party, redo the cabin, I don't know, but when have we ever been at a loss for words?"

Penny hurried down the hall, returning with a tote bag of necessities, a cosmetic bag, something to sleep in, and something to wear the next day. She filled a second bag with noshes though I told her I had plenty. She waved me away from the counter and added a bag of oatmeal chocolate chip cookies from Lou's Bakery meant for her kids.

We ran to my boat. The gusting wind and flights of clouds dusting the moon added mystery to our spur of the moment party. A dark and stormy night, huddled in the cabin, just being besties. We grinned happily as the boat bounced across the open water.

Penny helped me dock. With an eye at the roiling sky, we lashed the boat to the pier and unloaded. Solar lights lit our way to the cabin. I lit the light strings around Roy's Deck, then double-checked the gas level in the generator and topped it off, already wishing for the missing five gallons of gas.

Thunder rumbled, three miles away by my count. The wind thrashed the trees, but it wasn't a blow. A bolt of lightning jigged across the sky. Thunder. Getting closer. We carried the tote bags into the cabin.

I donned a waterproof poncho in case of rain and returned to the dock, leaving Penny humming as she happily searched for bowls and plates. I moved the boat, parallel parking it next to the jetty anchored to the rocks, and chained it fore and aft. The last thing we needed was the boat to float free or be swamped.

I checked the padlock on the propane and gas cage. The memory of Tim impaled, Finn packing the wound fore and back, raising Tim's shoulders to keep pressure off the rod embedded through his chest overcame me. I shut my eyes, the vision so real I willed it away. In a flash, in the dark, I remembered Dad's words. Brad and Roy. A boat motoring up the lake. Our boat adrift.

As the storm picked up steam, I joined Roy at his marker on the promontory. He sat next to me on the bench, blocking the wind. When I reached for him, my hand grazed cement. A moment later, something warm glissaded down my fingers. I told him then that he should have cut Dad some slack, that whoever took those pictures had helped our family evolve. Mom was happy, Dad was happy, and I was getting there. I asked him to cough up his secrets.

Lightning struck the water and lit the area. The rain came, squalls of it. I kneeled and dug out Roy's cookie tin, paddling the dirt behind me as I dug out all that remained of my adored brother.

Cookie tin tucked under my arm, I swished, swatted, and waded my way up the trail to the cabin. The generator was humming. The lights on the deck swayed in the wind. Branches whacked against the roof and slapped the outhouse door. I latched the door on my way to the cabin. Once, in the dry kitchen, I placed the tin on the table.

The poncho dripped on the faded, separating linoleum tile squares with flowers at each corner. A feast was spread across the front room table, plates of pickles, olives, chips, dip, carrot, and celery sticks, and more. Penny sliced a baguette of French bread at the kitchen table, placing the slices in a basket. I walked through to open the front door and let the storm-driven breeze flow in then out through the kitchen for cross ventilation. Outside, the canopy of the trees swirled, slapping and creaking until it seemed they might shear.

I cleared a spot on the front room table for Roy's box. A carrot in one hand, Penny kissed two fingers on the other and pressed them to the cookie tin.

"Roy and I almost hooked up."

"Almost?"

"We were always interrupted. You, because you were jealous, Meg, even Brad. Sometimes I still wonder what our life would have been like. If Roy would have stayed in Canada or if we would have moved to the US. I do know we would have summered here, our kids and yours and Mike's rousting around together."

It would have been, perhaps, as it should have been. The wind roared in, blowing a strand of lights off their hook on Roy's Deck. They bobbed, flashing off and on. I read the Morse code of it. Not because it was a signal, but because it was ingrained in me. CL. CL. CL. CL. Station Closing.

"Sorry, the lights," I said, returning my attention to Penny.

"I can't decide if they are signaling station closing or signaling an all stations call."

"You, too."

"It's odd, is all."

I sighed. "I am sorry I was a pest. Roy and I hung out together nine months of the year. He protected me at school, tutored me, took me sledding with him. The minute we hit Lower Bay, though, I was on my own."

"Not true, anyone could see how much Roy cared for you. But I do know Roy went a little crazy up here. You know it, too. He took some foolish risks, Boo. Roy scared Mike with some of his antics. Mike's no pansy. And, he is not slow, either."

I dipped a chip. "Silvie Dixon spread that rumor, correct?"

Penny sipped a soda, staring into the howling night, as the lights on the deck continued to flash. The wind tore at the roof, like a giant can opener peeling back the cabin's tin roof. Lightning lit the surface of the lake. A boat appeared then disappeared into the deep after-flash dark. What kind of fool boats on a night like this?

Penny nodded. "Poor Mike. He was forced into the vocational track at school. We rode the bus together. I walked into the school building, he went out back to the garage that housed the auto shop, welding, and plumbing courses. Girls discounted him because of the stigma. Everyone on Lower Bay knew, but Roy overlooked it. They invented things together, Mike taught Roy to weld, Roy taught Mike to dance. They were great friends."

A branch screeched across the roof as the rain renewed. By now, whoever was in the boat had made land. I reached for Penny's near hand. She took mine. Then I picked up Roy's tin. I said a little prayer to Roy as I pried the lid and dumped the contents on the table.

A whistle. A dirt-encrusted Hot Wheels car. A folded letter. A red and white float with his favorite plastic worm hooked in the swivel. A small bag of hair taken from his comb, my offering. Add to those things the photo, the SD card, and my grandfather's gold watch. Bits of nothing. Roy, with his blue-blue eyes and hangy-down hair, was bric-a-brac.

"It's like a séance, isn't it?" Penny asked. "Roy communicating from the dead."

"Not, really. Mom, Dad, and I filled the tin. And your brother." I showed Penny the watch. I added the photo of Finn and Roy to the pile and ejected the SD card from my computer. "The photo was added later, too. It's one of the last pictures on the SD card."

"Roy loved that camera. A Nikon with a brown leather case, right? Finn's flair for photography annoyed Roy to no end. It was his thing until Finn showed up. When Finn's dad started pedaling Finn's pictures in town, Roy got hot about it. It was kind of cute how jealous he was. Roy sold a few of his pictures, too." Penny glanced at the photo over the couch.

"It's Finn's," I said.

"Oops. I bet your mother thought it was Roy's. I went with Roy on one of his loon photography sessions. The moon was silvery, reflected by the lake waters. It was all very romantic, except for the part where Roy avoided any physical contact with me. He brushed my elbow once then apologized. The next day, I whined to Mom that I had done everything but throw myself across his lap. The day after that, Roy kissed me on the cheek. I was so confused."

"I bet you didn't wash that cheek for a week, like that time, Finn touched you on Sturdevant Beach."

Penny's eyes caught mine. "That day, that day was the beginning, Boo. At least, I always thought so. Up until then, everything was like always, no animosity, no scary doings, same old same. Remember?"

I stared at Pen. Dred, Mary, Lou, Mike, Tim, and my parents had handed me a mirror cracked long ago. Each of their slivers held only a fragment of the reflection. I shook my head, unable to conjure anything from my shaft of the broken mirror. Penny gave a lopsided smile.

"Mike and you were starting to hang out. It was all so tentative. When Sturdevant ran his eyes over your tasty little frame," Penny kidded, "Mike noticed, and Meg noticed Mike noticing. Roy and Brad noticed, too. Everyone reacted differently. For instance, Mike upped his game with you. Meg followed Roy until he paid attention to her even though he was semi-dating me. Brad and Roy started bullying Finn. And the summer continued like a clock being wound tighter and tighter until the spring broke."

I considered her comments as I concentrated on Roy's treasures, not much for seventeen years of life. A stolen watch, an SD chip, and a love or possibly loss letter from his mother. A photograph of a confrontation. A hank of hair from his sister in hopes he could be reproduced. My only thought as I stuffed strands of hair from his brush in that plastic bag and slipped it in the cookie tin. Had Dad thought the same when he included the leather bag containing a quarter-cup of Roy's ashes?

Penny grabbed the letter and slit the sealing tape before I could stop her. She read the note, then gazing out the window, she slapped it unconsciously on the table.

"Pen?" It miffed me more than a little that she opened the letter.

Penny saw my hurt. "Sorry, Boo, I recognized Meg's writing. I wonder how the letter got into the tin?" She slid the note across to me. I read it—a four-couplet poem about a kiss on the promontory.

"The meter is off," I commented, taken aback by the longing in the few hand-printed stanzas. "This never happened, Pen. It's pure fantasy. Poor Meg." I folded the note.

Penny glanced out the window, bobbling her head. "Poor Roy."

"What does that mean?"

"Well, he's dead. Maybe Meg should have given Roy the letter while he was breathing. If she had, Roy might still be alive. For instance, instead of swimming the lake that night, he might have been with Meg in a boat. That's all."

"Using that reasoning, if I hadn't responded to Finn as he appraised me on the beach that day, his father and Roy would be alive?"

"Maybe. And I would be married to Roy, you to Mike and Meg, I guess, would be left with Brad."

I huffed as I considered her words. We sat side by side at the table, Penny munching a cookie, me swilling beer, lost in our own thoughts.

"Meg," we both said.

"What goes up the chimney..." Penny began, then tipped her cookie toward the front window. The porch boards creaked. Penny and I exchanged a glance, fully aware we were visible through the wavy glass of the eight-paned front windows.

The screen door squeaked open. Meg followed. She removed a wet windbreaker, tossing it back out the door onto the porch boards.

"What a night! Brad's out, and his kids are overnighting at Dred's. So, I went to Penny's hoping for some company. No one was home. I was leaving when I saw the lights on Roy's Deck flashing. I thought what fun. I hope you don't mind me joining you?"

Penny smiled graciously, waving the cookie she held over the food, inviting Meg to partake. "We are checking out the contents of Roy's cookie tin. Not very revealing. By the way, how's Tim? I thought you planned to drive to Ottawa to spend the night with him.”

“Too stormy. I called the hospital, they told me Tim was resting in preparation for tomorrow. I asked to speak to him, they let me. He begged me not to come in this weather.”

“Join us then,” I responded. Greg had made Tim’s condition clear to me. Unless Tim O’Dell had super-powers, it was unlikely he begged or even spoke to Meg. “We found this note from you to Roy in the tin.”

“Your mother put it in for me. It was kind of her.” Meg said, munching on a cookie.

“I read it,” I said softly.

A branch slammed onto Roy’s Deck, taking the still blinking lights down with it. Penny cocked her head, reading the changed message as I had. We laughed as the lights flashed out *B-o-o*. When Meg glanced out the window, the lights blinked off and on, one last time. We cocked our heads. S-O-S? Maybe not.

“Crazy,” Meg said, opening the refrigerator door with a shake of her head. “The poem must sound so juvenile now. It is just—well, Roy and I met all the time, usually on the promontory. We had a bit of a thing going. We were super secretive about it. It made it hard for me to say my good-byes to him.”

“Where’s Brad?” Penny asked, as though minutes ago, she hadn’t revealed her own relationship with my brother.

“Friday night in Canada? Who knows! This is going to be so much fun. Just us girls, like old times. The storm just makes it better!” Meg shut the refrigerator door, a quart of milk in her left hand. I went into the kitchen and brought her a glass. “I hope you don’t mind, Boo. I raised the dock and locked it in place. The waves were pounding it."

Milk in hand, Meg settled into my preferred chair at the table and picked through the cookies. Penny paced the room. I leaned in the kitchen doorframe.

"Well," Meg said, "Besides the tin, and the random Morse Code being tossed out by the lights, which I admit is eerie. Station Closing. Boo. SOS. Like a séance. What were you guys up to when I came knock, knock, knocking on the front room door?"

Smiling at her joke, I scooped Roy's gifts into the tin and jammed the lid down. Meg had been on the island long enough for the lights to blink out all of the messages before they went dark.

"Everything is in the tin, plus some. Your letter, the photo, and my grandfather's gold watch, none of which the family contributed. It's like Roy's tin was a lost and found box in Gare Centrale de Montréal."

With a laugh, Meg threw her hands out, palms up. The polish on her fingernails was chipped. Her carefully coifed hair was fly-away as a result of bouncing across the water. I sat next to Meg, who took my right hand in her icy left. Boating at night can do that.

"Like I said, your mother put the letter in for me, I haven't any idea how the other items got in the tin, but it does seem odd."

"Especially the photo of Sturdevant pushing Roy. It feels like an indictment of Sturdevant. Almost as though someone was trying to leave an eternal, *I told you so.*"

The next time I called my mother, I needed to ask her if she had put the letter in the tin for Meg. It would have been years ago, maybe shortly after Roy's death. Not that it mattered. Mike and possibly Meg had opened the tin. Mike swore Brad took the SD card from him. If so, Meg could have had access to it and switched the SD cards when she deposited the letter if she had.

"Hmm, the eternal I told you so!" Meg scoffed. "Finn Sturdevant killed your brother, Boo. I think the photo's appropriate, don't you? What if something happened to your whole family before the tin was opened?"

"I see your point. I guess. Damnation by photo."

Penny pursed and scrunched her lips; something had piqued her curiosity, she asked, "If you sold the land, Boo, would you take the tin with you?"

"I'm not selling the island, Pen. I admit Mike and Tim's accidents and a few other incidents have made me wonder if I should sell. But Roy is still here, he needs me, and I believe he protects me. Besides, he sends photos of his exploits from time to time. I would miss those." I reached for the Star Wars lunchbox.

"Oh, rubbish," Meg poo-pooed with a wave of her chipped fingernails. "Roy's not here, he's not in the box, he never made it off the dock. He left the island long ago. Roy told me one night when we were out taking photos of the loons that your father forced him to come that summer. He said he was ready to leave Booth Island until after college."

I doubted that Roy would have told Meg something so personal, but then he was furious with Dad.

Penny threw her head, her eyes filled with doubt. "I never knew you two were such an item."

"Oh, we were. I told you we kept it a big secret. It is the very reason I am so sure that Roy has vacated the promontory. Frankly, it was the last place he wanted to be and certainly not forever." Her choice of words rankled me.

"You're wrong, Meg. Despite anything Roy told you that night, he loved it here. Roy wants to stay. All I need is a strip of land carved out of Sturdevant Peninsula and the beach, and I am set. Besides, I am not sure Finn is interested in selling it anymore."

Penny choked on her soda.

"He has a contract with the realtor, so I doubt he will change his mind. I really do. Plus, there is that mess in Detroit. It's all over the national news now," Meg noted.

"What mess?" Penny asked.

"His juvenile records were released," I said, "The newspaper had a heyday. His military records, too. He's being crucified in the media."

Meg snorted and changed the subject, "Enough. Your favorite memory!"

Penny sat in the chair farthest from Meg. The air cleared as though the worst was over, not outside, but in. "The time we took out the canoe and got so bloody lost Boo's Dad had to come looking for us," Penny laughed.

The fun of that day flooded me. Starting early, we paddled well up into Upper Bay, took a tributary, paddled up it, took another. With each turn, we thought we could portage the canoe back to Upper Bay and paddle home. Not so. Dad found us by driving around all the lakes connected to Upper and Lower Bay, stopping when he noticed three girls waving with a canoe beached between them.

We were hot, sweaty, mosquito-bitten, dehydrated bundles when he loaded the canoe on the roof rack. Dad thought to bring water, we swilled it. Penny even dumped a bottle over her sweaty red hair. Meg drank and stared out the window.

Dad prattled on about how we could have been killed and never found while Pen and I laughed our butts off at the adventure. Penny's mom, Mary, met Dad's car the minute we turned up Gagne Lane. Dad delivered Meg to the farmhouse door. Mr. Dixon opened the door for Meg, and she stepped into the house.

Dad patted the front passenger seat even though the drive to the dock was short. I scurried up from the back. He threw his right arm around me and pulled me close, kissing the top of my head. I snuggled into his sweaty armpit.

"I had double chores for a week. But it was fun, we were so lost," Meg said, "If we'd had a cell phone, we could have called one of the boys to come and rescue us. That would have made it even better. Hey, how about the day on Sturdevant Beach? You know the one? You two were so jealous when Sturdevant touched me the way he did."

Penny's eyes narrowed, her baby blues barely showing. The look said everything, up to and including I told you so.

"I remember Sturdevant loping along the beach. Remember how we giggled? We knew our brothers so well. Sturdevant wasn't rough or scratchy or even boyish," I said, trying to explain what Finn had brought to Lower Bay.

Penny approved, laughing, "I do. He even had an infant five o'clock shadow."

"You both sound like you were smitten." Meg smiled, her eyes on mine. "And you, Boo, you're on his rounds."

"He saved Tim, Meg. You do know that? You should be thankful."

"Are you suggesting that we did ourselves a favor by sending him to the Marines instead of prison for life?"

Penny cocked her head. "He was nearly killed by an IED blast, Meg. That is how he knew how to help Tim. It wasn't a free ride."

Meg stared at Penny over her milk glass, then sighed, "Finally, real Sturdevant justice."

A bolt of lightning shattered the still, followed by a gust of cold wind that rocked the cabin on its foundation and chilled the room.

"Wow," Penny said, all chipper, "I just brought knit shorts and a T-shirt for sleeping. Should we light the wood-burning stove?"

"Feel that," Meg said, "Warm again."

"How about a game or two of cards?" I asked.

"How about poker?" Meg chuckled.

"How about a nice friendly game of Crazy Eights, instead?"

I lifted a deck of cards from the bookshelf, shuffled then dealt five cards to each of us.

We sorted our cards accompanied by the deafening drumroll of rain on the tin roof. Penny played the first card of the game, a club, face-up next to the draw pile. Meg added the three of clubs, I played the ten of clubs. Penny drew two cards then played.

During Meg's turn, Penny fabricated, "Boo and I tried to remember if you were at Dixon Landing the night Roy died. You left the dance after the Karaoke contest. I told Boo that you met us, but she's not sure."

"Poor Boo, it's amazing she remembers anything about that night. I was at Dixon Landing when you arrived," Meg said, "All the commotion. Oh, my goodness. I was groaning in my bed, a hot pad for company when the noise started. I dressed and ran down to the dock. Boo's dad had just tied up their boat. Mike's head was bloody, and Brad looked scared. I wondered where Roy was until your father lifted his limp body out of the boat. I thought he was unconscious. Except, no one seemed to be hurrying. Boo's dad took Roy to Westport. Dred pulled up, you two tumbled out of the car. I ran over to you. We held hands."

Penny squinted at me. Had we held hands? Penny ticked her head no. I might have, though--I might have held Meg's hand.

"I *was* there," Meg emphasized. "Unlike Sturdevant, who swam off." She blinked and bobbled her head. Glancing out the window to Roy's Deck, Meg added, "This would make such a great park."

Dixon Park. Dixon Park was printed across the top of the plans on Alice's desk. The drawing encompassed the eighteen acres of the Sturdevant Peninsula *and* Booth Island. Upside down, what I assumed was the stump bog at Sturdevant Peninsula was Beaver Course connecting Booth Island either by a bridge or a short causeway to the Peninsula. Filling in Beaver Course would be easy. Heck, the island beaver had almost managed it more than once.

"I'm not selling, Meg. So, no, park. According to Alice Cornish, Sturdevant's crumbling warehouse will have to come down and might be a hazmat site. The cleanup will be costly."

Meg took three cards from the draw pile before she could play. "I don't know why Sturdevant is here. The sale could have been managed via phone. Maybe one last trip down murder lane."

"Finn didn't murder anyone." I played the five of

clubs, Penny the five of diamonds. Meg took a card and played it. The eight of clubs. She requested spades.

"Finn?" Meg glanced at me over her card hand. "Really, I swear the charges state that Sturdevant left your brother to drown. No different than Lyle Sturdevant, who cheated my family out of our land. For heaven's sake, Boo, Sturdevant's father hooked up with your mother, right there."

Meg pointed in the general direction of Sturdevant Peninsula. Penny's eyebrows shot up. She hadn't known.

"For all I know, Don Sturdevant hooked up with my mother, too. No doubt, Lou and Mary tattled to you that my mother was hooking up with someone on the Peninsula. It's okay. All of Lower Bay knows."

"According to Lou, your mother was seeing an Alberta cowboy." I played the last card in my hand and my only spade. "Don Sturdevant didn't know your mother existed."

Penny's eyes went so round I thought her eyeballs might pop out. She lowered them, shuffling the cards to hide her surprise.

"That's what you know!" Meg screamed, throwing her cards at Penny. Penny scooped them up and added them to the shuffle. "And you!" she pointed at me so there would be no mistake. "You cheat."

Penny dealt five cards. Meg stared at me. I sorted my cards by number rather than by suit, I always had. My mother taught me how. Now, it felt like some tainted card trick handed down from Lyle Sturdevant.

"I don't cheat. And Don Sturdevant wasn't your mother's lover," I answered. "It must have been horrible standing guard over your mother's body until the rest of the search party found you. I can't imagine."

"You can't imagine! You moon over your brother's cement marker like he was something other than a teen with a libido."

It wasn't the accusation, or the tone of her voice, or the implied knowledge, that stopped me; it was that she had been watching me. I flashed on the shadows and scurried movements at the marker.

"Still, you were so young," I countered.

Meg huffed. "My mother had melted on the rocks, like a rag doll. There was blood all over her face. I still wonder why she was running in those rocks." Meg shrugged. "I tried to put her right."

"Did she know you were with her?" Penny asked.

Meg ticked her head. "Maybe for a moment. I thought she looked at me. It was like she had a question she wanted to ask."

"You didn't see her lover?" I countered.

"Lover, s-lover. They fornicated. That's all. In and out. Out and in. Huffing and puffing."

Meg must have shadowed them, peering through windows and trees, watching. She was a child of eight.

"Well, that is the long past," Meg laughed, "More current, the Sturdevants virtually left their land untended off and on for three-quarters of a century. Tim's just the latest in a series of groundskeepers. The property has been deserted for so long, it is a public hazard. The Township can confiscate it, as is, or receive it should Finn Sturdevant die without an heir. Either way, it's ours."

"Or you could buy it," Penny said, playing a card.

Meg played, sorted her cards, and answered, "Don't be silly, neither the Dixons nor the Township has that kind of money."

"Don't get your hopes up because Finn Sturdevant

doesn't plan on dying anytime soon." I snapped. With Finn in the clinic surrounded by knives, needles, and potentially lethal drugs, Meg's words worried me.

"Then he should just gift it to the Township. Come on, let's have fun. What say we make boy talk off-limits and let our hair down."

Penny shifted in her seat and played her next card. Meg won the next few games. It took Penny and I combined to make it happen. While playing, we snacked, drank, remembered, and gossiped until Penny yawned, which was surprising considering the amount of soda she had downed. I made up the couch for Meg. She stood next to it, watching as Penny snuck off, changed, and climbed into the bed. I stayed with Meg.

"You and Sturdevant, what's that?" Meg pried.

I shrugged. "It's a bit disconcerting how easily people come and go off this island." And how easy it would be for someone to photograph him...us.

"Word is that you brought him to the clinic. They say he's a nut case. They had to sedate him. May as well give him a gun and let him shoot his brains out. He'll do it sooner or later."

"Someone sent Sturdevant's juvenile records to the *Detroit Free Press*. He came up here, hoping to find a way to put this all behind him. It seems coincidental that Brad is here, too."

"Sturdevant wasn't supposed to survive the Marines. Everyone wanted him gone for good. Oh, Boo, he changed everything. Nothing was ever the same. Damn Sturdevants, damn them."

I stared out the picture window, listening to the wind howl and the rain clatter on the tin roof, feeling Finn's arms around me. No boats had stirred since Meg tied up at Booth Island. As we jousted and played cards, the pounding waves fought to erode this water-bound hill of granite and finish the job the glaciers had started.

With nothing more to say, I squeezed Meg's hand. She acknowledged it with a smile. I wandered into the kitchen to close up for the night. Meg laid on the couch, covering up with the blanket that had warmed Finn only the night before.

XXXV

I LEANED OUT THE kitchen door to flip off the generator, which had burned through most of a tank of gasoline. By the light of the propane sconce in the kitchen, I checked that the three burners on the range and the oven dials were off, then turned the propane line to the stove off for good measure. Satisfied, I turned off the remaining light in the kitchen.

As the light hissed and faded, I noticed an empty peg next to Roy's Steeler's hat. I sighed. The keys for my car and the dock were in my purse on a bar chair in Penny's great room. Though I was thankful that Meg raised the floating dock from the storm's heaving waters, her boat was now the only way off the island.

I handed Meg a flashlight for midnight runs, then turned off the propane light in the front room. Meg thanked me. I checked Roy's Deck before locking the front door. After dimming the light in the bedroom, I scrambled into a pair of old cotton shorts and a T-shirt because the wind off the water had dropped the temperature by ten degrees.

I snuggled in the bed next to Penny. I thought she

was asleep until she rolled over, threw an arm over me, raised up, and whispered. "Why isn't Meg with Tim? I mean, they told you Tim has surgery in the morning. Didn't they? If it were Joe, they'd have to get a wheelbarrow to get me out of his room."

"I think she's been stalking me, Pen, well, keeping a pretty darn close eye on me."

"Or Sturdevant. She really wants that property and the island, too."

I shrugged, whispering, "The key to the dock, the boat, and the locks are in my purse on a chair by your breakfast bar."

"We're screwed if we need to get off Booth Island," Pen said with a hand signal that made me laugh.

"We can still swim for it."

We lay side by side on the old horsehair mattress, staring at the ceiling. The storm raged. Wind-driven water smashed from different angles against three sides of the island, creating an explosive cannonade of booms.

Penny reached for my hand. "It isn't funny, is it?" I shook my head. She sighed, "It's like one of those dodgy horror movies, three women stranded on an island in a storm."

"Try to sleep."

"How exactly?"

"Close your eyes and think of Joe and the kids. We are okay, Pen. We are."

"And what are you going to think about? Mr. Sturdevant sleeping peacefully in a warm bed at the clinic?"

"Meg. I think. She could have snapped the photos of Mike and me and Finn and me. She could have."

Penny changed subjects, "I'm thinking of my kids,

I'm loving Joe and his stupid water phobic waterdog."

I laughed. "Good, good beginning."

I thought of Meg. She followed her mother, watched her make love, then found her dead at Sturdevant Beach. She had seen my mother and Don Sturdevant hooking up.

Meg claimed a relationship with Roy. The photo of Meg in Roy's arms in the office at the Dixon farmhouse sprang to mind. The polka-dot bathing suit Meg wore in the photo was Penny's. The original snapshot of Roy hugging Penny was on Roy's SD card. Someone had carefully inserted Meg's face on Penny's body. It wasn't much of a jump from that to Roy's photo stitched into modern scenes, especially if she had either the SD chip my mother put in Roy's tin or the one stolen from Sturdevant's screen porch.

Different shards from a broken mirror. The squall had passed, the wind slowed. I sighed.

Penny stirred, whispering, "Meg took Mom's necklace, Boo."

I stared at Penny until the memory loaded. The three of us were having an overnight, like this one, only at Gagnes'. Their boathouse had a spare room. We set up cots preparing to make a night of it. Penny's mother, Mary, brought us lots of salty and sweet snacks and sodas. Water lapped beneath the floorboards as we romped and told boy stories.

About ten o'clock, all three of us went for a walk, hoping the guys would turn up, getting ever closer to Sturdevant Beach. Finn was at peninsula point, taking night-time photos of the rippling waters, silhouetted fishermen, and the black and white loons. Penny squealed. Finn pointed the camera our way, not to snap a picture, but to use his telephoto. Seeing us, he waved.

We turned en masse and ran along the shoreline, past O'Dell's, back to the Gagne boathouse. We talked about Finn lit by moonlight for the rest of the sleepover as only besotted, goofy, fifteen-year-old girls can. Penny and I fell asleep holding hands.

After midnight, Penny woke me, whispering that Meg was gone. We assumed Meg had returned to Sturdevant Beach to stare at Finn, as she proclaimed, but she hadn't. We found her crossing the lawn from the main house, stuffing something shiny in her left pocket. We teased her until she admitted she had gone to the house for a flashlight so she could read while we slept.

"If she brought a flashlight back, I never saw it, and Meg never used it," Penny whispered.

Penny's memory jarred loose one of my own. I held Penny's hand as I had that night, remembering. Meg had taken my mother's engagement ring and under almost the same circumstances. Mom took it off to do the dishes at night and put it on each morning after the breakfast dishes were dried. She noticed the ring gone after one of our sleepovers. Penny, Meg, and I searched for it, as did my whole family.

"She took your Mom's ring, too," Penny hissed, her memory substantiating mine. "Then claimed she saw Finn lurking in the shadows. Why?"

"Sturdevant justice? Meg wanted him to like her, he didn't, so she set him up, not once or even twice, but repeatedly."

"What are we going to do?" Penny asked. I squeezed Penny's hand, she squeezed back.

"Hey," Meg called from the front room, "Sounds like you're gabbing. I'm coming in to join you. I'll sleep across the foot of the bed. Remember how we used to do that?"

Meg opened the door and stood in the doorway.

"I do. You didn't fit and took a thrashing from our feet. We could make Penny take the short side."

"No way! I may be short, but I'm wide," Penny laughed.

"We could bring the blankets in from the couch. I could sleep on the floor," I offered.

Meg made a U-turn, returning with the one blanket and a pillow. I dutifully laid them out and crawled into the makeshift sleeping bag, ready for a wretched night on the floor. Penny resumed her side of the horsehair mattress. Meg stretched out beside her.

"Aren't we going to chat?" Meg asked. "You and Penny have always been better at chatting."

If making me feel guilty was her intent, it worked. I reached up and touched her right hand. Thinking of Joe must have worked, small wuffles filled Penny's side of the bed.

"Nothing to chat about?" Meg asked.

"Talking won't help. I just can't sleep. The storm. Poor Tim. I'm going out to the promontory to visit Roy. He always comforts me."

"Want company," Meg asked.

I nodded, yes, surprised after Meg's insistence that Roy was gone from the island. I unlatched the screen door in the kitchen and headed down the path to Roy's marker in my sleepwear, old shorts, and a T-shirt. Meg followed similarly dressed.

The night animals were still. Not a whisper of their usual cacophony clicked, rubbed, or called above the wind. Clouds scudded across the moon, to the west, thunder rumbled, and lightning crackled from cloud to cloud, signaling more rain to come.

Checking the shadows for any interlopers, I bounced off a tree. Meg laughed then selected a long, thick branch to use as a walking stick. She handed it to me. A few steps later, she found a similar limb for herself.

Soft footsteps rustled to our right through the groundcover. Like rabbits, our ears pricked as something or someone scurried through the brush. I stared down at my fisted right hand.

Several moments later, Meg urged me on with a poke of her stick, whispering, "Raccoon."

The path narrowed. Meg hesitated, giving me the lead, then fell in behind me.

"Quiet, isn't it?" Meg commented, reaching past me with her stick to hold a wet limb out of my way.

"Too," I answered.

"Not for long," Meg mumbled, checking the roiling sky through the canopy of trees. A clap of thunder let loose a ten-pin rumble, jangling my nerves. A branch covered in wet leaves struck me in the back, nearly downing me. I turned, ready to fight. No one was there, just the squalling night and Meg.

I hurried. Meg kept pace. I came to a hard stop on my toes like a deer at the cliff's edge. Roy's marker was rubble, shattered shards of cement even Mike would be unable to mend. Roy's bench was knocked over, its seat broken. Hate had been here.

Meg hated me because Mike kissed me, Finn watched me, Roy rejected her, and my Dad loved me. The thought stunned me, but I knew it was the truth. Ensnared in the gill net wrapping Lower Bay in hate, my mother did her best to protect me until she could escape it, leaving me to struggle free on my own.

I turned to Meg.

"No reason to keep Booth Island now, is there?" she said, softly, "Roy's almighty cookie tin with all its secrets is empty. The rest is just rubble, freeing Roy from your obsession with his death. You two were...sickening. So exclusive!"

"Not intentionally. This is the first I knew about you and Roy. I would never hurt you or Penny. I never have."

"But you did. You were all the boys ever wanted!" Meg screamed. "And pudgy little Penny, what a nothing! I hate them, the Gagne with all their money."

"Your family could have had as much."

"Five-percent of one hundred percent? Hardly. Your rumrunning relatives came up here, stole our land, and thought parties were a fair exchange. They made a fortune breaking the law, without regard for whose money they took. Booth Island is mine, all mine, we owned all this until George Booth swaggered in and made a deal with the Lapps who had no right to sell it. Lyle Sturdevant witnessed the signing, then swindled my family out of eighteen acres. The Peninsula is mine, or I take Sturdevant Distillers in payment."

Lightning bounced off the water, illuminating the promontory. Meg, her eyes on me, her hair whipping in the wind, tapped her chosen branch against her leg.

"Roy's standing behind you now, Meg," I said, hoping she would bite. Her eyes never left mine.

"Stupid Booth bitch," she snarled, "Have to have everything, don't you? Everything, including your period, had to have it first, didn't you?"

I scoffed, seeing the vile words written in the pages of the visitor's notebook.

Meg swung.

The branch hit my right temple. I pitched forward

into the refuse of Roy's gravesite. Shards of cement dug into my stomach, another tore into my leg. Blood trickled toward my open mouth. I lay still, waiting for the killing blow. Lightning bounced off the lake, lighting up the planes of Meg's face.

I reached for a jagged chunk of Roy's marker. Meg slammed her walking stick two-handed across my shoulders. Air rushed out of my lungs. Roy's cement dug into my collarbone and chest.

My last thoughts were of Mike holding my hand, Tim smiling at me, and Finn leaning in the doorframe to the kitchen, the refrigerator humming behind him, his eyes a soft velvet brown. I wanted to climb in them...

XXXVI

RAIN WOKE ME.

I opened my left eye, the right one wouldn't obey my command. The night sky flickered first yellow then orange. I rolled to my left side, facing the cabin. Flames shot ten, twenty feet into the night. The stately hickory trees ringing the bedroom cringed away, then back in the onrushing wind.

"Penny!" I meant to scream; instead, a hoarse whisper emerged.

"Penny can't hear you," Meg said, a shadow in the swaying trees. "Not anymore. What a waste, remodeling her house, spending the Gagnes' bribe. Justice served."

I wrapped my left hand around the chunk of cement I still held, working the piece under me, my movements shadowed by the quivering fire. A rush of wind caused Meg to look up as a branch slammed into her back. "Roy!" I croaked

"Really? Give it a rest, Treader." Meg brandished a new branch, thick as her arm, shattered at the end into deadly slivers. Hickory, the hardest of the hardwoods.

I watched the branch in Meg's left hand. I should have watched her eyes; I could have used the lead time. The stick connected with my right shoulder, driving me back to the ground. Clinging to the fist-sized rock in my hand, I rolled. Her next blow landed in the rubble.

I scrambled awkwardly to my feet, my ears ringing, random flashes of light spangling my vision. I shook my head.

Meg swung, knocking the wind from my lungs and buckling my legs. My left knee hit the ground. A shaft of pain coursed up my already bleeding thigh.

At the crest of the island, the seasoned timber of the cabin crackled, embers swirled into flames. A sinuous, flowing shadow whirled across the inferno's stage, mesmerizing me. Meg's next blow drove me face-first into the dirt.

The stench of burned horsehair rippled on the crazed night air. Penny had died for me, consumed in bed. The sharp cement chunk, Roy's gift to me, dug into my stomach.

Meg knelt, fingering stray hair from my cheek. Leaning down, she placed a hand on the back of my head and ground my face into the dirt. Rocking, rocking, smothering me. I inched my left hand back until it was even with my right, then pushed up with all the might left me. Enough to throw Meg off her haunches and onto her side.

My turn. I struck.

Meg's eyes flashed a moment of recognition, no, realization. She hit the ground with a slack thud. I slammed her head to the ground, my hands around her throat. Roy swayed with the wind, susurrating, whispering, his wind-driven hands on my shoulders. No, no, no.

"For Penny then," I begged, my hands tightening around Meg's throat. Fingers dark with soil, leaves dancing from the tips, soothed my back, relaxed my cramped fingers. I fell back on my haunches, searching for breath, the swirling wind enfolding me, winding around my shoulder.

Leaving me, the wind roared over the crest of the island, high into the trees. I clambered to my feet, my hands on my knees, gathering the strength to drag Meg to a sturdy birch tree. I sat her up and tied her hands behind the tree with the torn hem of my shirt. I used a bowline—every boater's best knot. I checked for a pulse and found one.

When Meg roused, I said, "Remember this. You're alive because of Roy. Remember that for the rest of your life."

Meg laughed. Somehow, I found the discipline to remove my hands, one from her nose and mouth, the other from her throat. A hand closed on my shoulder. I touched it. Felt it, clasped it.

"Roy?" Meg croaked. I gasped at the longing in her voice.

I gained my feet and turned for my brother. A swirl of smoke led me uphill. I ran for the engulfed bedroom, prepared to throw myself into the flames to save my dear friend. An arm grabbed me around the waist, depositing me away from the fire.

A dark head signaled me toward the outhouse. Someone lay there in a crumpled heap--Penny by the shiny light hair. She was asleep, breathing softly. I smelled her breath, remembering Meg handing Penny soda after soda until she yawned.

I trotted back uphill to the single dark figure fighting the flames. Stomping, swatting, holding them at bay. I twisted the outdoor spigot. The generator was off. Without it, there was no pump, no pressure, and no water. I coiled the hose, looped it over my shoulder, dropping the sprayer head to the ground as I passed the bedroom and ran to the raised 125-gallon water tanks.

I unscrewed the stopper in the tank closest to the cabin. Water poured out and ran in a torrent to the bedroom wall fanning out at the base, running down the left side. The rest slopped down the back wall to the kitchen stairs, pooling at the cement blocks and seeping into the ground. All along the fire line, the flames guttered and slowed. Finn smothered them with whatever was available. I screwed the hose into a tap on the third tank.

Finn picked up the sprayer before I could reach it. Water trickled then surged out, relying on gravity for delivery. A bolt of lightning shot across the sky. The rain came, pummeling us. Wet to the skin, we fought the flames into submission with the help of the drenching squall.

As soon as Finn had the fire under control, I ran to the Aldis Lamp and flashed an SOS. I prayed that Brad Dixon was in the farmhouse and wasn't the shadow that passed at Roy's marker. I flashed SOS again, hoping brother and sister weren't driven by the same rage, that Brad would help. On the third SOS, Brad rapped out: *help coming.*

I returned to the cabin. Finn, smudged head to foot in soot, kept watch with the sprayer head. The bandage on his left hand was dangling and singed. I lifted his hand into mine and turned it palm up. The glue holding the initial wound closed was laced with red-hot blisters. I wet a kitchen towel under the hose, then wrapped his injured palm.

Side-by-side, we surveyed the remains of the Booth cabin. The aged hickory half-logs of the shared wall were blackened but standing. The back corner of the bedroom was ashes. Nothing of real value had been lost, old clothes, pillows, things stored for summer, and the horsehair mattress trekked to the island by the great-greats. Finn shot a stream of water as an ember gusted to life.

"How did you get to the island?" I asked.

"I'll show you in the morning." He leaned down and kissed the top of my head. "Meg?"

I nodded, then bucked my head toward the promontory. He gave a snort I took as approval. I snuggled under Finn's right shoulder until he draped his arm over me. "Thank you, thank you for saving Penny. But how did you know?"

"I got nervous when the OPP dropped by to tell me that the request for my juvenile records had come from the Township Council. Then, when Greg O'Dell checked on me, he mentioned that Meg hadn't followed Tim to Ottawa. The minute Greg was out the door, I dressed, snuck out the back door, and stole Greg's car. I saw him park it. I hope he doesn't file charges."

Finn gave me a reassuring squeeze. "I drove straight to Penny's. Your boat was gone. I knocked on the door hoping for Joe. When no one answered, I used an old ATV track through Gagnes' property to the peninsula and swam from the beach. You look a bit worse for wear," he said, sliding the back of his bandaged hand over my bloody temple as he sprayed down an ember with the right.

I shied away from the pain.

My father's Bermuda shorts and madras shirt would never be clean, soot was ground into the fabric, small holes had burned through in places. Finn's loafers were gone, his bare feet covered in the slime of wet ash.

"Penny!" he said, turning for the outhouse.

He managed the still unconscious Penny onto his shoulders in a fireman's carry and slogged through the rain to the kitchen door. I opened it, he entered, continuing into the front room. It was dry, little else. He lowered Penny onto the couch.

I covered her with the sheet blanket.

Finn took me into his arms, his hands crossed at the wrists, not touching me or his own palms. I lay my head against his chest.

The Word of the Day

xxxvii

BRAD WAS TELEPHONING THE fire department, the OPP, and Joe Withers as I flashed the SOS. The OPP arrived in force within an hour. Joe and Brad powered in on the pontoon boat fifteen minutes later.

The OPP found Meg where I left her, alive, cold, wet, and tied to a tree. Her eyes were bleak, her lips chapped from babbling sweet nothings to Roy's smashed grave marker. When I heard, I thought of Tim, who had loved her, cared for her, knowing she was damaged. He had supported her to health. I destroyed that and nearly Tim.

The summer begun twelve years ago had finally ended. Don Sturdevant brought Finn to meet Roy and me that summer. That gesture was the catalyst for all that followed. Nothing had changed. Roy was still dead. Finn's father, Don, as well. My parents were still divorced, though it was my mother who betrayed my dad.

Now, Brad helped Meg to her feet and into a red windbreaker. The OPP cuffed her then let Brad accompany her back to the station. Meg shoved Brad away with a hip when he attempted to walk with her. When he offered an arm to steady her down the stairs, she spat into his face.

Brad wiped the spittle from his nose, held his arms out palms up, and grinned as years washed off his face. It was finally over for him, as well.

As Joe walked us to the smoldering cabin, he repeatedly apologized to Finn for not being home to protect Penny and me. Finn hung an arm over Joe's shoulders and whispered something meant only for Joe.

Penny awakened on the horsehair couch to find Joe seated at the kitchen table. She sniffed the sofa. The whole cabin smelled like wet, singed horsehair

By the time Penny attempted to sit up, Joe had her in his arms. When she tried to stand, he wrapped her in a plaid flannel-lined canvas barn coat then carried her to the pontoon boat. He climbed in next to her, lowered her head to his shoulder, then rested an arm at her waist. As Joe gunned the motor, he signaled a victory sign to Finn.

Finn grinned. I think. His whiskers were wet, ash-covered, and smelled of smoke. "Joe promised his eternal fealty. Anything. He said anything. I'll think of something suitably appropriate to get him off the hook. I like that man, Boo."

"The best for my best friend. Penny worried Meg would come for me, Finn. That's why she was on the beach that night with Joe's dog and why she proposed the sleepover. To be here, for me. Instead, I almost got her killed."

"Almost only counts in horseshoes and, apparently, curling," Finn commented. "She's alive, she's with Joe, and soon with her kids. You're a bruised, bloody mess. Let me smear you with salve for a change."

We strolled back up the hill to the cabin. Where,

over Finn's protests, I smeared the oily salve all over his left palm and rewrapped it in yet another ripped T-shirt. He checked over my bruises and abrasions, kissing each one. His beard tickled.

I led him to the couch, he laid down, I went to tuck him in, he pulled me down beside him. At first, it felt uncomfortable, spooned so close to a man that I could feel him. I relaxed as his exhaled breath ruffled my hair.

We wakened to the twin smells of smoke and the sulfur of scorched horsehair. Finn and I dressed as best we could, me in a T-shirt and shorts, Finn in a pair of Dad's slightly singed shorts complemented by his naked, nicely muscled, slightly scalded chest, and worn water shoes.

Though I wanted to sit with him at the dining table and share breakfast, the OPP investigating officer had warned us not to turn on the generator or light any fires. Actually, not to touch anything. My boat was still chained, the dock still up, and neither of us was in any condition to row.

I shrugged at my single-cup coffeemaker. A cup of coffee would have been nice. We might still die but of starvation. Instead of searching for grubs to eat as my dad would have advised, Finn threaded my right hand through his left elbow and walked us to the promontory.

We skirted Roy's shattered marker, making a left at a buckeye bush. Finn pushed several branches aside with his right arm then swept his left hand toward a hidden path.

We descended the steep track slowly. Taking care on the slippery, muddy ground. I grabbed a spindly tree to stop myself from sliding feet first down the side of the island. I came up hard on the bush where I had found the bit of cloth the day after Roy's death. It hadn't been an animal who slipped on the slope. It had been Finn rushing to help Roy. I glanced back at Finn. He was working his way carefully down to me, tree by tree, protecting his left hand as best he could. When he reached me, he gave me a hand, I should say wrist, back on to the foot-wide trail.

After scrambling down the island's slope, we emerged at the lake's edge exhausted. A wooden platform constructed from a pallet wedged then tied between two boulders welcomed us. The platform had stood the test of the seasons, unmoved by the winter snows or the summer waves.

It was another one of Roy's creations. If proof were needed, it still bore his initials. He chose its location carefully. Rocks, visible through the diamond clear water, provided a natural staircase onto the platform. Roy wasn't the only one who knew a good spot when he saw it. An animal had dug a den into the hillside above the spring water line.

I helped Finn settle onto the planks without putting pressure on his burned hand. When I sat, pain radiated up my spine and into my head from Meg's blows.

The Lapp Peninsula, where Misty grew up, was directly across the Strait from us. We swung our legs, two hungry, bruised people lost in our own thoughts. Noticing it, we shared a chuckle. The knee I fell on ached. My back was a black and blue mess, and according to Finn, I had a welt across the back of my head. He lost his glasses. I hadn't seen them for days. I touched the scar on his temple then the missing tip of his left ear. He didn't respond. He hadn't seen my hand, and he couldn't feel it on the scar. I sighed.

"Glasses?" I asked. He turned his face toward mine. "Glasses?" I asked again.

He cleared his throat. "Haven't a clue. I have a spare pair in my suitcase." With a puzzled look, he asked, "Why?"

"Quite the hero for a half-deaf, half-blind man. Have you actually seen or heard anything for the last two days?"

That made him laugh.

I clambered to my knees and crawled into the den. Finn grabbed my right ankle attempting to stop me from being eaten.

He was right to try. Anything might have been in the cave, including, yes, a fisher revved to gnaw on me. When my fingers brushed something soft, I squeaked but kept going.

At the far reaches of the den, my hands felt a waterproof bag. I dug behind it, feeling a box within. Even then, I knew what it was. The moment my hands cleared the hole, Finn grabbed his camera. The leather case was nibbled on by a rat, raccoon, or fisher, though, any self-respecting fisher would have eaten the case *and* the camera.

Finn pulled his camera from its case. Dark head down, he worked awkwardly with the one hand bandaged until an SD card emerged from the slot. Satisfied, he slid it back in for safekeeping.

We ascended the steep hill to the buckeye bush, using the trailside trees as a railing. Finn's jaw tightened each time he grabbed, though it was a bit hard to tell under what now qualified as a beard.

Back at the smoldering cabin, we found it overrun with volunteer firemen and one insistent medic. The medic refused to let us go until he tended to us. He was fast, efficient, and not in the least sympathetic. Done, he announced we both needed to go to the clinic posthaste.

Joe returned with my purse. But not before he lowered the dock and unchained the boat. In the kitchen, Joe let us know the OPP expected us at their office in Westport at 2:00 p.m. the next day. I knew then that Joe and Brad had already been interrogated.

"Did Brad finally admit that Roy was alive when he left him to meet my dad and Mike?" I asked.

"Yes. And that Roy's head had been bandaged when they found him but missing when they returned with your dad. When Boothe arrived this week, Brad tried to warn her off with a note and the fire on Roy's Deck."

"So," Joe continued, "I guess Finn's exonerated. No doubt there was mischief the night Roy died, but nothing planned, not with malicious intent." Joe patted Finn's back. "Finally, Penny sends all her good thoughts and begs Boo's understanding because she's still head-over-heels for Finn. I better get back. If I don't, Penny will be out here with a casserole and cookies. She also said once you've finished in town that you are welcome to stay with us."

Finn shook his head. "Between us, we have one cabin standing. We'll go there if we don't head home."

At a loss for words, I said, "I need to rebuild the cabin and finish the dance floor. Tell Penny we've got lots of time. Lifetimes." Penny would say I was jumping the gun, planning what great friends our kids would be.

"I'll let Penny know. She did announce, hands on her hips, as supreme ruler over her Pennydom, that you were expected for dinner. We eat at seven." Joe waved and trotted to join the other volunteers working their way through the debris.

Mid-day, the firemen left assuring us the propane line was operable, and the generator was safe to use. The birds started to chirp, one finch to warble, a crow to caw. The bugs kicked in, buzzing loud enough to wake the dead or keep the living from sleep.

In the post-storm humidity, steam and streamers of smoke curled skyward from the burned-out bedroom. I checked the water tanks, all empty. So, I reset the plugs, flipped the generator on at the kitchen door, turned on the pump, then listened. I heard the distant hum. Water reached the first tank with a gurgle and a splash. By tonight, all 375 gallons of water would be restored, and the water system fully operational.

Finn was waiting for me at the dining table, wearing his glasses, retrieved by one of the police at Joe's request. I studied him. He tipped his head then slid his camera card into the SD slot in my computer. I pulled the pictures up onto the screen. The first photograph wasn't of a loon or a perfect moon glade, it was of me—a fifteen-year-old girl in a madras bikini. Finn grinned a sly little grin. I liked how it lit his face.

"Mom told you I'd be up here, didn't she?" I accused.

He shook his head. "In all honesty, I've never liked your mother." He cocked his head. I liked that he was checking my feelings. I shrugged my okay with his distrust of my mother. We shared it. I would tell him later. "Now, I know why. She took Pop from me."

"My Dad, then?"

"Your father called me out of the blue. If I were to sum it up, I'd say he believed that we needed closure to move on with our lives." He tipped his head, right ear up, and sighed. "I would never have left Roy on that dock even for a moment if Brad and Mike hadn't been with him. I thought he was safe.”

“I know,” I said, scooting into the cusp of his right shoulder. He pulled me closer with his right hand, the left burned, still infected, and rebandaged, safely tucked in another towel sling. He kissed my closest ear. “The *Detroit Free Press?*”

“You asked me why I went to the OPP. I was following up on my juvenile records, reasoning that as a Councilperson, Meg was the only one who had any access to court records. Boo, the newspaper was sent my records only after Meg and the Council toured my property.”

“By the way, is Finn short for anything?”

He shook his head. “Go on, you’re dying to show off,” he urged, having another go at my ear. “Let me hear your reasoning.”

“Here’s what I’ve pieced together from what my father calls fieldwork. Ready?”

Finn laid his chin on my head, forcing me to pull away to see his face. He cocked his head, so I continued.

“Meg was stalking Roy on the night he died. He could hear her oaring behind him as he swam. Roy stroked into Lapp Strait to his secret place, knowing she couldn’t dock there. He slid your camera into the den and started up the hill in a hurry, not wanting Meg to know what he had done. You jumped out of the bushes.”

I hesitated. When Finn made no comment, I continued, “Meg saw him fall, saw you pull him out, skulked around in the boat, tying up somewhere near New Landing, and pretended to fish. The minute Brad ran up the hill to meet Mike and Dad, Meg smothered Roy then disappeared through the bushes to her boat, accidentally leaving Roy’s camera behind. The camera thing is a long shot, but it explains why Roy's camera was on the dock. Either way, Meg piloted the boat that Dad remembers motoring toward Upper Bay."

"I guess we'll never know if she killed Pop or why."

"I'm sure she did. Mary Gagne saw them set out. She thought it was Brad. Seated and in the dark, it would be hard to tell them apart. Meg is fond of pushing and blunt force trauma." I felt the bumps on the back of my head and on my temple.

"My guess is she told your father she had pictures of him with my mother. Your dad wouldn't have wanted you to see the photos, not until he was ready to break the news. From everything I heard about your dad, he would have jumped at the chance to get them. Information was the one thing Meg had that could get him in a boat with her. Meg may even have suggested rounding the stump bog, claiming as a local she knew where the fish hung out.

"At the bog, she smacked your dad with an oar and shoved him overboard. After that, who knows. As for why she did it? At eight, Meg watched her mother make love with an unknown squatter on Sturdevant Peninsula. Seven years later, she photographed my mom and your dad doing the same. Your dad morphed in her mind into her mother's lover. A Sturdevant. Worse than owl dung."

Finn humphed.

"I know it's crazy. Remember, Meg was impressionable when she saw her mother hooking up with the cowboy. No one can prove it, but I bet Meg killed her mother, just pushed her in a rage. It felt good. Just like seeing my mom and your dad made her lash out again. She had some fantasy about Roy, too. Did you ever see them out together at night taking photos?"

"I saw them once." Finn kissed my left cheek. "Meg swam out to Roy's boat. She made a lot of noise, both swimming and getting in the boat. He made her row. Roy was tracking and photographing a pair of mating loons. I was sitting out on the point at the beach. The next day, Roy yelled that I better not be photographing his loons. He knew I saw him with Meg, and the next thing I know, Brad's pressuring me to ask Meg out. I suspect Meg put him up to it."

"Poor Meg. She was indoctrinated in what my dad calls the creation myth. Which is that the Sturdevants were rumrunning, no-good weasels, who stole property from her family. She became obsessed with getting even."

"But why harm you? She couldn't get Booth Island, not with your mother alive?"

I stroked his right cheek. "Jealousy, I guess. Mike, Tim, you...even Penny. Who knew I was so alluring?"

"Well?" He studied me with those eyes, now a soft velvet brown. "After a while, like three days, when we're on the mend, might you..."

"Depends." I stopped him before the question was asked. He kissed me until my arches ached. When I tipped my head, he bobbled his head to egg me on. "Do I get the beach and beach access?"

He ran his right hand up under my loose-fitting blouse. A ripple of relaxation swam down my back. I shivered. "Well?" I managed.

He nodded, which wasn't an answer. A moment later, he responded, one dark eyebrow visible above his horn-rim glasses. "Play your cards right, and you might win the whole Peninsula." He ran a finger down my spine. My eyes closed with the pleasure of it.

"It's been done, I hear." I kidded.

"Funny." He licked my nearest ear.

With concentration, I asked, "You once implied you knew who was responsible for Roy's death. Were you right?"

"I could lie, you'd never know, but honestly, I thought it was Brad."

"What about Roy's shirt, hat, and bandanna?"

"I'm guessing Meg grabbed the shirt and hat from your boat that night and the bandanna as she left Roy. Remember, she was framing me. Lucky for her, she kept them. They came in handy to gaslight us and try to frame me. Again."

"Who taped all of the photos to doors and windows?"

"Meg."

"But why?"

"To wrench Roy from Penny, to get even with you for being you. The plus was it seemed so obviously my handiwork. And the jewelry. A prohibition choker and a Booth engagement ring bought with rumrunner's proceeds must have seemed to her like vengeance and rightfully hers. All to set me up."

"Humph. So, the answer to your initial, unasked question is this. I'm only interested in someone who coaches the Grosse Pointe swim team."

"I hear I have the butt for it," he laughed.

I raised my eyebrows.

"I still have connections, so I'm sure it can be arranged."

Finn fingered my lips, reared his head back, tilted it, studied me, put a finger under my chin, and drew my lips to his.

I stroked his beard. It was growing on me. "You're a loon expert like Roy was. What does a loon call? Woe, loss? Why would my dad write that of all things on Roy's stone? Why?"

His smile warmed me from head to toe. "A loon calls so that the others can find him in the dark, Boo." Fluting his voice, Finn called, "Here I am. Here I am. Come to me!"

I rested my head on Finn's right shoulder. Even now, I could feel my brother's presence in the caressing breeze and the fingered leaves of a hawthorn bush brushing my back. I sighed.

Happy, the word of the day: contented, carefree, joyful...at peace.

Acknowledgments

First things first, I love Ontario, Canada. It is gorgeous, the people are generous, funny, and family, eh?

Over the years, our lake neighbors have told many wild tales about the doings on the island my husband's family has owned since the early 1900s. Wild, fun, crazy plots, up to and including secret graves and mob dentists. Their tales inspired this story.

I love the storytelling of it all, as much as I love the place. I hope all who read this understand that the goings-on and the characters, except their wonderful Canadian-ness, are from my imagination. But not the beauty of the island, lake, mighty Westport, the Rideau Canal, or the nastiness of fishers.

Just don't try to sell your U.S. citizen-owned island without deeded or purchased lake access. That part is true!

Losing a sibling is tough. Losing one suddenly haunts you until you come to peace with the loss. An island, a storm, a ghost, and a killer. The perfect recipe for finding yourself and saying goodbye.

Please remember:

Reviews help keep authors writing and publishers publishing them. Please take the time to post a review.

About the Author

D. Z. Church was raised in the mid-West, she has lived in the Eastern, Southern, and Western United States and Barbados, adding several during a stint in the U.S. Navy. She has since been an award-winning Advertising Creative Director, and worked in educational assessment, specifically the evaluation of writing. And she fell in love with Ontario, Canada, the Rideau Canal System, and one little island in a big, big lake.

She currently lives on the West Coast and in the Sierra Nevada Mountains.

Facebook:
https://www.facebook.com/mysteryhistorysuspense

Learn More and Sign up for Newsletter at:
https://www.dzchurch.com

D. Z. Church
Thrillers

Perfidia

A California teacher's search for her missing father begins when a dead cousin, a jeweled key, and a call from a Bajan lawyer lure her into a deadly tug-of-war over a threatened plantation, inheritance, and lost treasure in 1970s Barbados.

Saving Calypso

Swagger meets savvy. Runaway Calypso Swale holds a key to end climate change. Big Oil wants her found, her secret, and her dead. Now, the hunt is on, and the man in the lead is the reason she ran.

Historical Thrillers
Cooper Vietnam Era Quartet

Dead Legend

Two estranged brothers, one Navy, one Marine, one war, two ways to fight it. One way back. Find their father's killers. A military family's journey through the Vietnam War begins. Cooper Quartet: 1967

Head First

Two brothers, two children lost, two wars, Vietnam and the war at home. The stakes are high, one Naval career and two lives. Cooper Quartet: 1972.

Pay Back

Two promises. One way out of Saigon as it falls, deliver on both, as the Vietnam War comes home to roost. Cooper Quartet: 1975.

Coming Soon: **Don't Tell**. Cooper Quartet: 1975

Made in the USA
Middletown, DE
20 February 2021